LET ME IN

ALI PARKER

BRIXBAXTER PUBLISHING

Let Me In

First Edition.

Editor: Eric Martinez
Cover Designer: Ryn Katryn Digital Art

FIND ALI PARKER

www.aliparkerbooks.com

DEDICATION

Thank you to all of my incredible readers. It's been a wild ride for the last 6 years, and I'm grateful that you've been on it with me. I'm a sucker for stories where one of the characters is hardened to love and ONLY love helps them mend, heal, and change. This is one of those. Hope you fall in love with it.

<3 Ali

CHAPTER 1

XANDER

Ten years ago

I kept my sunglasses on, protecting my eyes from the hot San Diego sun. I was early and in no hurry to get to my next class at UCSD. In fact, I was dreading it a little. I knew it wasn't going to go well. It never did. My professor had taken a strong dislike to me from the moment I darkened his door. I didn't know why, and I didn't give a shit. I just needed the damn grade.

My book bag was slung over one shoulder as I walked along the cement sidewalk. I sipped the iced coffee I carried in my other hand. It was a gorgeous sunny day. As soon as I was done with class, I was going to the beach. A cold beer and some good music were exactly what this day needed.

"Wait up," I heard from behind me.

I slowed my walk, waiting for Charlie Pugh to catch up. The guy was two years younger than me. We had met last year, his freshman year, and I had taken him under my wing.

"I didn't think you had class on Fridays," I said.

He grinned. "I don't, but the hot chick I'm after does. I'm going to accidentally run into her and see if I can convince her to go out with me tonight."

"Good boy," I teased.

"Did you do it?" he asked.

I patted my hand against my book bag. "I did."

"Xander, he's going to fail you," he warned.

"I don't care. It's good. If the old goat could pull his head out of the nineteenth century, he would know it was good."

He sucked in a breath through his teeth. "You are a rebel."

"No, I'm smarter than the average bear and this asshole can't see it. He hates me and is looking for a reason to fail me. It isn't going to work. Even if he rejects the project or gives me a shitty grade, I'll still pass."

"What about your dad, though?"

I rolled my eyes behind my dark shades. "I don't give a shit about that either. I'm passing. I'm not a college dropout. I'll graduate and he can get over it."

"You are a bad ass," he joked.

"Who is this girl you have the hots for?" I asked.

"She's a little older than I am, blonde, and sexy as hell. I've had my eye on her for a while. I have accidentally run into her a couple times. I make her laugh."

"Because you look funny," I quipped.

It was funny because Charlie looked anything *but* funny. He was young with a lopsided smile and a laid-back surfer attitude. His black hair and crazy blue eyes made him a standout. Girls panted after him, but he always set his sights on the ladies he couldn't have, the ladies that were not interested in his charms.

"I'll wear her down. I'll flash my blue eyes and smile a lot. It works every time."

I shook my head. "I would be very careful boasting about that. Someone might lynch you one of these days."

"I'm too cute to lynch."

"We'll see," I said and continued on my way.

"So, the project, did you change it at all?" he questioned.

"Nope. It's good. I know it's good. The professor can fuck off. It's people like me that are going to change the world. He is too set in his ways. He isn't innovative. He wants to keep doing things the way they have always been done. He's wrong."

He let out a low whistle. "I hope you didn't include that in your research."

"No, but I should have."

"You are close to being done with all this. Don't rock the boat," he said before bursting into laughter at the pun.

"That's the thing. My boat won't be rocking. My boat—ship rather —will carry ten times the cargo today's ships do. My ships will use half the fuel. They are lighter, faster, and more efficient. If he can't see that, he's an idiot. Hell, I already know he is an idiot. He doesn't have the ability to look ahead. He is stuck in the past."

He shook his head. "I hope he doesn't ruin your chances of graduating. You are so close."

"He can't. He doesn't have that kind of power. He only thinks he does."

We stopped walking. My class was off to the left. "Good luck," he offered.

I shrugged. "I don't need luck. I don't give a shit what he thinks. I know I am right. If I had a decent professor who understood the first thing about engineering, I would be getting an award. My idea is solid. As soon as I graduate, I am taking it to a company that can put it to work. One day, I'm going to laugh my ass off atop my piles of millions. I'm going to come back here as an alum and make sure I point out that the asshole tried to keep me down."

He laughed. "Gee, tell me how you really feel."

"I'll see you later. Good luck with the girl."

"I don't need any luck," he shouted as he walked away.

I headed for class. It was my only class for the day. I had a feeling I was going to need a stiff drink afterward. I was so looking forward to the end of the semester. I was done with school. Getting my engineering degree had been a long, hard process. I told myself it was better than the alternative. At least for me. I was not military material. My dad insisted I was. I wasn't. I knew myself better than he did, whether he believed that or not.

I pulled open the door and walked down the hall filled with posters about graduation, classes for next year, and so on. I ignored them all. I had short-timer syndrome. I was so close to being finished. I popped into the restroom before going to class. I was early.

I pushed up my sunglasses and took a look in the mirror. One of the reasons the old goat didn't like me was he felt I didn't take life seriously enough. Maybe I didn't. I thought judging a book by its cover was wrong. My hair was too long. I liked the shaggy look. I supposed I probably looked like one of the millions of surfers that hung out at the beach with light brown hair that hung in light layers just above my shoulders.

I dressed like a surfer, I supposed. It was my senior year of college. The dress standard depleted with each passing term. I was lucky to find clean clothes, or mostly clean. I didn't give a shit whether I matched or if they were wrinkled.

I smirked as I used my fingers to comb my hair down. I could admit my lack of concern for my image was a direct insult to my dad and family that had sticks way too high up their asses. I was the proverbial black sheep and I didn't care.

Putting off the inevitable wasn't going to make it go away. I left the bathroom and walked the few feet down the hall to the class. I actually felt nervous. I shouldn't feel nervous. If my professor was worth a shit, he would see I was onto something. Instead, the guy hated me. I was convinced he was intimidated by me. He didn't want me to be successful.

"Mr. Holland," the professor greeted me with a stern look on his face. "Are you here to turn in the final?"

I nodded and opened the messenger bag. I pulled out the black binder that contained the paper that would be the final piece of work turned in. "It's right here."

"I hope you changed course," he murmured as he took it from me.

"I didn't," I said defiantly.

He scowled at me and flipped it open. The first page of the report was a mock-up of the ship I engineered. "I told you at the beginning this was not an acceptable project."

"And I'm telling you the research is sound."

"This shit will never work," he snapped and tossed the binder on his desk without bothering to look at the research.

I looked behind me. There were a few students already seated. They were trying to hide their laughs. I was not the guy that was ever going to win Most Popular. I didn't care. I trusted my work. I knew what I had, even if none of them could see it.

"It will work," I argued. "You just need to look at the research."

He shook his head. "It's assholes like you that think you are going to change the world because you are smarter than anyone else. Look at history and science. You won't. This is a failing paper."

I wasn't going to win him over. I knew that. He wasn't my target audience anyway. "That's cool. I don't need your grade anyway."

He glared at me. If he could have put his hands on me, I was sure he would have. He wanted to shake me.

I smirked, daring him to do it.

"Punk kids like you will destroy our world," he said.

I buttoned my bag. "Lucky for you, professor, punk kids like me can see into the future. We aren't stuck in the past. We are what's going to save your ass one day. You are a shitty professor and you are going to be the one destroying our world if you don't pull your head out of your ass."

"You are a low-life punk. You will never amount to anything. Maybe I'll visit you on the dockyard one day. That's where you'll be, swabbing decks."

I turned and walked out. I was done with his class. There was no reason for me to go back. He could teach me nothing new. I got what I needed—a passing grade. I earned my degree, no thanks to his ass. He could fuck off. I was going to prove him wrong. I was going to prove them all wrong.

· · ·

Present Day

My tie was choking me. I hated wearing fucking ties. I didn't let on that I was totally uncomfortable. I sipped from the crystal glass. It was only water. I was sticking to water for the night, at least until I got what I came for. Then, I was going home and having a stiff drink. Several stiff drinks.

"With that said," the speaker said from his place at the front of the ballroom, "please, everyone, give our honored guest and Champions of the Earth award winner, Xander Holland, a big round of applause."

Showtime. I got to my feet and tried to smile. I had a feeling it probably looked more like a grimace. I made my way up to the front to collect the plaque with my name emblazoned on it. I nodded at the audience that was still clapping and held up the plaque. "Thank you," I said and walked away from the stage.

The room fell silent as I moved toward the room exit at the side. I didn't stop going. I walked right out the door and got into my car. No one said I had to give a speech. I didn't do speeches. I didn't do public gatherings much at all. Over the years, the introvert thing appealed to me more and more. The older I got, the more I discovered I didn't really like people.

I drove through the gates of what my one and only friend, Charlie, called my compound. It was my compound. It was my safe place with a very high fence all the way around the damn place. I liked my privacy. The fence and the always-locked gate were a symbol of how I lived my life. I kept everyone out.

CHAPTER 2

EVIE

I loved Pinterest. It was such an amazing website. I could literally spend the entire day staring at the endless pictures and ideas. I didn't like to steal anyone's great ideas, but I liked to take what I saw and add my own special spin. It was what made me good at my job.

I loved themed parties. They were so much fun. It gave me an opportunity to fill every fantasy. I could be under the sea, in Paris, or on the moon. I was known for planning parties that were ridiculously over the top. No detail was missed. When someone told me they had this idea, I took it and ran. One day, I would own my own business. For now, I worked for one of the top party planning agencies in the country. At least, that was what we advertised.

I took a quick screenshot and saved it to my file of ideas that I didn't need right away but was hoping to use eventually. I clicked off the site. I had to. It was too tempting to keep open. I pulled out the file for the party I was preparing a proposal for. It was a sweet-sixteen party for a very wealthy young girl, but it wasn't happening for another year. The family was very serious about the party being the best of the best.

"Evie," my boss, Clara, said as she walked into my small office.

I greeted her with a smile. "What's up?"

She sat down in the soft chair across from my desk. "I have a bit of an issue. I am hoping you can help me."

"What do you need?"

"We have a last-minute party request," she said with a grimace. "Like this weekend. Saturday."

I raised my eyebrows. "Last minute is right. How big?"

"Two hundred."

My mouth fell open. "Two hundred?"

She nodded. "It's for a cargo-shipping company. Apparently, they are pulling in some pretty good business and the owner wants to throw a party to celebrate and recognize his employees."

"Ah, that's sweet," I said, completely ignoring the fact the party he wanted would normally take weeks, sometimes months, to plan.

"Yes, sweet, but seriously, this is a big deal. I've tacked on a fee for the short notice. This could be a good account. We were the only planners willing to take it on. If we prove we can handle it, we will earn their regular business."

"Okay, what do you need me to do?" I asked. I loved a challenge.

"I want you to handle it. I have that wedding this weekend. I cannot possibly spare a minute for this. I have Amber and David with me as well. You would be on your own."

A knot formed in my gut. "Me? Alone?"

"I know you can handle it. They don't want a lot of flair. You can do it, right?"

It wasn't like I could say no. "Yes. I will not let you down."

"Thank you. If you need help, reach out, but this wedding is a big deal. I can't let down this family."

I nodded. The wedding was right up there with the likes of Will and Kate and Kim and Kanye. It was big. I had been picking up the slack while Clara focused all her energy on the one wedding. It was great for me, giving me a chance to grow and gain some experience. "I will give it my best."

She breathed a sigh of relief, her shoulders sagging forward. "Thank you. I knew I could count on you. This wedding will be the death of me."

"I have seen some of the plans. It is a doozie. They are going to love it."

"They better. I'll send you the details in the next ten minutes."

"I'll get right on it," I assured her.

She left my office. I slapped my hands over my face. "Oh shit," I breathed. "You can do this, Evie. You can do this."

I quickly cleaned up my desk, putting away the sweet-sixteen folder. I needed organization. I needed everything in its place. I pulled out the yellow pad I insisted on keeping notes on and tore off the top page. It wasn't written on, but it wasn't pristine. I liked pristine.

I heard the chime alerting me to a new email. It was from Clara. I took a deep breath and put myself in the right frame of mind to tackle a new project. A big project. I opened it and immediately printed the document. We used a standard form and then the planner would reach out and get more information from the client.

I pulled the forms from the printer, put them in order, tapped them on the desk to get them perfectly even, and put a staple in the corner. Only then did I start to read through the forms. I made little notes on my yellow pad about things I needed to clarify.

With the notes made and an idea already forming in my mind, I packed up my things. I needed to do a little window shopping. I needed fresh air and a change of scenery. It was the way I worked. I needed to get my juices flowing.

I knew just the place—my favorite bar. I wasn't a heavy drinker and I rarely liked day drinking, but my best friend in the whole world worked at the bar. It was really the only time we got to chat. She worked nights. I worked days and sometimes nights.

Right now, it would be nice and slow in the bar. The few regulars and the guys having really bad days would stick to their corner of the bar and I would hang out at the other side. I said my goodbyes to the small staff that worked in the office and headed out into the beautiful San Diego sun. I slid on my sunglasses and walked to my car. The heels I wore were sensible, which was a necessity considering how much I was on my feet most days.

I made it to the bar, parking in back next to Nelle's car. I went around the front. The bar was in one of the better neighborhoods of the city, tucked in between several other bars. It was where the college kids came to do their pub crawls. Nelle's bar was more of a sports bar by day and a millennial hangout by night. It was where the young people with man buns and skinny jeans liked to hang out. A lot of rich kids hung out in the place as well, which was really how Nelle paid the bills.

"Hey." I greeted her with a small wave as I walked through the doors. The place was plenty bright in the late afternoon hours. At night, the lights were down, and the music was up.

"Uh oh, you got a new job," she said with a bright smile. She knew me very well.

Her long, shiny, blonde hair was pulled back in a ponytail. The woman could have been a model. She was gorgeous. I admired her beauty and the perfect figure she had but it was the beauty on the inside that made her special. She was kind and ferocious enough to run a bar and deal with stupid, sometimes mean, drunks.

"I did," I said with a grin.

"You are happy, so it must be especially challenging," she commented. She quickly filled a glass with my usual diet soda and put it down in front of me with a little square napkin underneath.

I took a sip of the soda. "I am. It's for a big party this weekend."

Her perfectly sculpted brows, darkened with the skilled hand of a makeup expert, arched up. "This weekend? How big?"

"About two-hundred guests," I answered. I was excited and couldn't hide it.

"Wow. That's not a small gathering."

"Nope."

"You will, of course, pull it off," she said with a bright smile.

"You bet your ass I will. It does mean I'm going to be working around the clock for the next six days."

I pulled out my yellow pad, ready to jot down ideas as they came to me. I took another drink and looked around the bar. The usual suspects were gathered around their table talking about football. I didn't even think it was football season, but what did I know? It was the middle of July, hot as hell, and shaping up to be even hotter next week.

"What kind of party?" she asked as she filled a glass with foamy beer before handing it to one of the regulars.

"Shipping."

"Shipping? Like the post office?"

"No. Cargo ships. I have to do a little homework, but they ship things all around the world on their really big boats."

She didn't look very excited. "How boring. What kind of theme?"

"No theme. I'm thinking I'm just going to have some big ropes, anchors, and stuff like that around the room."

"Where is it being held at?"

"One of the local hotels down at the waterfront. I've worked with the rooms so many times before, I already know what I'm going for. It's going to be tight quarters, but I'll make it work."

"Of course, you will."

I put my pen down and focused on her. "How have you been?"

"Good, busy. You know how the weekends are."

"I know. You work yourself to the bone. I was going to ask you to go shopping with me yesterday, but I figured you would be sleeping most of the day."

She laughed. "I was. I got home just after four on Saturday—I guess that would technically be Sunday—and slept until about two. Got up, ate, showered, and went right back to bed. There were back-to-back concerts Friday and Saturday. You know how they flock in here, all hyped up on music and alcohol."

"Did you have to kick any ass?"

She winked. "Just once. Two young bucks thought they were going to fight in my bar. They now know better."

"I bet they do," I said with a giggle. "Being attacked by all one-hundred-twenty pounds of you must have terrified them."

"I think it might have been Martha that really scared them," she said with a grin. Martha was her bat. It was her lucky bat. She'd played softball in school and kept it behind the bar. Her Louisville Slugger was not to be messed with.

11

"Martha is an intimidating gal," I agreed. "I want a beach day. I'll be busy this week, but what about next week?"

"I'm off Tuesday," she answered.

"Then a week from now, we have a date. I have a feeling I'm going to be running my ass off this week and probably won't see you."

"Don't work too hard," she cautioned. "You know how very Type A you can get. I don't want you having a breakdown or something."

"I won't have a breakdown. I promise."

"Famous last words."

I took another drink. "I've learned. I've gotten more organized. I've gotten better at scheduling. Now, there is no need to panic. Everything will be done on time. It will be last minute, but it will be done."

She nodded. "Good girl. I don't want you having a stroke at the ripe age of twenty-eight."

"I won't."

"Speaking of Type A, how is your dad?" she asked.

I shrugged. "I have been busy. He's been busy. I have barely talked to him at all. I really wish he would relax a little more."

She rolled her eyes. "That's the pot calling the kettle black. You two are both wound very tight."

"He made me this way," I protested.

"Yes, he did."

"Now that you mention it though, I probably should check in on him. He works way too much. When he isn't working, he is doing something else that is far from relaxing."

She gave me a knowing look. "Yeah, weird. It's like I know someone just like him."

"Ha. Ha."

An idea popped into my head. I quickly jotted it down. When I looked up, she had her arms folded over her chest. She was right. I did work hard. I worked a lot. I liked working.

CHAPTER 3

XANDER

I picked up a tool that I had no idea what it was. I examined it and put it back down on the table alongside Charlie's workstation. I looked around the massive warehouse with various parts of cargo ships being manufactured or repaired. I knew exactly what I was looking at when it came to the bits and pieces of the ships.

"This baby is almost finished," Charlie said, lovingly patting an engine housing.

I walked around the massive piece that would eventually be a part of one of the cargo ships I had designed. "It looks good."

"Of course, it looks good. I made it."

"I designed it," I reminded him.

He grinned. "Damn straight you did. And I'm glad you did. If you didn't, I wouldn't be working as much as I have been. Look at this place. We have work lined up for the next two years. Your fancy ships are the bee's knees."

I rolled my eyes. "When did you turn ninety?" I asked, referencing his very old, outdated phrase.

"Do you want a tour?" he asked.

I shook my head. "Nah, once you've seen one, you've seen them all."

He flashed a smile. "That isn't even remotely true."

His mind was in the gutter. "Please do not regale me with tales of your latest girlfriend or whatever it is you call these women you date for a few weeks."

"I call them my ladies," he said with his boyish grin. "How was the trip to LA?"

I groaned. "As expected."

"What exactly were you doing up there?"

"I was presented with an award. I wasn't going to go at all, but my assistant told me it was a big deal. Then other people told me it was a big deal. I went to get it fucking over with."

"What kind of an award?"

I shrugged. "I don't know, some environmental thing or something."

He slapped a hand to his forehead. "How do you not know what it is for?"

"Because," I answered. It was a lame answer, but I had no good answer. "I went, I got it, and that's that."

"Where is it?"

"In the backseat of my car, I suppose."

"It's pretty clear you have never actually got an award before," he mused.

"Why do you say that?"

He smirked. "I bet the best award you ever won was one of those pretty little participation ribbons."

"Fuck you."

"It's an award, man! A really cool bit of recognition. You did good! Celebrate it. Be proud of what you have accomplished."

I supposed I was proud. Somewhat. I just didn't see the need to boast. "I am proud," I argued.

"You are a billionaire, and don't deny that you are. I know you are. You don't act like it, which is a good thing, I guess, but damn, be proud."

I scowled at him. "You want me to act like a peacock? Should I strut around boasting about my wealth?"

He slowly shook his head. "Never mind. I'm just glad I knew you when."

"When?"

"Before you became this guy. You are one step away from a big, bushy beard and living off the grid in a tiny little shack."

That made me smile. "That isn't a terrible idea."

"Living is a good thing," he started the lecture he usually doled out.

"Don't," I warned. "I've heard it. I like my life just the way it is."

"Alone."

"Unencumbered," I shot back.

He laughed. "That's a big word. But I guess coming from a guy that designed the ships that are changing the world, I would expect nothing less."

"How is business?" I asked as my eyes scanned the massive building once again.

"Good. Like I said, I'm not worried about being laid off anytime soon. In fact, I talked with the plant manager and he and I are going to discuss hiring more people."

"Damn, that's awesome."

"It is awesome. I can't wait to see what else you have up your sleeve."

I smiled, shrugging a shoulder. "Not a lot. I should probably get going though. I am supposed to meet with a private client that wants to hire me to design a boat for him."

"Wow, you still do that?"

"Not like I have a lot going on."

My phone started ringing in my jeans pocket. I pulled it out, expecting it to be the man that I was going to be meeting with. It wasn't. It was one of my top clients. "Hello?" I answered, praying there wasn't an issue with one of my ships.

I felt like they were all my babies. I had designed every element of the cargo ships and felt a connection to them. There were times, not often, when there was an issue. The people who bought my ships, although I didn't technically build them, trusted me to fix any problems. That was why I was successful.

"Xander, this is Al Sampson."

"Hi, Al," I said as I took a few steps away from Charlie. "What can I do for you?"

"We are having a party, a celebration to thank our hardworking crews and employees in all facets of the company. I wanted to invite you to celebrate with us. After all, it's your ships that have given us our most profitable year in the company's history."

I grimaced and looked over at Charlie. "A party?" I repeated.

Charlie's eyebrows shot up. "Where?" he mouthed.

I frowned and shook my head. "I can check my schedule," I said, ready to makeup an excuse for not going.

Charlie's eyes grew round. I didn't get a chance to hear what Al said because Charlie pulled the phone from my hand. "Hello, this is Charles. I'm Xander's personal assistant. He had to step out for a moment. What is it you wanted to ask him?"

I shook my head as Charlie nodded, grinning big. I waited while Al spoke.

"You know, that is an excellent idea," Charlie said. "He would love to attend. There will be a plus one included with the invitation I gather?"

I groaned, putting a hand to my head. Charlie turned his back to me. "He will be there. Thank you so much. Take care."

Charlie turned back to look at me with a very satisfied expression on his face.

"What did you do?" I asked.

"We're going to a party! Free alcohol and food."

I rolled my eyes. "I don't need free food and alcohol."

"But I do."

"No, you don't."

"Okay, maybe I don't need it, but I want it. I like to party. It will be a great way to meet new people."

I let out a long sigh. "You mean new women. I think you've about run through most of the women in San Diego."

"Not even close, my friend, not even close."

"What did you get me into? When is it?"

"Saturday," he answered.

"This Saturday?" I asked with surprise. "What if I had plans? That's not a lot of notice."

"You don't have plans. You and I know both know that."

I didn't have plans. I never had plans. It was why I liked my life.

"Boring," Charlie said. "You have got to live a little."

I took a dramatic inhale. "I'm living just fine."

"Gee, that sense of humor will definitely have the ladies falling at your feet."

"I don't care if they fall at my feet or otherwise," I said. "What kind of party is this? Do I have to wear a tux, and how long do I have to stay there?"

"No tux, but a suit would be a good idea. You have to stay for… let's say an hour. You can survive an hour, can't you?"

"I don't know if I can," I complained. "I hate these things."

"You hate anything that pulls you away from your giant house, AKA your compound."

I couldn't help but smile. "I like my compound. We could have a party there."

He curled his lip. "Gee, your company is good and all, but I was looking forward to a little action and I don't mean sex."

I wasn't going to get out of it. He wanted me to go and I had been very neglectful as a friend. I was a hermit. I rarely went out with him. I preferred to hide away from the world. He was a social butterfly. "Fine, I'll go."

He slapped my shoulder. "It will be fun. Free drinks are always a party."

"Do you need a ride?" I offered.

"Nope and neither do you. Free drinks. That means we are going to be drinking. We'll call a taxi."

"No thanks. I'll hire a car."

He laughed. "We both know you are going to cut out early and leave me. I'll be taking a cab."

I wasn't going to deny it. "All right. I better get out of here. I'll talk to you before Saturday."

17

"I know where you live," he warned. "Don't try and hide. I'll climb that fence."

I knew he would. "I won't stand you up."

I walked out of the massive warehouse and headed to my car in the parking lot that housed the cars of the many employees. I checked the time and pointed my car toward town. I didn't necessarily need the business to build a single boat, but I was looking forward to a new challenge.

I thought about the upcoming party. I really wasn't looking forward to it. It was hard for an extrovert to understand an introvert. I considered myself an introvert. I had always been a loner. In college, I did party a little. I did date and I did have fun. After I graduated, I began to become more closed off. Mostly, I was closed off because I was always working on the design for the ship. It took a couple years to fine tune the idea I had come up with during the last year in college.

Every day I stayed alone in my own little bubble, the easier it got to stay in that bubble. The few women I dated were not right for me. They didn't like being cooped up. They wanted to go out and hit the clubs. They wanted to be seen on my arm. I knew I was wealthy, and a lot of the women thought they were getting a real catch. Then they got to know me.

Sometimes, they made the excuse to leave. Sometimes, I made the excuse. None of the relationships had necessarily ended badly but they did end. I couldn't ever remember being sad about them ending. I supposed that was part of the problem. I should have been sad. I should have cared a little more than I actually did.

I convinced myself some years ago I was meant to be single. I was going to be a bachelor all the rest of my days.

The worst part about it—I didn't care. I wasn't worried about being alone.

CHAPTER 4

EVIE

I parked my car in front of the small antique store. I often shopped at the place when I was looking for that little something special to make a party theme complete. I had a good relationship with the owner and appreciated the many stories he had about the old days.

I walked in, the bells on the door alerting him to my presence. The bells were a necessity. The shop was packed, wall to wall. In some places, things were stacked so high one couldn't see more than a few inches in front of them.

I walked inside, being careful not to knock anything over with my purse. "Bob!" I called out the owner's name.

I heard a muffled reply. "Back here."

I followed the sound of his voice. He was kneeling on the floor, unpacking a box of what looked like skeleton keys.

"Those are awesome!" I exclaimed.

He softly chuckled. "These are trendy right now," he commented. "The rustier, the better. I'll sell these in no time."

"They are very cool," I agreed. I considered buying some just to have them. I was thinking they could be great for a Halloween party or a steampunk party. I pushed the thoughts aside. I was there for the shipping party. Skeleton keys were not that hard to find.

He very slowly got to his feet, brushing off his knees. "You're here for the boat stuff, right?"

"I am. What do you have for me?"

He walked me around a pile of stuff to an area where there were some thick ropes piled on the floor. "Check out this anchor," he said.

I grimaced and shook my head. "I think that is a little on the large side," I told him. The anchor was a hair shorter than I was. "I was thinking of something a little smaller. I do like the ropes. I'll take those."

"I've got this old wheel," he said, moving around to point out the carved-wood piece.

I wasn't an expert, but I didn't believe it was an authentic wheel. It looked close enough for my needs though. "I'll take that as well. What else?"

He looked thoughtful before he put a finger in the air. "Ah, the old light. This came off an old freighter."

He held up the brass spotlight that was old and tarnished and absolutely perfect. "Yes, that works. I'll take that."

He showed me around, offering up a few more pieces. I was already imagining their placement in my head.

"Well?" he asked.

I smiled. "This is perfect. Now, let's get down to business. How much?"

He threw out an outrageous number. Initially, I thought he was joking. Then I realized he was very serious. "Bob, no. That is never going to happen."

"These are some great pieces!"

"They are nice pieces, but none of them are all that rare. I can go to any one of the many shops around the waterfront and find these."

He scowled at me. "You won't find half of this."

"Bob," I warned. "I love giving you my business, but I can't pay way over the market value. I have a business to run as well."

He shook his head. "You used to be nice."

I laughed. "I still am nice. I'll tell you what. I'll rent that big anchor from you if you give me a better deal on this other stuff. We'll include a little tag that says the anchor is for sale at your shop. It's free advertisement for you."

He mulled it over. "Fine, but don't go blabbing to everyone that I gave you a good deal."

"I would never do such a thing. You are my secret weapon."

That seemed to help. He smiled and nodded. He helped me load the small things into my car and promised to have the anchor delivered to the ballroom. It was a huge piece and would be the statement for the party. I had planned on a ship replica, but the anchor was going to be much better. I got in my car and pulled out my iPad. I made the checkmark on my list of things to do today. One down and about a million to go.

I loved lists. They were so rewarding. Every time I checked a box, it was like I was winning the game I played with myself. The final preparations were coming together. I needed to check with the caterers, but I was confident all would be well. I had a select group of contractors I worked with all the time. We had developed a trust that made my life easier. They did a good job and I rewarded them with more work.

With everything pretty much handled and running smoothly, I felt confident I could call Clara and assure her everything was well in hand.

"Hi," I greeted when she answered the phone, sounding out of breath. "Are you hanging in there?"

"Oh god, I swear. This is it. This wedding will kill me."

I softly laughed. "You are going to be fine. I just wanted to let you know the shipping party for tomorrow is rolling along. Everything is set and I don't foresee any problems."

She let out a long sigh of relief. "Thank god. At least one of us is doing our job."

"How is it going? Is there anything I can help with?"

"No, no, you have a full plate. We'll make it through. This bride? My lord, she is a piece of work. The nerves are getting the best of her. She actually wanted to change her bouquet this morning. I explained it wasn't possible. She cried. Her father yelled and I am now busting my ass to try and find a florist that has the flowers in stock. Then, she saw the shade of pink and didn't like it. I'm going to need a vacation and a lot of alcohol once this is over."

"I'm so sorry," I empathized. "It sounds like a nightmare."

"That's lasted a year," she muttered.

"Take care of yourself. I'll see you next week."

"Are you going back to the office today?" she asked.

I bit my bottom lip. "I wasn't going to. I need to check on my dad. If you need me to, I can."

"No, no, it's fine."

"Thanks, Clara," I said and ended the call.

She was a great boss. We all worked long, hard hours. Cutting out a little early on a Friday wasn't a big deal, especially considering we generally worked weekends. We all worked a lot, especially during the spring and summer seasons. We also worked our asses off throughout the holiday season as well. Our slow time was late winter, but even then, we were busy planning big spring weddings.

I drove to my father's house in La Jolla. It wasn't one of the big, fancy homes, but it was comfortable. It was older. It was my child-hood home and held a great deal of memories. It was small, but as a single dad, it was all he could afford. I pulled into the driveway and cut the engine. It was clear he wasn't home. I made my way up the cement walk with little cracks that were in need of repair but would likely not get done anytime soon.

I collected the mail from the box and used my key to go inside. "Dad?" I called out, just in case his car was in the shop.

There wasn't an answer. I put the mail on the small table near the front door. It was where the mail went. It never went on the dining table or on a kitchen counter. It always went on the table. My slightly obsessive nature was absolutely the product of my father's upbringing.

I looked around the living room that was clean and neat. It was who he was. Organized. He could give Marie Kondo a run for her money. I walked into the kitchen and noticed a few dishes in the sink. I quickly rinsed them and put them in the dishwasher.

I opened the fridge to see what he had been eating. I wrinkled my nose when I saw the meager contents. He was clean and organized but he ate like shit. He would get so caught up with work, he would skip meals. He did eat a lot of takeout, which I did not recommend. He was getting up there in years and I didn't want him keeling over because he ate like shit.

The fridge offered no hope. I opened the freezer and found some chicken. I pulled it out, popped it in the microwave to defrost and rummaged through the pantry to find something to pair it with. I tapped my fingers on the counter, trying to figure out what I could make.

"Chicken casserole, it is," I decided.

I quickly mixed it up, popped it in the oven to cook, and went to check the laundry. I tossed in a load and folded what was in the dryer before carrying it into his bedroom. His bed was neatly made. A book sat on the nightstand, along with his reading glasses. I left the folded clothing sitting on his dresser and walked out.

My bedroom was pretty much the same as it had been when I lived there. He had put a desk in one corner and was calling it an office. He left the bed, just in case I needed a place to crash. It was sweet. I had been in my apartment for years and had my own bed, but he always wanted me to have that safety net.

I walked down the hallway, pausing to stare at the picture of my mother. I missed her. Well, not really her because I never really knew her. I missed the idea of a mother. My dad had done his best, and I never lacked for love or attention, but a mother offered a little something different. Her life had been cut short on a quick run to the store. A car accident had taken her from us when I was three. My dad never remarried. It was not a subject he entertained.

I puttered around, picking up a little before I heard the oven timer. I pulled out the casserole, covered it with foil, and popped it back in the oven on the warm setting. I wasn't sure when he would be home, but I didn't think it would be too much longer.

I grabbed the notepad from the drawer to leave him a note.

Hi Dad, I stopped by, but you weren't here. I made you a chicken casse-

23

role. There's a load in the wash. Make sure you toss it in the dryer before you go to bed. I have an event tomorrow, but I will call you on Sunday. Take care of yourself. I love you, Evie.

P.S. I tossed the Chinese. It is high in sodium! You know better!

I left the note on the counter and left the house. I had learned to cook at an early age. I wasn't ever going to be Pioneer Woman good, but I could hold my own with the basics, like casseroles. I could cook the hell out of a casserole.

I had to get home and get back to work on all the little details for the party, including what I would wear. I had a full wardrobe specifically for events. As the planner, I needed to be in attendance, but the rule of thumb was not to stick out like a sore thumb. A lot of clients wanted their guests to have the impression they planned the whole thing. If I was standing in the corner, directing traffic, and wearing an earpiece while looking like a drill sergeant, that would not work.

We wanted to blend in. The client knew who we were. The caterers, the musicians, and all the hired help knew who we were. That was all that mattered. I flipped through my closet, trying to decide what to wear. I didn't want to stick out, which automatically eliminated the full-length gowns.

My color wheel included lots of blacks and blues. The blue made my eyes pop. Black was just my thing. I had a couple pastels but nothing red. Red was a no-no. Red screamed siren. Sirens upstaged party hosts. I went with the black, beaded gown that fell just above the knees. It had a halter-style neckline, which meant I didn't need to worry about the girls on my chest spilling out. No wardrobe malfunctions for me.

With my outfit picked out, it was time to make myself something to eat before digging into all the tiny little details that could make or break the party.

CHAPTER 5

XANDER

The car pulled to a stop in front of the hotel. I could see Charlie pacing in front of the building. He was irritated. Pissed, judging by the flurry of texts he'd sent over the last twenty minutes. I was late. I could admit I nearly backed out. I wasn't thrilled with the idea of going to the stupid party. The only reason I was going was because of Charlie.

I got out of the car, buttoning the suit as I moved toward him.

"It's about fucking time," he said. "You need a better watch."

"I don't need a better watch."

"You are late."

"I know. See? My watch works fine."

He growled. "Why didn't you text me back?"

"Because I knew what you would say. I was on my way."

He shook his head, clearly still pissed. "Can we go in? I need a damn drink."

"You could have gone in," I told him.

"No, I couldn't. You are the one invited. I'm the plus one."

I nodded and moved to open the door. I gestured for him to go inside. "Let's get a drink."

"I'm going to get a drink. And some damn good food."

"I'll go in. I'll get you settled. Then, I'm probably going to bail."

He stopped walking. "Xander, it cannot be that bad."

"It can be," I told him. "I really don't like this kind of thing."

"Tell me one thing that you hate," he said.

I shrugged. "People."

"You don't hate people."

"I don't mingle. I don't like networking. I'm uncomfortable talking to strangers."

A slow smile spread across his face. "You put on this air that makes you seem invincible. You don't appear shy or uncomfortable. You come across as aloof, like you know you are good and you don't give a shit."

I grinned. "That last part is probably true. I don't try to be a dick."

"I didn't say you were a dick. I'm saying loosen up. I think you might actually have fun if you let yourself."

I sighed. "I'm going in. I'm getting a drink and we'll see how things go."

"Fine," he said with exasperation. "I'm going to look into putting you in therapy."

I laughed, knowing it would never happen. I gave my name to the man standing guard at the door. He looked at Charlie, waiting for his name. "I'm with him," Charlie said with a wink.

The man nodded and opened the door. I didn't care that he thought we were a couple. The room had lots of twinkling lights with a slow strobe moving like a lighthouse. The music was a typical cover band playing the usual Top Forty hits. People moved around the room, carrying glasses as they talked in groups. I was immediately looking for a quiet corner that was out of the way.

Charlie grabbed a glass of champagne from a passing waiter before snatching a few crab cakes from another tray. Champagne wasn't my thing. "I'm going to the bar," I told him.

"Don't leave," he warned.

It took him about three seconds to find a beautiful woman to talk to. I ordered a scotch from the bar and was about to recede to my chosen corner when I was stopped. "Xander," a very large man said with a great deal of enthusiasm.

I looked at him but had no idea who he was. "Hey," I said, trying to pretend like I knew him.

He reached out to shake my hand. "Damn, it's been a few years. You have certainly come a long way. I remember the first time you showed up in my office with your plans for a lightweight ship. I damn near laughed you out of the building."

A light went on. "Gary."

He grinned. "How have you been?" he asked.

"Good, you?"

His belly jumped up and down as he laughed. "I'd be better if I would have listened to you all those years ago. I don't know if I can afford one of your ships now, but good job. Really good job."

Another man that was vaguely familiar joined us. "Congratulations," he said.

I wasn't sure why he was congratulating me. "Thank you."

He turned to Gary and smiled. "You did hear about the award, right?"

Gary nodded. "I certainly did. We are standing in the midst of greatness."

I had to believe he was buttering me up. Now that I had finally made a name for myself and managed to become the designer everyone wanted, I could pick and choose my clients. I was not going to pick Gary. Something about the guy irritated me. That, and I remembered the meeting in his office. He practically laughed me out the door. I didn't like him. He would pay full price and he could get in line behind the other companies clamoring to get one of my ship designs.

"I'm not sure about greatness, but I appreciate the compliment."

"You are a smart guy," Gary said. "Us old guys are just not as smart as you. We never would have considered making a lighter boat that could carry more cargo."

"And use less fuel," I added. I wanted to make sure he knew exactly what he missed out on.

Gary grinned. "Less fuel, which makes these little shindigs possible. Al is swimming in cash. I guess Al is the second smartest man in the room. He saw what you had and jumped on it."

I nodded. "He took a chance on me. I'm grateful to him for being willing to trust a young, shaggy-haired guy."

They both laughed. It was true. There were a lot of Garys. I'd had more doors slammed in my face than I cared to count. My success was the best revenge. I had made my money despite the hurdles, despite the lack of support. In my mind, it was the hurdles and lack of support that propelled me forward. I was more determined than ever to be successful. I knew my shit. I trusted my research.

"We all are very happy Al took the chance," Gary said with a laugh. "I'm not a gambling man. I didn't want to see one of my ships sink to the bottom of the ocean."

"Lucky for me, the ship didn't sink. None of them did. If you excuse me, I need to say hello to someone." I walked away, anxious to get away from them.

I moved through the crowd, nodding at a few familiar faces. Charlie made his way to me. "See? It's not so bad."

I glowered at him. "It is painful."

"Nah, it's not so bad. I've already met two very lovely ladies. I could introduce you."

"No thanks, I'm good."

"Incoming," he said in a hushed voice.

"Xander," Al, the man hosting the party and the owner of the company, said. "Thank you so much for coming."

"Thank you for inviting me," I replied. "This is nice."

Al smiled and looked around. "It is nice. We owe my lovely wife Deidre the credit."

The woman stepped forward and smiled. She had Texas-big hair. "Hello, Xander. It's nice to finally meet you. You've made my husband a very happy, wealthy man."

I smiled. "I'm happy to help."

"We owe this tremendous year to you. Your ships changed our entire business model."

"I'm glad I could be a help to you," I said, doing my best to sound pleasant.

"It's more than just a little help," Al said with a laugh. "I look forward to talking with you again. I have some grand plans."

I slowly nodded. "I look forward to that."

"Great, I'll be in touch. Take advantage of the food and drinks."

"Thanks," I said.

He walked away, leaving me and Charlie alone. "Look at you, drumming up business without even trying."

"My designs sell themselves."

"Not arrogant at all," he said with a laugh and slapped my back. "I'm going to see how many more ladies I can meet. I'm keeping my eye on you. Drink and have fun."

I held up my glass. "I am."

"Now get to the part where you have fun."

He walked away, leaving me alone in the swarm of people. I swallowed the last of my drink before getting a fresh glass. With my glass full, I slowly extracted myself from the crowd, moving to the corner I had been eying since I walked through the door.

I leaned against the wall, my eyes surveying the people that all seemed to be having a good time. They were all laughing and chatting. Part of me wanted to be like that. Then there was that part of me that had no inclination to be one of them. I liked my life just the way it was.

The slow spotlight, which was a soft blue hue and didn't blind a person, moved over me. It was kind of soothing. I had noticed the little touches. The old-school lanterns and the lights that would have been mounted on a ship were strategically placed around the large room. There was no missing the giant anchor in its prominent position in the center of the room.

It wasn't a terrible party. I had certainly been to worse. There was, however, a certain vibe in the place. It seemed like the people were truly enjoying themselves. It was obvious the attendees were the real people that ran the company. They did the work and they were being justly rewarded. It won Al some points in my book. He was a good boss.

"Bored?" a female voice cut through my thoughts.

I turned to my left to see a beautiful woman approach me. She had an air of confidence about her that I was immediately attracted to. "Nah, quite the opposite," I told her.

"You don't look like a wallflower," she replied. She came to stand beside me, casually leaning against the wall. I caught a whiff of vanilla. I didn't know if it was her hair or her skin, but it was intoxicating in the best way. I found myself inhaling through my nose to get a better whiff.

"I don't know that I am a wallflower," I answered.

I barely looked at her. I didn't want to look directly at her. Her blue eyes were stunning and could suck a man in. Her black hair was long and curly, hanging well past her shoulders. It wasn't just her eyes that could pull a man in. Her body was smoking hot, curvy and supple. I could imagine the weight of those breasts in my hands.

"I noticed you seem to be rather popular," she commented.

I looked around. "Why would you get that idea?"

"I've seen the looks. People are looking at you like you are a big deal."

I shrugged. "I don't know why."

She softly laughed. "I have a feeling you do know. Humility is a good thing."

"I honestly don't know what you are seeing. I'm standing alone, unbothered. At least, I was alone."

She laughed again. "Prickly. You are not a wallflower, more of a wall cactus."

I couldn't help but smile. She didn't know who I was. That was refreshing. "I believe that is an apt description. I'll take it."

Her pretty smile reached her eyes, crinkling just a little at the corners. I liked that she was a pretty smiler. So many of the women I dated had this idea that smiling caused wrinkles. They would offer weird lip movements instead. I liked genuine people.

"Everyone seems to be enjoying themselves," she commented.

I nodded. "I agree."

"Ah, you are a man of few words."

"I thought I was a prickly cactus?"

She giggled, sounding very young. "Yes, yes, you are."

She was definitely not like most of the women I encountered. Maybe the party wasn't so bad after all. I didn't mind passing some time with her. That was all I was doing, passing the time until I could leave.

CHAPTER 6

EVIE

The man was handsome as hell. I had a feeling he knew it as well. Not that he acted stuck up or arrogant but there was a vibe about him, like a "don't bother me, I'm too sexy for my suit," kind of thing. He seemed bored, like he attended parties like this all the time. My party was another in a long line of boring engagements he was forced to attend. I wondered if he was part owner of the company throwing the party. Maybe he was the pain in the ass brother that lurked in the shadows.

I turned, leaning my shoulder against the wall as I faced him. His hair was a little too long for him to be one of the usual suits that ran a big company. His eyes were a light shade of brown, almost a yellowish gold tone. His brows were thick and his lashes were long. His jaw was square and chiseled. I liked that he had a hint of a shadow along his jawline. He was definitely not the average suit. Every other man at the party, not counting those that had beards, were freshly shaven.

Not him. I was guessing he shaved that morning and called it good enough. The faint hint of brown stubble was actually very attractive. The man was large and very tall, and underneath the suit, I could tell he was built. Maybe he was one of the ship workers. That had to be it.

He was the kind of guy that would be shirtless and sweaty with his muscles bulging as he tossed heavy ropes and cargo.

"You seem bored, like this is something you do often," I commented.

He smirked. "Too often for my liking."

My theory he was a ship worker was dashed. A ship worker would not be the kind to attend fancy parties on the regular. "Most people enjoy a good party."

He shrugged. "I think it's a pointless waste of money. And time. There are about a million other things I could be doing right now."

"Having fun isn't wasteful," I argued. "Fun is living. Nothing is more important than that."

"Look around you," he said, turning his shoulder to lean against the wall. Now we were face to face, getting a good look at one another.

I turned, scanned the area, and looked at him again. "I see people having a good time, enjoying the product of their hard work. They deserve to let their hair down and get to know their coworkers better."

"I bet half these guys would be just as happy in a bar, wearing their comfortable jeans and kicking back, playing pool and watching a game. They can't let their hair down in a stuffy party like this. Someone is making a great deal of money off Al's company's success. There's always someone wanting a piece of the pie, whether they earned it or not."

"What do you mean?" I asked. I was a little offended. I wasn't going to let on I was offended. He was clearly one of those people that could find fault with anything.

"Al can say what he wants, but I know his wife didn't put all this together. Some overpaid party planner decided what food to serve and made sure there was plenty of alcohol flowing. That person saw Al's deep pockets and decided to go crazy. That's what happens when you write a blank check."

I smiled to hide my laughter. "That same person probably splurged on all the silly decorations as well."

"Exactly," he agreed. "These people work in or on boats. Their entire lives are devoted to boats. Why in the hell would they want to be surrounded by the same shit they see day in and day out?"

I pursed my lips and nodded. "You have a very good point. There should have been something more exciting." I was going to take his criticism as constructive. He didn't mean it that way, but that was the way I would apply it to my next venture. I should have done something a little less work-like and more fun. I could have done a tropical theme or something that took the people away from their everyday lives.

He seemed pleased with my assessment. "Exactly," he said again. "This would have been much better in a bar or a club or even a fucking bowling alley. Don't you think?"

I softly shrugged the shoulder not pressed against the wall. "Maybe, but I think ladies and even some of the guys enjoy the chance to dress up once in a while. Does a party in a bowling alley really say thank you for making me a very rich man?"

That seemed to hit home. "I suppose not. I bet they would have been just as happy with a bonus check. He could have saved the money and split it between the employees."

"True, but I bet most of these people would have used the bonus to pay off a bill or something responsible. This is all about them. This is about them getting to mingle and have a nice time away from the kids for the night."

He looked thoughtful but unconvinced as he sipped on his drink. "What do you do for the company?" he asked.

I took a drink from my glass of plain soda and smiled prettily. "I'm the overpaid party planner."

He turned a bright shade of red. I thought he would choke on the drink he had just taken. "Shit," he breathed. "I'm sorry. I didn't mean—fuck. I'm so sorry."

I shrugged. "Don't be. I am an overpaid planner. These things can be fun."

He scoffed. "Not in my experience."

"That's because you are hiding out in a corner," I told him.

"I don't know any of these people," he said.

I scanned the crowd. "Don't you work with them?"

"No," he said, offering no explanation.

"Are you a party crasher?"

He gave me a dry look. "Do I act like a party crasher? Wouldn't I be enjoying myself a little more?"

I looked at his drink. "You're enjoying the free liquor."

"I'm here under duress," he claimed.

I laughed. "I don't see the chains."

"I came because I was invited and my friend insisted I show up."

"You were invited but you don't work for the company?"

He looked uncomfortable. "No."

I waited for him to explain. He didn't. "Are you related to Al?"

"No."

I burst into laughter. "I think I understand a little more about why you are here in the corner. I feel like I'm giving you a root canal."

He shrugged. "I told you I'm not a big people person."

I studied him. I felt like I was pretty good at reading people. I had to be in my line of work. I had to be prepared to jump in and rescue a bride that was on the verge of hysteria or a bitch fit. When I read him, I saw a guy that was uncomfortable but could be fun given the right circumstances. "You haven't found the right people."

"Pardon me?"

"You said you aren't a people person. I'm saying you haven't met the right people. I bet you could enjoy things like these if you had someone to hang out with."

He looked amused. "Is this your professional opinion?"

"It is. Like me. I'm fun. You are talking to me."

I saw a flash of amusement in his eyes. "I'm not sure if that's what I would call this."

"This?" I asked.

"This," he said, gesturing between us. "I think you are doing the talking. I'm just here to agree."

"I want to touch you," I said, earning a shocked look from him.

"Uh, that's different."

I heard myself giggling again. I couldn't even explain why I was laughing. It really wasn't that funny. He was just so damn dry, it made me laugh. "I don't want to *touch you*, touch you. I want to know if you are truly as prickly as you come off."

He smirked. "Yes."

"Yes?"

"I'm prickly. I'm a dick. I'm arrogant, aloof, introverted, and all the other words. That's me."

"Liar. I don't think you are. I think you think you are. I bet you know how to have fun."

"Maybe." He scanned the crowd before finishing his drink and standing up straight. "I'm going to find my friend and go. I've had as much fun and excitement as I can handle."

"You keep saying you came here with a friend, but I have yet to see this person. Is this a girlfriend?"

"No."

"Why are you in such a hurry to leave?" I questioned.

He shrugged. "Because I find my own company to be far more entertaining."

"Ah, but we have free booze."

"Which is why my friend is here. He likes the free shit. Personally, I have much better booze at home. And I don't have to wear a suit. I can sit around on my very comfortable couch and drink good scotch."

I was intrigued. I didn't know why. The man had done nothing to interest me. He had not given me even the slightest idea he might like me. In fact, he was making it very clear he would rather be anywhere else than in that room talking to me. Yet, here I was, wanting to spend more time with him. It made zero sense.

"I have an idea," I said, pulling away from the wall and looking into his eyes.

He stared back at me. I wanted to believe I saw a hint of desire, but I couldn't be sure. "What would that be?" he asked in a husky voice.

Yep. I had detected desire. I would use that to get what I wanted. "I have an idea about how we can get you out of that shell you are in."

"I'm not in a shell," he replied.

"Okay, shell isn't the right word. Let's soften your pricklies."

He raised an eyebrow. "What?"

"You are a prickly beast. You use those proverbial quills to keep people away. I know how we can soften those sharp ends."

"Why would I want to do that?"

"Because."

"Because?" he pressed.

I didn't have an answer. "Because it will be fun."

Instead of telling me to take a flying leap into the ocean, he slowly nodded. "All right, what's this grand idea?"

"Let's go to Balboa Park. I'll meet you there at ten tomorrow."

He really looked confused then. I decided that was my cue to leave. I needed to leave him hanging. If I gave him the chance to argue, he would talk himself out of it. I wasn't going to give him the option. I walked away without a backward glance. Curiosity was killing me, and I had to know what he was doing. I waited until I was tucked safely behind a curtain to take a peek.

He was still standing in the same spot looking very confused. Confusion was good. It was better than anger or irritation. I checked in with the caterers, made sure there was plenty of appetizers coming out, and made my usual rounds around the room.

I stopped, turned, and looked for my mystery man. I realized in that moment I never even got his name. I never gave him my name. I would probably never see him again. He didn't shut me down, but he didn't exactly say yes. I wasn't sure how that made me feel. I couldn't explain why I had any interest in him at all. I really had nothing to go on.

The guy wasn't the kind that gave a girl the warm and fuzzies. But, as usual, I was attracted to the wrong kind of guy.

CHAPTER 7

XANDER

I parked my BMW in the parking lot, not caring I was stuck at a spot way in the back. It was the parking lot she designated—no ordered—me to be at. I was actually on time, which surprised me a little. I couldn't explain why I was there at all. The woman intrigued me. That was why I was there. She had challenged me. I did not turn down a challenge, especially from a beautiful woman.

I tapped my hands on the steering wheel, staring out at the cars in every size and color, and wondered once again why I was there. I shouldn't have come. I moved to start the engine, ready to get the hell out of there when there was a knock on my driver's side window. I nearly jumped out of my seat.

It was her. She was peering at me through the heavily tinted window. How did she know it was me? I pushed the button to roll down the window and looked at her. "Are you going to sit in your car all day? That really wasn't what I had in mind."

I shook my head. "No."

"Then come on," she said, reaching for the door handle. "I'm parked right in front of you. How crazy is that? With these windows, I never would have been able to see you. Are these even legal?"

Her rambling put me off my game a little. I climbed out of the car, leaving my shades on. "Do you always talk this much?"

She burst into laughter. "I do. I have a feeling I have to talk enough to make up for the both of us. You don't strike me as a great conversationalist."

"Not really," I replied, closing the door and hitting the lock button. "I don't mind the peace and quiet."

"I love a little peace and quiet as well, but a conversation isn't really noise."

It was to me. "I suppose that's one of those things everyone has a different opinion on."

"Subjective," she agreed. "Thankfully, I am not one to care a whole lot about other people's opinions."

I inwardly groaned. What in the hell had I gotten myself into? "Isn't this place kind of touristy?" I asked, noticing the families taking pictures of every fucking thing.

"I love it here, tourists or not. We all have our little space in the world."

"Seems awful crowded in my space," I complained.

She patted my arm. "I promise you will be okay. No one will invade your space."

I looked down at her hand touching my bicep. "Good to know."

"I'm sorry. I had to know."

"Know what?" I asked, quickly growing tired of the back and forth. She was exhausting me. I had only been with her for less than five minutes and I felt like I could use a drink.

"If you were really prickly," she said before bursting into laughter.

Her laughter was contagious. I found myself laughing a little. "And?"

"And you don't feel prickly at all."

My short-sleeved T-shirt barely hid the tat, the standard barbed-wired, around the upper part of my arm. "Good to know. So where are you taking me? What is it you think is so special about this place?"

I gave her a look. "I grew up in San Diego or the general area. Yes, I've been here."

"All right, all right, I was just making sure. I thought there was a chance you spent your days in a dark dungeon."

She was making a joke. Teasing me. That was definitely different than the other women I dated. I quickly reminded myself it wasn't a date. It was—hell, I didn't know what it was. "I suppose you want to walk through the shops and stuff?"

"I was thinking we could go on a short walk and then to the Japanese Garden first," she said with way too much enthusiasm. "I love going there. It is absolutely beautiful. Have you been before?"

My brain felt like it had just been tossed on a hamster wheel. I was trying to keep up with the onslaught of talking. "Yes."

"Great! Then I won't have to explain every little thing."

She was already on the move. I took a second to check out her ass in the shorts she was wearing. The shorts weren't the booty shorts that had the cheeks hanging out. They were a respectable length that showed off plenty of leg without being too much. She was wearing a pretty pair of sandals with little jewels on the straps. The sandals showed off her toes that were painted with a bright red polish. The shirt she wore was fitted around the waist and flowing in the middle with massive shoulder cut-outs. Her long black hair was pulled up in a ponytail. She was beautiful.

"Are we in a race?" I asked.

She stopped walking and turned to look behind her. "Your legs are twice as long as mine are. Keep up."

My brows shot up. She was a bossy thing. "What exactly are we doing here?"

"We are enjoying the beauty of the world we live in."

"Why?"

"Because we can," she shot back. "Are you always this obstinate?"

"I suppose I am. Are you always this pushy?"

She laughed again. "I am."

"Why me?" I asked the question that had been on my mind all night. "Why are you insisting I come enjoy life with you? I'm not the most personable man."

"You've got that right," she said.

"Then why me?"

She let out a long sigh, slowing her pace to fall in line with me. "Because I see a man in need of saving."

"Saving from what?"

"Yourself."

"I'm fine."

"You are fine, but you are not great," she answered. "I guess I can't walk away from a project. I see a man in need of a boost. A man that needs to see the brighter side of things."

"I see things just fine," I replied.

"You see things in black and white and maybe a hint of gray, I suspect."

We kept walking, finding an easy pace that allowed us to talk without sprinting. "What's wrong with that?"

"Nothing, if you are at work or working on a project. I am a very black and white girl Monday through Saturday. Sunday, I like to see color."

"What the hell does that mean?" I asked.

"It means on Sundays, I like to come here. If I don't have a job on Saturday, I will take the whole weekend and go up the coast. I love to get out in nature and recharge. Nature is the place that reminds me how lucky I am to be alive. I need the color. I need the lively activity of nature. It's like a reset once a week."

"You work six days a week?" I asked.

"Most of the time. Sometimes, I take a Monday or Tuesday off, but during our busy season, it is usually six days."

I slowly nodded, having a newfound respect for her and the work she did. "I had no idea a party planner worked that hard."

She made a choking sound. "We work our asses off."

"Where are we going?" I asked when I noticed she wasn't taking the usual route to the garden.

"I wanted to show you something," she answered.

"If this was reversed, me taking you to some off-the-beaten-path place, it would be the premise of a horror film."

She laughed as she started to walk a little faster. "I promise I will not violate your body in any way."

"Too bad," I mumbled under my breath.

Her head whipped around to look at me. "My goodness—" She stopped talking. "I get that you want privacy and you are a closed book, but can I at least know your name?"

I chuckled at the fact she only then realized we didn't know each other's names. It had certainly taken her long enough. "My name is Xander Holland."

She stopped walking and extended her hand. "Nice to meet you Xander. Officially, that is. My name is Evie Marsh."

"Evie, where are we going?"

"Just a little farther," she promised. "The view is gorgeous and there are not a lot of people up here."

"Why are you wearing sandals?" I questioned.

She looked down at her feet as if she just realized they were there. "I always wear sandals."

"Even to go hiking?"

"This isn't hiking," she said with a laugh. "It's a nice walk. The sandals are comfortable. Far more comfortable than the heels I usually wear."

I shrugged. "If you say so."

We continued walking up a slight incline. I couldn't remember ever visiting this particular section of the park. It was pretty. It was calming—minus the endless chatter from my walking companion.

"It's just up here," she pointed.

I didn't know what it was, but this was her show. I was only along for the ride. We rounded a corner and came upon several benches set apart from one another. An older couple was sitting on one of the benches and looking over the view that stretched out below. She took a seat on the bench farthest from the couple and patted the spot next to her.

"Is this what you brought me here for?" I asked.

She smiled and pushed up her sunglasses. I did the same. The area was shaded and provided a nice place to cool down after the rather brisk hike up the hill. "Yes and no. Don't you ever just like to sit and be?"

"I think I do that pretty often," I replied.

"Outside?" she questioned.

I grinned. "I have a pretty nice backyard." I didn't go into details, but my backyard rivaled the park in my opinion. I didn't have acres of gardens, but I had the ocean and that was better than anything else.

She rolled her pretty blue eyes that were as blue as the ocean on some days. "Your backyard is not the same as this."

I wrinkled my nose. "It's pretty damn close."

She looked skeptical. "What exactly is it you do?"

"I'm an engineer," I answered. "I design ships."

"Aren't ships pretty basic?" she questioned.

I smiled. I loved to talk about my work. Few people, besides those that were interested in buying my ships to increase profits, really understood or cared. "Yes and no. I design ships made with materials that are much lighter. The usual ships are made of heavy steel. Because they are so heavy, the ships can't carry much cargo."

"Because they would sink," she said with a nod.

"Yes. My ships are lighter, a little smaller, but yet, they carry more cargo. Because they are lighter and smaller, they use less fuel."

She smiled. "Well, aren't you a smarty pants?"

I shrugged. "Maybe not smart but forward thinking. Too many people get stuck in the way things are and don't know how or don't want to look forward."

"Why boats?" she asked. "You are a forward thinker, so why not solar energy or something like that?"

"There are lots of people working on solar energy and I like boats."

"Do you own a boat?"

I had to smile. "I do."

"Like a little speedboat or a big boat?"

"It's not a yacht, but it isn't a speedboat."

"So, a big boat."

I had to laugh at her persistence. "It's a good-size boat. I could probably live on it if I needed to."

She nodded, seeming to file away the information. "Would you like to show me your boat?" she asked.

The woman always talked in a way that made me feel like she was dropping sexual innuendo. I wasn't sure if that was the case and didn't want to stick a foot in my mouth by saying something inappropriate. "I would like to show you my boat."

She grinned. "Then it's a date."

CHAPTER 8

EVIE

I t was a fairly cool morning, or as cool as it could be on a summer day in southern California. I appreciated the shade that made it comfortable to sit outside while listening to birds and the happy sounds of kids enjoying nature.

"What about you?" he asked.

I turned to look at him, taking in the profile of the man that had caught my interest. "What about me?"

"You're a party planner. How did you get to be that?"

The way he said it made it sound like it was a dirty word. "That?" I said with a laugh. "I think I always knew that I loved parties. Didn't you like parties as a kid?"

"I don't think I remember a lot of parties when I was a kid."

"Birthday parties?" I questioned.

He slowly shook his head. "No. Not really. I think we had one for my younger brother when he turned five, but that's about it."

That struck me as odd. I couldn't imagine a childhood with no parties. "Did you ever go to parties?"

"I went to a few homecoming parties."

I wrinkled my nose. "Not a kegger. I mean a party to celebrate something."

"A homecoming party celebrates a military person coming home," he explained.

"Oh, I see. Were you in the military? Navy, right?"

"No. I wasn't. My dad was a Navy man."

It was becoming clearer. "And you probably moved around a lot, so you didn't have a lot of friends and therefore not a lot of parties."

"Actually, no. My parents moved around a lot when my dad was first in the Navy, but he quickly climbed the ranks. Most of his time in the service was spent here in San Diego. When he had to go out, he went, and we stayed."

"That had to make your life easier," I reasoned.

He shrugged. "I suppose."

It was a subject he wasn't going to discuss. That much was clear. "I love a good party," I said, starting up the conversation again. "Parties, especially the themed ones, are a chance to go all around the world. You can be anyone. I love to create these imaginary worlds where a person can forget who they are just for a few hours."

"Themed parties?" he questioned. "Like the boat thing?"

I laughed. "That was not a theme. That was decorations. I will admit I probably missed the mark with that one. I should have done something a little more fun. To be fair, I got exactly six days' notice and zero direction from the client."

"Does that happen a lot?"

"Short notices?"

"Yes."

I shook my head. "No, not really. Usually, in my world, a short notice is a month or two."

"It takes that long to plan a party?" he asked with surprise.

I laughed, nodding. "Yes, at least our parties do. It isn't always parties. It can be a wedding, an anniversary, a grand opening, and things like that."

"Do you plan weddings?"

"I do," I answered. "I do it all."

"Do you go to school to become a party planner?"

I didn't get the sense he was asking it to be rude. He seemed genuinely curious. "You don't technically have to. I have a degree in public relations with some business admin classes as well."

"I never knew it was such a serious industry."

"Have you ever been to a wedding?" I questioned. I had a feeling I already knew the answer.

"I've been to a couple."

"Weddings are ridiculous to plan, big weddings that is. There are so many details. Add in people's nerves and feelings and it can get pretty crazy. We take away the crazy."

"I don't envy you," he said. "It is not a job I would ever want."

"Yeah, I kind of get that from you. I don't see you being a real people person, handling a hormonal bride that cries when there is a single bead out of place on her veil."

"Oh my god," he said with shock. "Does that actually happen?"

"It does. A lot."

He shuddered as if he was truly repulsed. "No fucking way I could do that job."

"It's not all bad," I assured him. "Sometimes, it can be so much fun. I love the big budget kid parties. I love the princess parties with castles and fairies and stuff like that."

"Whimsy," he said.

"Whimsical and dreamy," I corrected. "Tell me more about your boat."

"Why? It's a boat. It floats."

I burst into a fit of giggles. "Do you try to be funny or is this the real you?"

"I'm not trying to be funny. This is the real me."

I slapped at my knee. "You are so dry."

"Is that an insult? It feels like an insult."

"It isn't, I promise," I said, trying to hold back my laugh. "You have a very dry personality and it is actually very funny."

"Okay," he said as if he wasn't sure he believed me.

We fell into an easy silence. I noticed him scanning the area. I remembered the first time I had come upon the benches. I sat down and probably sat for an hour. I was taken with the beauty of it all. "It's hard to resist, huh?"

"What?"

"The view."

"It's nice," he agreed.

"It's beautiful," I answered. "I love the contrast between the park and the city. When I was younger, I used to pretend we were in a dome. Like a terrarium of sorts."

"It is a very peaceful place," he said.

"Sometimes, especially after a particularly long week, a little bit of peace is necessary. What do you do to unwind after a long week?"

He shrugged. "I don't know. I go down to the beach."

"Do you surf?"

He scoffed. "No. It's the hair, right?"

I grinned. "It's a little bit the hair. What do you do on the beach?"

"I walk. I swim. I just kind of chill."

"Do you live near the beach?"

His coy smile told me he did. "You could say that."

"Stop being so cagey. You have one of those big beachfront mansions?"

"It's not as big as some of the others. I preferred more land and less house."

My eyes widened. "Oh my god, you are being serious!"

"Yes, I am. Why would I lie?"

I turned to look at him, making a big show as I did. "The boat business is that good?"

"It is," he said with a soft smile as he nodded.

"That explains a lot," I said, putting all the pieces together.

"What does?"

"You are one of those wealthy, eccentric types."

"I don't think I'm eccentric at all. I like to keep to myself. I don't go out a lot. I don't care to go out a lot."

"Because you don't like people. I remember. Do you live in San Diego?"

"Yes," he answered. "I live in the La Jolla area."

"Wow, no kidding. I grew up in the general area. Not in one of those big fancy mansions on the beach but the general area."

"I grew up on base mostly. We did finally move off base to a house just outside the city."

"That's pretty cool. Which base?"

"Pendleton," he answered.

"Oh, yes, I know where that is."

He smirked but didn't say anything about it. "Can I ask how old you are?" he asked with slight discomfort.

"Why do you want to know that?"

"Because you look young," he answered. "Maybe a little too young. I don't want to be accused of anything."

"I'm twenty-eight, plenty old enough. How old are you?"

"Thirty-two."

"What do you think you would be accused of?" I asked.

He shrugged. "I don't know. It always surprises me."

"Are you saying you have been accused of doing things with young girls before?" I asked, only half-joking.

"Fuck no!" he answered. "It's more about young women see me and think I'm their ticket to an easy life."

I raised an eyebrow. "Now you are trying to piss me off."

"No," he quickly said, turning on the bench to face me. "I'm not trying to do that at all. I don't think you are doing that. I'm saying the younger ones, they tend to do that."

"Really?"

He nodded. "Yes. They get this idea we are going to date and I'm going to fall all over them because they are young and interested in me. I'm not a fucking dinosaur just yet."

I smiled, having a new understanding of him. "I imagine there are some ladies, young and old, who would be attracted to the money. I'm not."

"Then why did you talk to me?"

"I talk to everyone. You intrigued me. I didn't know who you were. Honestly, I thought you were one of the ship laborers."

He burst into laughter. "Really?"

"Yes, really."

"And you still talked to me?"

"I'm not like that," I told him. "I really am not interested in anything. I just saw a guy who, for whatever reason, appealed to my need to want to help. Not help but get to know."

"Am I charity?"

"No. I can't explain it."

He didn't seem convinced. "Me either."

We sat for a bit longer before we decided to make our way back down the trail. I asked if he wanted to visit the gardens, but he declined. I had pushed him enough for one day. "Was it terrible?" I asked when we reached our cars.

"Was what terrible?"

"Taking a walk with me?"

He offered me a very small smile. "No, it wasn't terrible."

"Can I borrow your phone for a second?"

He frowned. "Why?"

I held out my hand. "Paranoid much? I'm going to put my number in."

"Oh," he answered and fished it out of the pocket of his cargo shorts. He handed it to me after unlocking the screen.

"Call me if you would like to do this again," I said and handed him his phone.

"Would you like to do it again?" he asked as if it was completely crazy.

"Yes, I would. Maybe we can get to one of the gardens next time."

He stared at his phone. "I would like that. Should I give you my number?"

I smiled and nodded. "Yes, please. If I think of anything exciting to do, I'll give you a call. Unless you call me first. Let me grab my phone."

"You didn't take it with you?" he asked.

"Nope. When I am on my walk, I am not on. I have to unplug, or I will go crazy."

That seemed to surprise him. I grabbed my phone and saw a missed call from my dad. I would call him later. I handed him the phone and watched as his large hands held it and punched in the number. He handed it back. Our eyes locked. My breath caught in my throat. He was intense. I had a fleeting thought about what sex would be like with him.

I quickly pushed it out of my mind. I could not think like that. "Thank you," I said in a whisper.

"Thanks for today," he answered, still holding my gaze.

My mouth felt dry. "Okay."

"Okay," he repeated.

I found the energy to make my feet move and stepped away. I got into my car, suddenly feeling very hot. I started the engine and blasted the AC. Damn. The man got under my skin. I sensed there was so much more to him than what he presented to the world. I wanted to get to know him better. I couldn't explain why. It was just something I had to do. I had to know him.

"Xander Holland," I repeated his name aloud. I looked in the rearview mirror and watched him drive away.

There was something about him. Something raw. Something that appealed to my very soul. He was nothing like the men I usually dated. Nothing.

CHAPTER 9

XANDER

Charlie was sitting outside the building where he worked. I was meeting him for lunch. Technically, I was bringing him lunch to make up for ditching him at the party the other night. He wasn't truly mad. We both knew from the very beginning there was no way I was going to stay the entire time. It didn't matter. He was a little pissed. I would make up for it with burgers and fries, and all would be well.

I parked my car, hanging the parking pass from my rearview mirror before climbing out. I sauntered across the parking lot, carrying the bags in my hand. He was staring at his phone, obviously texting someone.

"You can't ignore me forever," I told him.

"It won't be that hard," he said, dropping the phone down. "You don't talk much."

I sat down and pushed a bag toward him. "I brought a peace offering."

He reached into the bag and pulled out one of the burgers. I grabbed one for myself. The waxy paper the burger was wrapped in was covered with grease stains, ketchup, and melted cheese. He took a big bite before wiping his mouth. "Where did you go?" he asked. "I saw you talking to some woman and then you were gone."

"I told you I was leaving," I reminded him.

"I didn't think you were serious."

I shrugged. "I was."

"Who was the woman? The way you were looking at her seemed like you were enjoying yourself."

"How was I looking at her?"

"Like you wanted to eat her."

I almost choked on the burger. "Bullshit."

He grinned. "You had that look in your eye."

"What look is that?"

"The look that says you want something. I've seen you get that look in your eye before. That car, your boat, an excellent ship. You want her."

I ignored his accusations. "What about you? Did you hook up with the lovely lady you were fawning all over?"

He groaned. "I lost her."

"What do you mean you lost her?"

"We agreed to go back to my place. I told her I was going to grab one for the road. She said she was going to grab her purse. This, mind you, came after a rather hot and heavy fifteen minutes crammed in a bathroom stall in the ladies' room. I walked outside and saw my Uber. I waited for her. She never came out."

"You lost her," I said with understanding.

He sighed. "I lost her. I went home alone with a serious case of blue balls. She was hot. She was wild. And I lost her."

I had to laugh. "I cannot believe you lost a person. That is a new one."

"What about you? Did you get her number?"

"Why would you ask that?"

"Because like I said, I saw the way you looked at her. She was also looking at you like you were a scrumptious snack."

I grabbed a box of fries and snatched one. "I don't think so."

"I saw her."

"I insulted her," I confessed.

"What do you mean you insulted her? What the hell? You cannot be that bad at flirting."

I smirked. "Apparently, I am. I was talking shit about the party planner. I mentioned how much of a waste it was. I even insulted the decorations."

He shrugged. "So?"

"She was the party planner."

He burst into laughter. "Damn, that's bad."

"It was, but it wasn't really that bad."

"I know you are a novice at this dating thing, but trust me. That is bad. You insulted the woman."

"I got her number," I smiled.

"No, you didn't?"

I grinned and nodded. "I did."

"Do not try and convince me you've got game. You have no game."

"I will not even try to convince you, but I did get her number. In fact, we hung out for a while on Sunday."

"Did you have a sleepover on Saturday?" he asked and waggled his brows.

"No, asshole. I'm not you."

"Then what happened?"

I quickly told him about her order to meet her at the park, which he laughed about. "It wasn't bad."

"You make it sound like you went for a root canal," he said with a laugh.

"I have to admit, that's what I thought it would be like at first. She talks a lot. And she moves a lot. She's just a lot in general."

He took another bite. "You are far from high energy."

"I have energy," I replied.

"I have never known you to be bubbly. Ever. Not even when you are drunk."

"I do not claim to be bubbly. She's bubbly. I just kind of effervesce in her presence."

He laughed harder. "Stop. You're going to make me choke."

"We walked up to a spot on a hill and just sat there. Well, she talked, but we sat."

"Tell me more about your lady."

"She is not my lady," I shot back.

"What did you do?"

"Nothing. We talked a little about her job. We talked about my love of ships. Normal stuff."

"Wow. I'm impressed. Now that you have her number, you have to make a move."

I shrugged. "Why?"

"Sometimes, I want to slap the shit out of you," he mumbled.

"Why?"

He sighed, making a big show of wiping his hands. "Because you have no clue. Zero clue. How long have you been single?"

I thought about it. "I don't know. Forever."

He nodded. "How many dates have you been on in let's say the last three months?"

I shrugged. "A couple."

He groaned, sounding pained. "I go on a couple of dates a week. You sit at home. You aren't getting any younger. You need to enjoy your youth. You need to date and have some fun."

"You always say that."

"I'm serious. You are in the prime of your life right now. You've got beauty, brains, and money."

I wasn't sure how to handle that statement. "Thanks. I think. You are not hitting on me, I hope."

"I don't want you, thanks. I'm saying, you have plenty of women that are more than happy to date you."

"They want to date my checkbook."

"I don't believe that's true for all of them," he insisted.

"Not for Evie," I said, her name rolling off my tongue.

"Evie," he repeated her name. "You like her."

"I don't dislike her."

"That's high praise coming from you."

I laughed. "She's not bad. And do you know what the best part is?"

"What?"

"She didn't know me. She thought I was one of the employees that worked on the ships."

He raised his brows. "Are you sure? You don't think it could be a trick to make you think she didn't know you."

"No, I don't think so. I only gave her my full name after we met at the park."

"Really? That's weird."

It was weird. "I guess it just didn't come up. You know me. I'm not really very good at the people thing. She seemed to get it and didn't pressure me."

"Hell, this one is a keeper," he joked.

"I think I'm going to offer to take her out on the boat," I said.

He stopped chewing, his eyes going wide. "No shit?"

"Why not?"

"Take her."

I studied him. "Why?" I asked, knowing he was up to no good. He had a plan.

He grinned. "Because no woman can resist a nice ride on a boat. You can offer her some of your fancy wine. Serve her expensive cheese. She'll crawl into bed with you so fast, you won't know what to do."

"I'll know what to do," I growled. "I'm not that out of practice."

"Then act fast. I saw her. She's gorgeous. Those curves. Another rich man is going to take advantage of that woman if you don't get in there."

"She's not a prized horse to win at an auction," I retorted.

"I don't know what you saw, but I saw a nice prize standing two feet in front of you. If it had been me, she would have been in my bed before the night was over."

I couldn't explain why, but hearing him say that pissed me off. It made me jealous. "You won't fucking look at her."

He grinned, his eyes sparkling. "Oh, touched a nerve. Look at you. You are already smitten."

"I am not," I argued.

"Don't wait too long," he warned. "I'm serious. She seemed to be a rare one."

I slowly nodded. "She is. I will."

"Good," he said, wiping his hands on a napkin before tossing it in the bag. "Now, I've got to get back to work. Call her. Don't fuck this up."

"I will." I nodded. "I will."

He got up from the table, grabbing his trash. "I'll call you later. Thanks for lunch."

I walked back to my car. For once in my life, I was going to take some advice. I pulled my phone out and quickly found her name in my contact list. This was where things got tricky. Did I call or text? I was really bad at the dating thing. I held the phone in my hand, staring at her name.

I was going to text.

Still want to go out on the boat?

It wasn't exactly smooth. I wasn't a smooth talker. It just didn't come naturally to me. Maybe I was a product of my upbringing. I didn't know how to be any other way. My father was a drill sergeant —literally. Well, we never dared call him that. He was Navy. He was an RDC and never let any of us forget it. He was a hard man. He didn't offer colorful words or soften his opinion. When he was pissed, he was pissed and didn't hide it.

She replied. *I would love to. When?*

My schedule was wide open. I didn't want to sound too eager and decided to play it cool. *Thursday?*

Perfect. Afternoon? Evening?

I would love to show her the sunset, but that would be very late. I decided late afternoon was best. If it turned into a long night out on the boat, so be it. I sure as hell wouldn't mind. I would love to spend the evening with her.

She agreed to call me on Thursday morning to establish a time. In the meantime, I would secure a couple bottles of the best wine and cheese. I didn't often flaunt my wealth, but I wanted to show her a good time. If I had the means, I may as well use them to my advantage. God knew I needed all the help I could get.

I wondered if I should text her again tonight. I was so bad at this. I should have gotten more tips from Charlie. No, that would be a mistake. Charlie was kind of a one-track man. I wasn't interested in fucking a woman just to fuck her. I tended to be a little more careful when it came to things like that. Sex could be just sex, but to me, it was an invitation into my life.

I liked to keep my life locked down. Very few people were allowed into my inner circle. I wasn't a saint by any means, but a hookup with a woman in a back alley or at her place was not the same as spending time with her, talking with her, and talking about myself.

Taking Evie out on my boat was a big step. Charlie was the only other person in the world that had been on my boat. Not even my brother had stepped foot on it. Granted, he wasn't in the country, but still. It was sacred ground. I was suddenly having second thoughts about taking such a big step. I wasn't sure I wanted her in my personal space.

I started the car and headed for my offices. Maybe I did want her in my personal space. I did want to let her in, just a little. It was a trip out on the boat. It wasn't a fucking wedding. I really needed to get over my knee-jerk response to the very idea of a relationship.

CHAPTER 10

EVIE

I walked into Nelle's bar just after six with my laptop bag in one hand and my phone in the other. It had been a crazy day. The day was spilling into my evening, which it tended to do. Nelle's bar was semi-busy with the after-work crowd sitting at tables and complaining about their shitty days. I was going to sit at the bar and complain about my day.

I sat on my usual stool at the very edge of the bar, farthest away from the action. It was where Nelle took a break when the action was slow. It was the best seat in the house as far as I was concerned. I could see everything and everyone, and yet, no one really paid much attention to the corner.

I ended my phone call to the flower shop that insisted they couldn't get the tulips my client wanted. I very nicely told them to look harder. I flopped down on the stool, my laptop bag on the bar. I looked around and knew there was no way I was going to get any actual work done. I was fried and really uninterested in hashing out the details of an all-vegan, gluten-free menu. That needed to be done on a fresh brain. I was beat. I slid it under the bar between my legs and the solid wood and waited for Nelle to notice me.

"You can drink coffee or water, but you are not getting another damn drink from me," Nelle snapped.

There was an older gentleman leaning forward in a drunken stupor as he lifted one finger to waggle it in her face. "Listen, young lady. You might be pretty, but you can't tell me what to do. Only my wife gets to do that, and she isn't here."

"I'm not telling you what to do," she replied and leaned closer to his face. "I'm telling you what you are not going to do. You're drunk. You are not getting another drink. Have some coffee."

"I don't want coffee," he replied, sounding a lot like a spoiled kid who refused to eat his dinner. "I want a beer."

"No."

"I want one."

"No," Nelle said again and poured him a cup of coffee. She put it in front of him and waited.

He looked at it and frowned. "That's not a beer."

"No shit?" she said with feigned surprise. "Pretend it is and we'll both be happy. Be good or I will call your wife. You know what she said last time."

That seemed to sink in. "You don't gotta call her," he slurred.

"Then drink the damn coffee!"

He pouted but did as he was told. Nelle sighed and came toward me. I smiled at her, noticing she barely looked ruffled at all.

"Just another Tuesday, huh?" I asked with a small laugh.

"He lost a big account or something," she said with a shake of her head. "I felt bad for him but now he's pissing me off."

"Poor guy," I said.

She shrugged. "What about you? You have been working your tail off again."

I sighed. "Yes. The normal. I didn't work Sunday though. Not all of Sunday anyway."

"Did you go to the park?" she asked.

I smiled and nodded. I was excited to tell her about Xander. "I did. And I didn't go alone."

"Your dad?" she asked as she filled a glass from one of the taps and handed it to a waitress. Nelle was the best multitasker I had ever met in my life. She did it effortlessly. She could carry on three different conversations without missing a beat.

"Nope, a guy."

She stopped wiping the bar and gave me her full attention. "Woah, woah, woah. When was there a guy in the picture? I talked to you last week. There was no man."

"I met him at the event on Saturday," I said, unable to hide my smile.

"Who is this man?"

I shrugged. "I don't really know all that much about him. I didn't even get his name until we were at the park."

She held up a hand. "How did you get to the park with him?" Her eyes bulged. "Oh my god, did you stay the night with him?"

"No! I met him there. Sheesh, I'm not that easy."

She raised an eyebrow. When I scowled in return, she laughed. "I'm kidding. So, who is this guy?"

"I really don't know. I noticed him alone at the party and struck up a conversation with him."

She nodded. "Because that's what you do. You see a wallflower and you decide they must be drawn into the fun."

"Exactly. That's what I do. Literally. That's what I do."

"Okay and then it went well from there?"

I grimace. "I think well is a strong word. It didn't go terrible. He is a really quiet guy. A real, genuine loner. He clearly preferred his own company."

"And yet you hounded him until you got him to go to the park with you," she said with a laugh. "I will never doubt your power of persuasion."

"I didn't hound him," I protested. "We chatted a bit and then I suggested—maybe demanded—he meet me at the park. He left right after we talked. While I was making my rounds around the party, I heard some of the other people talking about him. One of them mentioned he won some big award."

"You went to the park with a man whose name you didn't know

and you didn't know shit about him?" she questioned. She was giving me that stern look. It was the same look she gave me when I was a little tipsy and considering going home with a guy.

"It was the park," I insisted. "It wasn't that bad."

"What's this guy's name?" she asked, pulling her phone from the back pocket of her skinny jeans.

"Xander Holland," I told her. I should have Googled him. I didn't even think to do it. I really needed to get with the times and learn how to internet stalk better.

I waited while she typed in the name. Her brows shot up. "Not bad," she murmured. "Not bad at all."

"Let me see!" I grabbed her phone to check out a picture of him. It was one of those awful company pictures with a forced smile and him in a suit. He looked like he was getting a tooth pulled.

"That's him." I smiled.

"He's hot," she said and took the phone back. "Let's see if we can find any real dirt on him." I waited while she slid her finger over her screen, scowled, and pushed another button.

"Well?"

"He has no social media, unless he uses a different name. There is nothing on him. How boring."

"That sounds very much like the man I spoke with," I said, oddly happy that he wasn't one of those guys that bragged all over social media. "He's very closed up. He doesn't talk much."

"I bet you do plenty of talking for the both of you."

I laughed. "Odd. He said the same thing."

She put her phone back in her pocket. "Why him?"

"I don't know. There was just something about him. It's like seeing a pretty box with intricate wrapping paper. I wanted to know what was in the box. I am dying of curiosity to know him."

"Because he's hot," she said.

"He is handsome."

"Now what?" she questioned. "Was it a one-park date or is this going to be a thing?"

"I'm going out on his boat with him on Thursday," I told her.

"Wow."

"Is that a bad wow or a good wow?" I questioned. Her opinion mattered. I valued her advice and her experience. She was a little more world-wise than I was.

"I think you have to go with your gut," she answered. "You like him. You were drawn to him. You have had one date with him and it went well. Go for it."

I grinned. "Thank God. I was really hoping you would say that. I'm excited."

"What kind of boat is this?"

"Not a yacht but not a little boat. I think he has money. I don't know how much but he said he lived on the beach. We know how much those houses are."

"This is what I need you to do," she said, leaning on the bar like she had to give me the details of a top-secret mission.

"What?" I whispered.

"I need you to find out if he has a brother."

I burst into laughter. "I will certainly ask."

"I'm happy for you. It's been a while since I've seen you crush on a guy."

I shrugged. "It is slim pickings out there. A lot of the guys I meet are just so—I don't know—irritating. They want sex and someone to take care of them. I like a man that can stand on his own two feet. I like sex, but I would like to think I am more valuable than a basic pin cushion."

She sighed, shaking her head. "I hear ya girl. Boy, do I hear you. All the good ones are taken or gay."

It was our usual complaint. "I'm not sure if this is a boyfriend thing, but I do want to find out. Like I said, he doesn't exactly ooze information. He's not even an onion that I need to peel back layers. He is more of a coconut. I need to hammer at that hard shell he has just to get to the part where I can see who he really is."

"He's your new project."

I smiled. "Maybe."

"You are a natural-born nurturer. You nurture your dad and now you are looking for a man to nurture. You are going to make a good mommy one day."

I groaned. "Shh, you are going to remind my biological clock that time is ticking away."

"You've got time. You better. We are the same age and I'm not about to leave this world without having a child."

"I should probably go home and try to get some work done," I said on a long sigh.

"You work too much."

"I know. I do. But if I'm at home, I can work with a glass of wine in my hand. It doesn't feel like work so much then."

"Go home, relax a little, and daydream about your hot new man."

"I don't think I can call him mine—yet."

"Not yet, but you can certainly dream about him. I just might."

I frowned at her. "Hands off, woman. He is mine."

She winked. "Thought so."

I grabbed my laptop and headed out. I was in the mood for sweats, wine, and Netflix. And maybe a little daydreaming about Xander. It was hard to dream too much when I knew so little. I didn't know what it was like to be touched by him. I knew he was a hard man in a very literal sense. My touch to his arm gave me a little clue about what he was hiding underneath the invisible armor he wore to keep people at arm's length.

I was not the kind of person who really respected those rules. I could admit I tended to be more of an in your face person. I liked people. Most of the time. There were very few occasions when I truly disliked someone.

I was going to find out what made the man tick. And then maybe, just maybe, I would like what I found. If I was lucky, he would reciprocate the feeling.

"Or it could all be one giant waste of time," I muttered to myself.

I drove home and parked in the designated spot in my apartment building before going up. I opened the door to my one-bedroom apartment just on the outskirts of the La Jolla neighborhood. I wanted to be close to my dad but couldn't really afford the rent in his area.

My apartment wasn't luxurious, but it was in a newish complex and it worked perfectly for me. I loved the pool and the outdoor amenities which was why I chose the building over some of the cheaper ones.

I put down the laptop and went into my room to change before settling in for a dull but comfortable evening on the couch.

CHAPTER 11

XANDER

I was on my back, messing with the wiring for the stereo on the boat when I heard footsteps. It was a busy marina. I didn't think anything of it until I heard her voice.

"Knock, knock," she called out.

I had to smile. I slid out from where I was mostly hidden from view. "I'm here," I said, getting to my feet.

She looked at the screwdriver in my hand and then back at me. "Um, I think I might take a raincheck."

"Why?"

"You are working on your boat. That isn't a good sign, is it?"

I grinned, shaking the screwdriver. "I was fixing the stereo. The boat is fine. She isn't going to sink."

She looked skeptical. "I don't know. I'm not a great swimmer."

"It's going to be fine. It isn't going to sink."

She gestured at the boat with one hand. "What about the engine? Is it sound?"

She was nervous. It was very different from the confident, bubbly woman I had met at the party. It was too good to pass up. "I have rations on the boat. They will last at least four days. We can live three weeks without food."

Her mouth fell open. "What?" she gasped, looking absolutely horrified.

"I'm kidding," I teased.

She studied me as if she was trying to decide whether I was truly joking. I put down the screwdriver and climbed off the boat. I grabbed her shoulders and bent my knees to look directly into her eyes. "It's going to be okay. It's a fairly new boat."

"You were teasing?" she whispered.

I nodded. "I was."

A slow smile spread across her face. "You're an ass."

I grinned and stood up to my full height. "I've been called that before. I'll take it. Now, come on."

I took her hand and helped her onto the boat. It gently rocked with our weight before quickly leveling out.

"I can't believe you joked about something so serious."

"It was a joke," I said. "You look terrified."

"So you kept going?" she asked, putting a hand on one hip.

I shrugged. "I'm sorry."

She laughed. "No, you are not."

I took a second to look her over. She was wearing a pretty blue tank that was tucked into the low-rise jean shorts. Again, the shorts were a little longer than the usual style. Her legs were tanned and shapely. The flat boat shoes she wore were appropriate for the occasion. Her hair was left loose, hanging over one exposed shoulder.

"Are you ready?" I asked.

She took a deep breath. "I have a confession."

"What's that?"

"I've never actually been out on the water. I've been on boats for parties and stuff, but I've never actually gone out to sea or anything."

"Are you truly nervous?"

"A little," she admitted.

I was happy she could admit her fear. The first two encounters with her made me feel a little less than. She seemed to have it all together. She had a very confident air about her. She wasn't perfect.

"It's going to be okay. I'm good at what I do. I've been out on the boat a hundred times."

"Okay, I trust you," she said.

"Great. Would you like the grand tour now or when we are out on the water?"

I shrugged. "Now is good."

I thought so as well. I wanted her to be comfortable. "All right, we'll start up here."

I showed her around the boat before taking her below. There was a small kitchen, living area, and a single bedroom. By the time we made our way back upstairs, she seemed a little more relaxed. I was curious as to why she wanted to go on the boat if she was afraid of the open water.

"Go ahead and have a seat," I told her. "Get comfy."

I started the engine and sat down. I navigated out of the marina and headed for the open water. Thankfully, the water wasn't too clogged with other boats. Once we were out at a comfortable distance from the shore, I set the anchor and moved to sit down with her.

"This is nice," she said.

"Are you feeling okay?" I asked her.

She smiled. "I am. I was a little apprehensive, but this isn't bad at all. And you showed me the lifejackets, so I'm good. I can float."

"Good to know. I'm going to grab a drink. Would you like a glass of wine? Water? Something else?"

"A glass of wine would be very nice."

"I'll be right back."

I went downstairs and quickly opened one of the bottles of wine I had brought along for the trip. I poured two glasses, grabbed the cheese tray I'd picked up from the deli, and walked back upstairs. I handed her one of the glasses and put the tray on the small table.

"This is so relaxing," she commented.

"It is, especially when there aren't a lot of other boats out here. Sometimes, it can get really packed. Other boaters think it's a great place to party out here. They blast their music, scream, and just kind of ruin the tranquility for the rest of us."

She sipped her wine. "It sucks when a few bad apples ruin it for everyone."

"I agree. And it is just stupid. Unsafe. Reckless."

"Gee, tell me how you really feel," she said with a laugh.

I crossed one leg over the other and relaxed into the comfortable couch. I did enjoy a nice evening out on the boat. I realized in that moment, it was even better with a little company. "Are you busy planning another party?"

I smiled. "Always. There is always another one."

"Any more shipping parties?"

"No. If I do another with a ship theme, it is going to be all in and it will not be for a shipping company."

"I hope you didn't take what I said seriously. I'm the last person you want to take party advice from."

She pushed up her sunglasses. I did the same. "It was true. You were being honest. Brutally honest."

I cringed. "I tend to be a little tactless."

"It's okay," she assured me. "It was deserved."

"How come you have never been out on a boat?" I asked. "You said you lived in the area all your life. It's kind of hard to avoid the water."

She shrugged. "We didn't have a boat when I was growing up and it really never appealed to me. I like the sand beneath my feet. I like solid footing."

I slowly nodded. "I understand. I'm sorry if I pressured you into coming out."

"No!" she said, sitting forward. "Absolutely not. I wanted to come out. I think I kind of pushed my way onto the boat."

"I'm glad to have you aboard."

"I'm happy to be aboard," she said with a smile.

A cool ocean breeze lifted her hair. I wanted to know if it felt as silky as it looked. I turned my gaze away before she could see what I was thinking about. The tank she wore was tight, hugging her ample breasts. It was hard not to be that guy. The guy that stared at a woman's breasts instead of her eyes.

"Do you work in an office or do you work from home?" she asked.

"I do have an office," I answered. "I have a staff that runs things."

"Do you work out of it?"

"Sometimes," I answered truthfully. "I don't get involved with much of the actual business side of things. I have a finance guy, an assistant, and a handful of other employees that take care of all that. Mostly, I take meetings, I design, and I decide how much a design is worth. I can do that from my office at home. I get a lot more work done at home than in the office."

"I get that," she said. "I like to do a lot of work from home or a restaurant or my friend's bar."

"A bar?" I questioned. "I didn't take you for a barfly."

She softly giggled. "I'm not a barfly. It's about the only time I can talk to my friend, Nelle. She works nights. I work days."

"Ah, I see."

"Why don't you show me how to drive this thing?" she asked.

"You don't just drive a man's boat," I told her.

She burst into laughter. "I won't drive it. How about I steer?"

"It's like driving a car without pedals."

She got to her feet. "Show me."

I got up and walked to the driver's seat. I sat down and patted my leg. She raised one eyebrow before smiling and taking a seat on my leg. Her perfect, round ass settled against my thigh. It was hard to focus on what I was actually supposed to be doing.

I grabbed her hand and put it on the wheel before taking her other hand and putting it on the throttle. "Ready?"

I pushed the button to pull up the anchor. Once ready, I showed her how to apply the throttle and we slowly started to move forward. She squealed with delight once we started moving. We headed farther out to sea before she decided she had enough.

"Why don't we settle here for a bit?" I told her.

She stood up from my lap. "That was amazing. I feel so alive."

"I'm glad you enjoyed yourself. Would you like another glass of wine?"

She smiled and nodded. "Absolutely."

I moved to grab our empty glasses and headed downstairs. She followed me down into the kitchen. I opened the wine and began to pour. The entire time, she stared at me. Her heated gaze was going to be my undoing. I truly never meant to take Charlie's advice, but if she kept looking at me like she wanted to eat me, I was going to push her up against that wall and pound myself into her.

I put down the wine bottle and looked at her, really looked at her. I didn't hide my desire. Her lips parted, her pink tongue darting out to lick them as if she suddenly had a very dry mouth. I could fix that. I took a step toward her. She made no move to escape.

I paused, inches from her, giving her the chance to move. She didn't. Her chin went up and she stared directly into my eyes. I saw the same heat reflected there. The tension between us was thick with need. There was no fighting what was happening between us. I waited a single breath before I reached for the back of her head.

My mouth closed over hers. I only meant to give her a small kiss. I wanted it to be a simple kiss that would take the edge off. Part of me wanted to rebel against what Charlie told me to do. Fuck that. One kiss wasn't enough. I growled low in my throat as my mouth opened wider to devour her. I burned for the woman. I could feel the fire low in my belly, urging me to take more.

Her hands moved into my hair, holding my head low against hers. I couldn't release her. I refused to release her. Some otherworldly force was driving me on. My tongue dueled with hers. It was a clash to see who could get whose tongue in the other's mouth. She gave as good as she got.

CHAPTER 12

EVIE

I was not going to let myself think about the fact I was kissing the man in his kitchen, on his boat. I was letting go of all my rules and inhibitions. I was living in the moment. Holy hell, what a moment it was. His mouth moved over mine like a man that had been searching the desert for water. His hands, holy shit, his hands were everywhere.

I struggled to keep up. My hands roamed his body, getting my first real feel of the muscles in his arms and stretched across his back. He was powerful and hard and so damn hot. He reached for the hem of my shirt and tugged at it until it was halfway up my body. Our mouths tore away from one another while he quickly removed it before diving right back in.

One of his large hands grabbed my breast, lifting the weight of it. He groaned low in his throat and attacked me with new enthusiasm. I wanted the same. I pulled at his shirt, essentially trying to tear it from his body. I didn't want to take it off the usual way. I didn't want to lose his mouth against mine.

He pulled back just a little, his mouth still on mine as he pulled the shirt up, yanked it away, and tore it off before devouring my face once again. My hands stretched out across his pecs before running around to touch his back. His skin was hot and smooth and taut across the rippling muscles.

"I need you naked," he growled. "Now."

His hands were stripping off my shorts, taking my panties down with them. Clearly, he wasn't interested in doing a layer by layer. I attacked his shorts with my fingers. I fumbled with the button until I yanked, popping the damn thing off. He was wealthy. He could buy more shorts.

Within seconds, we were both stripped naked. He stood in front of me, his chest heaving up and down as he dragged in heavy breaths. I could see the passion in his eyes. I could feel it radiating off him. It was intense and made me want to climb him like a tree.

I stared at him, waiting to see what he would do next. I would probably die if he had a change of heart at that point. My eyes pulled away from his and drifted over his body. He was hard and tattooed. That was unexpected. I saw the band around his arm and what looked like writing on the underside of his arm. That had to be a painful place to get a tattoo. I wouldn't know from personal experience, but I imagined so. There were small tattoos on his chest, including a ship that I suspected was one of his.

Once the inspection of his torso was complete, I dropped my eyes lower. I sucked in a breath when I saw the size of him. His heavy cock was jutting forward. He was a big man in every sense of the word. I was a little intimidated. I wasn't an innocent virgin, but he was definitely one of the largest men I had ever been with.

"Are you okay with this?" he asked on a breath that made him sound as if he was choking.

I met his eyes and gave him a slow nod. "Absolutely."

He sprang into action so fast, I barely had time to blink. His hands were on my ass and then one was sliding between my legs. His mouth slammed over mine again, his tongue pushing its way in as his finger worked its way inside me down below. It was a double whammy. I gasped, inadvertently sucking his tongue deeper into my throat. I lifted one leg, bending it at the knee to give him better access like a complete wanton.

"You're so fucking wet already," he whispered.

I was a little embarrassed, but seriously, had he seen him? He was sex on a stick. He was a Greek god. He was every woman's wet dream. Of course, I was wet. I was also about to climax. I tried to fight it. I didn't want him to know just how badly I wanted him.

"Oh no," I whimpered.

"Already?" he rasped the word, pushing his finger higher inside me.

"Oh no," I repeated when I felt the spiraling of beautiful sensations soaring through my body. "Oh god. Oh no."

"Yes, fuck yes," he growled. His mouth covered mine, attacking me with a new ferocious need. It was more than I could take. There was no holding back the orgasm. It burst through me with a violence that had me arching against him, rubbing my breasts against his chest.

His mouth pulled away from mine and sucked on my neck as his finger continued to work inside me. I shouted out as the ecstasy sent me on a journey into the stars. Before I had the chance to come down, he lifted me up, pushing me against the wall and shoving his giant dick inside me. The orgasm eased his entry, but he was still big.

I winced, cried out, and dug my nails into his shoulders. He paused about halfway inside me. I lowered my mouth to his from my new vantage point and thoroughly kissed him. My body relaxed, blooming like a flower in the early morning sunshine. He slid deep inside and held perfectly still.

My chest heaved up and down as I struggled to cope with the onslaught of passion and ecstasy. It was overwhelming in the best way. "Good?" he asked on a strained breath.

"So good," I moaned.

He began to move, slowly at first as he pushed my body against the wall. His length stretched me and filled me to completion with every stroke. I felt like I weighed no more than a feather as he held me with an arm around my waist and the other on my hip. He rocked into me, picking up the speed, grunting with every thrust.

"Fucking hell, you are so goddamn wet," he whispered.

"You are making me that way," I managed to get out. My brain felt foggy, saturated with lust and need. I could feel myself already on the climb to another orgasm. Sex with him was way too good. It was addicting.

He pounded into me a few more times before releasing a frustrated growl. He pulled me away from the wall and carried me across the small expanse to the wraparound couch. With me mounted firmly on his dick, he used one foot to move the small coffee table out of his way before lowering me onto the couch.

I had no idea how we were both going to fit, but he made it work. His body slid into mine once again. I raised one leg, resting my foot on the back of the couch and spreading wide for him. I didn't care if it wasn't ladylike. I wanted him and didn't give a shit about rules. He made me feel wild, just as crazed as he was acting.

"Wider," he snapped. "Open wider. I want to be deep, deep inside you."

I put my other foot on the floor, spreading my legs wide until I worried I would break a hip. He lifted himself up on one arm. He stared down at me, his eyes focused on my breasts that felt swollen and achy. His other hand reached up, kneading the sensitive flesh before tweaking my nipple.

I whimpered, my back arching as I wiggled under him, trying to take him deeper inside. I dug my nails into his back, encouraging him to move. I needed him to move. He did as I asked without words. His hips moved in a slow roll. I looked up at the man's marvelous body. His hair fell forward a bit. His jaw was set tight and his eyes focused on me. The intensity of his gaze turned me into liquid fire. I was burning for him. It felt like molten lava pumping through my veins.

I was hot and flushed, and my skin felt stretched. He kept moving, the slow glide in and out of my body. "Xander," I said on a whispered plea. I needed more. I could feel my body ramping up to another explosive orgasm. I wasn't going to be ashamed of my body's response to him.

"Fuck me, another one?" he growled.

I reached for his biceps that were straining under the weight of him supporting his body over me. I squeezed, digging my nails into his flesh once again. "Yes," I cried out as the orgasm broke over me once again.

He roared, his body going stiff as he exploded inside me with such force it triggered another orgasm, piggybacking on the first. I felt as if I would black out in that moment. It was too much pleasure. Too much ecstasy. Everything went dark and then exploded into light.

He fell on top of me, kissing my neck and cheek before kissing my forehead. "Holy shit," he breathed.

A weird laugh crossed my lips. "Yeah, holy shit."

He moved his chest off mine a bit and looked at me. "That was unexpected. Good, but please don't think I lured you out here for that."

I smiled. "How do you know I didn't do the luring?"

He grinned. "I suppose I don't."

He rolled off me and got to his feet in all his naked splendor. I had a very good view of the man's body and I wasn't about to look away—until I realized he was looking at me with one leg still resting on top of the back of the couch. I felt myself turning bright red as I quickly closed my legs and sat up.

We both quickly dressed. The awkwardness between us was thick and uncomfortable. I didn't like to feel that way and felt it was better to address a situation head on. "I don't want to complicate this," I said once I had my clothes on.

He shrugged, pulling on his T-shirt. "I don't see it as complicated."

"I mean, this," I said, gesturing between us. "It was nice, but I am not sure I'm in a place in my life to be involved."

"Neither am I. We're friends."

"Friends with benefits?" I asked.

He smiled and stepped toward me. His hands rested loosely on my hips. "Only if that's what you want. I don't do serious. I'd like to hang out with you again, but we don't need to make it a thing."

I breathed a sigh of relief. "That works for me."

He dropped a kiss on my forehead. "I should probably get back up there and start us on our way back."

I smiled and nodded. "I'll clean up down here."

He walked away, and for some really stupid reason, I felt sad. I couldn't explain it. I was the one who said no strings attached. I think a part of me was hoping he would insist on us being something more. I wanted him to say I'd like to see you again or something like that. He didn't. That was a good thing because I really was not looking for a boyfriend.

We were pals, buddies, friends. That was it. Nothing more. We had sex. Amazing sex. That was it. People did this all the time. I wasn't one of those people. At least, I didn't used to be. I was now. I had stepped into the world of sex with no strings attached. I wasn't sure how I felt about that.

CHAPTER 13

XANDER

I walked into the restaurant where I was supposed to meet Charlie. He was taking a long lunch and had the time to actually leave the plant where he worked—managed, really. He was good with his hands and had a hard time keeping to the managing. He liked the doing.

He put up his hand. "Xander," he called.

I made my way to the table and took my seat. "Did you order yet?"

"Two BLTs."

"One is for me, right?" I joked.

"Maybe."

"Asshole."

He chuckled. "How have you been? I haven't talked to you in a week."

"I was out of town for a few days and then I was working on that other job for a client," I told him.

"Your pet project?"

I smiled. "Yes. It's nice to do a little something different."

"Whatever happened with the party planner?"

I took a drink from the glass of water. My first option was to play dumb. "What do you mean?"

He chuckled, shaking his head. "You know exactly what I mean.

You being dodgy tells me something did happen. You said you were going to take her out on the boat."

"I did. We had an enjoyable evening."

The waitress brought two plates of food and set them down in front of us. After making sure we had everything we needed, she hurried away to help another group of men.

"Okay, now that there are no ears to hear, tell me the truth. You can speak above a PG rating. I think I can handle the dirty details."

I took a bite from the fry. "I am not giving you any dirty details."

"What happened?"

"We had a good time."

I felt like a shithead for talking about it. Then again, I knew she had probably told her friend Nelle all about the encounter. Women did that. Guys did it and it was called locker-room talk.

"You hooked up?" he asked with a grin.

I sighed, knowing he wasn't going to give it up. "We did."

"On the boat?"

"Yes, on the fucking boat," I growled. "Where else?"

He held up a hand. "Where on the boat? On the couches on the deck?"

I frowned. "No, why does it matter?"

He grimaced. "On the couch in the living room?"

I didn't necessarily consider it a living room, but I knew what he was referring to. "I'm really not sure why it matters. Do not expect me to give you details. I'm not going to give you a blow by blow."

"Now I have to clean the boat," he said with disgust.

"What are you talking about?"

"You sullied the boat. I sit on that couch. Hell, I lay on the damn thing. I need to know where the bleach goes."

I chuckled, taking another bite. "You should probably just get a hose. It would be more efficient."

He groaned. "Oh my god. Gross."

"You'll survive."

He took a bite of his sandwich. He looked thoughtful as he chewed. "You don't expect me to sleep with you every time you take me out on the boat, do you? I think you are a cool guy and all, and you are mildly attractive, but you are just not my type."

I ignored him and ate my sandwich. He didn't let up. He outlined all the acts he was willing to consider and those he was adamant against. If he made a move on me, I would knock his ass out. Both of us knew that.

"Are you done yet?" I asked him when he paused for a bit.

"I just want it made clear. I like your boat, but I could buy my own boat."

"You could build your own damn boat," I told him.

He nodded. "I could, but that's not the same. It wouldn't have all those nice finishes. Any boat I would build would be utilitarian and not comfortable."

Before I could offer to go boat shopping with him, his phone rang. Because of his job, he needed to answer his calls. "This is Charlie," he answered.

I finished my sandwich while he nodded and made various grunts and noises.

"I'll be there as soon as I can," he said and ended the call.

"Gotta get back to work?" I asked.

"No, not exactly. We've got a dead duck out in the water. They want me to chopper out there and see if I can get it running before they have to call a tug."

"How far out are they?"

"I'm not sure. They were going to send the chopper to pick me up."

"I can take you out on the boat," I offered.

He laughed and shook his head. "I think the chopper will be faster and more sanitary."

"Is it one of mine?" I asked.

He nodded. "Yep. She's only been in service for a couple of months. I'm sure it will be an easy fix."

"I'll go with you," I offered.

"You must be bored," he joked.

"It's one of mine," I said, being very serious. "I need to know if there is an issue."

"I doubt it is anything you did in the design. It is probably something stupid like they didn't plug something in or some shit."

I wiped my mouth, grabbed my wallet, and dropped a hundred-dollar bill on the table. "Let's go."

My reputation was everything. I refused to have rumors spread about my shitty designs or subpar ships. It only took one poorly designed ship to sink my business. While I would still be okay financially, I refused to take the hit to my reputation. My reputation was everything. My reputation was a million times more important than the money in the bank.

There were a lot of people who would love to see me fail. I refused to fail. I refused to let them see me crash and burn and live up to what they thought would happen. My success was fueled by my need to prove everyone else wrong.

"They will be at the plant," he said as we walked to our cars.

"I'll follow you over there. Let them know you'll have a plus one."

He laughed. "Glad I can return the favor."

I was too irritated with the idea my designs had failed to laugh. I was already going through the potential causes in my head. I had no information to go on, but I knew what the likely suspects were. I prayed it was manufacturer or user error. If it was something I did, I would be very pissed at myself.

Thirty minutes later, we were in the air and flying out to the ship that was stuck out in open water. They had only left the dock a few hours ago. That told me it had to be a failure of some kind. I brought along my iPad with access to the file containing the design specs, including the engine specs. Charlie built them from what I designed. He knew them just as well as I did, but he knew the way it sounded and how it looked when it was all put together.

The helicopter landed on the massive deck. Charlie and I climbed out and made our way over to the ship's captain. He led us into the engine room and quickly told us what was going on.

"We'll get you back up and running in no time," Charlie told him.

"I have no doubt in my mind you will. I need to go up and check on things."

81

Charlie and I were left alone to diagnose the engine trouble. He was running through his list of diagnostics, but I could see the problem almost immediately. I checked the specs against what I had on my iPad and determined it to be the issue. It took less than five minutes to right the wrongs with me directing Charlie on how to fix it.

"Damn," he shouted over the sound of the humming engine. "You are good."

I shrugged. "I can be."

We left the noise of the engine room and set out to find the captain. He was already barking orders to his crew, making ready to get back on course.

"Thank you," he said, shaking my hand. "I have to say, when I made the call, I wasn't expecting the damn engineer to show up. You're a lifesaver."

"It's no problem," I told him. "Charlie is the guy who fixed it. He's good at what he does."

Charlie was more than happy to accept credit for a job well done.

The captain shook his hand. "Thank you," he said. "You really saved my ass."

"Not a problem at all," Charlie answered. "Happy to help. You shouldn't have any more problems."

"If I do, I'm calling you two," he joked.

"Please do," I replied. "I take my ships very seriously. I want to know if there is an issue."

"These puppies sail like a dream. This is only my second run with her, but she's been a really great ship to captain."

"Glad to hear it," I told him.

"We better get out of here," Charlie said.

We said our goodbyes and headed back to the helicopter. We climbed in and were back at the plant in no time.

"Thanks," Charlie said. "I would have figured it out eventually, but you were a big help."

"Sure, it isn't like I had anything else to do," I teased.

"We didn't get to finish talking about your new lady," he said.

"Yes, we did. I said all I had to say."

"What's up? Are you guys dating?"

I thought about it. "No."

"It was just a hookup?" he asked with a skeptical look.

I shrugged. "Yes, I guess it was."

"Bullshit."

I frowned at him. "Why do you say bullshit?"

"Because I know you."

"I have had one-nighters before," I said, suddenly feeling like I *was* in a locker room.

"Haven't we all, but you don't do it much."

"We agreed not to complicate things. I'm really not interested in a relationship. I don't want all the baggage. I like things just the way they are. I don't want the messy stuff."

He shook his head, a disgusted look on his face. "It sounds like you already got messy. Little late to turn that one back."

"Whatever. She's got her life and I have mine. Neither of us is interested in making this a thing. It was an itch that needed scratched and that was that."

He rolled his eyes. "You'll see her again."

"Care to wager on that?" I asked him.

He grinned, never one to turn down a bet, especially one he thought he could win. "Fifty bucks says you will see her again. Not just see her but sleep with her."

I extended my hand. "You're on. Now, I have to get to work."

"No, you don't."

I laughed. "No, I don't, but you do."

"I'm checking on you and I will know if you are lying about seeing her again."

"I doubt it," I called as I walked away. "And I won't be seeing her again, at least not in that way."

I heard him laughing as I crossed the lot and headed for my car. It had already been a week. I had not heard a word from her. Granted, I hadn't texted or called her either. We both agreed to keep things simple. I wouldn't mind another hookup with her, but it would be a repeat of the boat incident. We would both get what we wanted, and life would go on. I wasn't interested in dating or getting serious. That took a lot of effort and I didn't want the hassle of going through those early weeks in a relationship.

I didn't want the getting to know you stuff and all that. She was fun. She was fucking gorgeous and she seemed to be on the same page as I was. Neither of us made any commitments to call.

Why did I suddenly regret that?

CHAPTER 14

EVIE

I closed the dishwasher and turned it on. Being a single lady that was rarely home and didn't eat a lot at home meant few dishes. I had to practically wash my dishes before putting them in the dishwasher. If I didn't, they would be crusty and gross by the time I got a full load. I put the towel on the counter and shut off the light.

I had plenty of candles going. I loved candles. Anytime I got a chance to burn candles, I did. I carried my glass of wine out to my itty-bitty balcony and sat down. It was a warm evening with some serious humidity.

I settled in, putting my feet up on the railing and staring out at the pool below that was packed with tenants taking advantage of the warm weather. My phone chimed, alerting me to a text. I didn't want to look. I didn't want to deal with a client bitching at me. I was completely chill at the moment. Not a minute later, the doorbell rang.

"Nelle!" I said, already knowing it was her.

I walked barefoot to the door and pulled it open. "I didn't know you were coming over."

"I thought I would stop by."

"You're off on a Thursday?" I questioned.

"I am."

"Do you want some wine?" I offered.

"No thanks. What are you doing?" She looked around at the many candles and then me.

"I have to do some more work, but I'm taking a break before I dig in again."

She slowly nodded. "I see. Rough week?"

I sat down on the couch and stretched out my legs. My feet were aching. "Yes. I have a party this weekend and took on two new clients with events scheduled in a couple of months. It's been crazy."

"Sounds like it."

I sighed, knowing my break was over. I needed a few more things for the event on Saturday. It wasn't an event I was looking forward to. "I need to find some cigars," I said, thinking out loud.

"Taking up smoking?" she teased.

"It's for some corporate thing, all men. A few women, but mostly men. I'm doing an old twenties kind of vibe. I need some good cigars."

She quickly named a place. I opened up my laptop and pulled up the name of the store. "Hey, you are right. How did you know?"

"I work in a bar. I know things."

I laughed as I quickly typed in my order. "Of course, you do."

"How is Xander?" she asked.

I looked up, catching the sly smile on her face as she stared at me from her place in the chair. "Subtle," I said.

She shrugged. "Subtle is boring and it takes too long. Have you talked to him?"

"Nope."

"Why not? I thought you liked him?"

"He's all right, but we are just friends. We both agreed to keep things neat and tidy. Neither of us wants the baggage. I work all the time and a boyfriend would quickly feel ignored. I have been down that road before. It's better if I just stay single."

"That is the dumbest thing I have ever heard," she said.

"It isn't dumb, it's practical."

"You liked him."

I nodded. "I do like him. He's fun to hang out with. He has a very

86

dry sense of humor and it makes me laugh. He isn't wild. He isn't boisterous. He doesn't try to impress me. He's just him. It's refreshing to be with a man that doesn't care what anyone else thinks. He's his own man and that's that."

She was smiling. "You really do like him. Did something happen that has you running scared?"

"No," I assured her. "It isn't that. Now, I'm going to get my shoes on. Will you run me over to that cigar place?"

"You've been hitting the bottle pretty hard?"

I laughed. "No, I had one glass of wine. Trust me. I deserved it. I want to pick up the cigars before they close. Then I need to stop by the party rental place and pick up some stuff."

"Your wish is my command," she said and got to her feet.

I quickly put on my shoes, not caring that I was very dressed down. I had been going for what felt like four days straight. I needed some casualwear and my feet were begging for the comfort of my tennis shoes.

She drove to the cigar store where I quickly picked up my order, along with a few accessories. Then it was to the party rental place to pick up more decorations for the gig. It was almost seven before the last of my errands were done.

"Let's grab something to eat," she said once we were back in the car.

"Sure," I answered. I was so ready to go home and crawl into a hot bubble bath, but she was obviously not ready to call it a night.

She drove us to a restaurant that specialized in wings. "So Xander," she started again.

I rolled my eyes. "I knew there was a reason you wanted to sit down and eat."

"I usually sit down and eat," she replied.

"No, you don't. You are always on the go."

"Anyway," she said, steering the conversation right back to the place I didn't want to go.

"I already told you," I insisted. "I like him well enough, but you know how much I work. I don't have time to date regularly. I rarely sleep as it is."

"I bet your dad would like him," she commented.

I rolled my eyes. "I don't think my dad would ever like any man I brought home to meet him."

"But this guy sounds like he's got his shit together. He's an engineer. He's wealthy. He's not wild and dumb. I think the two of you would be really good together. He would tame you and you would liven him up."

"You haven't even met him," I protested.

She shrugged. "I don't have to. You told me all about him."

"I can't take him to meet my dad. For one, we are not even close to being at that stage, and for two, no way. You know how critical my dad is. Xander would cut and run before we even get started. My dad would find fault with a royal prince. There will never be a right man for me in his eyes."

She smiled, sipping on her diet soda. "That's because he loves you. He wants the best for you."

"He wants me to be a spinster."

"I think he just wants to make sure you are with someone that is going to treat you right. He loves you. He raised you. He has some very high standards. It's normal for dads to be picky about who their daughters date."

"My dad takes that a little too seriously."

"You won't know until you try," she said.

I shook my head. "Nope. I have not taken a man to him yet and I don't plan on doing it now. Not until I am a million percent sure he is going to be the man I am going to marry. Then, I will be more willing to fight for the man."

"Makes sense, but I think your dad is also a good judge of character," she said. "He might be able to see something you can't."

"Oh, yes, you are right there. He can see all the negative in a person. He doesn't see good in anyone. If I need to know the flaws of someone, all I have to do is ask him."

She softly giggled. "I'm afraid to know what he thought about me."

"You have passed his high standards but just barely. The fact you work in a bar is still one of those things he is less than thrilled about."

She rolled her eyes. "It isn't like my parents were overjoyed either. I simply remind them I get paid more than a lot of people with shiny college degrees. I don't have the student loans dragging me down. I'm very content with what I do."

"I know you are and that's all that matters," I told her. I hated that people looked down at her because of what she did. She was one of the smartest women I knew, and she loved what she did and was paid very, very well for it.

"Hey," she said and pointed to a TV mounted on the wall behind me. "Isn't that your man?"

I sighed, shaking my head. "I don't have a man."

"Just look." She pointed.

I turned around to look up at the screen. There was an image of Xander and another man getting off a helicopter. I squinted to read the text. "What does that say?" I asked.

"He saved a ship or something?"

"I can't see," I complained. I got up and walked closer to the TV to be able to read what was running across the bottom of the screen.

"Look at that," Nelle said from behind me. "Your man is a hero."

I had to smile. "He's still not my man and I'm proud of him. He is a good guy."

"He builds ships. That is crazy. I really didn't think it was true."

"Yes, he does. He is smart."

"I told you, you like him."

I sighed and headed back for our table. "I do like him, which is why I'm not taking him home to Dad. He would turn and run in the other direction before I could blink twice."

"I hope you won't let that stop you from enjoying time with him," she said.

I shrugged. "I don't know if it even matters. I haven't talked to him since the boat incident."

"It isn't an incident. It was sex. Damn good sex, judging by how red you got when you told me. Maybe you should reach out to him. We aren't in the Stone Age anymore. You can call him. Text him. Whatever. I'm not saying marry the man. I'm saying have fun with him. You have said repeatedly you like him."

She had a point. "Maybe I will next week. I have to get through this weekend."

"Take him to the park again on Sunday or maybe ask for another boat ride, and by ride, I mean—"

"Don't even say it," I told her, cutting her off.

"Call him."

"I will. Sunday."

"I'm going to keep hounding you until you do it," she warned.

"I know you will. Now, if you are done trying to set me up, I need to get home. I have a few more details to iron out before I go to bed."

We finished our late dinner and headed for her car. After she dropped me off, I couldn't stop myself from doing a little more Googling. I wanted to know more about the man that had captivated my attention. I couldn't quite figure him out. I got the impression he wanted to make people think he was the tough, unfeeling guy. I didn't think he was all that tough. Definitely alpha male but not tough in a mean way.

I clicked off the image of him that appeared on his company website. I wondered if maybe, just maybe, he could pass my dad's litmus test. He was successful and well spoken, at least when he wanted to speak. If there was ever going to be a man that could get close to measuring up to my dad's very high standards, I had a feeling it would be Xander.

What could it hurt to have a little fun and a casual relationship? Spending my one day off a week with him would be fun. We could agree not to be the kind of couple that fawned all over each other every minute of the day. We would be the kind of couple—not couple, friends. We would be *friends* who needed a date for a party on occasion and could call one another up without explaining where we've been the last week or two.

CHAPTER 15

XANDER

I flipped off the TV and walked outside. I had my swim trunks on and was ready to dive into my pool. I had gone down to the beach earlier, but it was packed. I couldn't wait until school picked up and some of the tourists drifted away.

I dove in headfirst, the cool water washing over me. I swam a few laps before drifting to the edge of the pool and holding on. I waited to see if I heard the sound again. My brain could be playing tricks on me.

When I heard the birdsong again, I sprang out of the pool, using my arms to lift myself up. That was Evie's ringtone. I felt a bit like a teenage girl, but I wanted to make sure I knew when she called. I picked up my phone. "Hello?" I answered, pretending to be totally cool and casual.

"Hey, it's me, Evie."

I smiled as I picked up my towel and rubbed it over my head. "Yes, I gathered that. What are you doing?"

"I am calling to ask you for a huge favor," she said.

"What would that be?" I asked, praying like hell she didn't ask me for money. I didn't want to think she was using me. I would never trust my judgement again if that was the case.

"Are you busy tonight?"

"I don't think so," I said hesitantly.

"You don't think so? That sounds like you are keeping your options open."

Busted. "Not entirely."

"It's not terrible," she said. "Well, not too terrible."

"Now you are making me a little worried."

"Would you like to go to a party with me? You wouldn't have to mingle. I need a man to save me from the other men."

I rubbed the towel over my bare chest. "What? What does that mean? Is someone bothering you?"

"No, no, nothing like that. I have an event tonight, a corporate party for a bunch of lawyers at one of the big firms here. It's mostly men. Married, single, and in between. I've done other parties for them. The men are very, um, flirty. Very handsy. If I had a guy there, posing as my boyfriend of sorts, it would help deter the constant barrage of flirting and hitting on me."

I was immediately jealous. "Yes," I heard myself say. "I'll go."

"You will?" she asked with surprise.

"Where? Should I pick you up?"

"I have to be there early to get everything set up. If you could meet me there, that would be great."

I couldn't believe I was willingly agreeing to go to a party, but here I was, signing up for an evening of hell. "Text me the address. What do I need to wear?"

"A suit will be fine," she quickly answered. "You can wear the one you wore to the other party."

I smirked. "I own more than one suit."

Her soft laughter floated through the phone. "I wasn't sure, and I didn't want to assume. Wear whatever makes you comfortable."

"Nothing," I replied. "I like my birthday suit."

"I like your birthday suit too, but I'm not sure the men there would appreciate it though. You'll give them a complex."

I smiled, looking down at my bare chest and rubbing my hand over it. I liked that she liked my body. I wasn't sure why I cared, but I did. "Then a suit, it will be."

"Thank you so much for doing this. I'll owe you big time."

"I'm going to remember you said that," I warned her.

She giggled again. "Is it crazy that I am looking forward to you calling in your debt?"

"Nope. I'll see you tonight."

We ended the call. I was not looking forward to another party, but it didn't put me off as badly as it usually did. I wasn't required to mingle. I was going to be there acting as the bouncer. I would absolutely bounce any asshole that messed with her.

I headed inside to take a quick shower. I had been planning on a night in and was going to work on the design for the client on the side. I would work on it until it was time to go to the party. I was truly looking forward to seeing her.

I wasn't familiar with the feeling of missing someone. I was never close to my family and therefore didn't miss them when my parents moved out of state and my brother was shipped overseas.

I missed Evie. I didn't really know her that well, but I wanted to know her better. On a strictly friend basis. I spent the rest of the day watching the clock. I couldn't believe I was actually looking forward to a party. I dressed for the event and called a car to take me to the downtown address. The party was being held in one of the tall office buildings. I found the right floor and took the elevator up.

The doors slid open. The law firm was throwing the party but was obviously too cheap to spring for an actual venue. My eyes scanned the area that was much larger than I thought it would be. It appeared most of the typical office furniture had been removed. There were a lot of suits. A lot. It wasn't hard to spot Evie. She was wearing a blue dress with a very high neckline and sleeves. It was the kind of dress I would expect to see on a woman going to church.

I moved toward her, watching as a man, probably in his forties, leaned in close. She stepped back, clearly uncomfortable. I walked up, put my arm around her waist, and dropped a kiss on her lips. My back was to the other man, making it very clear he didn't matter.

"Hi," she breathed when I pulled away.

"Hi," I replied.

I turned to stand beside her, my arm around her waist. The man who had been hitting on her disappeared.

"Thank you," she said on a sigh.

"No problem. Is that normal?"

"With this group, yes."

I looked around at the men talking and laughing. Some had removed their suit jackets and loosened their ties. Others were still buttoned up tight. "They are lawyers?" I asked.

"Yes. The expensive kind. They have one of these parties every few months. They always ask for me. Every party is always the same. The married men are on the prowl. They are worse than the single guys."

"What do you mean?" I growled.

"They are relentless. They think they are god's gift to women. They do not understand the word *no* or what marriage vows mean."

"Assholes," I murmured. "I'll make sure they know it is not okay."

She smiled up at me. "I think you being here is definitely going to change things. I've claimed I had a boyfriend at past parties and they don't care."

"They will now."

"There's one of the partners. I need to talk with him."

"I'll go with you," I insisted.

Her pretty smile made me very happy I showed up. "Thank you. I think he is one of the worst of all."

That didn't make me happy. I stuck by her side as she crossed the room. I glared at a few of the men that were checking her out. "Mr. Calhoun," Evie said. "How is everything?"

The man was looking at her tits. I wanted to throttle him. I cleared my throat to get his attention. He looked at me. I glared back at him. "Everything is fine," he said, looking away from me.

"Great. This is my boyfriend, Xander. He's here to help me tonight."

"I thought you hired caterers," he said, clearly not happy to have me there.

"I do," she said. Her smile never slipped. "He's here to help me put out any of those little fires that tend to pop up with events like these."

The man's face turned red. "I'm sorry about that incident. We've talked with our team, and I assure you, there will be no more drunken antics that not only embarrass the parties involved but the firm as a whole."

"I appreciate that. Xander will make sure of it."

He looked at me once again. I didn't know what the incident was, but I didn't like where my mind was going. I was going to ask her. She walked away, and like a good bodyguard, I stayed right beside her.

"What was that about?" I asked in a low voice when we were out of earshot of anyone else.

She shook her head. "It was no big deal."

"What was no big deal?" I pressed. The more she held back, the angrier I got.

"One of the partners got a little drunk. No, very drunk. He seemed to be struggling with the concept of no."

"Did he touch you?"

She was blushing. "Nothing terrible. He was pulled away."

"Why do you keep doing their parties? Why not tell them to fuck off?"

She burst into laughter, quickly covering her mouth. "Because I like my job and I think I'm better able to handle it than anyone else at my company. It was a drunken moment and I don't think it will happen again."

"But you wanted me here to make sure it didn't happen again?"

She wrinkled her nose. "Yes. You are kind of an intimidating man."

"I certainly can be. If one of these yahoos touches you, I will put him down."

She touched my arm. "I appreciate that, but don't go too caveman. I do need to work."

"I'll do my best," I told her.

The looks that were directed her way all night were exhausting. For every leer, I returned a glare. I made it clear she was mine. I couldn't understand how she could put up with that kind of bullshit. I hoped after tonight, she didn't have to. Then I realized she probably had to put up with this kind of thing all the time. She was a stunning woman and any man would want to get his hands on her.

"Things are wrapping up. If you want to go, you can. Thank you so much for doing this for me tonight. It really helped."

"I'm good," I told her. "I don't mind sticking around a while longer."

She smiled and reached up to touch my cheek. "If you don't mind breaking curfew, we could go out for ice cream. A little token of my gratitude."

I gently wrapped my fingers around her wrist, keeping her hand against my cheek. "I would love to break curfew."

She grinned. "Then it's a date. I need to talk with the caterers and then get with the cleaning staff. I should be ready to go in thirty minutes."

"I'll be right here," I told her. "Trust me, with the amount of alcohol these assholes consumed, I'm not letting you out of my sight."

She laughed as she walked away. I was serious. I didn't want to have to put any of the men on the ground, but I would. I watched as she talked with the staff. She was so genuine. Everyone seemed to like her. She was definitely my opposite. We were the proverbial night and day.

"I think I'm ready," she said after she finished talking to the partner from earlier.

I put my arm around her shoulders and led her away. We made it to the elevator in record time. I could see she was exhausted. She leaned against the wall of the elevator and let out a long sigh. "Are you sure you want to do ice cream?" I asked her. "You look exhausted. We can do it tomorrow if that works better."

She smiled and slowly shook her head. "No way. I'm okay. I really want ice cream. I want to go for a walk on the beach and enjoy the beautiful night."

It sounded like the perfect way to end the night to me.

CHAPTER 16

EVIE

W e carried our bowls of ice cream to a bench that overlooked the ocean. I sat down first, with Xander sitting down beside me. It was a warm night with no wind. It felt good to get off my feet for a while. I took a bite of the chocolate chip cookie dough ice cream and let it melt in my mouth. It was my guilty pleasure. One of many. Life was too short and stressful to not indulge in ice cream.

"Tired?" he asked.

I turned to look at him. He had loosened his tie and undone the top button of his shirt. The gel he had put in his hair was slowly failing, allowing the long layers to fall loose around his ears and forehead. The light from a streetlight nearby cast him in a soft, bluish tone. He looked absolutely handsome. "I am tired. I always like this moment."

"What moment is that?"

"The moment the event—whether it's a party or a wedding or whatever—it's the moment I can sit and relax without thinking about what I need to do. It's a chance to go over the event and identify what went wrong and how I will keep it from going wrong again."

"Tonight went very well," he offered.

I smiled and nodded. "It did. It was an easy one really. Tonight was a little different with the twenties theme, although none of them really dressed up."

"It was cool. It would have been even cooler with some Tommy guns."

I rolled my eyes. "Of course, it would have."

"It was great, and judging by the smiles and the laughter, they all had a good time. No one was complaining."

"They were too drunk to complain," I said with a laugh.

"True."

"I saw you on the news," I said.

He groaned. "I don't know who called the news. It wasn't exactly exciting stuff."

"They called you guys heroes."

He took another bite of his ice cream. "It wasn't a big deal. Charlie did the work. We happened to be at lunch when he got the call."

"He works with you?"

"No, he works at a plant that builds the ships I design."

"Ah, you guys are quite the team."

He smiled, taking another bite. "We are. We have been for a long time."

"How long have the two of you been friends?"

"I was a junior in college and he was a freshman. So, ten, eleven years. I'm a little embarrassed to admit he is probably my only friend."

"Because you don't like people," I said.

He chuckled. "It isn't that I don't like people as a whole, but in my experience, I have found most people are assholes. Greedy assholes."

I burst into laughter. "Well, gee, when you put it like that."

"I don't mean only greedy with money. I mean in general. Greedy with my time, their time, their needs. All of it. I'm not normal. I'm not like you. I could never talk to everyone in the room and remember their names or treat them like I give a shit about them. You do that and you do it very well."

I thought about what he said. "I think because I like people in general."

"Charlie is like that as well."

"You are naturally drawn to social butterflies, it sounds like," I told him.

He made a choking sound. "I don't know why. We are totally incompatible."

I felt a clenching in my stomach. He was probably right, but there was something between us. I felt like we clicked, like we were drawn together. "I have a proposal for you," I started.

He groaned. "Are you going to take me to the zoo? A crowded, nasty concert?"

I ignored his questions. "I get these parties, or similar parties, about once a month, sometimes more often," I said. "How about we do a little trading of services?"

He lips quirked at the corners. "I think that might be illegal in California, but I won't tell if you don't tell."

I softly giggled. "Aren't you funny?"

"I don't try to be."

"You don't have to be," I told him. "It comes naturally."

"Odd. Few people have ever found me to be funny."

"You are. My proposal is you go to some of the parties, the ones where I am most likely to be relentlessly hit on, and I'll show you how fun life can be. We'll go out and explore some of the fun stuff there is to do in San Diego."

He slowly licked the plastic spoon. "You are a very confident person."

"I guess," I said, not sure why that mattered.

"You are so convinced you are going to be hit on," he said, a little gleam in his eyes.

He was teasing. Oh, the man kept me on my toes. "History predicts the future. Look at me. I'm dressed like a pastor's wife. I hate that I have to hide my boobs."

"Why do you? They are nice boobs."

I almost choked on my ice cream. "Thank you. I hide them because I don't want to encourage the flirting. I am very professional when I am at work. Sometimes, the guests get confused about who I am. A little harmless flirting, someone offering to get me a drink, that's okay. It's the guys that are looking for a hookup that piss me off. They are the ones I want to avoid."

He slowly nodded. "I see."

He was suddenly very serious.

"If you truly don't want to go out in public, that's okay," I said. "I don't want to force you to do stuff you really don't want to do."

"No, it's fine. I'm not a total hermit. I do go out. Just not often."

"I think me and you will have fun."

"I think so too. I think you bring the fun."

I smiled again and leaned against his shoulder. "That's sweet."

"It's true."

"Will you do it?" I asked. "Will you pretend to be my boyfriend?"

"I will, but I don't need anything in return."

"I know how much you hate wearing the suit and mingling. Some of the events might be black tie. Do you have a tuxedo?"

He groaned. "I'm afraid to answer that."

"You do," I surmised. "A man like you would have to own one. How often do you get roped into benefits and fancy gatherings?"

He shrugged. "Not as much as I used to. In the beginning, I was more open to shaking hands with the people I needed to buy my designs. I shook a lot of hands. I couldn't turn down an invitation and risk coming off as rude or ungrateful."

"But now, you don't have to?"

"No, not really. I still do some because I do like to support a good cause. I just don't stay all night. I show up, drink some champagne, shake a few hands, write a check, and get the hell home."

"It's nice that you show up."

"What about you?" he asked.

"What about me?"

"Do you go to parties and benefits? Ones that you are not putting together. Just as a guest."

I thought about it. I had been to so many parties and big gatherings, they tended to blur together. Sometimes, I became so immersed in a particular job, I almost felt like I was part of the celebration. "I've been to a couple with my dad, or for my dad."

"Is your dad a corporate bigwig?" he asked.

I smirked. "No, definitely not."

"I bet your closet is filled with fancy dresses," he commented.

I had to laugh. "It is. My closet looks like I have a very active social life with ballgowns, cocktail dresses, business casual. I have to remind myself I am not a part of the parties I throw."

"When is the next gig?" he asked.

"I'll have to check my calendar. The weddings and anniversaries are fairly safe territory."

"I guess you'll just give me a call when you need me?" he questioned.

I thought about it and decided I didn't want to wait that long. "Are you busy tomorrow?"

He turned to look at me. "Nope. You?"

"Want to hang out? Get started on this fun adventure?"

He shrugged. "I can do that. Do you promise to go easy on me?"

There was a hint of sexual innuendo in that sentence. "I don't know," I said in a sultry tone. "You seem like a tough guy. Easy might be boring."

"I can be tough. I can be tender. I can be just about anything. I'm up for whatever it is you want."

"Great! Are you free all day?"

He gave me a skeptical look. "You are making me nervous."

"Don't be nervous," I assured him. "You will be in good hands. I will make sure you have lots of fun."

"How can you know if I will have fun?"

"Because I think I know you, not well, but I know you can smile and laugh."

"I'm not a zombie. Of course, I can smile and laugh."

"Good, because I want to see it."

He was quiet for a bit while he finished his ice cream. "What is your grand plan?"

"For tomorrow?"

"Yes. Should I wear a suit?"

"No. Definitely no suits."

"So, you have a plan in mind?" he questioned.

I turned my body toward him, bending my leg and pulling up my skirt a little. "I always have a plan."

"What does that mean?"

"You'll see. You just have to trust me."

"I think I do trust you," he said in a low voice.

I wasn't sure if he meant to speak the words aloud or if they were just private thoughts. "You can trust me," I said and grabbed his hand.

He looked at me with those eyes that were so good at hiding what he was thinking. "I hope so."

I gave his hand a good squeeze. I didn't have to say anything. We sat in silence, staring out at the water and the couples taking advantage of the nice night by walking along the beach. Young love, old love, and budding romances all played out in front of us. I wondered what we were and then quickly reminded myself we weren't anything. We were just a couple of people hanging out.

"Penny for your thoughts?" he said after a while.

I smiled and looked down at where my hand was still resting on his arm. "They aren't worth a penny. It was just random thoughts."

"You look beat," he said.

I smiled. "Thanks. That's exactly what every girl wants to hear."

"You are still beautiful, but you need some sleep."

He was right. "I am exhausted," I admitted.

"Let me take you home," he offered.

I was so glad I decided to Uber to the party. I could admit part of me was hoping to go home with him or take him home with me. It was a small part. I was glad the larger part of my brain knew better. It was too risky to go home with him or vice versa. The boat was one thing. If he was in my space, it would be much harder to forget about him.

I needed to keep him at arm's length. At least for now. I wanted to know him better. Then I would know how to move forward, with or without him in my life.

CHAPTER 17

XANDER

I parked my car in the lot of the IHOP where Evie wanted to meet. It was packed, as expected on a Sunday morning. The hostess knew exactly who I was asking about when I described Evie and led me directly to her table. Every time I saw the woman, I was taken aback by her beauty. Her hair was piled on top of her head with little black curly strands hanging loose. She had on another one of those blouses with shoulder cutouts and looked absolutely beautiful.

"Good morning," she greeted with a bright smile.

"Good morning," I said and took my seat at the table. "Coffee, please," I said to the hostess who was waiting to hear my drink order.

"I wasn't sure you would make it," she said, taking a sip of her own coffee.

"I got hung up on a phone call. I'm sorry."

"Don't be. I was early. I'm always early."

"And I am almost always late," I replied.

"I'm glad you showed up," she commented. "Otherwise, I would be eating a lot. I took the liberty of ordering you breakfast. I hope you don't mind?"

I raised my eyebrows. "You ordered my breakfast?"

"I ordered big, just in case. Are you much of a breakfast eater?"

"I can be," I answered. I wasn't sure how I felt about her ordering for me. I wasn't used to being controlled. I supposed it wasn't really control, but I got the idea she was used to things being done her way. That could be an issue.

"I'm sorry," she blurted out.

"For?"

"I shouldn't have ordered for you. I order for my dad all the time and Nelle. I get this idea in my head that I can read people better than they can read themselves. I was looking at the time and just thought it would be more efficient if I ordered since I was already here." She looked flustered and was rambling.

"Hey, it's cool," I said. "I don't think you can go wrong with breakfast. It took me by surprise. That's it."

"Are you sure? We can always ask the waitress to stop the order."

I offered her a smile. "I'm sure. I'll be surprised when it shows up. I am hungry and now I don't have to wait as long."

She breathed a sigh of relief. "I won't do it again."

"Maybe you do know me better than I know myself," I said. "Maybe you ordered me something I normally wouldn't have, and I'll love it."

"I hope so," she said and took a deep breath.

"What are we doing today?" I questioned.

She grinned. "I have it all planned."

"You are truly a planner, right down to your very core."

She grimaced. "I am. I plan every minute practically. I use calendars and lists and apps to keep me on schedule. I like to know what I am going to be doing on a given day. I like to know where I should be and what comes next."

That sounded a little intense for me. "Not me," I told her. "Definitely not me."

"I suppose you are the type that wakes up and just goes with the flow?"

I shrugged. "Not quite that loose, but yes. I don't know what's on my schedule for next week."

"Do you have an assistant who keeps you on track?"

"I do," I admitted. "She mostly sets up the appointments and shoots me a text when I have a phone conference or something. Most of my days are spent going with the flow. I don't plan."

She visibly shuddered. "I guess you could say I am very Type A. I think I would have a nervous breakdown if I didn't have a schedule."

"Do you color code charts and stuff?" I asked, half-joking.

"Not anymore."

"Wow."

"I can be a little neurotic. I know it. I try to lighten up, and I think I have a little more over the last couple years, but I get very anxious when I don't know what's coming next."

"I've met people like that before."

She burst into laughter. "You make it sound like we are zoo animals or something."

I grinned. "It would be interesting to see you in action. How do you know when you are going to have fun? Don't you like spur of the moment stuff?"

"I'm not wound that tight," she joked. "I do things all the time that are not otherwise scheduled. I have to have some flexibility in my day to handle all those little emergencies that arise. It's more about I know when I'm going to be at work and what I'm going to be doing for the day. I know what needs to happen on a given day. I don't go to bed or leave work until the tasks that I have outlined for the day are done."

"Were you born like that?" I asked, genuinely curious. "I ask because my dad is that way. We did have color-coded charts. Our chores, our classes, everything was plastered on a chart for us to look at every fucking day."

She grimaced and shook her head. "I have been like this for as long as I can remember. I cannot imagine being a kid and having that thrust on me."

"He liked order. No, that's not accurate. He demanded order. Things were scheduled right down to when we could shower. I'm surprised he didn't tell us when we could take a shit."

"I'm sorry."

I realized that was a pretty dumb thing to say. "I'm sorry. That was crass."

"I get it. That would have been very difficult to deal with. I don't think I'm that strict. I craved organization when I was younger because my world was chaotic. It was the only thing I had any control over."

"Why was your world chaotic?"

She sipped her coffee. I did the same, waiting for her to explain. The waitress delivered heaping plates of food, including a stack of pancakes for each of us. It was a lot of food. I wasn't a huge breakfast eater, but it looked good.

She took a bite of bacon and then put it down. "My mom died in an accident when I was very young. It kind of turned our worlds upside down. My dad, bless his heart, he tried so hard. I could see him struggling to keep our little household running. I think I was already planning dinners by the time I was five."

"You're joking? Not about your mom. That's awful. Were you really making dinner at five?"

She smiled. "No, not usually. Every night my dad would ask me what I wanted for dinner. I started to pick up on the fact it stressed him out when he didn't know what to make. I wanted to make things easier for him. I didn't write, but I remembered I would spend my day with a babysitter or at school and think about what I wanted for dinner. When he asked, I would have an answer."

I was amazed. "Wow. That's young to pick up on that."

She shrugged. "My dad worked hard, and I wanted to do my part. My mom used to let me help her in the kitchen a lot, so I had a pretty good understanding of meals and cooking."

"I don't know if I should feel proud and impressed or really sad for you," I told her.

"Don't be sad. We all have our little hardships. I had mine. I got through it by figuring out how to make things easier. As I got older, I began to see how much easier our lives were when I knew what was coming. I took over meal planning and made grocery lists until I was old enough to do it on my own. I liked being able to help ease the burden on my dad."

I felt like an asshole for complaining about my childhood. She had it much worse. She had lived through the loss of her mother and endured a lot of struggles and was still a happy person. I really felt like a self-absorbed prick for being the way I was. In the grand scheme of things, I had it good. "You're amazing."

"What about you? Did your dad demand you be the man of the house and that kind of thing?"

I laughed. "Not really. He didn't deploy often. He was always around. He made it very clear it was his house, his rules. We either fell in line or got out. My mom was kind and gentle. She always had a hot meal on the table and made sure we knew we were loved, even if my dad couldn't say it or show it."

That seemed to make her happy. I felt like I knew her so much better now, with one small conversation. We ate our breakfast, talking about the weather and different events happening around the city. The trip down Memory Lane to our past was enough. I wasn't interested in reliving those days and I doubted she wanted to either.

"What kind of fun do you have planned for the day?" I asked her.

She wrinkled her nose. "I think I mismanaged our time."

"How so? Do you need to postpone our day of fun?"

"No, I have grand plans to make you smile and laugh and maybe even yell."

I leaned forward. "If you are talking about another trip out on the boat, I'm up for it. I will yell as loud as you want."

Her cheeks stained red. "Not that," she said with a smile. "Something wilder."

I raised an eyebrow. "Really? I'm game."

She rolled her eyes. "You are such a man."

"I'm not going to take that as an insult."

It was her turn to lean forward. "I want to hear you scream."

"I thought you were the one who was supposed to scream."

"Oh, I'll scream all right. I usually do."

I was growing harder by the second just thinking about getting her naked again. I didn't plan on a day of sex, but in the grand scheme of things, it was probably about the best way to spend a day. "My place?"

"You are bad," she said with a grin.

"I can be anything you want."

"Stop, you are making me blush," she hissed.

"You are making me hard."

She closed her eyes and shook her head. "You are killing me."

"Do you want to reach under the table and feel what you are doing to me?"

She waved a hand, as if she was swatting at me. "What has gotten into you?"

"It's more like what I want to get into you."

Her mouth fell open. "We better go, or we are going to end up embarrassing ourselves in the bathroom."

"I wouldn't be embarrassed," I told her.

"Let's go," she said, and for a brief second, I thought she meant to the bathroom. When she headed for the door, I was more than happy to follow the woman wherever she led me. I quickly paid the bill and followed her outside.

"Well? Where to?" I looked up and down the road. "There's a hotel."

She slapped at my arm. "We are not going to a hotel. I have other plans."

I groaned. "But you've kind of got me in a bad way here."

"Take a deep breath and then release slowly. That's what I did. I'm feeling much better."

"I know exactly what will make me feel better," I told her.

"Come on, mister. We'll take my car."

"To your place?" I teased, knowing it was off the table. I had to try though.

"To Belmont Park," she announced.

I stopped walking. "What? Really? You want me to ride roller-coasters?"

"Yep and other things," she said with a playful smile.

I caught up to her and leaned down to whisper close to her. "You? You want me to ride you?"

Her answer was a sharp intake of breath. I had never been the kind of guy that flirted and talked like that. With her, I didn't feel like I had to hide what I wanted. I wanted her. I felt safe talking like that with her because I knew she knew I was playing. She wasn't going to ask or expect anything more from me. It was freeing.

CHAPTER 18

EVIE

My stomach felt funny. It had nothing to do with the breakfast. It was him. He made me feel all wet and gooey. He'd been so flirtatious. It was fun. With any other man, I probably would have dumped my orange juice in his lap. With him, I wanted to climb onto the table and beg him to have his way with me.

"I'm paying," he insisted when we got to the ticket booth.

"No, this is my idea."

"I'm paying," he said again and left zero room for argument. He handed a credit card over and bought the passes that gave us unlimited rides.

"I was thinking we could visit some of the attractions first. Let our breakfast settle a bit before we go on anything that will give us the milkshake treatment."

He smirked. "Yeah, I'm not sure why we had a big breakfast if this is what you had in mind."

"Because there is plenty to see and explore while we let our breakfasts settle," I told him. "I suppose I should have asked if you were afraid of heights?"

He gave me a look. "I'm not afraid of heights."

"What about rollercoasters?"

He shrugged. "It's been a while since I got turned upside down, but I'm not afraid of the things."

"Good, because I love rollercoasters."

He didn't look like he shared that same opinion, but I was hoping he would have fun. It was a risk to bring a grown man to a theme park, especially one that was so serious. We spent the next hour and a half roaming the park and checking out the many attractions. I felt like my stomach was ready for a rollercoaster.

"Are you serious about this?" he asked when we got in line.

"Are you backing out on me?" I teased.

He slowly shook his head. "Nope."

When it was our turn, we climbed into our seats and waited to be locked in. He seemed nervous. It was strange to see a big, burly man like him nervous. "All good?" I asked.

"Evie, I'm fine."

I wondered if it was possible to truly not enjoy a rollercoaster. The element of fear was what made it exciting. When the ride started to move, I looked over at him. He looked as if he were sitting in the backseat of a taxi. There was zero emotion. He didn't look scared, but he also didn't look like he was enjoying himself. I was not ready to give up on him yet.

When the ride was over, with very little reaction from him, I decided to up the ante. "How about the big one?" I asked.

He looked at me. "I'm not sure you can handle another one."

"Oh, I can handle it. I'm just getting started."

He smiled and shrugged. "Okay. But if you are going to toss your cookies, you have to aim the other way."

I rolled my eyes. "I am not going to toss my cookies."

It was several rides later before the man started to thaw a bit and let himself go. He seemed to be enjoying himself and was having a good time. "I think you broke my eardrums on that one," he commented as we walked away from the coaster.

I laughed. "That one gets me. I can handle being upside down, but backwards kind of freaks me out."

He put an arm around my shoulders. "That was fun."

"Finally," I said. "I thought I was going to have to take you to the hospital and have them check your pulse."

"I could use something to drink," he said. "How about you?"

"Absolutely. All that screaming has left me a little parched."

He flinched, inhaling a sharp breath through his nose. I knew exactly what he was thinking. Sex. The man had sex on the brain. It made me feel sexy and wanted. Definitely not something I was used to feeling. We made our way to one of the little shops outdoors and ordered a couple of root beer floats before finding a place to sit.

"This was fun," he finally agreed.

"Good. I was beginning to worry a little. Have you been here before?"

"Yes, a few times when I was much younger. My mom would bring me and my brother here on occasion. We didn't usually ride all the rollercoasters in one visit though."

I smiled. "You bought the full-day pass. Can't let it go to waste."

"What about you? Is this somewhere you spent a lot of time with your dad?"

I slowly nodded. "It is. Usually on the weekends. He would bring me here for a ride or two and then we always got a corndog followed by an ice cream."

"I bet those are some fond memories."

"Aren't your memories fond?" I questioned.

He shrugged. "I guess. Usually, my mom would bring us here when my dad deployed. She said it was to take our mind off what was happening, but I think it was really for her."

"I imagine it would be hard to be a military wife."

"I think the hard part was him being who he was," he said. "They were married for more than thirty years, but I never got the feeling they really loved one another. They didn't act like it."

"I think some people are just like that," I mused.

"Were your parents?"

I slowly shook my head. "I don't know. I don't really remember. My dad never remarried, so I am guessing he loved her a lot. He changed after she died. That, I do remember. He didn't laugh as much, and he didn't smile as much."

"I'm sorry," he said in a soft voice. "I lost my mom about five years ago. I can't imagine losing a mom at that young age. We weren't exactly close, but it was a loss."

I had wanted to ask him about his mom, especially since he talked about her in the past tense. I stopped myself from pushing. It was none of my business, and if he wasn't ready to talk about it, I wasn't going to pick the scab off a festering wound.

"I'm sorry. Death is sad no matter the situation."

He nodded but said nothing more on the matter. "Is this another one of those things you do often? To decompress?"

I laughed. "No, definitely not. I don't know if this is really decompressing. The fun does rejuvenate me a little though. It's exhausting but it feels good to scream and just kind of let loose. Don't you agree?"

He smirked. "I suppose. There are other activities that can lead to screaming and letting loose."

He was so different than he had been before our outing on the boat. I was convinced I was getting to see the man behind the mask. "Yes, I suppose there are."

"I'm sorry," he said, looking away.

"For what?"

"I'm being an ass."

"I don't think you are," I assured him.

"I don't normally talk like I'm a horny teen," he said with smirk.

I used my straw to stir the float. "I can't believe I'm going to say this, but I don't mind."

"I'll try and curb it."

I nudged him with my shoulder. "I think I like it. It's fun. I know you aren't being serious." I popped out my bottom lip. "But I think I like it. It makes me feel like I'm a teen again."

"Then I won't stop," he said in a husky voice that sent goosebumps spreading over my body.

I sipped on my float and watched people mill about. I was always fascinated by people. "Dang," I muttered when a young couple that was clearly very enamored with one another passed in front of us.

"Is this the part where we yell at them to get a room?" he joked.

"Something like that."

We finished our drinks but neither of us made a move to get up. "I have to go out of town tomorrow morning."

I turned to look at him. "Oh?"

He nodded. "I should only be gone for the week. When I agreed to our little deal last night, the meetings slipped my mind. I hope I don't leave you hanging."

"I'll be fine. I don't have anything on the calendar just yet."

"Can we do this or something next weekend?" he asked. "I'm hoping to be back by Friday, Saturday at the latest."

"I would love to. I don't actually have anything going for this weekend."

"Really? Is that a first?"

"Yes, it is actually. I just hope my coworkers don't decide they need me."

"Maybe I can take you out to dinner?" he offered. "We can go to McDonald's or something."

I laughed. "I don't know. I'm kind of a BK fan."

"But do they have the awesome playground?" he teased.

"Some do."

"Then Whoppers, it is."

We both rose from our seat and slowly meandered back toward the parking lot. We got to my car and headed back to the restaurant to drop him off. I got out of the car, for whatever reason. I wasn't sure where to go from here. We had been dancing around the sex subject all day, but now that we were at the end of our time together, it didn't feel like that was where we were going.

In many ways, it felt like a first date, which was silly because we had spent a lot of time together.

"Thank you for hanging out with me today," I said.

"Thank you for dragging me out," he said with a smile. He was standing in front of me, keeping a safe distance.

"I guess I'll wait for your call?" I asked.

He nodded. "I will call."

"Good."

He didn't move. We had come to that part of the date. To kiss or not to kiss. Considering we had already crossed way over that line, it seemed a little silly to be so stressed out about what to do in that moment. I decided it was on me. After all, I was the one who made it clear I didn't want us to be a thing. He was respecting the boundaries I had set forth.

I stepped forward and went up on my tippy toes to drop a kiss on his cheek. "I'll be waiting for your call," I said and stepped back.

He stared at me, heat in his eyes, but he didn't make a move. I got into my car and waved. He lifted a hand and watched me pull out of the parking lot. As soon as I was down the block, I blew out the breath I had been holding. That had taken every ounce of willpower I possessed. I was dying to kiss him, really kiss him. I wanted to take him up on the many offers for sex.

I was damn proud of myself for not jumping his bones. I could be just friends with him. If we had sex all the time, it would blur the lines of our casual relationship. It was probably a good thing he was going to be out of town. I needed time to cool off. If I knew he was in town, I was going to be tempted to call him up and offer my body to him.

Distance was best. I would see him again and we would do something completely safe and nonsexual. It was going to be hard, but I could do it. I couldn't let myself fall for the man. I didn't need that in my life. I liked things neat and tidy, just the way they were, without complications.

But damn, I really liked sex with him.

CHAPTER 19

XANDER

My jet landed just after one my time and four Miami time. The car I hired for the duration of my time in Miami was waiting at the airport for me. It was moments like these I appreciated the wealth I had made. It was a hell of a lot easier than navigating a busy airport and trying to hail a cab. I leaned my head back against the headrest and closed my eyes.

The difference in weather was night and day. I would never get used to the humidity in Florida. We had our days in San Diego, but Florida gave humidity a whole new meaning. I shrugged off the suit jacket I thought I would wear to the meeting. I wasn't going to wear it. The other engineers I was meeting with could think what they wanted.

I unbuttoned the top few buttons of my shirt and aimed the AC vent directly at my face. The car stopped in front of one of the many Miami high-rises. I climbed out and headed inside. The driver was going to be delivering my luggage to the hotel while I got through the first meeting of the week.

I hated fucking meetings. I hated having to deal with other engineers who wanted to tell me how to do my job. I was here as a courtesy. I was brought in to help the company figure out what the hell they were doing wrong. No one liked to be told what they were doing wrong, especially arrogant engineers.

"Gentlemen," I said as I walked into the conference room.

The owner of the ship company got to his feet. "Mr. Holland, I'm glad you could make it."

No one else seemed glad. I shook his hand. "I hope I can be of help."

What sounded an awful lot like a scoff came from one of the older gentlemen at the table. I knew his type. Old, set in his ways, and uninterested in hearing what a young buck like me had to say. I took a seat at the table and opened the binder that had been sitting at the open spot.

"We were just going over the latest design options for our fleet," the owner explained. "We can't seem to get a unanimous opinion on how to design the hull. We've got plenty of ideas, using some of the elements from your designs. We'd love to hear what you have to say."

I scanned through the various specs and drawings that were in the binder. There were elements of my designs, but none were really exact duplicates, for obvious reasons. "What are you proposing to use for the skin?" I asked.

The older engineer sighed. "The skin isn't the problem. It's the hull. Reinforced steel is the best option."

"It's also the heaviest option," I replied without looking at him. "Isn't the goal to streamline your ships? Cut costs? Save fuel?"

"Yes," the owner answered. "However, if the cost of production exceeds the cost of operation, I don't see the benefit."

His response triggered an argument. All the engineers began to talk at once. One of them got up to draw on the whiteboard in an attempt to get his point across. I wasn't listening. Truthfully, I didn't care all that much. I would let them have their say and then I would tell them the right answer. If they listened, great. If they refused to, so be it. It was no skin off my nose.

I felt my phone vibrate in my pocket and quickly pulled it out. It was a text message from Evie.

Did you land safe and sound with all of your parts attached?

I smiled and quickly sent a reply. *All the important parts are present and accounted for.*

Good. There's a particular part I was most concerned with.

I had to bite back my laugh. She could be saucy when she wanted to be. I loved playing the game. The men around me were arguing about something. I focused my attention on Evie.

Working? I texted.

Always. You?

I looked up, noticed no one was paying any attention to me, and returned to the text conversation that was far more interesting.

I'm sitting here, listening to men bicker back and forth about shit they don't have a clue about. It's riveting.

She replied with a series of laughing emojis. I found myself smiling. We exchanged a few more messages before I decided I better pay attention. They were paying me a lot of money for my opinion and advice. I had taken one look at their proposed designs and knew almost immediately what the problem was.

"Mr. Holland, is he wrong?" one of the engineers asked.

I looked up. "Is who wrong?"

"Carl suggests we increase the sheer," he said.

I shook my head. "I would not advise increasing your sheer. I would suggest you consider a long span between the perpendiculars. The belly of the ship is too heavy. The weight needs to be more evenly distributed. Using the building materials I suggested last week would also be a huge benefit."

"Steel is best," the old guy shot back.

I shrugged. "In some cases, it is. In this particular case, it isn't."

The man shook his head. "You kids think you are so much smarter. I have history on my side."

"I wouldn't brag about that," I muttered.

"All right," the owner said, slapping his hands on the table. "I think that will be enough for today. Why don't we meet back here tomorrow at ten? I have a couple of my ship captains coming in to offer their opinions."

I inwardly groaned. Just what we needed, more opinions. I got up from the table and took the binder with me. I said nothing on my way out. I was ready to get to the hotel and hop in a pool or a cold shower. My hired car was just pulling up to the curb when I stepped outside. I practically ran to get into the back of the car. I directed him to take me to the hotel without making any stops.

When I got to my room, I was stripping out of my clothes before the door closed behind me. I headed directly for the shower, stepping under lukewarm spray. The huge shower gave me ample room to turn and make sure every inch of skin was the recipient of the soothing spray.

After finally cooling off and feeling human again, I pulled on a pair of underwear and nothing else. I grabbed a beer from the minibar, not caring that it probably cost twenty bucks, and flopped down on the sofa. I had barely taken the first long drink when my phone began to vibrate on the table. I got up, expecting it to be Evie—hoping it would be Evie.

It wasn't. It was a number with a whole lot of digits, which told me it was from overseas. There was only one person that could be. "Kade," I said with a smile on my face.

"How did you know it was me?"

"Because if ISIS is calling me, we've got a problem."

"How are you?" he shouted into the phone. He was clearly somewhere loud. I could hear a lot of background noise and the usual static.

"I'm good. I'm actually in Florida right now. What about you?"

"I'm in a place with a lot of fucking sand," he said with a laugh. "I'm going to need to go through a pressure wash to get the sand out of my ass."

I had to laugh. He managed to keep a positive attitude all the time. I knew it sucked where he was—wherever he was. He was never allowed to tell us exactly where, but I suspected Afghanistan. "I'll be happy to shoot you with one. Spread your cheeks, little brother."

His laughter broke up over the shitty connection. "Are you still living in San Diego or did you finally move?"

"I still live there, same house."

"Mansion, you mean. You live in a fucking mansion."

My house was not a mansion, not by far, but it was certainly bigger than any house we ever lived in growing up. "You can always come and live with me," I offered.

"Yeah, right. These fuckers own me for another two years."

I knew he loved being in the Marines. He would likely sign up for another four years when it came time. He was a lifer, career military, just like our father. "I can buy you," I joked.

"Oh yeah, I forgot you had more money than God," he joked.

"Not quite, but I'm working on it."

He chuckled, the line crackling a little. "I'm coming home next month," he announced. "I'm hoping I can see you."

"Home to Cali or home to Oregon?" I questioned.

"Oregon," he answered. "I don't know if I can make it down there."

"Kade," I said. "If I go up there, it's only going to cause drama. I don't want to fuck up your time at home."

"Just say yes. It's been too long. There won't be any drama. If there is, we'll all get over it."

"I'll do what I can," I said.

"Bullshit. That's a pussy answer. Man up and face the guy. What's the worst he can do?"

I scoffed. "Easy for the Golden Child to say."

I waited for him to tell me to just do it. I waited several seconds.

"Hello? Kade, are you there?"

There was no answer. I put the phone down and leaned back against the couch. I was happy to see my little brother but not quite as thrilled to see our father. I knew his leave would be short. He wouldn't have time to fly down to see me. The best-case scenario would be me going up there. That was about the last thing I wanted to do.

My brother was a good guy, but sometimes, it was hard to stand in his shadow all the time. Granted, he was about four inches shorter than me, but he was a Marine. In my father's eyes, Kade walked on water. He was the golden boy. He was the son who made him proud.

He carried on the family name and made sure the Holland family name would always be associated with service to our country.

"Fuck," I groaned. I finished my beer and went in search of the room-service menu. I needed something to distract me. I was going to be thinking about the not-so-happy family reunion coming soon. Maybe I could fly in, meet Kade at a restaurant, and then fly home without ever having to see my father.

I thought about texting Evie and talking to her about the situation. I couldn't do that. We barely knew each other. Although she probably knew just as much about me as Charlie did. She was one of those people that could make you spill your guts with very little effort. She would have made a hell of a therapist.

I checked the time, my watch showing it was just after five at home. She was probably still working anyway. I didn't want to bug her. I didn't want to be that guy. The guy that texted or called every hour on the hour. We weren't that couple. I was not going to be the needy type.

Instead, I ate my dinner in silence and watched some really stupid show on TV. It was pretty much how I spent most of my evenings. The only difference was I was on the other side of the country. I was hoping I could get the meetings wrapped up early and get back home. Maybe I would surprise her.

CHAPTER 20

EVIE

I walked into Nelle's bar, my face glued to my phone like a true millennial. I was smiling as I sent back a lips emoji in response to something Xander had texted. I barely looked up as I walked through the door, navigating my way around the tables to my seat at the end of the bar.

"No," I heard Nelle say.

I looked up and found her staring at me with her hands on her hips. "What?"

"Don't you dare turn into one of those zombies."

"I'm not a zombie," I protested at the same time my phone vibrated in my hand. I had to look down and see the message.

"Yes, you are. Put your phone down."

I smiled and put my phone on the bar, facedown. "There, happy now?"

She frowned at me. "I'm not sure. Do you want a drink?"

"A glass of red would be nice, thank you."

"Are you off for the night?"

I nodded. "For the whole weekend."

"Wow! That has to be a first."

"I know and I cannot wait to just unwind for two days in a row."

She laughed. "I can't even imagine what that would be like."

"It's going to be awesome."

She drifted away to take care of her other patrons. I buried my nose back in my phone, texting back and forth with Xander. He was in a meeting, which you would never know judging by how much he was texting me. I told him he should be paying attention. He told me he didn't need to because he already knew what the answer was and was waiting for the rest of them to quit talking so he could tell them.

That was Xander. Just a tiny bit arrogant. I liked it. The man was smart and deserved to be revered. All week, we had texted back and forth. Every night before I went to bed, there was a message from him. It was really getting hard to remind myself we were nothing serious. We weren't in a relationship. We were just friends.

"You have barely taken a drink of your wine that I took such great care in pouring for you," Nelle said.

I looked up from my phone. "Busted."

"Is this the man that is not your boyfriend that has you so preoccupied?"

"He is not my boyfriend," I said as much for her sake as my own.

"I don't think I have ever seen your face stuck to the phone that much. Not even when you are working are you that focused."

I grinned and finally took a drink of my wine. "He's a fast texter."

"It isn't like his texts will evaporate if you look away," she said dryly.

"Maybe they will."

"You look happy," she commented. "Like really happy."

"I am happy. I'm usually happy."

She shook her head and pointed a finger at my phone. "That has made you a very different kind of happy. You have a little sparkle in your eyes."

"I do not," I protested.

"What's the deal? I thought this was nothing? It certainly seems like something."

I shrugged. "I don't know. I don't think it's something, like we are an official couple. It's just a blooming friendship."

"With a side of sex."

"That only happened one time," I corrected.

"But you want it to happen again." She grinned.

"It wouldn't be terrible if it did, but I think this distance thing is for the best. I get to know him without being near him. When I'm around him, sex is pretty much all I think about. Him too, judging by the way he looks at me and some of the things he says."

"Of course, he is thinking about sex with you," she said. "Have you seen you?"

I smiled. "Thank you. That is very sweet."

"And very true. Why aren't you seeing him?"

"He's in Florida this week," I answered. "He comes home tomorrow, and we are supposed to try and get together."

"Oh, a date," she cooed.

I couldn't help but smile. "Kind of. He isn't sure what time he will be back. Nothing is set in stone."

"How does that make you feel? You are the type of person who needs confirmed plans."

"Usually, yes, but I'm off tomorrow. I can be a little flexible."

My phone vibrated again. I couldn't resist flipping it over and checking the message. I quickly tapped out a reply and put the phone back down. When I looked up, she was watching me. She had a sly smile on her face.

"What?" I asked.

She shook her head. "This seems serious."

"No," I immediately answered.

"Yes, it is."

"He's just fun to talk to. I'm having fun."

"Good. I think you should have fun. You are young and this has been a long time coming."

I took another drink. There was a feeling of contentment I had never experienced before. "It's weird," I said. "I keep asking myself why? Why him?"

"Because he piques your curiosity," she answered. "You know you are like one of those psychics. You can read people. You have this weird empath thing and you know what people are thinking even before they know what they are thinking."

I smiled. "True."

"And you can't read him."

"Not as well. I get different vibes from him."

Someone waved a hand to get her attention. She stepped away to quickly fill a beer before handing it off and coming back to me. "I watched a movie once," she said. "Or maybe it was a television show. Anyway, the vampire could read minds, but when he met his soul-mate, he couldn't read her mind. That's how he knew she was his soulmate."

I raised my eyebrows. "Are you calling *me* a vampire or him? I'm confused."

"Neither of you are vampires, but in my hypothetical situation, you would be the vampire."

I grinned. "I think I could be a vampire when it comes to him."

"Dirty, dirty," she chided.

"You saw his picture," I said, feeling a little warm. "It's hard to resist."

"I think it's cute," she said. "I'm happy for you."

"Don't be too happy," I warned. "I don't think this is anything to write home about."

"I don't know. I'd be willing to place bets on it."

"Stop," I said, not wanting to entertain the idea. I needed to keep my expectations in check. If I let myself get caught up in the idea that there was a chance at happiness with him, it would be hard to let it go. I couldn't even begin to entertain such thoughts.

My phone vibrated again. It was a phone call. My immediate reaction was it had to be him. "Oh, it's my dad," I said when I saw his number. I slid off the stool and headed toward the back corner of the bar near the restrooms to hear better.

"Hey, Dad," I answered.

"Evie? Is that you?"

"Yes, Dad, who else would have my phone?"

"I hear a lot of noise. Are you working?"

I looked around the bar. "No, I'm at the bar."

"Oh, visiting Nelle," he surmised. It was only a little embarrassing that my father knew how straitlaced I was and knew I wouldn't be hanging out at a bar on a Friday night. I never did get that rebellious streak. I sometimes wondered if I missed out on something good.

"Yes, I am visiting Nelle," I answered. It was sad I wanted to lie and tell him I was there drinking and hanging all over men. I was not normal.

"Do you have anything going on tomorrow night?" he asked.

I bit my lip. I was hoping to spend some time with Xander, but we had made no firm plans. My dad was my number one priority in my life, which meant I needed to be there when he asked me to. "Nope. I have no events tomorrow."

"Can I take you to dinner?" he asked.

Again, how could I say no to my dad? Xander and I weren't a thing. We had no official plans. I could always go see Xander after dinner. Yes, that was what was known as a booty call, but it was what it was. "I would love to!" I said with excitement. "I've missed you. You are supposed to be taking the summer off, not working harder."

His gentle laugh warmed my heart. "I will see you tomorrow. Our usual place. Let's say six?"

"I will be there. I'll talk to you later. Get some sleep, and if you are eating Chinese for dinner tonight, I will know, and I will lecture you."

"I'm not having Chinese," he said.

"Oh no, pizza?" I groaned.

His laugh told me I guessed right. "There are vegetables on the pizza. That is healthy."

"Not when you dump cheese and greasy meat on the damn thing."

"I worked hard this week. I deserved a pizza."

"Fine, but tomorrow, I am making sure whatever meat you eat is steamed."

"Don't threaten me with that or I won't show up at all."

I laughed. We both knew he would show up. "I'll see you tomorrow."

"Good night. Tell Nelle I said hi, and if you drink, you call a ride."

I nodded as he spoke. It was the same old lecture. "I know, Dad. I know."

I hung up and took my seat at the bar again. Nelle was busy pouring drinks for a new crowd of young men that had come in. I drank the rest of my wine and waited for her to get done with her job. She was only going to get busier. I could stay and watch her swat away the flirts and propositions all night while dodging a few myself, or I could go home and crawl into my jammies.

I knew what appealed to me more. I was already thinking about what I would eat when I got home. I had some gourmet cheese I picked up yesterday from a place I was going to use for appetizers for an upcoming event. They had given me some samples and I couldn't leave without buying some for myself.

I had a fresh bottle of merlot and there was a new episode of Grey's Anatomy I could watch. The more I thought about it, the more anxious I got to get home. I waited until Nelle was finished and made her way back to me. "I know that look," she said.

"What look?"

"That look that says you are going home and curling up on your couch with the remote in your hand."

I grinned. "You know me so well."

"Yes, I do. What did your dad want?"

"He wants to get dinner tomorrow."

"Uh oh," she said.

I frowned. "Why uh oh?"

"Aren't you supposed to be meeting up with Xander?"

I shrugged. "I don't know. He didn't say anything definite. You know I can't turn my dad down."

"Why not take Xander with you?"

"I can't."

"Uh, yes, you can," she insisted. "You'll get to see Xander and your dad will get to meet him. You'll find out what he thinks, and you can go from there."

"That's not a terrible idea," I said as I mulled it over.

"It's a great idea. Then when you realize you and Xander are actually a couple, you won't have to worry about whether or not your dad will like him. You will already know."

"It's scary," I groaned. "You know my dad. He can be so critical. I don't want to scare Xander off before we have even got started. I don't think it's the right time."

"It's dinner. It's better to have the meeting go down in public. That way, your dad has to be on his best behavior."

I rolled my eyes. "My dad does not give a shit if we are in public. If he doesn't like someone, he doesn't exactly hide it. He does not have a poker face."

She burst into laughter. "He didn't like me at first, but he came around. It might be like that with Xander."

"And it might not be. I don't know. I'll have to think about it and then I'll have to ask Xander. I don't want him to think I'm taking him home to meet the parents after one night of great sex."

"Ah, but we both know it is so much more than that."

"No, it isn't," I protested, even though it was weak and without conviction.

I left the bar and headed home. It would be the perfect opportunity. Now, I just had to figure out how to broach the subject with Xander.

CHAPTER 21

XANDER

After a false start home yesterday due to some stupid storm, I was finally home. The pilot had called me bright and early in the morning. He informed we had a small window to take off. I packed my shit and made it to the small airport by five. In California time, that was two. My body was screwed up. I hoped to go back to sleep but it was impossible.

I cracked a few eggs into a pan before popping some bread into the toaster. I wasn't a chef. I didn't cook a lot, but I could cook a few things. My eyes felt gritty from the lack of sleep. I made another cup of coffee, thankful it took less than a minute to be ready to drink and sipped it while my breakfast cooked.

I sat down at the kitchen bar with my iPad propped up on a holder. I took a bite of the eggs while scanning through the headlines for the day. The world was going to hell in a handbasket, as my father would say. It was depressing to read the news.

My phone rang, interrupting my quiet morning. It was still early for a Saturday morning. I hoped it wasn't a ship emergency. I didn't have the brain power to deal with any engineering problems. Not until I had at least two more cups of coffee.

"Hello," I answered without paying attention to the number.

"Hi," Evie's perky voice came through.

I almost choked on the eggs. "Hey," I said, checking the time. "You are up early."

"It's eight. That's not early. Did I wake you?"

"No, I've been up since two, or five, I suppose."

"Really?"

"I didn't get to come home last night like I planned. We got in early this morning."

"Oh, I'm sorry. I should let you get back to sleep."

I took a drink of coffee. "No, I'm up. I was just eating some breakfast."

"Are you up for company?"

I looked down at the wrinkled jeans and even more wrinkled T-shirt I was wearing. I hadn't showered yet. I lifted one armpit and sniffed. It didn't smell bad. "Sure."

"I can wait if you want to try and get a nap."

"Nope. Come over. I'll text you my address."

"I'll see you soon."

I quickly sent the address and then went out to push the button to open the front gate. I scarfed down my breakfast and then rushed upstairs to brush my teeth. I put on a fresh slide of deodorant and then spritzed on some cologne before dashing back downstairs.

I did a quick run through the house, picking up the shit I had tossed around when I walked through the door earlier. A few minutes later, Evie was ringing the doorbell.

"Hi," I said as I opened the door. My eyes drank in the sight of her. She was wearing a pair of beige capri pants and a plain black T-shirt with a pair of black sandals. Her hair was pulled back in a ponytail once again. I liked it like that. I liked her shapely neck.

"Oh," she pouted. "You look tired."

I ran a hand through my hair. "I'm fine. Come in."

I gestured for her to enter the foyer. She stepped inside, her eyes scanning the area. "Can I get you a drink? Coffee?"

"I'm good. Your house is beautiful. Now I understand why you don't like to go out."

"You have to see the view," I told her and led her toward the sitting area that stretched along the length of the house that faced the ocean. There was no privacy, and if any boat out on the water aimed a telescope or binoculars my way, they'd get an eyeful.

"Wow!" she said, coming to a stop in front of the massive sliding doors that were blended in between the windows. "This view is amazing. I think this is what they are talking about when they say a million-dollar view."

"Step outside. Smell the ocean."

She followed me onto the patio. I watched her chest expand as she inhaled. "This is stunning. Just absolutely beautiful."

"The pool is over here," I gestured. "It's protected from the breeze that can come off the ocean and be a little too chilly. And it provides some privacy."

"Do you do a lot of skinny dipping?" she asked with a grin.

I winked. "Define a lot."

I showed her around the rest of the house before we ended up back in the living room. "I have to say, I thought your house would be much bigger," she said. "You are this rich guy that lives in—I hate to say it—but kind of a normal house. I was thinking you would live in one of those mansions that you need a map to navigate."

I laughed. "I'm a single guy. I don't need a big house. I don't need a giant house. I don't want a giant house. That's a waste of space and furniture. It would take me a week to get from one end to the other. I checked out several of those mega-mansions before I settled on this one. They all felt cold and very isolating."

She nodded as she looked around what I thought was a fairly normal house. "How many rooms do you have?"

"Four."

"It's a beautiful house. I like that it's comfy and you don't have silly vases that cost more than my car sitting out on a table. I've had to work with clients that insist on parties at their houses and then freak out when one of those stupid things gets broken. Your house looks like a home."

"Land was more important than house. I would have been fine

with a one-bedroom house if I could have plenty of space between me and the neighbors. I wanted comfort. I wanted to walk in the door, kick off my shoes, and just chill."

"You and your lack of liking people, right?" she joked.

I smiled. "It's more about my like of privacy and quiet."

"Your stairs go directly down to the beach?" she asked.

"Yes, they do. It's steep, and it can be a hell of a workout, but it is well worth it. One of these days, I might buy a house that is right on the beach."

"I've always dreamed about living on the beach," she commented as she took a seat on one of the overstuffed white couches. "Not this beach because it is always so packed but maybe a little more up north. Better yet, a deserted island."

"Now, you are talking," I said with a laugh.

"Do you have people that try and sneak up here?"

"Not a lot. There is a locked gate below, but you know drunk kids."

"You need an island," she said with a nod.

It did sound appealing. "I might just look into that."

"Then you wouldn't have to worry about sharing your beach with anyone else," she reasoned.

"It does get packed during the summer, but during the fall and winter, it's pretty quiet down there. I like to go down and just spend the day doing nothing."

"That does sound nice," she said with a smile.

"So, what does your schedule look like for today?" I asked her.

She shrugged. "No schedule."

"You don't have a checklist of things you need to get done?"

She laughed. "I have things that I could get done, and I do have a few errands to run, but nothing hard and fast."

"You don't have plans to drag me to Disneyland or some other wild and crazy place?" I asked with a smile.

"Not today, but now that you put that out there, have you been to Disneyland?"

I nodded. "A few times when I was younger but not in recent years. You?"

"I went a few years ago with my friend. It was fun. We should go sometime. We could get a hotel and stay overnight. Maybe stay the weekend."

She was making plans for us. Plans for the future. "I think that sounds like a great idea. And today?"

She shrugged. "I have no plans for today, but I was thinking about this evening."

"Oh? Would you like to go to dinner? Movie?"

She chewed on her lower lip, telling me she was nervous about something. "Dinner, yes, but, um, well, I have plans."

That took me by surprise. "Oh, I see. Maybe another night."

"No, actually, I wanted to know if you would like to go to dinner with me. And my dad."

"Your dad?" I asked, automatically leaning away from her. It was not what I expected. I would have never predicted that would come out of her mouth.

"Yes, my dad."

I cleared my throat. I needed to clarify some things without coming off like a total asshole. "Evie, I like hanging out with you, but I want to make sure we are on the same page here."

"What do you mean?"

"Meeting your dad," I said, knowing it was blunt.

"Oh," she said. "No, no, no."

"No, no, no, what?"

"I wouldn't be introducing you as anything other than my friend. We are friends, right?"

"Yes, we are."

"If it bothers you, that's cool. I probably shouldn't have asked. I didn't mean to make you uncomfortable. My dad asked me to have dinner with him tonight. I was hoping me and you could have dinner, and well, it just seemed like why not do both?"

I mulled it over and decided I may as well. "Okay."

"Really?"

I shrugged. "Sure, why not? It's just dinner."

"Right, just dinner between friends."

"What should I wear? Is this an Applebee's kind of restaurant or should I wear a suit?"

She groaned. "I'm so sorry. You hate suits, and here I am, constantly asking you to wear a suit."

"Hey, it's cool. I don't really mind the suits. It's just not something I could wear every damn day for twelve hours a day."

"Are you sure?"

"I'm sure."

She leaned forward and dropped another one of those chaste kisses on my cheek. "Great. I'll see you tonight then."

"You're leaving?" I asked with surprise.

"You need to sleep," she said, putting a hand up to my hair.

"I suppose I should probably try and take a nap. I don't want to look like a zombie when I meet your dad for the first time."

"Get some rest and I'll see you tonight."

I walked her to the door and said goodbye. I watched her leave, a little disappointed that she wasn't sticking around a while longer. I had missed being around her while I was gone. I went upstairs and caught my reflection in the mirror.

"Shit," I muttered. I did look like hell. No wonder she ordered me to get some sleep.

I headed for bed. A couple hours would do me good. I lay down and pulled the light blanket up and over me. I thought about the coming dinner. I was a little worried about meeting her father. I didn't do that kind of thing. I didn't meet the parents.

It was no big deal, I told myself. We would sit down, have some steak, talk about the weather, and then go home. Nothing to it. Easy-peasy.

If it was so fucking easy, why in the hell was I so nervous?

CHAPTER 22

EVIE

I was a nervous wreck. I couldn't believe how nervous I was. I wasn't sure if I was nervous about seeing Xander or nervous about Xander meeting my father. It was new territory for me. He would be the first in a long, long, long time. I couldn't even remember when I brought a man home. A boy. I think the last time I was probably sixteen and going to the Homecoming dance with an upperclassman. That had been a fucking nightmare.

I stared down at the three dresses I had pulled from my closet and laid on my bed. I couldn't decide what to wear. I was acting like it was my first date with Xander. It was, but it wasn't. It wasn't a date. It was dinner with my dad and Xander would be along for the ride. Not a date.

I decided to hop in the shower before it got too late to do it and then I would really be freaking out. I showered, shaved, and slathered lotion from head to toe. I put on a matching bra and panty set that made me feel sexy. I was going through way too much trouble for a date that was absolutely not going to end in sex.

I couldn't help it. I wanted to impress Xander. I wanted him to want me. I stared at the dresses again and decided none of them were right. I went back into my closet and started the hunt all over again. I was wedged in between the blues and blacks when I heard the doorbell. My first thought was it was Xander. Then I remembered he didn't know where I lived.

I walked to the door with my robe on and peeked through the door. "What are you doing here?" I asked Nelle.

"I am going in late tonight and thought I would stop by."

I grabbed her arm and pulled her inside. "Thank god you are here. I need help."

"Help with what?"

"I don't know what to wear!"

"You have one of the healthiest closets I have ever seen. How can you not find something to wear?"

I groaned and dragged her into my room. "I think there are too many choices."

She looked at the dresses on the bed. "I like that one," she said, pointing to a blue and black bandage dress.

"Really?"

She nodded. "Absolutely. It hugs your body. It's perfect for a date."

"This isn't a date," I reminded her. "I'm having dinner with my dad."

"And Xander, the guy you are banging."

I put a hand on my hip. "Stop. It isn't that."

She shrugged. "You are acting like you are getting ready to introduce your boyfriend to your father for the first time."

I sighed and flopped down on the bed, pushing the dresses out of the way. "I am, aren't I?"

"Yes, you are. You are nervous because you like this guy and you need your dad's approval."

"It would be nice if they could get along. I don't expect them to hang out or go to football games, but I want my dad to like him. My dad is far more world-wise than I am. I have to trust his judgment and his experience."

She didn't look like she bought into that line of thinking. "You are not exactly a naïve little country bumpkin. You have dealt with a lot of people and know how to handle just about anyone."

I sighed. She was right. "But how weird would it be if Xander and I did want to date or hang out more often and my dad hated him? I would always feel like I was lying to my dad."

"Evie, you are twenty-eight, not eight, not eighteen. Your dad should trust your judgement. He knows he didn't raise an idiot. You are more than capable of making sound decisions."

I worried my bottom lip. "I know. He knows, but he is still the kind of man that questions everything. He has some pretty high standards. I don't think there is ever going to be anyone that passes muster."

"Except for me." She grinned. "Your dad loves me."

"Now, he does, but trust me. He wasn't thrilled with the idea of you in the beginning."

She waved a hand. "It's a good thing I don't give a shit. I've got enough people judging me. I don't need any more."

"Maybe I should cancel," I said. I had been running through various scenarios all day about what could happen. There were very few times the little run through came out good. Most of my imagined scenarios ended with my dad tossing his napkin onto the plate and walking out. In some cases, he grabbed me by the arm and made me go with him.

"You can't let your dad ruin this," she warned. "You like Xander and that's what really matters. You said Xander is a bit of a slow burn. You need to start the burning process if you ever want your dad to like him. Let them meet and see if it's a clash of the titans or more of one of those horribly awkward encounters where no one talks."

"As a friend," I reiterated. "I like him as a friend. We are just friends having some fun."

"Whatever you say. Keep telling yourself and maybe you will believe it."

"Nelle, I can't let myself fall for him, not now."

"Why not now?"

I groaned and looked up at the ceiling. "Because I made a big deal out of wanting to be friends only and he went along with it. Hell, he jumped at the chance. I offered him no strings attached and he was thrilled. I can't change my mind now."

"You are a woman. That is your prerogative. It's kind of a known fact that women can and will change their minds frequently. It's what we do."

I shook my head. "It isn't what I do. I'm not wishy-washy. I say it and I mean it."

She rolled her eyes. "Whatever. Dumb. You would stick to your guns just to prove a point, even though it made you miserable?"

"I don't know."

"That is really stupid. If you have strong feelings for this guy, which I can tell you do, have another conversation with him. Talk to him about maybe casually seeing each other. Ease into the whole thing. Don't show up at his house wearing a wedding dress and carrying a magazine about babies. Go slow and easy and see if he's the skittish type."

"You make it sound like I'm approaching a rabid animal," I quipped.

"I have found most men resemble scared little beasts," she answered. "A tranquilizer gun might be needed."

I burst into laughter. "I'm not going to tranq Xander and drag him back to my place and tell him he will be mine."

"I think there is a movie about that," she mused aloud.

She had effectively lightened the mood. I felt a little better. Not a lot but enough to be my usual rational self. "Okay, now, I need a dress."

"Wear that dress and your black heels. Leave your hair down and make sure you go a little darker on the eye makeup than usual."

I got up and picked up the dress. "Don't leave," I said and went into the bathroom to quickly dress. I slid the tight fabric down my body before turning left and right in the mirror. I did love the dress.

I walked into my bedroom once again. Nelle handed me the shoes. I slipped them on and held out my arms before doing a slow turn. She gave me a thumbs-up. "Perfect. He is going to be blown away."

"Is it too much?" I asked, smoothing the dress over my stomach. "I think it might be too tight for a dinner with dad."

"It's not too tight. I see women wear those to the office all the time. It looks good. I love that dress."

"Thank you. I'm so fucking nervous."

"I know you are," she said, looking me directly in the eye. "Nervous is okay. Try and relax. Get through the introduction and then let the chips fall where they may. If your dad doesn't like him, it doesn't mean anything. You have already said your dad likes very few people. It doesn't mean Xander is a bad guy. You have to find out whether you like him. Don't worry about daddy just yet."

"I hope he does like him. I do value my dad's opinion."

"I know you do, and that is perfectly understandable, but don't let his opinion ruin something good."

I sat down at my vanity and started to do my makeup. "He can't ruin something that isn't there."

"Keep lying to yourself," she teased. "I do have to get going. Good luck. Call me tomorrow and let me know how it went. Remember to breathe. Use those skills you have worked so hard to develop to smooth out any problems."

I smiled. "You are right. It will be fine."

She patted the top of my head and left. I looked in the mirror and hoped I was right. I wanted them to get along.

I didn't want to be late. That would make my dad crazy. I fluffed my hair and then headed out. I got to the restaurant a full fifteen minutes early. My father was already seated, his glasses sitting on the end of his nose as he scanned the menu.

"Here you go, miss," the nice waiter said as he pulled out my chair. "Can I get you a drink while you browse the menu?"

"Just a diet soda for me," I answered. "We'll need a third seat."

My father lowered the menu. "Excuse me?"

I smiled up at the waiter. "Please?"

"Yes, ma'am."

He rushed away and returned a minute later with an additional chair and silverware wrapped in a napkin. "Can we have a clean set for our mystery guest?" my father snapped. "Maybe a fork that hasn't been rubbed against the leg of a chair."

"Dad," I scolded.

"I'm sorry, sir," the waiter said, looking mortified. "I'll be right back."

He rushed away, giving me a chance to scowl at my father. "Dad, don't be like that."

He didn't get to answer. The waiter returned, putting the new silverware at the place setting before scurrying away. "Who did you invite? Nelle?"

"No, it's actually someone else. A friend. I would like you to meet him."

"Him?" he asked, taking off his glasses and resting them on the table. "A boyfriend?"

"No," I told him. "Not a boyfriend. Just a friend."

He looked at me with those eyes that saw too much. "A friend? Since when do you have men that are friends?"

"I have plenty of guy friends."

"None that I've ever met," he said, obviously not happy.

"This guy is different. I think you might actually like him. You have some things in common."

He offered a small smile. "Is this friend a serious friend?"

I giggled. "Dad, I swear he is just a friend."

"I don't think you dressed up for me," he said with a small smile.

"Of course, I did."

I heard my phone vibrate in my purse. I quickly pulled it out. "He's going to be here in a few minutes," I said. "I'm going to go out and meet him."

"I guess I'll be waiting here," he said with a silly smile. "This should prove to be an interesting evening."

"Promise me you will be nice," I said.

"I'm always nice."

I raised my eyebrows. "Dad, you are rarely nice."

"I am a man with standards. I don't have a high tolerance for stupidity, disrespect, or arrogance."

I slowly nodded. "I know, Dad. I know. I'll be right back."

I got up and walked out of the dining room to wait for Xander. I was having second thoughts about bringing Xander to meet my father. Serious second thoughts. I sometimes forgot how abrasive he could be. He was very abrasive.

I prayed everything went well. It just had to.

CHAPTER 23

XANDER

I pulled my car up to the valet and got out, handing him the keys. Evie was standing outside the restaurant, waiting for me. I walked toward her, putting one hand on her waist and dropping a kiss on her cheek. "You look stunning," I told her.

The dress she was wearing hugged every curve. It gave her an hourglass figure, a la Marilyn Monroe. I liked it. If only we weren't having dinner with her father. My imagination was running wild. There was so much I could say to her that would get her juices flowing and get her into that bathroom stall with me pounding deep inside her.

"Thank you."

"You are meeting me outside," I commented. "Does that mean your dad isn't here yet?"

"No, he's here. He's always early."

I grimaced. "And I'm always late."

"You're not late tonight. At least, not that late."

"Sorry," I murmured.

"It's fine."

She didn't move to go into the restaurant. I could sense her discomfort. "Is everything okay?"

"Yes, of course. Great."

I touched her cheek, being careful not to press too hard and ruin the makeup she had so carefully applied. I liked the look on her. It was very dramatic. "If everything is great, why are you out here and your dad is in there?"

She sighed and looked down at her feet. "Because I felt like I should warn you."

"Warn me about what?"

"My dad. He can be, uh, off-putting sometimes. He really is a good guy, and he has a beautiful heart and soul, but he can make it difficult for people to see it."

I smiled. "Evie, I have dealt with men like him my entire life. I know how to fly under the radar and avoid saying things that will piss them off. I've told you my dad wasn't the easiest to get along with. I survived him. I can survive your father."

"You're right. I'm making a big deal out of nothing."

"If you are that worried about the two of us meeting, I can make up an excuse and bow out. I don't want you uncomfortable. I agreed to come because I thought you wanted me to. If you would rather we not do this, I'm cool with it."

She softly laughed. "I'm sure you are. No one wants to meet the parents."

"But this isn't that," I reminded her. "We're not doing an official meet the parents. This is me meeting your dad in a very casual way."

She nodded. "You're right."

"Should we go in or do you need a minute?" I questioned.

"I'm good. Thank you for asking. Just remember, he is all bark and no bite."

"Is he going to dislike me on principle?"

She gave me a look that said that was exactly it. She was so friendly and open, I couldn't imagine her coming from a man that was the total opposite. "Maybe. He dislikes most people when he first meets them. It isn't anything personal. It's just the kind of man he is."

"I'm going to be fine," I assured her. "If he doesn't like me, I will survive. I'm not going to get too hung up on another person's opinion of me. I learned how to ignore that shit a long time ago."

"I wish I was as thick-skinned as you," she said. "I try and tell myself I don't care what people think about me, but I do."

"You are perfect the way you are."

She looked up at me and smiled. "Thank you. Let's do this."

I opened the door for her and let her pass in front of me, taking a minute to appreciate the fine ass that was hugged and lifted in the dress. I looked away. I wasn't sure where her father was sitting. I didn't want him to see me checking out his daughter's ass the first time he met me. I wasn't sure what she'd told him about us, but I didn't want to do anything that would embarrass her or make her uncomfortable. We were friends that had never seen each other naked as far as I was concerned.

Evie wound around a few tables. I could see the top of a man's head with a menu shielding his face and assumed that was where we were headed. There was a slight hint of nerves in my belly as I stopped in front of the table.

"Dad," Evie said.

The man lowered his menu and looked up at his daughter. Nerves turned to anger as I stared at Dr. Fucking Marsh. "You are fucking kidding me," I mumbled under my breath.

Evie scowled at me. "Xander, this is my father, Dr. Philip Marsh. Dad, please meet Xander Holland."

I stared at the man who had attempted to derail my dreams of becoming a ship designer. "Mr. Holland," he said, his lip curling in disgust.

"Will you sit, please?" Evie pleaded with me.

I realized the people at the other tables were taking notice. I sat down, making a big show of jerking my chair away from him. "Marsh," I said his name.

Evie sat down. I looked at her and could see the confusion on her face. "Do you two know each other?" she nervously asked.

I looked at Professor Marsh. "Do we, professor?" I sneered.

Marsh looked at his daughter. I could see the irritation in his eyes.

I would not let him make her feel bad for this encounter. "I know this punk, yes."

"Dad!" she exclaimed. "Stop it."

"This is one of the worst students I have ever had the displeasure of having in one of my classes. He is the kid I measure all the other horrible students against. I have yet to meet a student that is as arrogant, rude, and antagonistic as him. This is your friend? Evie, we need to have a very long talk. You must choose better people to call friends."

"It's funny you say all that about me because that is exactly how I feel about you. Although I think I would add stubborn and archaic to my description of you."

Evie held up her hands. "What the hell is going on? You were in his class?"

The question was directed at me. "I was. It was the worst four months of my life. I hated the class and I found every reason to avoid going."

"Yes, because you were a spoiled, entitled brat who thought you knew better than anyone else," he snapped.

I sneered at him. "My billions of dollars sitting in my bank account would say I did know better than anyone else, most especially you."

"Bullshit," he seethed, spittle forming in the corners of his mouth.

I slowly shook my head. "It isn't bullshit. I made it, despite your attempts to hold me back. You did everything in your power to hold me down. I rose anyway. The cream always rises."

He smirked, shaking his head and looking at Evie. "See? Arrogant. This kid thinks he is the smartest person in the room. He thinks he knows so much more than the guy with the PhD."

"I do," I quipped.

He looked at me with pure disgust. "You aren't good enough to know my daughter's name. You are not good enough to be in her presence."

"Fuck you, old man," I seethed.

"Wait, hold on," Evie said, clearly very confused. "Please stop. Both of you. I'm so confused right now."

"Get rid of this punk before he drags you down," her father warned.

I scoffed. "Oh yeah, because I'm wallowing in the gutter. Think again, Dr. Marsh. You don't know shit. You didn't know shit then and you don't know shit now."

"Xander, please," Evie begged. "You were in his class?"

"Yes. My senior year. Like I said, it was some of the worst days of my life."

Marsh looked at me. His scornful gaze would have made a lesser man squirm. I didn't flinch. I glared right back at him. "Did you go after my daughter to get back at me?" he asked.

I rolled my eyes. "Why would I waste a minute of my time doing anything to get back at you? I don't have to get back at you. I'm more successful than you will ever dream of being. That's my revenge."

He scoffed. "Everyone gets lucky once in their lives."

I shook my head. There was no way I could sit down and have a meal with the man that had tried to destroy my life. I looked to Evie. I could see the shock and despair in her eyes. I hated that she was his. I hated that because of my past relationship with her father, she and I would never be friends. I had listened to her talk about her father and I knew they were close. There was no way I was getting in the middle of that.

"I'm sorry," I said to her. "This isn't going to work. I don't want to ruin your dinner."

"Xander, wait," she said.

"I have to go."

I got up from the table and walked out without looking back. The valet looked very surprised to see me. "I'm leaving. I need my car."

He nodded. "Yes, sir."

I stood on the sidewalk and waited. If my car didn't appear within the next few minutes, I was going to fucking walk home. Secretly, I was hoping she would come out and try to explain. She never did. I shouldn't have expected anything different.

My car arrived. I slipped the valet a twenty and took off. I rolled down the window, letting the summer breeze blow through the car. It did little to calm my racing heart. I was so pissed. I was pissed at Marsh. I was pissed at myself for thinking Evie was a woman I could actually learn to care about.

There was no way she and I could ever have a relationship. We couldn't even be friends. I couldn't imagine how fucking Marsh managed to have a daughter like Evie. She was light and he was darkness and misery. No wonder she was drawn to me. They said women were attracted to versions of their fathers.

Fuck me. I was her dad. I was sour and dour and a real asshole most days—just like Marsh. I slapped my open hand against the steering wheel. All day today, I thought that maybe there was a chance Evie and I could take this thing up a notch. I thought maybe we could casually date. Nothing serious but a step above friends that got together once in a while.

That hope had been dashed. I could never date her knowing her father was filling her ear with bullshit stories about me. The man hated me for no good reason. He had carved out a little piece of my soul in the short time I knew him. He had made me second guess myself. He made me think that maybe I wasn't as smart as I thought I was.

He damn near made me feel like the piece of shit he thought me to be. There was no way I could let his negativity back into my life. There was no way I would subject myself to that again. It really was too bad. I did like Evie. I had looked forward to spending more time with her and getting to know her better. Not now. That ship had sailed.

"Easy come, easy go," I said aloud. It was something my dad always said to us. He was convinced the only things in life worth having had to be obtained through blood, sweat, and tears. He didn't believe in luck or fate. If something came to us without us busting our ass to get it, it wasn't worth having.

I supposed he was right. Wouldn't he be thrilled to know that? Dad was right. In a way, Marsh was right. I didn't deserve Evie. I didn't have to fight for her. Therefore, by my dad's theory, she was never meant to be mine.

CHAPTER 24

EVIE

I was stunned—speechless. I didn't know what to say or think. I turned my head, half-expecting Xander to come back to the table. He was joking, right?

My dad and him had gotten together beforehand and came up with a practical joke. That was the only explanation my brain could come up with. I looked around the restaurant, wondering if Nelle had a hand in this. She knew how stressed out I was about introducing Xander to my dad. This was something she would do.

I didn't see Nelle, though. My father looked like he had just dined on glass. Xander wasn't coming back. It wasn't a joke. No one was going to jump out and laugh at the fact I had been pranked. This was my real life. All my fears about introducing a man to my father had just come to life.

I turned back to look at my father. His cheeks were red, and his eyes were flashing with anger. His hands were clenched in tight fists resting on the table. For a brief millisecond, I stopped to notice I had never seen him so angry. No one would ever call my father jovial, but he never showed extreme emotion in any direction. He was just always the stone-faced man in my life that had been my rock through some very tough days.

"What the hell just happened?" I asked him.

"Don't speak to me that way," he growled.

"Dad, I am trying to understand what is going on here. I don't even know where to begin. Let me start by saying you were awful to my friend. I have never seen you treat anyone so awful."

"That—that person," he spat out the words as if they tasted foul. "He is not worthy of your time. He is nothing more than a piece of shit. He is an arrogant little prick that thinks his shit doesn't stink. His type thinks they should just have everything handed to them. He thinks he is better than everyone and so much smarter than everyone else. He insulted me in front of my class. That lowlife scum deserves nothing."

My mouth fell open as I listened to him talk. I couldn't ever remember him talking so vulgarly, especially about a person. A person that was none of the things he said.

"Why would you say that?" I asked.

"Because it's true. That punk probably stole whatever design he claims made him rich. He refused to listen to me back then. He came into my class thinking he was God's gift to humankind. I took him down a peg or two."

"Dad, you are wrong. He is not like that at all. He did engineer a new series of designs for ships. He has won awards for his innovative designs. I don't think he stole them from anyone. Why would he do that?"

"Because he is a piece of shit that does whatever he wants without regard to anyone else."

I slowly shook my head. The man he was describing was not the same man I knew. "Are you sure you don't have him confused with someone else?" I asked, hoping to explain the situation away as a misunderstanding.

"I would never forget that name or that face. I know exactly who he is, just as he knows who I am."

I felt defeated. I had so wanted things to go well between them. "I thought you two would get along," I murmured. "You share a lot in common. I just… I just can't make sense of it all."

"I can't believe you brought that man here to my table."

"This was supposed to be a nice dinner. I cannot believe *you*. I have never witnessed you act so disgracefully. I'm shocked and angry. Why? Why would you do that?"

He shook his head. "You better not even think about dating a man like that."

"Why not?" I asked defiantly. "You don't even know him."

"If you want to date him, then you can just forget about me."

He was full of piss and vinegar. I had never seen him behave so terribly. I was embarrassed and angry. "This is ridiculous," I told him. "I'm ashamed of your behavior. You can eat dinner alone."

I stood, grabbed my purse, and walked out of the restaurant, hoping I could catch Xander. I looked up and down the sidewalk, looking for any sign of him.

"Excuse me," I said to the valet.

"Yes, ma'am," he said, waiting for me to hand him a ticket.

"I'm looking for a man, very tall, shaggy light brown hair. He was wearing a black suit with a red tie."

"He left a few minutes ago," the young man answered.

I sighed. "Thanks."

"Can I get you your car?"

I handed him my ticket. "Thank you."

I waited under the canopy, half-expecting my father to come after me. My mind reeled as I replayed their heated conversation. I would have never imagined they knew one another. What were the odds? It was fate, but fate did not like me. I wasn't sure what I had ever done to deserve the shittiest luck on the planet, but it was getting old.

I got in my car and aimlessly drove away from the restaurant. I had to assume Xander went home. He was likely very pissed at me. I didn't want him to be angry with me. I couldn't control my father. I needed Xander to know I didn't think he was any of those things my father said. Just thinking of the venom he had spewed made me ill.

I found myself driving to Xander's house. I doubted I would be welcomed, but I wanted to try and apologize. I needed him to know I didn't think that way about him. I wanted to ask more specifics about the drama between them but I was a little worried about what he would say. Part of me was a little angry with Xander as well. He could have been the bigger man. He could have tried to be calm or set aside past grievances. Both of them had behaved badly.

The gate to his driveway was open. I hoped that meant he was home. I parked my car and got out, suddenly feeling a little nervous. I pushed aside the nerves. I wanted the matter settled.

I rang the doorbell and waited.

Xander pulled open the door. His suit jacket was already off and his tie was hanging loose around his neck. He looked at me with irritation. "What?"

His greeting told me all I needed to know. He was going to stay mad. Well, guess what? I was mad too.

I put a hand on my hip and glared at him. "Don't *what* me," I snapped.

"You set me up," he barked.

"How could I set you up? I didn't know you knew each other!"

"I don't know that man. I don't *want* to know that man."

My temper was thoroughly piqued. "That man is my father. Have a little decency."

"He wasn't decent. He was an asshole and you sat there and let him talk to me like that!"

"What exactly did you expect me to do? Was I supposed to stuff my napkin in his mouth to make him shut up?"

He smirked. "I certainly considered it."

"Xander! It's my dad! Why do you hate him?"

"Your father made my life hell for longer than I care to remember. He is an asshole."

"He is my father!"

He shrugged a shoulder. "I'm sorry about that."

I shook my head. I couldn't understand how he could be so callous and horrible. "Wow."

"Yep, wow. I can't believe you are his child. I would have never guessed that. Not in a million years."

"Well, I am his child. I'm his only child."

"Sucks to be you," he shot back.

I bit my lip, thinking about what to say next. Unlike him and my father, I didn't feel the need to lash out and say hurtful things. I refused to resort to name calling. "I guess it's probably for the best if we leave this right here," I said.

"This?" he asked, folding his arms across his chest.

"Us. Whatever this was or wasn't."

He slowly nodded. "You're probably right."

"Goodbye, Xander."

"Bye," he said and stepped back inside.

I turned and made my way back to my car. I refused to look back. I didn't hear the door close behind me and was unsure if that meant he was watching me or if I just didn't hear it.

I felt sad. Whatever we almost had was never going to happen. I reached for my door handle, refusing to let him see how sad I was about the way things had gone down.

"Wait," he called.

I turned to look behind me. He was walking across the black pavement toward me.

"What?" I snapped. "I will not stand here and listen to you insult my father or me. Whatever beef you have with him, that's on you. I want nothing to do with it."

"Why don't we go get some real dinner?" he asked, completely ignoring everything I said.

"Dinner?" I asked with surprise. "Are you kidding me?"

He shook his head, that slow smile spreading over his face. "You promised me dinner. I'm hungry."

I stared at him, wondering what the hell was going on. He was mad, and now he wasn't. My dad's warning echoed through my head. "You want to have dinner with me?"

"Yes."

"You do remember who my father is, right? You're not worried I might be tainted in some way?"

"Can we just get some food?" he asked on a sigh.

I thought about it and decided I was hungry. "Fine, get in, though.

I'm picking the place and I'm driving. I don't want you ditching me again."

He grinned. "Not a chance in hell. Not when there is dinner involved."

He walked around the car and got in the passenger side. I had no idea what I was doing. Playing with fire seemed like an appropriate term. Maybe it was my rebellious side finally showing up ten years too late. My dad didn't want me to have anything to do with Xander.

Could that be the appeal?

I slid my key into the ignition and glanced over at him. His jaw was set, and I could see the anger was still there, hovering just below the surface. He was making an effort. Or was he?

Was he using me to piss off my dad? I took a deep breath and made the decision to do it anyway. Maybe I was the one using him to piss off my dad.

"Ready?" I asked.

He turned to me and offered me that playboy smile he brought out on occasion. "I am. I don't think there is anything worse than what already happened."

I scoffed. "Gee, thanks."

"Just drive," he ordered.

I put the car in drive and pulled out of his driveway. I was probably going to regret spending another minute with him, but I couldn't seem to bring myself not to do it. I didn't know if it was him or the idea of him that was pulling me in. I didn't want to think about it just then.

I was hungry and I wanted food. I wanted to live in the moment. I would worry about the consequences of my decision to share a meal with the enemy later. Hell, I had done the whole sleeping with the enemy thing. *If my dad only knew,* I thought with a small smile.

"Where are we going?" he asked when I took a turn that would lead us into a part of town I doubted he knew existed, considering his wealth.

In my experience, the best places to eat were the places no one knew about, except for the locals.

CHAPTER 25

XANDER

When she pulled into a parking lot that was half gravel, half blacktop, with weeds growing through the endless cracks, I wondered if she had lost her mind. There were some rather unsavory characters sitting at one of the outdoor tables. They were looking at us like we were the enemy.

We were invading their territory. I wasn't really up on the gangs in the area, but I didn't want to step onto anyone's turf. Could she be setting me up? Was she pissed at me and thinking to drop me off in a bad part of the city and hope I would get my ass kicked?

"Um, is this some kind of payback?" I asked. "Are you planning on ditching me?"

She smiled and shut off the car, indicating we were staying. "No, this is dinner. I'm not paying you back for anything, nor do I need to."

I looked around the area once again. I looked at the building with the flat roof and rather unappealing appearance. The bars on the windows really gave it that ghetto-chic look. "Is it safe? I mean to get out?"

"If you mean, are we going to get shot or shanked, the chances are fifty-fifty. Just don't glare at anyone and we should be okay."

"Are you fucking serious?" I asked. "What the hell are you up to?"

She laughed and took off her seatbelt. "Relax. It only looks rough. It's fine. I come here all the time. I have no bullet holes in me yet. This is the best place to get tacos. Real tacos with homemade everything. It only looks scary. That's part of the charm. It keeps the riffraff away."

I was going to have to trust her. Plus, what man could resist tacos? I was starving and some authentic Mexican food was too good to pass up. "The riffraff?" I looked at the men still eyeballing us.

"Yes, the tourists and those annoying little manbun men," she said. "You are going to be just fine. No one is going to maul you."

"Fine, but for the record, I like my body the way it is. I'm not interested in extra holes being added."

"Me too," she shot back before she realized she was flirting with me. "I like your body just as it is." She looked at me, her eyes roaming over my body before reaching my heated gaze again. She was teasing me.

I was on the verge of pulling her into the backseat and showing her exactly how much I liked *her* body. *There is hope.*

I got out of the car, quickly pulled off my tie, and tossed it in the seat before closing the door. I felt really overdressed. Evie's tight dress was attracting a lot of attention. The men were staring at her like she was on the menu. I wasn't interested in getting into a brawl, but I shot the men a glare anyway. One of them smirked before turning back to his buddies.

"You have actually eaten here before?" I asked in a low voice.

"Plenty of times. I was brought here by a client a couple of years ago. I've been hooked ever since."

The smell of spices, the kind that made my eyes water a little, was a little overwhelming as we stepped inside the small building. It was painted the ugliest color of green with orange trim. I found it to be hideous, but it gave the place a very authentic feel.

I stood back while Evie ordered our meals. She spoke Spanish apparently and had an entire conversation with an older man I suspected was the owner. That was new. It wasn't long before she was carrying two sodas and moving to sit at a table inside. I was on high alert. I kept scanning the area, waiting to see a gun flash at me.

"This is different," I murmured.

"You should feel privileged I brought you here," she said with a grin. "I never bring anyone here. It's my secret. I take tacos very seriously."

It was a little nugget of information about her that I didn't have before. "I guess you do if you are willing to come all the way over here. Do you come here by yourself?"

"All the time," she said with a grin.

A few minutes later, the short round man she had been talking to at the register delivered a tray filled with foil-wrapped tacos.

"Gracias, amiga," he said with a nod of his head. He gave me a look. It was the kind of look I would expect to get from a father, warning me to treat his daughter right or else. I offered a very small smile in return, hoping he didn't decide to kill me.

"I promise you are going to love it," she said when I looked at the assortment of food that was delivered to our table.

"I like tacos," I said.

"These are not just tacos. These are so good, you will never want another taco from some other place again. Manny's tacos are the bomb."

I chuckled, taking my first tentative bite. The meat was moist and flavorful. There was a kick of heat but not to the point I needed to guzzle a gallon of milk. "Good," I said with a full mouth. "Very good."

"Told you," she said with a grin. She wiped her mouth and took a drink before looking directly into my eyes. "Can you tell me what happened between you and my dad?"

I groaned. "He didn't tell you?"

"No, not really."

I had nothing to hide. I really didn't feel like I'd done anything wrong. "As he said, I took his class. I was a senior and it was the last semester. I aced his class—well, up until the final paper. He had a reputation for being really smart and stuff but kind of a dick."

She frowned. "Really?"

"I'm sorry. I don't want to talk shit about your dad, but I think your dad at home is very different from your dad at school. Have you ever been in his class?"

"No. I went to a different school."

"He's smart, really smart, and he knows his shit, but he's dated."

She laughed. "Dated?"

"He can't see the future. He doesn't want to see the future. We clashed. I came up with the idea for the design for my ships while I was in school. He failed my paper because he didn't like it. We got into a rather heated discussion that last day, with him saying some pretty fucked-up things. I was a student. I was a good student and he hated me."

She was shaking her head. "It's hard for me to think of him like that. I suppose it shouldn't be that difficult. He can be kind of abrupt and abrasive."

I scoffed. "Yeah, you think?"

"He is very smart and tends to kind of speak before he runs his thoughts through a filter."

"Unlike you," I commented. "You are always so kind when you speak. I think I'm still grappling with the idea you two are related."

She grinned before taking another bite. "I get that a lot."

"Your dad pretty much hated me from the moment I walked through the door of his class that first day. He took one look at me and sized me up."

She wrinkled her nose as if she didn't believe me. "Really? Did you flip him off or something?"

I smiled, shrugging a shoulder. "I am sure I was a little cocky back then. Guys like your dad don't like guys like me. My hair's too long. I dress sloppily, so I've been told. I'm tall and big and it apparently grates on their nerves."

"I get that," she said. "Women can be the same way when they see a beautiful woman. They make assumptions about her. My best friend Nelle is a total knockout. Even I assumed she would be a snob, but she is the coolest chick I know."

I was surprised she didn't relate to the feeling. She was fucking gorgeous. "Your dad, Marsh, as I called him on my good days, was convinced we were all cogs in a wheel. He was educating the future generation with the tools of the past. He wanted us to keep doing what has always been done. We were all just supposed to slide into the next spot when someone retired. I couldn't do it. I didn't fit the mold. I couldn't conform to the status quo."

"You rebel!" she teased.

"I suppose I am."

She smiled, her blue eyes sparkling as she looked at me. "I guess every generation needs a few people like you or we would never move forward. I think it's cool. I'm a conformer. I slid right into my designated spot in the system and I don't mind a bit."

"But you make your spot in the system awesome. You make people happy. You are changing lives and giving people memories they will never forget. I didn't want to work day in and day out sitting behind some desk and doing the same thing that had been done a million times before. Just thinking about it makes me anxious."

"Thank you."

I finished off my second taco and reached for the third. "What did your dad say after I left?"

The look on her face told me it wasn't good. "I think you figured out he doesn't much care for you."

"Yeah, I kind of got that from him."

"He suggested—no, demanded—I not have anything to do with you."

"I'm shocked," I said with heavy sarcasm.

She finished her taco before taking a long drink. She was giving me that look. I knew that look. It was the look of desire. Part of me had to wonder if it was the rebellious side of her coming out to play. "He basically gave me an ultimatum. You or him."

I felt like a gauntlet had been thrown down. What could a man do when he was challenged? He rose to the challenge. "I like that dress," I replied.

She looked down at her chest and then back at me. "Thank you."

"Got any plans?"

She slowly shook her head. "Nope."

"Want to go back to my place?"

She held my gaze. "I do."

I quickly dropped the remainder of my final taco on the foil wrapper. "Let's go."

She got up. I followed her out to her car. Neither of us spoke as she drove back to my place. The tension in the car was thick. I was halfway to being rock hard just thinking about stripping the dress off her. My ears were tuned to her breathing. Every breath she took reminded me of the soft gasps she had made when I was buried deep inside her wet heat the first time.

I wanted it again.

She parked her car. Both of us bailed out like we were in a race. Both of us were desperate for the other. It was a feeling I had never experienced before. I reached for her, grabbing her around the waist and yanking her body against mine so hard it knocked the breath from her.

Her mouth opened wide, her hands moving through my hair as she ravished me. I kept walking toward the front door with her body glued to mine. One arm acted as a band around her, holding her against me as I used my other hand to unlock the door.

I had barely pushed the heavy door open before she was attacking the button on my pants with a fierceness that belied everything I knew about the gentle woman. I felt the button pop open and had a feeling it was going to be a case of another missing button. The woman could be very impatient.

I managed to kick the door closed behind me at the same time she pushed my pants down. Clearly, we weren't going to make it upstairs to my bedroom. Not for the first round anyway.

CHAPTER 26

EVIE

I did not feel like myself. I felt crazed. Wild. Unhinged.

I needed him, and I had never needed anything so desperately in all my life. I couldn't get him naked fast enough. My hands were furiously pushing down his pants, freeing his erection that was slightly hidden by his shirttails. His shoes were in the way, keeping me from getting the pants all the way off.

I dropped to my knees and helped him. While he kicked off the shoes, I yanked the pants off. When I looked up at him, there was a shift deep inside me. He was staring down at me with those golden eyes, his need matching my own. My eyes dropped and I found myself face to face with what I craved most. I immediately reached for his dick, engorged and straining under the shirt.

My hand wrapped around him, pulling a sharp inhale of breath from him. I looked up and saw the hunger in his eyes. His jaw was clenched, and his nostrils flared. He was just as desperate for me as I was for him. My tongue lashed out, lapping over the round, swollen head. He cursed under his breath, his fingers threading into my hair.

I leaned forward, swallowing his length until he was scraping over the back of my throat. I drank from him. I sucked on him, my cheeks indenting with the force of my suction. I couldn't get enough of him. I pulled him deeper into my throat. His fingers massaged my scalp, pulling me against him.

"Fuck, I can't," he roared and fell to his knees, pulling himself from my mouth. A popping sound echoed around the expansive entryway.

I was shaking as he pulled me against him and kissed me. His tongue shoved into my mouth, replacing the dick I had just been enjoying.

His hands reached behind me and pulled the zipper down. He shoved the dress down my shoulders until my torso was exposed. I leaned forward, rubbing my breasts against his chest. The lace scratched over my hard nipples. I rubbed harder, needing more friction.

It wasn't enough. I reached for his shirt and decided he could afford another. I yanked it open, sending buttons flying. I shoved it down his shoulders, pinning his arms at his sides. He growled low in his throat, struggling to get his arms free. I held them down while my mouth moved to his neck. I slid my tongue over his collarbone and bent lower to suck on his chest.

His strength was no match for mine. His arms were freed with one powerful jerk. In a flash, he had me flat on my back, the cool tile pressing against my back. He grabbed the dress and yanked it over my hips. My chest heaved up and down as he looked down at me. The matching lacy black panties and bra were new, a treat from one of the online lingerie stores.

The way he was looking at me told me they were worth every penny.

"How much do you like these panties?" he asked without looking at me. His gaze was locked on the thin black triangle of lace covering my heated core.

I looked down at my body. I wasn't sure what he was asking.

I didn't have to wonder for long. There was a tug, followed by another, and then they were torn from my body. I sucked in a breath, and the cool air from the AC vent washed over my bare flesh. It was a stark contradiction to the heat that was clinging to my skin.

With zero gentleness, he pushed one leg, opening me to his view.

His hand stroked up my inner thigh, one finger parting my folds before pushing in. "I fucking knew it," he hissed.

My back arched, pulling the finger in deeper. "Knew?" I managed to get out.

"You're wet. You're swollen. I bet you are on the edge."

I moaned, closing my eyes to block some of the sensory overload I felt. I couldn't look at him. Looking at him was too much. He was too hot. Watching him watch himself slide his finger in and out of me was beyond erotic. I felt a million pinpricks as my body wound tighter. "Oh god," I cried out.

The orgasm broke free. My body arched as he pushed a second finger inside, stretching and filling me. "More," he shouted at me.

My eyes popped open. He was intently staring at me, his fingers working in and out of my body, stroking over the sensitive nub and sending me higher and higher. My body clenched, clamping down on the fingers as sensual sounds of ecstasy escaped my lips.

"That's it," he coaxed. "God damn, I like to watch you come."

I whimpered as the grip of the orgasm relaxed, allowing me to finally breathe again. It didn't last long. He was sliding over my body and pushing the cock I had just had my mouth on inside me. Unlike the first time, my body was much more receptive to his invasion. He slid inside, pausing only briefly before he began to jackhammer inside me.

I slid across the smooth surface of the floor with every thrust of his hips. "Fuck," he angrily growled before pulling out of me. He jerked me forward, manhandling me until I was on all fours in front of him.

My body ignored the sharp pain of the hard surface beneath my knees. I felt no pain as he once again slid his body inside mine. I felt my breasts fall forward. He had released my bra and was already reaching around to hold one in his hand as he began to pound inside me. He held my hip, keeping me steady as he continued to fuck me.

I didn't feel like myself. It was like I was having an out-of-body experience. Me on all fours in the entryway of his house was not what

I did—except with him. I pushed backward with my hands, ramming him deeper inside me.

"You little vixen," he hissed.

I felt naughty, daring. I crawled away from him before turning to look at him over my shoulder. He was on his knees, a shocked yet slightly angry expression on his face. I got to my feet and waggled my finger at him.

He sprang to his feet, nearly knocking me on my ass with the force of him grabbing me.

"I'm so not done with you yet," he whispered before lifting me and carrying me out of the entryway and to one of the couches that faced the massive bank of windows. He dropped me to my feet in front of him before turning me around once again. "Bend. Now."

He was very bossy. I loved it.

"Like this?" I asked as I put my hands on the back of the couch and bent forward. I gave my ass a little shake for good measure.

He swatted my ass before soothing the spot with his fingertips. "Just like this," he said in a husky voice.

One knee nudged my legs open. I felt the back of his knuckles scrape over my flesh as he guided himself inside me once again. I dropped my head forward, letting him have his way with my body. He was much slower and far more purposeful with his strokes.

I could feel the tension vibrating through his body directly into mine. I moaned, rolling my head back and forth between my shoulders. It was too good. I never wanted to stop. "More," I heard the word cross my lips.

"Not yet," he rasped on a strained breath.

"I need to," I whimpered. I could feel the next orgasm building. I could feel the familiar coiling low in my belly.

"Not. Fucking. Yet."

The more he ordered me not to, the more I wanted it. The more my body craved the orgasm. I couldn't stop it. I could no more stop what was happening than I could stop a speeding bullet with my hand. He knew it. He was doing it on purpose.

"Xander," I cried. I completely surrendered to him. I had never fully surrendered to any other man. He demanded it. I willingly gave it.

"Again!" he shouted. "Say my name!"

"Xander!" I cried as my world broke apart. It was a full-body meltdown. Every muscle, every nerve ending was on fire in the best way possible.

"God dammit," he hissed. "Fuck me. You turn me inside out."

I couldn't reply with words. I could only answer with my body. I was caught up in a sea of ecstasy and I didn't want to leave it. I felt him explode inside me. He shouted out with his release. His body rocked forward, pushing me against the couch. I slumped forward, my head resting against the soft couch with him still seated inside me.

I felt him spasm once and then again. The spasms continued to rock through my body. I couldn't tell if they started with me and ended with him or vice versa. We stayed joined together for at least another minute, neither of us speaking.

He slowly stood up from where he had draped himself over me. He lifted me as well and slowly turned me to face him. He pulled me into his arms and held me close. Again, words were not needed.

"Wow," I breathed.

There was a low chuckle in his throat. "No shit."

There was the sound of a ringing phone. "Not mine," I said when he didn't move.

"It's mine," he said with a sigh.

He stepped away from me, taking several long strides back to the front-door area where his pants lay in a crumbled heap. He was gorgeous. An Adonis. His body was toned and tanned.

I stared at the tattoo of what looked like Chinese writing on his side, directly on his ribcage. That had to have been painful.

I couldn't resist the allure of him. I told myself I was only walking toward him because I needed my clothes. Then I noticed the name on the screen.

"My brother," he said.

"Are you going to answer it?" I asked.

"No. He'll leave a voicemail."

He reached for me again. My naked body pressed against his. My nipples were still sensitive. The hardness of his chest against my breasts sent a shiver of desire racing down my spine. His mouth nuzzled my ear, and I sucked in a breath. I couldn't stop myself from leaning into him. I rubbed against him like a cat. I actually purred, demanding to be stroked.

"Ready?" he whispered.

I turned my face toward his. "I think the real question is, are you?"

"Think I could get a quick drink?" he asked with a sexy grin.

"I think that sounds like a very good idea. I don't want you to get dehydrated."

His hands rubbed down my back before grabbing healthy handfuls of my ass. "Stay," he said the word as a command.

"Are you sure? I don't want to break any rules."

"Stay," he said again. "Let's have a drink and then maybe we can go for a swim."

"I didn't bring my suit," I teased.

"That's right. You didn't."

"I'll stay," I agreed, feeling a little flustered at the idea of spending the night with the man I had repeatedly claimed was just a friend. A sleepover wasn't really in the friend zone, but I would worry about that later.

I reached down to grab my dress.

"Leave it," he ordered.

I turned to look toward the windows, feeling a little exposed. No, *a lot* exposed. "But, um, maybe you can close the blinds?"

He smiled. "No one can see in here, but if it makes you feel better, I will."

He moved to a touchpad on the wall and pushed a button. There was a mechanical sound followed by blinds sliding down over the windows. *Ah, to be rich.*

CHAPTER 27

XANDER

It was beyond strange to wake up with a woman in my bed. I had lain awake for several minutes trying to process everything. Evie in my bed, in my arms. It was not how I'd expected things to happen yesterday when she asked me to go to dinner with her and her father.

Her being in my arms was a little confusing. I wasn't sure what to think of it. Or what to do about it. Did I have to do anything?

For now, I was going to be cool and casual. Just play it off like I did this kind of thing all the time. Or maybe that was the wrong approach. I didn't want her to think I did this all the time. I didn't. Not even close.

That was not the right approach. I would just go with whatever she did.

She sighed and stirred against me. "Ugh, what time is it?" she asked in a sleepy voice.

I looked over at the clock. "Just after eight."

She let out a long breath again. "I should get up."

I didn't disagree. Lying in bed naked was only going to lead us to another sex marathon. "I'll make some coffee."

"Oh, you don't need to do that."

She pulled away from me and sat up, keeping the sheet pulled over her breasts. I smiled up at her. "Evie?"

"Hmm?"

"I think I've seen every glorious inch of you," I told her. "You don't have to hide from me."

"But it's the morning after. This is always the weird part."

"Always?" I asked, raising an eyebrow as I folded my hands behind my head. "This is normal for you?"

"No!" she exclaimed. "No, no, no. That's not what I meant."

"I'm kidding. Do you want breakfast? You don't have to slink out of here like you are doing the walk of shame."

She grimaced, running her free hand over her mass of curls while clenching the sheet to her chest. "I am doing the walk of shame, aren't I?"

"No," I said, sitting up and giving her a quick kiss.

She slid off the bed, pulling the sheet with her and exposing me in the process. I looked down at my nude body and then back at her. She was a dark shade of red. "I'm going to find my clothes."

I got out of bed and walked to my dresser to pull on a pair of clean underwear. I walked downstairs to find her shimmying into the dress. I noticed the scrap of black lace that had been the thong she'd been wearing. I grabbed the torn panties and held them up. "I'll buy you more," I told her.

Her eyes went wide as she snatched them out of my hands. "Let's not start doing IOU's for torn clothing. I think I might owe you more than you owe me at this point."

I couldn't help but grin. "You do get a little wild when it comes to getting my clothes off."

She blushed all over again. "Maybe you should start wearing those Velcro pants basketball players wear. It would make things easier."

I stepped toward her, cupping her cheek in my hand. "And maybe you should just go commando. It would absolutely make things easier."

I felt her shudder. I had her going again.

"I should go," she whispered.

"I'll walk you out," I offered.

"You're only wearing your underwear."

I shrugged. "So?"

"Your neighbors?"

"They can't see the driveway," I told her. "Remember, I told you I liked my privacy. No one is peeping."

"Okay."

I walked her to her car, standing barefoot on the black pavement that was fortunately not hot yet. I gave her a kiss as she stood inside her open car door. "I was thinking about taking the boat out sometime this week. Would you like to go along?"

"I would like that. I'll need to check my schedule first."

"Do that. I'll call you tomorrow."

"Call your brother," she said. "Didn't you tell me he was overseas?"

"He is."

"You can't miss his calls!" she exclaimed and slapped at my shoulder.

"It's fine," I assured her.

She got in the car and left. I headed back inside. I was in a great mood. A really good mood. Evie put me in a great mood. I didn't want to get ahead of myself, but the idea of her staying over again was very appealing.

I walked into the kitchen to start some coffee before dropping a couple pieces of bread in the toaster. I grabbed my phone and listened to the voicemail. "What the hell?" I said aloud as I listened to the message.

I hit the return call button.

"It's about time," Kade answered.

"Sorry, I was, uh—what are you doing back already?" I asked instead of telling him I was busy with a woman.

"There was a last-minute change and the whole unit was sent home a couple weeks early."

"That's cool. That had to be a welcome change."

"It was. Usually, we get extended."

"Where are you?"

"We're up north right now," he answered, keeping to the vague answers I expected from him. It was all about OPSEC. I had been trained from a young age not to ask questions about my father's whereabouts.

"For how long?" I asked.

"I'm taking two weeks," he said. "Then I'll be heading to Cherry Point for a while."

I nodded, knowing the base well. "I bet Dad's excited."

"As excited as an old Navy guy can be," he joked. "Come home and visit. We'll grab a beer, eat some crab and that amazing chowder at that place near the beach."

"Kade," I warned. I did miss the clam chowder from Mo's. After our parents had moved to Oregon, it had become my new favorite restaurant.

"I'm serious. I want to see you. It's been over a year. You can get away for a day or two."

I grabbed the carafe from the coffeemaker and poured myself a cup. "Dad doesn't want to see me. I don't want to ruin your visit home by ruining the reunion. Why don't you come down here?"

"He will want to see you," he insisted. "I don't want to waste my leave flying up and down the west coast."

"You are full of shit," I answered. "The only thing our old man wants to see from me is failure so he can scream he told me so."

"Come on. One of you has to swallow your pride and put all the bullshit behind you. You know he isn't going to do it. He is old and set in his ways. He can't do it. You have to be the one to try and move forward."

"I've been doing exactly that. He just can't seem to accept that. He thinks I'm a loser."

"He doesn't think you're a loser," he said. "He just doesn't know how to relate to you. The service was his life. It's all he knows."

"I design fucking ships," I snapped. "He's Navy. Shouldn't that be something we could talk about?"

"One would think, but it's Dad. I know you two love each other.

I'm not sure why you two butt heads so bad, but I think it's time to bury the hatchets."

"I don't know," I said. "I don't think it's possible. Mom was the mediator. With her gone, I feel like we speak different languages."

"I'm not home very often. I might not be back on the west coast for another year or longer. Please say you'll come up."

I sighed. "Fine. Call me when you are in Oregon and I'll either drive or fly up for a couple of days. But don't ask me to stay at the house. I'm not staying at that house."

"Got it. I've got to run. I'll talk to you soon. Answer your damn phone next time."

I smiled. If he knew why I had been unavailable, I doubted he would be upset. I ended the call, leaving my phone on the counter while I slapped some butter on my toast. I sat down on one of the stools. My muscles were a little stiff. Last night had been amazing and exhausting. I was sure we had only gotten a few hours of sleep.

My body felt used. My muscles were a little sore but relaxed at the same time. She had used and abused me in the best way possible. I regretted nothing, not even the bruised knees. She had been insatiable. Or maybe it was me that was insatiable. Either way, it had been a wild night.

I finished my toast and refilled my coffee cup before going upstairs. I was glad Kade was back stateside. That was always a relief. It was hard to think about him putting his life in danger somewhere far away.

I wanted to see him, but damn, seeing my dad would be difficult. I had never meant for us to drift apart. It just kind of happened. Years of listening to him praise Kade and look at me like a maggot had taken their toll.

It had been tough as a kid growing up in the shadow of my little brother. I used to ask my mother why Dad hated me. She always told me he loved me in his own way. I didn't know what that way was. I still didn't. I wasn't sure I believed her at all. The years of his constant insults that were thinly veiled but very present had made me into the teenager I eventually became.

I could admit I was rebellious. I didn't jump when he barked an order. I didn't call him sir. I stayed out too late. I drank and I wrecked two cars before I was eighteen. Every little thing I did to disappoint him only cemented his belief I was a lost cause. Kade was his son. He was the son my dad always wanted. I was the failure in his eyes.

When I decided to go to college, it was the last straw. It was a little ironic that a parent would be pissed that their kid chose college over the military, but that was my dad. I went to school and that was when our relationship really fell apart. He could barely stand to look at me when I did show up for holidays or other special occasions. The tension grew to a point I couldn't take it anymore.

I chose to avoid him. Then Mom died and there was no reason for me to visit. I didn't blame Kade for my father's behavior. Kade was a good guy. He was funny, kind, and I had no reason to dislike him, even if I was convinced my father tried to turn Kade against me. We were brothers and nothing would change that.

We didn't always see eye to eye, but we were never mean to one another. Kade used to apologize for our father's behavior, which was unnecessary. It wasn't his fault our dad was the way he was. I didn't hate the man, but I sure as hell didn't particularly like him. We had a strange relationship. It hurt my head to try and figure out why. That was one of those strings I chose not to pull. Pulling on it would unravel decades of hurt.

I preferred to keep my shit buried deep. I liked it nice and repressed. One day, I would probably need therapy, but for now, I chose to ignore those feelings of rejection and isolation. I knew those feelings were why I was the way I was.

I didn't care. I wasn't exactly failing at life. I was doing okay being my reclusive self.

CHAPTER 28

EVIE

"Finally!" Nelle said as she rushed around the bar to greet me. "I was beginning to think you fell off the face of the earth. I texted you last night."

"I know. I went to bed early. I was exhausted."

She looped her arm around mine and dragged me to my usual seat at the bar. "Tell me everything. Did your dad like him? Did they hit it off and talk all night and leave you out of the conversation?"

"No. The very few words they spoke to each other were rather ugly. They did *not* hit it off."

She frowned. "Well, that sucks."

"You're telling me. They hate each other."

She waved a hand and went back behind the bar to pour my usual glass of wine. "Did you smooth things out?"

I rolled my eyes. "There is no smoothing that train wreck out. Turns out, they know each other. Knew each other."

"Really? How? I can't imagine your dad hanging out with anyone younger."

"Xander was in my dad's class. You should have seen and heard my father. I have never seen him behave so badly. It was ugly. Horrible. I was so embarrassed and pissed at the same time."

She winced. "That bad?"

"Worse than bad. My dad has forbidden me from seeing Xander. In fact, he said if I have anything to do with him, I can count him out of my life."

That seemed to surprise her. I was glad it wasn't just me that was a little floored by my father's ridiculous reaction to Xander. "Seriously? What did Xander do? Was he one of those pranksters that superglued the chair or something?"

"No, much worse," I groaned.

She shook her head. "What? What did he do?"

"He was too smart."

She blinked. "What?"

I nodded. "Yep. Xander was too smart. Too innovative. Too arrogant. Too everything, and my dad didn't like him. Xander came up with his ship designs when he was in school. He presented them to my dad and my dad shot him down. Xander used the idea for his final grade in the class and my dad failed him. Fortunately, Xander had a solid A and the failing grade didn't prevent him from passing."

"Wow. And they still have beef?"

"Apparently. It was not a pleasant scene. Xander ended up storming out of the restaurant before we ever got around to ordering appetizers."

"Holy shit," she breathed. "I never saw that coming."

"Neither did I."

She waved a hand. "Then what happened?"

"My dad and I had some words and then I went after Xander. I found him at his place, we had dinner, I stayed the night, and yada, yada, yada."

"This was after your father forbade you from seeing him?"

I slowly nodded before taking a drink from the wineglass. "Yep."

"Holy shit. Have you talked to your father since then?"

"Nope."

She let out a low whistle. "Well shit. Twenty-eight years it took you, but you finally rebelled against your father."

"Yeah. I'm still in a bit of shock myself."

"How are you doing with it?" she asked, her tone gentle.

"Honestly, I don't know. I'm a little pissed at my dad. He can't forbid me from seeing anyone. To give me an ultimatum like that was pretty fucked up. I'm a grown woman. I have never, ever, ever made any crazy decision. I have never done anything bad. I always put him first. I always think before I act. He's treating me like I'm a twelve-year-old who sat next to the girl who wore eyeliner."

"Do you think there might be more to the story?" she questioned.

"I don't know. I have thought of that, and it would explain the extreme reaction on both sides, but neither one of them is saying anything."

"Sounds suspicious. But anyway, how did you get to the sleepover part?"

I grinned. "It just kind of happened."

"Does this mean this is a thing? Like you guys are going to be having regular sleepovers?"

"I don't know. We didn't discuss it."

"You like him," she sang the words. "Evie has a crush."

"Yeah, yeah. The real reason I stopped by was to ask if you can get someone to cover your shift here on Saturday night. I have an event and they want to have a bar. It's all very last minute. I was hoping you could step in."

She gave me that look. "Um, duh. Hell, yeah. Is it a swanky gig? I love the rich folks. The men always tip very well and the women tip even better to try and keep me from flirting with their men."

I rolled my eyes. "It's pretty swanky. It's for a doctors' group."

Her eyes lit up. "No way! Man candy! Hell yeah, I'll work it."

I laughed. "You know there are just as many women doctors nowadays."

"Yes, but that's okay. There are still plenty of male docs to choose from."

I wasn't really paying attention to her or thinking about the upcoming gathering. I couldn't stop thinking about Xander. We had such amazing chemistry. I couldn't believe my father wanted me to give all of that up. How could I possible walk away from him without a second glance? I didn't think I could.

"Hello? Earth to Evie."

I blinked and looked at Nelle, who was staring at me with one hand on her hip. "What?" I asked.

"You spaced out. I was talking to you about your doctors and you drifted away."

"Sorry," I murmured.

"Were you thinking about your man?" she teased.

I sighed and took another drink. "Yes, I was. Although I don't think I get to call him my man."

"You get to call him anything you want," she said. "You are way into him. I can see it all over your face. Are you going to keep seeing him?"

"I don't know."

"Why don't you know? Don't tell me you're going to let your father decide who you get to date. I know you're a good girl and you're a daddy's girl, but you are also a little too old to let him run your life."

"You would think," I muttered.

"Maybe you need to try talking to him about Xander," she suggested.

"I did. At least, I tried to. He doesn't want to hear it. He has made up his mind and that's that."

"He was angry. He was reacting to the situation. I'm sure once he has had a few days to cool down and realize he is mad at a guy for acing his class, he might reconsider. I have never known your father to be overly dramatic. You probably caught him on a bad day. He took it out on Xander."

"And me," I added. "He was awful to me as well. He's never been like that. I just don't understand how he can hate Xander that badly. Xander is a good guy. Just because he thought of something no one else had does not make him an arrogant prick."

She winced. "Ouch. That's harsh."

"That was one of the nicer things he said about him."

She slowly shook her head. "I really don't think you're getting the full story. There has to be more to it."

"Maybe, but it's ugly. Very ugly and I don't like it."

"Try and talk to your dad again. Be calm. Explain to him the man you know."

I rolled my eyes. "He is not going to listen. He is going to be furious if he finds out just how well Xander and I know each other."

"Make him listen. You are hung up on Xander. That is pretty clear to see. Maybe he is your true love and maybe he isn't. But you deserve a chance to find out. Don't walk away because daddy told you to. You are going to end up miserable. You are going to end up resenting your father, and eventually, you lose twice."

"Because I lose them both," I said.

"Yes. Exactly. Now, speaking of Xander, I need you to do something."

"What?"

She leaned forward. "I need you to find out if he has any friends. Single preferably, but if they aren't single, that wouldn't be a complete deal breaker."

I slapped at her shoulder. "You homewrecker!"

"Hey, if a guy is interested in me when he already has a girlfriend, that home is already broken."

"That doesn't mean you fuel the fire," I argued.

She shrugged. "I just want everyone to be happy. Ask him."

"No. Definitely not."

She pouted. "I'm not sure I'm available Saturday after all."

I shot her a dirty look. "Not cool."

She shrugged a dainty shoulder. "Ask him."

"He doesn't have any friends," I told her. "Don't you remember me telling you he was a recluse?"

"He has friends. I want a double date, but only if his friend is under, let's say fifty."

I wrinkled my nose. "Ew."

"Fifty isn't that old."

"It isn't that young. A fifty-year-old could be your father."

She grinned, her eyes flashing with mischief. "I believe that's why they call them sugar daddies!"

I burst into laughter. "You are so wrong."

"I have to get back to work. Ask him."

"I'm going home," I told her.

"Ask him," she said again from the other end of the bar.

I shook my head and walked out of the bar. I felt a little better after unburdening myself to her. The night with Xander had been amazing, but the last twenty-four hours had left me feeling horribly guilty. I hated that I'd defied my dad. I hated that I was doing something he didn't like or approve of. I wasn't that kind of daughter. I liked making him happy. I liked knowing he was proud of me.

He would not be proud to know I did exactly what he'd asked me not to. Not just that, but I went a little wild. I could admit that the excessiveness was a direct rebellion against him. When he told me I couldn't have Xander, it only made me want the man more.

I drove home, kicked off my heels, and poured myself another glass of wine. I needed to decide what to do. Nelle was right. I had to talk to my dad. I had to try and make him understand that Xander wasn't the man he thought he was. Deep down, I knew the likelihood of me changing my father's opinion on anything was slim to none. That left me right back at that ultimatum.

I could never abandon my father. Never. But could I really walk away from Xander?

We said we were just friends, but that was bullshit. I could say it a million times and it wouldn't make it true. Xander was so much more than a friend. I wanted him to be so much more than a friend. I hoped he felt the same way.

I wasn't well versed in the art of love and relationships, but when we were together, it certainly felt like there was something happening between us. I felt like our lives were slowly weaving together. I could almost picture the intricate stitching happening every time we talked, touched, and made love.

"Oh, Evie," I said on a sigh. "Why do you do this to yourself?"

I had no one to blame but myself. I shouldn't have asked him to the park that first day. I shouldn't have gone out on his boat and had sex with him. I shouldn't have gone to him after my father explicitly told me not to.

Unfortunately, I did all those things and now I was going to pay a high price for it. I smiled a little as my mind drifted back to Saturday night.

Truthfully, the price was kind of worth it. That night had been amazing, and it would be one I looked back on often with a great deal of fondness and heat.

CHAPTER 29

XANDER

I carried the cold beers out to the patio where Charlie was lounging in a chair. The grill was smoking, releasing an enticing aroma that promised some good eating was going to be happening soon. I handed him the beer and moved to the grill to check the status of our steaks. Both of us had managed to get off early and decided steaks and cold beer were exactly the way to finish the day.

My phone rang in my pocket. I put down my beer and fished it out. It was Kade. "Hey, little brother," I said. I nodded at Charlie as I walked by to go back in the house. It was the universal head nod that said I would be right back. "What's up?"

"I'm officially on leave!" he exclaimed. I could hear a lot of hoots and hollers and talking in the background. I was guessing he was at a bar with his buddies and celebrating their freedom.

"Awesome."

"Come up," he said, sounding just a little drunk.

I laughed. "It's kind of short notice," I told him. "I've got meetings all day tomorrow. I can't get up there just yet. I thought you were going to give me some notice."

"Ah, man," he said, and then I knew for certain he was drunk.

"I'm sorry. What about next week?"

"How about I go there?" he asked.

I stopped walking. "Really?"

"Yeah, why not?"

I smirked, shaking my head. I knew exactly what was going on. "Dad doesn't want me there, does he?"

He was quiet for just long enough to tell me that was the case. "I want to go there," he insisted.

"You're a fucking liar."

"Hey now," he said with a laugh. "It will be fun. I want to check out the house I have only seen pictures of."

"Great," I said, pushing down the hurt that threatened to spring to life after essentially being disinvited from my brother's homecoming. "I'll fly you down."

"I don't need your fucking money, Xander," he answered. He wasn't being mean or rude. It was his pride. I got it.

"Okay, then fly yourself down here."

I could hear him drinking and waited for him to answer. "I'm going to. It's not very warm here and the god damn wind. It's like being back in the desert with all the fucking sand in my teeth."

I had to laugh. "Get your ass down here. When are you coming?"

"I promised I would go fishing with Dad tomorrow. I'll get a flight for Saturday. Can you free up some of your precious time for your little brother?"

"Yes. Let me know the details and I'll pick you up."

"You fucking better," he slurred. "I can't believe you won't come see me."

"I will, but I can't be there right this minute."

"That's okay. I'm going to come there." He was definitely getting a good drunk on.

"All right, have fun and I'll see you soon," I told him before ending the call.

It was always the same thing when he got back from deployment. No one ever lectured the guys about drinking too much the first few nights they were on leave. It was one of those unspoken rules.

They got away with just about anything in those first few days, especially if it was a long tour or a tour that ended with a few of their buddies being shipped home in caskets. I couldn't begin to understand his life or what he saw or went through, but I knew it wasn't pleasant.

He was a strong man and stayed upbeat, but I knew he had his demons. One day, he would have to deal with it all. I just hoped he was ready for it. Fortunately, he did have our father to lean on. My dad had seen a lot during his time in the service and knew how to help Kade cope. I didn't. It was just another bond between the two of them.

I made my way back to the patio and found Charlie at the grill, pulling our steaks off.

"Done?" I asked.

"To perfection," he answered. "How's your brother?"

I laughed. "Drunk."

"I take it he's on leave?"

I sat down at the table and reached for my beer. "Yep. He's coming down on Saturday. Apparently, daddy dearest did not want the black sheep in the same state."

He winced. "Sorry, man. That sucks. Your old man is tough. I would think with the success you've had, especially in the last year, he would get over the fact you didn't enlist."

I shrugged. "I guess not. It's cool. I'm glad Kade is coming here. I'm looking forward to hanging out with him."

"Are we going to hit the bars? A Marine always gets the ladies. I'd be more than happy to serve as his wingman."

I had not seen my brother in a long time. I wanted to be a little selfish with the short time I had with him. "Actually, he's only going to be here a day or two. I was thinking about him and I reconnecting."

Charlie held up a hand. "No problem. That's good. You guys need to hang out."

"Maybe another time," I offered.

"Absolutely. I will look forward to it. How goes it with you and your new lady?"

The smile was an automatic reaction. There was no stopping it. "Good. Very good."

He chugged his beer. "No shit? I didn't think it would last."

"Why not?"

"Because you are not the kind of guy that dates a woman more than a couple times. And you are not the kind of guy who gets that cheesy, lovesick smile on his face when I mention the woman."

"I'm not lovesick," I protested.

"Have you guys hooked up since the last time?"

It was a direct question. It should have been an easy question to answer. I didn't want to answer it. It felt wrong to talk about Evie and I hooking up. I was beginning to see it less and less as a hookup. "We spent some time together over the weekend."

"Oh, that's right," he said with a nod. "You were supposed to meet her dad. How did that go?"

I groaned and finished off my beer before getting to my feet to retrieve another. "It went like shit," I said as I walked away.

I grabbed a couple more cold ones before sitting back down at the table. "You bombed the meet-the-parents thing?"

"I don't know if I told you her full name," I said.

He shrugged. "Maybe. I don't remember. Evie, right?"

"Evie Marsh," I answered.

He didn't get it. "And?"

"Evie Marsh is the lovely daughter of Dr. Philip Marsh."

I waited until the name sank in. His eyes bugged out and he choked on the beer he'd just taken from the bottle. "No fucking way! Are you shitting me?"

"Nope."

He burst into laughter, throwing his head back and getting it all out. "How in the hell do you find the one woman in the city that you can't have?"

"What do you mean I can't have?" I snapped. I didn't like being told I couldn't have something or someone. It made me want it all the more.

He shook his head. "Seriously. How are you going to have a relationship with her? I take it the meeting went about as well as could be expected between the two of you? Wait, did he even remember you?"

"Oh, he remembered me all right," I told him, remembering the moment we laid eyes on each other.

"Fuck. That sucks. What happened?"

I gave him a brief recap of what was said and me walking out. "He hasn't changed a bit. He's just like my dad. I have made myself a very wealthy man and I'm still not good enough in their eyes."

"What about Evie?"

"Marsh told her to stay away from me. She didn't. I don't know if she will ultimately cave in to his demands, but she stayed over on Saturday after she walked out on her dad."

He grinned. "That's my boy. Stick it to the man."

"It isn't like that. Me and her were friends before I knew he was her dad."

"And now? You think she will dump your ass because her daddy doesn't like you?"

"I honestly don't know. If she does, that's her choice. There won't be a damn thing I can do about it. I'm not interested in causing a family war. Marsh hates me and I'm not exactly his biggest fan. I don't see a future for me and her. It's just her and her father. Before I knew who he was, she talked about him a lot. They are really close. I can't get in the way of that and I'll be damned if I suffer through his bullshit on a regular basis."

Charlie was quiet for a few seconds. "That really sucks. I'm sorry."

"Don't be. It's not your fault."

"No, but I know you liked her."

"I do. I did. I don't know. I'm not going to boo-fucking-hoo about it. We said we were going to keep things cool and casual. I'm not pushing anything."

"I know you," he said with a smile. "You may not push it, but I think you like her. I think you want her. When you want something, you make it happen."

He wasn't wrong. "Maybe not this time."

He popped a bite of steak into his mouth. "Are you going to introduce her to Kade?"

"Fuck no!" I answered immediately.

He burst into laughter. "I thought so."

"What do you mean?"

"You are going to keep her all to yourself. Just like you won't introduce her to me. You are a selfish bastard and maybe a tiny bit insecure."

"I'm not insecure," I retorted.

"Then why don't you want her to meet me or your brother?" he asked with a shit-eating grin on his face.

"Fuck you."

"It's all good. I caught a glimpse of her. She's hot. I would keep her all wrapped up tight too. Especially around me and your brother. We make you look like chopped liver."

I rolled my eyes. "Yeah. Sure, you do."

"I know you didn't ask, but I also know you want it," he started. "You need to figure out how to play nice with Marsh."

"Fuck that. I will not kiss that man's ass."

"If you like her, you will."

I slowly shook my head. "I will never kiss any man's ass. There is nothing so valuable that I can't find another way to get. Marsh can kiss my ass."

"What about Evie?"

"What about her?"

"Don't do that," he said. "Don't minimize what you have with her and don't deny there is something. It's clear that there is. Figure out a way to please all parties. Maybe you can come to an agreement. You and her date and there is never talk of her father."

"I don't think that will work. Like I said, she is close with her father. Her mom died when she was very young. It's been just the two of them. That is not a bond I can break. I'm just going to take it one day at a time. We're supposed to go out on the boat this week. I'm not going to pressure her into anything. I don't want that kind of responsibility on my shoulders."

"Miracles do happen. Maybe you and old Marsh will become the best of friends."

"And pigs will fly, and my ships will sink."

He laughed and finished off his beer. "You really shouldn't have jinxed yourself like that."

CHAPTER 30

EVIE

I pulled open the door to the hall where my father's office was located. I knew he wasn't in class. I knew his schedule. He wasn't returning my calls, which really pissed me off.

He was the one acting childishly. I couldn't believe he was actually mad at me. He was the one who had acted like a tyrant. I was not going to let him get away with ignoring me.

I had mulled over it all week. The only way this was going to get settled was to hash it out. There would be some things said that would probably hurt. They needed to be said. We needed to clear the air. He knew it and I knew it, but he was avoiding it.

He couldn't hide from me. I was fully capable and willing to track him down. I didn't really have the time to do it, but I was doing it anyway. The week had been hectic and irritating. I was irritated in general. I was pissed I had not been able to see Xander all week. We never got the chance to go out on the boat.

This weekend was busy for both of us as well. I wasn't going to be able to see him until next week, if I was lucky. We had managed to exchange a few texts but nothing more.

I missed him. I missed his touch. I missed his kisses. I missed sex. The man had turned me into a bit of a nympho. I didn't have time to sort through what all that meant. I didn't want to acknowledge the feelings. They were there, but I kept shoving them to the back of my mind to be dealt with later. Procrastination wasn't really my thing, but when it came to matters of the heart, it was very appealing.

First things first. I needed to make my dad talk to me before I could delve into the feelings business. I needed to make him understand that I was a big girl and I could date whomever I damn well pleased.

If I was such a big girl, why did it feel like I was going to throw up? My palms were sweaty. I felt like I was going to my own trial and the odds were stacked against me. I walked down the hall, my heels clacking over the hardwood floors.

I could hear raised voices and slowed my pace. I turned my head, straining my ears to hear better. I cringed when I recognized my father's raised voice. I walked toward his office and confirmed it was definitely him. I leaned against the wall and listened to the heated exchange.

My father was on a tirade. I could hear the soft sobs of a female. It was clear it was a student.

"You should have majored in fashion or makeup or whatever it is that you actually do well!" my father said. "Why are you in my class? This is not what you care about. You are wasting my time and yours."

"Sir, I promise, I do want to be an engineer," the female insisted. "I'm trying."

"I've seen better effort from a wall. Get out. Figure out what you want to do with your life and don't come back to my class until you know."

The door opened and a young woman rushed out. She barely looked at me as she ran past me with tears streaming down her cheeks.

My dad stepped out and spotted me. "Evie," he said with surprise.

"Dad."

"Sorry you had to see that," he muttered.

"Me too."

"Come in."

I followed him into his office. I felt bad for the girl. I felt bad for Xander. I had been wearing blinders for a long time when it came to my dad. I was always apologizing for him. Usually, I didn't mind. It was second nature to me. I always chalked up his shitty behavior to his personality. I was beginning to see he really wasn't very nice.

"What was that about?" I asked.

He waved a hand. "Another spoiled brat thinking she has the chops to make it as an engineer. I swear, every year it gets worse and worse."

"I think you need to give some of these young adults a chance. You are judging them based on their looks."

"Is that what he told you?" he sneered.

I sighed. "Can we sit down and talk for a minute?"

He gestured to the hard wooden chair. I sat down and waited while he took his seat behind his desk. "What brings you by?"

"I was waiting for you to call me. You didn't. I figured an apology is best delivered in person."

"You don't need to apologize," he started.

I leaned forward, putting my hand on his desk. "I'm not apologizing for anything. You owe me an apology."

His eyes grew round. "You want me to apologize?"

"Yes."

He offered a small smile. "All right, I'm sorry you are upset that I tried to help you. As your father, I need to do things that you don't always like. It isn't always pleasant, but it is necessary. I think they call it tough love."

I should have known he would find a way around it. "You know that's not what I'm asking for."

"It's all you are going to get."

"Why do you hate him so bad? You can't give me a good reason for disliking him. You have all these assumptions about him, but you don't actually know him. Just like that girl that went running out of here. You assume the worst in people. You assume the younger generation isn't worthy of your teaching. Why? That is your job. You are supposed to be imparting wisdom on the next generation."

He studied me for several seconds. "I don't have to explain

anything to you. It is what it is, and I would appreciate it if you accept it and let me get back to work."

"Dad! Why are you being so hateful?"

"I'm not being hateful," he answered without any real inflection. "I know him. I know his type."

"You are wrong."

"Listen, Evie. You are a good girl. You have this natural inclination to like everyone. You see the good in people. I see the bad in people. I have lived on this earth a lot longer than you. I know people."

"I'm not naïve. I know people. It's what I do for a living. I read people. I anticipate their needs. Xander is not a bad guy."

He scoffed. "Yeah, right. He is using you to get to me."

"He didn't even know you were my father!"

"Bullshit. It isn't hard to figure out. Your last name. The college bio page."

It was my turn to roll my eyes. "That would be assuming he stalked you. Do you really think he has followed you all these years? I think you are giving yourself too much credit. He is a successful man. The last thing he cares about is what you are doing."

"So he says."

"He has said nothing. He hasn't said one word about you because he doesn't think about you."

"I don't think of him either."

"You sure do harbor a lot of hate for a man you don't think about."

"He is a pissant. A blip in my memory. Trust me. Stay away from him. He isn't a good guy. That is something you can believe me about. I'm with guys like him all day. I see and hear how they treat the young women in this school. I will not have you be the subject of disgusting locker-room talk."

"He isn't in school. He isn't the same as all the other guys you know."

His expression changed. I knew the look. He was done. The conversation was over. "Just listen to me on this. Walk away from the guy. There are hundreds of other men out there. You don't need this one."

I got to my feet and moved to the door. I paused and turned back to look at him. "You know, I think I'm a responsible woman. I have never done anything to make you think otherwise. I've never done anything that puts my life in danger. I've always been a good girl. I've always taken care of you. I've always toed the line. Don't you think you can trust me on this?"

"No." He didn't even try to soften his response. It was his usual no-nonsense approach. His way or the highway. It was no wonder him and Xander clashed. Xander was a strong personality. He was a little more subtle, but he was strong and stubborn and so much like my father.

"That's too bad," I said.

"Don't make this a big deal," he said nonchalantly. It was the same tone and demeanor he used when I was little and wanted an extra brownie. Or when I asked for a new car.

"It is a big deal. I'm going to date whomever I want. I trust my judgement. You raised me to be responsible and I am. You raised me to make decisions that I could trust. I trust myself on this."

He slapped a hand on his desk. "I am your father! You will respect me."

"I do respect you, but I respect me more."

"This is not how you talk to your father."

"I would expect my father to be supportive of my decisions." I walked out of the office and headed down the hall. I didn't stop walking.

I was so angry and hurt. I didn't think it was too much to ask for a little support from him. He was jaded and set in his ways. He could have chosen to set aside those ways and heard me out. He didn't. He had made me choose and I was not going to soon forget what he had done.

I got in my car and drove away. I wasn't sure if I wanted him to come after me or not. Part of me did. I wanted him to apologize and tell me he was okay with me deciding who I would date. I wanted him to say he'd like to try dinner with Xander again.

But that was never going to happen.

When I got home, I had shaken off the sadness and was feeling a little more independent. Of course, I had always been independent, but I felt empowered. I had finally stood up to my father. It had been a long time coming. It felt good. It felt right, but part of me felt a little guilty for doing it.

I needed a drink. I poured myself a glass of wine and sat down on the couch to mull it all over. I had told my dad I would date whomever I wanted. I might have jumped the gun a little bit. I wasn't even sure Xander and I were dating. I wasn't sure he wanted to date me.

That didn't matter. It wasn't about Xander. It was about me and my dad and our relationship. For too long, I had been living the life of the good little girl. I had always been obedient. I had always done what he asked me to do and rarely put up an argument. I should have stood up to him much sooner.

I hoped we could move forward now that I had set some ground rules. I wasn't all that hopeful. My father would wait for me to come crawling back. He would starve me of his attention until I couldn't take it anymore. Then, and only then would I cave in and step back in line.

"No," I said aloud. "I am not going to cave. I will stand strong."

CHAPTER 31

XANDER

I stood in the living room, looking around to make sure there wasn't any dirty socks, trash, or anything else. I was probably being ridiculous, acting like a little old lady expecting company, but I wasn't used to visitors.

I rarely got visitors. If I was being honest with myself, I got zero visitors. Charlie didn't count. I supposed I could count Evie. Two. Exactly two visitors.

After assuring myself the room was ready for company, I checked the kitchen. I was just moving the bowl of fresh fruit to a new spot on the counter when I heard the doorbell. I quickly made my way to the front door.

"Hi," I greeted.

Kade grinned and launched himself at me. He wrapped me in his arms, giving me a bro hug. I patted his back before he released me.

"Damn, did you get taller?" he teased.

I laughed. "I think you got shorter. All those years packing around a heavy ruck will do that to you."

I opened the door and gestured for him to come inside. He picked up the small duffel sitting next to his feet and followed me in. "This is a nice place," he said with genuine appreciation. "Are you right on the beach?"

"I am. Well, above the beach. Come on. I'll give you the grand tour. Do you want a beer?"

"Hell yeah, I do. I'm on leave."

"How could I forget the rules? Alcohol, alcohol, women, and then more alcohol."

"And sleep. Don't forget sleep. In a bed with a pillow and a warm fuzzy blanket."

I closed the door and led him into the wide-open living space.

He walked to the bank of windows and looked out at the ocean. "This is a hell of a view."

"It sure is," I agreed. "It's really what sold me on the place. One look out those windows and I knew I had to have the place."

He turned and slowly took in the rest of the house before I led him upstairs and then finally out to the patio area. There was an expanse of green lawn with plenty of shade trees to the left. The patio led to a deck that was multi-level with stairs off the side that led down to the beach. The outdoor living space was as big as the indoor living space, which was exactly what I wanted in a home.

"I'll grab us a couple beers," I said.

"Can we get down to the beach from here?"

"We can. I'm sure you are used to a little physical activity."

I walked into the house and grabbed a couple of beers before rejoining him on the patio. He was spacing out, staring at the ocean. I stood back and let him be. It was something else I learned from my father. Whenever he came back, he tended to do that. He would space out, lost in thought. We learned not to startle him. I waited a few more minutes and then cleared my throat.

He turned to look at me with the usual smile on his face. I handed him the beer. "Thanks."

"Ready to go down?"

He shrugged. "Maybe we can just chill here for a few."

"Works for me. I'm not sure I can keep up with you on those stairs."

We sat down at the patio table, both of us leaning back and hiding under the shade of the umbrella overhead.

"This is a really nice place," he commented.

"Thanks," I answered.

"No, really. This is prime real estate. The house is great but the view? The land? You have really, really done well for yourself."

His words were exactly what I had been craving to hear. I just wished it was my father saying them. He never would. He refused to acknowledge I had done anything with my life. He refused to accept the fact I had made the right choice by following my dreams instead of his.

"Thanks. Really, I appreciate it."

"You didn't say you lived in a house like this," he said. "Are you embarrassed?"

"No, not at all."

"Then why didn't you ever send me pictures?"

I shrugged. "I don't know. I didn't want to be a douchebag."

He laughed. "You are a douchebag. Sending me a few pictures isn't going to make it any worse."

"Good to know."

"Didn't you tell me you had a boat?"

"I do."

"Then why in the hell are we sitting here?"

I smiled and got to my feet. "All you had to do was say so. We'll swing by the store and get some food."

"And beer."

"And beer," I assured him.

Just over an hour later, we were heading out for open water. He sat on one of the couches, a beer in one hand and his other arm across the back. "This is good," he said with a huge smile.

"When you get out, you have to get a boat."

"I will. I'm going to."

"Have you thought about where you will land once you're out?"

He shrugged. "No, not really."

"Are you re-upping?"

He shrugged again. "I don't know. I haven't really thought about it. When I'm in the shit, all I can think about is getting back home and living a normal life. Then I get home and I miss being over there. Isn't that fucked up?"

"Not at all. You crave the action. You've made a life in the Marines. You have friends, or brothers rather. I think you need to do what is right for you."

"I have another year before I need to decide. I was thinking about going to officer school."

"Then you are considering making it a career?"

"I guess I am."

I drove the boat out a little farther before setting the anchor and moving to sit down on the other couch. "How is Dad?" I asked him.

"Good. All he does is fish, from the sounds of it."

I had to smile. "It's what he always wanted to do."

"He asks me about you a lot."

I wasn't sure I believed that. "Bullshit."

"No, really. When I call home, he asks if I've heard from you."

"He could call me himself," I said.

Kade took a drink from the bottle. "He could, but you know he's stubborn. He does care about you."

"I think he cares about me because I'm his son. He certainly doesn't like me. He doesn't like what I do or what I have become."

Kade laughed. "Remember when he used to run drills with us?"

I rolled my eyes, groaning at the memory. "How could I forget? He would get us up when it was still dark outside. Mom used to get so pissed at him."

"*Lance, they are little boys. You can't get them out of bed that early. They are going to need a nap!*" He said it in a falsetto voice, imitating my mother.

"*They are going to learn to be tough,*" I said in a deep voice, pretending to be my father.

Kade shook his head. "I think I was three the first time he taught me to do pushups."

"And running the mile, I think I was six the first time he started timing me."

"Mom always tried to get him to lighten up. Remember when I fell during the obstacle course?"

I couldn't help but laugh. "How could I forget? I thought Mom was going to beat Dad with a two by four. She was so pissed. She picked you up, hauled you to the car to take you to the emergency room, and left me and Dad standing there."

"The whole way to the hospital, I kept telling her I was okay. She wasn't having it. She was so pissed."

I thought about that day. It was one I remembered very well. "He was nervous," I told him. "He didn't let me quit but he told me to be careful. I think if it had been the other way around, he wouldn't have given two shits. He would have made me suck it up."

"Whatever."

"It's true. You were his favorite. You can't deny that."

"I didn't mean to be," he said apologetically.

"But you were. I don't blame you for it. You can't help being who you are."

"Hey, what the fuck does that mean?"

"You are perfect in every way," I teased.

"I am pretty damn perfect."

"It wasn't always bad," I said.

He shook his head. "No, it wasn't. All in all, I think we had a pretty good childhood. We weren't poor. Our mom was awesome. Our dad was strict, but it did keep us in line for the most part."

The *most part* was me. "I suppose."

"How come you aren't married yet?" he asked.

"Way to switch subjects."

"I don't have a lot of time. We have a lot of ground to cover."

He was right. Growing up, we had been pretty close. Over the years, we had drifted apart with him always gone and me working my ass off to make some money. "I haven't found the right woman to marry."

"Have you even looked?"

"It's not that easy," I told him. "I have found some women like me for one reason only."

He groaned. "Aren't we passed the days of comparing our sex skills?"

"Not that, asshole. I'm talking about money. Now that I have it, that seems to be the motivating factor. I don't think most of them even like me."

"You are hard to like."

"I suppose I am," I admitted. "There is one woman that likes me for me."

"Oh?" he asked, immediately intrigued.

"Yes."

"Who is she?"

I wasn't sure how much I wanted to say. Then I remembered he would be leaving soon and would have no one to tell anyway. "Evie. We met at a party. She's a party planner."

"Wow. This is a new development."

"It's nothing serious," I assured him. "We haven't even officially gone out. It's a very casual thing."

"It doesn't sound casual."

I smirked. "It might be on the way to a step above casual."

He laughed. "You're a pretty shitty liar. I want to meet her. Invite her over to your house or maybe we can go out to a club or something."

"She's working tonight."

"Damn. What about tomorrow?"

"No."

"What's the matter, big brother? Are you afraid I'm going to steal your girl?"

"Like you could," I shot back.

"There was that chick in high school. What was her name? Ashley? Amber?"

I scowled. "April. The cheerleader."

"She saw the better man and couldn't resist," he teased.

"Whatever. April wasn't exactly choosy."

"You're just jealous." He laughed.

We spent a couple hours out on the boat, reminiscing and catching up on the last year since we had seen each other. I drove us back to my house and showed Kade to the room he would be staying in for his visit. I had insisted on him staying with me instead of a hotel.

"This is seriously really nice," he said after we had gone for a swim in my pool and were now lounging on the patio with cold beers in our hands.

"It's my oasis. I don't go out much. I don't really see the need in going out. I like my house. I like being alone. I like the quiet."

"Your house is basically a five-star hotel. Speaking of, I'm hungry. This place have room service?"

"Do you want pizza? Chinese? Name it and I will have it here within the hour."

He sighed, settling in on the chair. "I have to say, that is one thing I miss most when I'm over there. Takeout. I miss being able to eat whatever I'm craving."

I imagined it would be a tough life. "I'll order a little of everything."

"What's the plan for tomorrow?" he asked.

"Anything you want to do, I'm open."

"I might just lounge poolside all day."

"We could go down to the beach," I offered.

"I'd like that."

"Sit tight," I said and headed inside.

I felt the urge to take care of him. When we had been really young, I always looked out for him. When he turned twelve or thirteen, he had kind of turned into this full-grown man that didn't need me taking care of him anymore.

He would always be my little brother and I sensed he was tired. Not tired like he needed some sleep, but tired as in life was wearing him down.

I had two days to spoil him and that was what I was going to do.

CHAPTER 32

EVIE

I finished pulling my hair up into a messy bun that would keep the heavy strands off my neck. It was going to be a warm one.

I sat down on the foot of my bed and put on my tennis shoes before standing up and checking my reflection in the mirror. I wasn't really all that concerned with my appearance. I was going for an extra-long walk today. I needed to walk off the frustration of the week.

I headed for the kitchen and filled my water bottle that I carried when I knew I was going to go farther than my usual spot in the park. Despite my declaration I wasn't going to work today, I needed to check my email. One peek.

When my phone started ringing, I slowly shook my head. "No. No way. I'm off."

I glanced over at the screen, unable to keep my curiosity from checking to see who it was. I smiled and grabbed the phone. "Hey there!" I answered.

"Hi," Xander's rich baritone came through. "What are you doing?"

"Uh, getting ready to go for a hike. What are you doing? Are you with your brother?"

"I am with my brother and I was wondering if maybe we could tag along, if you don't mind?"

"Really?" I asked with surprise and a bit of excitement.

"Yes, really. Kade needs to stay in shape." I heard laughing and assumed it was his brother in the background. "And he would like to meet you."

He'd told his brother about me. I wasn't going to get too excited about what that meant, but it was pretty damn cool. "Are you guys up for a hike?"

"To your usual place?"

"I was going to go a little farther."

I waited while he talked to his brother. "Yep. We're up for it."

"Do you want to meet in say thirty minutes? Is that enough time for you to get there?"

"Absolutely. We'll be there."

I ended the call, unable to stop smiling. He had called me. He wanted to see me. He wanted me to meet his brother. It was a lot and it was awesome.

All week, I had been worried my father had scared him off. I kept thinking I was going to miss the chance to be with someone awesome because my dad couldn't see past his own prejudices.

I went back into my bedroom and gave myself another onceover. This time, I added just a hint of eye makeup and slathered lotion on my arms.

I was wearing my running pants and a long tank that hung just below my ass. Technically, the outfit was made for running or maybe yoga, but I liked to wear it when I went hiking. The fabric protected my legs from scrapes from branches and the little bugs that loved to cling to sweaty skin.

I didn't want to be late, so I headed for the park. I parked in the same area I did the first time I met Xander. I got out of the car to stretch and text to see where they were. I heard my name.

I spun around to find Xander and a smaller version of him walking toward me. It had to be his brother. I waved and watched as they made their way toward me.

They were a couple of very handsome men. Both were wearing similar khaki cargo shorts and T-shirts. Xander's was a little tight in the chest area, while his little brother's was tight around his biceps. They were both built like gods.

"You showed up," I teased. "I wasn't sure you were up for this."

Xander put his hands on my hips and gave me a quick kiss before stepping away. It was so sweet and natural and had me feeling all warm and gooey.

"Evie, this is Kade," he said and stepped out of the way to introduce his brother.

I stepped forward, extending my hand, which Kade used to jerk me against him. "I'm a hugger," he said. "Nice to meet you, Evie."

I heard what sounded like a growl and stepped back. Xander was staring at his brother like he wanted to eat him. "Kade," Xander said the name in a warning tone.

"It's nice to meet you," I said. "Are you guys ready?"

"Let's do this," Xander said, wrapping an arm around my shoulders. We walked toward the trailhead.

I was not going to be able to walk the entire four miles with his arm banded around me.

"How long are you in town for?" I asked Kade, although trying to see him over Xander's arm was a little difficult.

Kade grinned and I had a feeling he was purposely teasing his big brother. "Just for today. I head back tomorrow."

"Oh, that's too bad," I said.

"Why?" Xander snapped. "Why is it too bad?"

I patted his broad chest. "Because you won't get to spend much time with your brother."

"Oh," he said, relaxing a little.

I could sense the rivalry between them. Rivalry and maybe a little jealousy. "I bet you two were quite the handful when you were younger."

Kade was the first to laugh. "I wasn't. Xander was."

"Not true," Xander protested. "You did just as much shit, but you got away with it."

"Because you were too big and obvious about it," his brother shot back.

I managed to extract myself from Xander's grip as the trail began to narrow. I began to fall in line behind him with Kade behind me. Xander grabbed me and practically lifted me, plopping me in front of him with Kade bringing up the rear.

"Did you guys get into a lot of trouble?" I asked.

"Xander did," Kade quickly answered.

"Will you shut up?" Xander snapped.

"He was always in trouble. Not when we were young, but when he turned about fourteen, he kind of took the rebellious thing to a new level. He was always doing shit to piss off our dad."

I turned to look over my shoulder at Xander.

He shrugged. "I never did anything that bad."

"One time, he purposely broke the lawnmower. My dad was gone, and my mom had no idea how to fix it."

"You guys lived on base?" I asked.

"Yep, and if the lawn isn't cut, you get in trouble. Our dad was pissed when he got in trouble for it."

"It wasn't that big of a deal," Xander argued.

"Yes, it was, and you know it," Kade retorted.

"You could have mowed the fucking lawn," he shot back.

Kade chuckled. "But that was your job."

The two bantered back and forth. Kade revealed more about Xander than I had ever known before. Their relationship made me a little sad. I never had a sister or a brother to have that fun banter with. I didn't have a person in this world that knew me like that. There was no one who had shared my childhood.

We made it to the lookout, each of us a little out of breath.

"I need to take a leak," Xander said, looking around.

I laughed. "There are no bathrooms up here."

Kade nudged me with his shoulder. "Sweetie, he isn't looking for a bathroom."

Xander walked off, disappearing into the trees.

I was a little shocked. "Oh. Okay. Wow."

"He likes you," he said.

"What?"

"My brother likes you. I've never seen him like that."

"Like what?" I pressed. I didn't want to interrogate him, but I was going to pump him for as much information as possible.

"He's possessive of you."

"That's just how he is," I replied.

"No, he isn't. I've stolen a couple of his girls before. He didn't care. He pretended he did. I think if I touched you, he would remove my arms."

I had to laugh. "Xander and I are just friends."

"He has never had a girlfriend to introduce me to, at least not in the last five or six years. I was beginning to wonder if he was headed over to the other side and didn't want to tell me."

My eyes widened and I laughed. "He's definitely not switching teams!"

He grinned. "I didn't think so. The fact he wanted to hang out with you and spend time with you in general says a lot."

"No girlfriends?" I couldn't stop myself from asking.

He shook his head. "None that he has ever mentioned and certainly never introduced me too. He's a private guy but I would have known if he had a girlfriend."

"He's a good guy. I have a feeling he's misunderstood."

Kade nodded slowly. "Absolutely. I'm glad he has you. I hate the thought of him being all alone."

"Aren't you alone?"

"I've got my brothers. And I hate to admit it, but my dad stays in touch with me. Him and Xander don't talk."

"What are you telling her now?" Xander asked, coming back into the small clearing.

"I was telling her you were the victim of a small penis," he said totally deadpan.

I almost choked. My cheeks flamed red. Xander looked at me with that sultry smile. "Yep," was his response.

He didn't argue or deny it. The three of us knew it was bullshit. I was certainly not going to jump to his defense and praise the size of his penis in front of his brother.

Kade was laughing, clearly enjoying himself. "My turn," he said and started to walk into the trees where Xander had just been. "Do you want to come with me, Evie?"

"Fuck you," Xander growled.

"I'm good," I told him.

"I don't even want to know what he told you," Xander said once Kade was out of the way.

"Nothing bad," I assured him. "I like him. I'm glad you have a brother. Trust me, you are lucky."

He rolled his eyes. "You didn't have to live with him."

I could tell he was joking. It was pretty clear there was a close bond between them. They loved each other. It was evident in the way they teased one another and, whether they realized they were doing it or not, the way they spoke about one another with a sense of pride.

Kade came back a minute later. "Are we going to keep going or you too weak?"

I rolled my eyes as they started to compare stamina and then size and everything else two brothers could argue about. I thoroughly enjoyed seeing Xander relaxed and having fun. By the time we made it back to our cars, I was sure they had covered every topic they could argue about.

"It was nice to meet you, Evie," Kade said, giving me another hug.

I smiled and hugged him back. "It was nice to meet you. When do you think you'll be coming back for a visit?"

He shook his head. "I'm not sure. These things can be hard to predict but I will most definitely be back."

"I'm going to hold you to that," I told him.

"I'll give you two a minute," Kade said before getting into Xander's car.

"Thanks for being cool with him," Xander said. "I know he can be a little obnoxious. It's how he blows off steam."

"He wasn't obnoxious at all. I like him. I'm bummed we couldn't hang out more."

He stepped close to me, heat from his body emanating against me. "Don't be too bummed. I don't consider myself a jealous man, but I will kick his ass."

"I am not interested in him like that," I told him, leaning forward and brushing my lips over his. "I only want what you have, no matter how small it is." I jumped away before he could grab me.

"Small, my ass. You can barely take me inside you." His husky voice dripped sex.

Just like that, I was wet. "I should go. Your brother is waiting."

He slowly nodded. "He is, but I bet he'd wait ten minutes while we climbed into the backseat of your car and I gave you that orgasm I can see building inside you."

I felt flushed. "Stop!"

He winked. "I'll call you tomorrow. I don't care what we have to do, but we need to see each other this week."

I nodded, gulping down the desire. "Yes. Definitely. Call me."

I got into my car and blasted the AC. He always left me feeling hot and achy.

CHAPTER 33

XANDER

I jogged downstairs. I had canceled my meetings for the day and was going to hang out with him until it was time for him to catch his flight back to Oregon.

I was going to make him breakfast. Something nice and greasy and completely unhealthy. I spoke to Alexa and asked her to turn on the morning news station.

While I was apprised of the events happening in the country and the city, I fried bacon and cooked hash browns. I cheated a bit and opened a jar of gravy and popped open a can of biscuits. The final touch was the scrambled eggs, a little on the wet side, just like Kade liked them.

I had thought he would be down by now. Neither of us was prone to sleeping in. Years of living on a military base and living with a military man stole away the whole sleeping in thing.

I went upstairs and knocked on the door to the room he was sleeping in. "Kade! Wakey, wakey, little brother."

There was no answer. I opened the door and immediately noticed the bed was neatly made. I didn't have to look around. I knew. He was gone. I walked into the empty room anyway and found a note sitting on the dresser. There was an old four-by-six picture resting on the dresser next to the note.

I picked up the picture first and was transported back to one of the few happy memories I had. I was probably ten or eleven in the picture. Kade would have been nine. My dad had his usual high and tight cut. I was holding up a large fish and grinning like I had won the lottery. Kade had his own fish as well. My dad looked so proud. I knew my mom was the one behind the camera.

I closed my eyes and let myself drift back to that day. My dad had just come back from a deployment. We went fishing and had a picnic. I could practically feel the cool breeze coming off the lake. I remembered the peanut butter and jelly sandwiches my mother had made and the chocolate chip cookies.

I remembered my father's laugh. He never laughed, but that day, he had laughed a lot. My mom had laughed a lot as well. It was strange that I had not remembered that day until just now. Just thinking about it made me feel very nostalgic and very lonely. I missed that life and those days. Growing up sucked. Hormones and being stubborn sucked.

I put the picture down, cursing Kade for his little trip down memory lane. I preferred to keep memories that made me feel sad or melancholy for the good times way back in a corner. I preferred to keep things on a nice even keel with no highs and no lows. I picked up the letter, wondering what words of wisdom he was going to impart on me.

Hey big brother,

Sorry to cut and run, but I got a call late last night from a buddy of mine. His wife left him, and he isn't handling it well. I caught an earlier flight. I should have woken you, but I didn't. I didn't want to see you cry. I know you'll miss me. I'll miss you too.

I had to laugh at his humor.

I left the picture because I think you need to remember more of the good times and less of the bad. I do. I like to think on the good stuff. You think about the bad stuff enough for both of us. I know things are rocky between you and dad. I get it. He's not an easy man to get along with.

He loves you. I know he does. He doesn't know how to relate to you. He wants to be a part of your life. I want you to be a part of his life and mine. Mom would have wanted us to make an effort to fix this. She would be pissed to find you and dad drifted so far apart.

It's just the three of us and we did have some good times. I'd like to have more of those good times. I want to go fishing with you and dad. I want us to go to Mo's and drink a beer around a campfire on the beach.

Say we can go back to those days. I know it is a huge ask but damn if I don't miss those days. I'm going to try and get back for a visit before I deploy again or PDS overseas. Don't make excuses. Just do it. I want to be like we were. This weekend was amazing. It reminded me of the good times.

Life is too short not to fill it with good times. Let's make a pact to outweigh the bad with the good. Do it for you. Do it for me. I'll call you before I head back east. Take care of yourself and take care of that beautiful lady. She's a good one. I like her.

Love, Kade, the good-looking one.

I smiled and put the note back on the dresser. My eyes drifted to the picture. He was right but I wasn't sure I could swallow my pride. There were a lot of hurt feelings. Every month, every year that passed, the gap between my father and me widened. I wasn't even sure I could fix what was broken.

"Well, shit," I muttered. I had a full breakfast downstairs and a clear schedule.

I went back downstairs and grabbed my phone. I doubted Evie was available, but I was going to call her anyway.

"Hello," she answered.

"Hey," I said, smiling as I took a bite of bacon. "What are you doing?"

"At this moment, I am going to a coffee shop."

"Do you have a packed schedule today?"

"Nope. I only have a few things. Why?"

"Want to play hooky?"

She softly giggled. "What do you have in mind?"

"I took the day off to hang out with Kade, but he ditched me. I was thinking me and you could do something. I think I'm due for a new lesson in having fun."

"I'm in. Let me go into the office and check on a couple things. Then I can be free, say by ten?"

"Awesome."

"What did you have in mind?" she asked. "Theme park? Beach?"

"How about the zoo?" I blurted out, surprising even myself.

"The zoo?" she questioned, sounding surprised.

"Yeah, why not? I don't think I've been there in forever."

"I'm excited. That sounds like a great way to spend the day. I'll need to go home and change. Do you want me to meet you at your place?"

"I can pick you up," I offered.

"I'll text you my address."

"See you soon."

I ended the call and felt hopeful. I wanted to take Kade's advice to heart. I wanted to fill my days with fun. I figured I had another thirty or forty years to make memories that would hopefully fill the void in my life. I tended to dwell on the negative. The less negative I had, the less chance I could dwell on the bad.

I put away the leftovers and went upstairs to take a shower. I changed into a pair of shorts and the usual T-shirt. I pulled out a pair of new tennis shoes that had been sitting on a shelf in my closet for weeks.

I wasn't a shopaholic. I didn't really like shopping at all and I absolutely hated shopping at the ridiculously overpriced shops that carried brands like Gucci and Prada. I had the money, but damn if I was going to pay five thousand for a fucking shirt.

I headed back downstairs and went into my home office to check emails and kill time until she texted. I hoped she hurried. I was looking forward to seeing her. It felt like forever before she finally texted and said she was on her way back to her apartment. I grabbed my keys and was out the door in a hurry. I didn't want to wait another minute.

Her place was only fifteen minutes from mine. I liked that she was close. I couldn't explain why it mattered, but I liked it. I parked my car and texted to let her know I was there before going inside.

She met me in the lobby instead of waiting for me to knock on her door. I wasn't going to read too much into it. She didn't want me in her place.

Watching her walk toward me in the pretty pink capris and the white flowing blouse made me think it was probably a very good idea I didn't go into her apartment. We would never get to the zoo.

"Hi." I greeted her with a kiss.

"Hi, yourself. This was a nice surprise."

"If the zoo isn't really how you wanted to spend your day, I'm up for anything."

"I'm absolutely thrilled to go to the zoo. Kade dumped you, huh?"

I nodded. "He had a friend in crisis. Those guys stick together. Kade is a sergeant and he takes his duties very seriously. He looks out for his team on and off duty."

"That's sweet. I can see him being like that. I think he wants to take care of you as well."

I rolled my eyes. "He's always been bossy. I've told him a million times I'm the older one. I'm the one who is supposed to take care of him."

"And I bet you did when you guys were younger."

I nodded. "I tried. Now, let's go before all the animals go down for their afternoon naps."

She wrapped an arm around my waist. I wrapped mine around her shoulders and pulled her against me. She was the perfect fit. We walked out to my car. I opened the door for her like a perfect gentlemen before going around and getting in the driver's seat.

"Are you sure you want to do this?" she questioned.

"What do you mean?"

"You don't like public places. I know you aren't comfortable doing public things. We could go somewhere quiet if you want. I don't want you to do this for me. I am perfectly happy doing anything, as long as you are there."

I reached across the center console and grabbed her hand. "I do want to go to the zoo. I have to confess something."

"Oh?" she asked, raising an eyebrow.

"I wasn't always reclusive. I've never been a social butterfly, but it just seemed easier to fade away than deal with questions and opinions. When you are around, I do feel a lot better about being in public places. Your social butterfly wings protect me."

"Okay, that works. Let's go to the zoo."

I put the car in drive and headed to the zoo. I shouldn't have been surprised to find the place very busy. With no school, there were a lot of kids and families. There was a tiny twinge of anxiety, but I quickly tamped it down. I was a normal guy, out for a normal date with a beautiful woman.

She took my hand and gave it a good squeeze. "This will be fun."

I nodded and handed over my credit card to buy our tickets. "Yes, it will."

CHAPTER 34

EVIE

He held my hand as we made our way from one animal exhibit to the next. He was saying all the right things and smiling and was acting perfectly normal. That was what bugged me.

He was too normal. He wasn't being his usual self. I could feel him trying too hard to be the normal guy. Xander was naturally reserved, but just then, he was being very—for lack of a better word—normal.

"Something to drink?" he asked with a friendly smile. That was when I knew something was definitely not okay.

"Yes, please."

I stood to the side while he got in line to get the sodas. I spotted a small table in the shade and took it over. When he turned to look for me, I waved my hand to get his attention. He carried the drinks and sat down. Again, I could see there was something on his mind.

"Hot?" he asked.

"It's not too bad. What about you?"

"Fine."

I sipped on the soda before I decided the best way to find out what was on his mind was to ask him directly. "How are you? Like really, how are you?"

He frowned. "Fine. Why? Do I look ill?"

"No, you look devastating," I said with a wink.

He grinned. "Devastating, huh? Does that mean you want to go in the bushes with me?"

He was flirting, which was definitely a good sign, but his smile didn't reach his eyes. He was reserved, holding something back. "You seem like you have something on your mind. Is it me? Work? What's up?"

He sighed, shaking his head. "Nothing."

"Okay. If you do decide it's something and you want to talk about it, I'm here. I know you're not a big talker and I'm not going to be a nag."

He offered another small smile before sipping his drink and staring off into space. It was evident there was something. I wondered if it was Kade's visit. Had they gotten in a fight? That could explain why he was suddenly available for the day. I hoped not. I hated to think of the two of them fighting.

They were very cute together. I loved watching the camaraderie. I loved that Kade accepted me with open arms. I could admit I let myself have a little fantasy about the three of us being pals and hanging out together in the future. And yes, I was already thinking about a double date with Nelle and Kade together. I had never been accused of not having an active imagination.

"You're right," he said. "I'm sorry if I'm being a killjoy."

"No!" I quickly answered. "You're not being a downer at all. I'm having a lot of fun. I'm only asking because I care, and I can see you have something on your mind. If you don't want to tell me, I get it. We can go on with our day. Sometimes, a day at the zoo is just what the doctor ordered."

"I appreciate you asking. I guess I'm not so great at hiding everything. It's just that seeing Kade got me to thinking about a lot of stuff. Stuff I have chosen to not think about for a long time."

I sipped on my soda, waiting for him to go on. He was a tough cookie to crack and I didn't want to push. "Stuff? Is that code for feelings and memories?"

"I haven't seen him in over a year. The last time I saw him, it was maybe ten minutes and he was out the door. The last five years, I've maybe seen him a few hours."

"Because he's been in the service?"

"That and because I didn't want to be around my dad. My dad and Kade are close. Well, as close as my dad can be to anyone."

"Are you jealous?"

He seemed to mull it over. "Maybe a little. It's more about me acknowledging I miss the kid."

"That is very sweet. I saw you two together. You guys have a great relationship. I don't think there is any breaking that bond. Now that you guys have reconnected, you have a chance to change."

"I suppose you are right. I don't want to fuck it up."

"Is he *gone* gone or back at your dad's?"

"I would guess he'll be at my dad's eventually," he said.

"Why don't you go too? You can surely take the time off work. Spend as much time with him as you can."

He grimaced and shook his head. "I don't think that is a good idea."

"Because you don't want to see your dad?"

"I don't think he wants to see me."

I hated to think of him feeling unwanted and unloved. It hurt my heart a little. "I'm sorry. I hate to ask, but are you sure? Is there a chance he is over whatever beef you guys had?"

He sighed. "It wasn't just one beef. It was me. He doesn't like me."

"I refuse to believe that. You are a very likeable guy."

He smirked. "You met my brother. He's likeable."

I grinned. "He is pretty damn likeable. Is he single?"

He eyes narrowed. "Excuse me?"

"I'm kidding. I was only teasing."

"Not funny," he mumbled under his breath.

"It is funny. You are the total package."

That seemed to make him feel a little better. "Thanks."

"I don't want to be nosey, and feel free to tell me to mind my own business, but what happened? That was too forward. I shouldn't have asked."

I thought he was going to tell me to fuck off. He didn't. "Kade is perfect."

I wrinkled my nose. "He's a nice guy and easy on the eyes, but perfect? That's a stretch."

"Okay, if you keep telling me how good looking my brother is, I'm going to feed you to the lions."

My smile erupted over my face. I liked his little jealous side. I liked that he wanted me all to himself. "Speaking of, let's go. They should be getting fed about now."

We got up, both of us carrying our sodas in one hand while we held hands. "You really are worthy," I told him.

"My dad doesn't see it that way. Him and your dad would get along very well."

That stung. "I'm sorry."

"Don't be. I rub people the wrong way."

"You rub me in all the right ways," I said.

"Be careful," he warned. "I am still thinking about taking you back into the penguin palace. There were plenty of dark corners."

"I'm thinking that could be a little cold. The chill might cause some performance issues."

He slowly shook his head as his eyes raked over my body. "I could never have any issues when it comes to you. I don't care how fucking cold it is. You make me hot. You would melt away all the cold."

"You are dangerous," I breathed.

"So I've been told."

"For what it's worth, my dad is kind of a dick to everyone. I don't even think he realizes when he is doing it. He's very abrasive. He's never really been that way with me, but I have seen him do it to countless people, students as well."

"His reputation at the school isn't great," he said.

"How so?"

"He's known as a hard ass. Everyone dreads taking his class, but it's a requirement to get almost any engineering degree. I don't want to talk too much shit about your dad, but he's hardcore. He fails more than he passes."

It was hard to hear that about my father. "I know I've said this before, but I'm sorry. I think I've had hero worship for so long, I wore blinders. I didn't see or I chose to ignore the rude behavior and his condescending words to just about anyone he has ever encountered. Truthfully, I have apologized for his bad behavior for the majority of my life. I think I just stopped seeing it. If I don't see it, I can't be embarrassed by it."

"My dad was a dick most of the time, but people expected it from him," he said. "He was in uniform almost always. People saw the uniform and just gave him a free pass. I didn't. I think that's why he and I clashed. I didn't think it was okay to treat people like shit."

"It is not okay, but I think we have to acknowledge our fathers are a different breed. I don't think either one of them is bad, but they are just a little harsher than most people. They don't have those soft edges we see in TV dads."

He rolled his eyes. "Not even close."

"Why do you think you guys clash?" I was prying. I did that even when I told myself not to do it. "I'm so sorry."

"My dad wanted me to go into the service. I knew from about the time I was thirteen I didn't want to be in the Navy. I didn't want to be in the Marines. I wanted to go to college. He kept telling me I could go to school after I did my four years. I tried to tell him four years was too long for me to wait. I didn't want to wait. I had been designing stuff from a young age. I always knew I wanted to be an engineer or an architect. I always knew I wanted to create. I wanted to design something I could see with my own two eyes."

I smiled as he spoke. He spoke with a great deal of passion. I loved hearing him talk about it with such enthusiasm. "I don't see anything wrong with that."

"Me either. He did. He called me selfish. He insisted I was making the wrong choice. He made me feel like I was not only letting him down but the entire country. He couldn't even look at me. When I left for school, it pretty much sealed the end of our relationship."

"All because you wanted to go to college?" I asked with disbelief.

"Yep. Just like your dad hated that I wanted to do something that had never been done. It's like they all wanted me to fail. Every step forward was a direct insult to them."

Things became very clear. We slowly walked toward the primate area, joining the crowd of people watching the beautiful apes groom themselves. "And Kade joined the service," I said.

"Yep. Kade was selfless. Kade put his life on the line for his country. Kade is the son that followed in my father's footsteps. He's carrying on the family name with honor."

"You aren't exactly a bum," I told him.

"Nope, but it doesn't matter how much money I have or how successful I am or the fact I'm technically changing the world. I will never be good enough in my dad's eyes. Or your father's eyes for that matter."

"I'm really sorry you feel like that."

I turned to face Xander, threw my arms around him, and rested my cheek against his chest. "You are a good man. You are selfless. He can't see it, but I do. I know what you are doing is helping our country. It is helping the entire world. Your ships are saving fossil fuels, and with less gas being used, less emissions. Right?"

He smiled, reaching up to cup my face in his hands. "Right. I just wish he could see it."

"I know, sweetie. I know."

"Sweetie?" he questioned, raising his eyebrows. "Did you just call me sweetie?"

"I did."

"I like it," he said after a few seconds.

"Good, because I think I like calling you sweetie."

He dropped a kiss on my forehead, mindful of the very young audience crowding around us before we finally made our way to the lion exhibit.

CHAPTER 35

XANDER

I parked my car in the massive parking lot reserved for the hundreds of dock workers. I checked my watch, wincing when I confirmed my suspicions. I was late.

For the life of me, getting to where I was supposed to be on time seemed like an impossible feat. I tried and I tried but something always happened.

I made my way down to the right dock and immediately spotted Charlie. He had his hands on his hips and was staring out at the massive cargo ship in the harbor. By his stance, I could see he wasn't happy.

He had called and asked me to come down and give him some ideas. Apparently, there was a ship coming in for repairs. Charlie was stumped and needed some fresh eyes on how to take care of the issue.

It was my thing. The ship wasn't one of mine, but I didn't mind offering some advice to a friend. It wasn't like I needed the money, so I never charged him a consultation fee. There were a few companies that I did charge because the owners or CEOs were dicks. Probably not the most professional way of doing business, but it was my way.

"Hey," I said, coming to stand next to Charlie.

"Look at that." He gestured out toward the water.

I watched the ship slowly make its way in. "What am I looking at?"

"See how tough it is for the captains to navigate in here?"

I nodded. "Always has been," I said, my mind already whirring.

"This is your thing," he commented. "Do you know how much time it would save if I could get these ships into dry dock faster? This one is coming in with a rudder problem. There are always rudder problems. It has basically left this ship incapacitated. Thankfully, the captain is an experienced guy and has been able to get her this far."

"Propeller?" I said the word without asking a specific question.

"It seems to be fine."

"These ships are losing valuable time having to come in here. This one should be halfway around the world and yet it's going to be sitting in my dock for at least a week. The company has to pay to unload it and load the cargo on a new ship. Valuable time is lost."

"I get it," I told him. "I do."

"Your ships seem to be doing okay with rudders. Granted, they haven't been in service as long as some of these antiques, but can't you come up with a way to fix this? Don't you have some genius plan that could make rudders flawless?"

"No."

He smirked. "All right, then."

"No, I don't have a plan yet, but I have some ideas. I'll come back once you've got her pulled out of the water."

"Really?" he asked, looking a little surprised.

"It's why you called me out here, right?"

"Yes, but I didn't think you would have any ideas that fast."

I smiled and patted him on the back. "It's why they pay me the big bucks. I need to do some thinking and a lot of math, but I will try and get something put together. I don't know if it will be in time for this ship but maybe for the next."

"Wait," he said, furrowing his brow. "I think I just turned you onto a new design. You are going to put it on your ships and make a shit-load of money. I might be owed a finder's fee or something."

"We'll see. I don't know if anything I'm thinking will work. I need some time."

"I can already see your wheels spinning. This is what you looked like back in college. You would space out and then come back with some wacky idea for a ship. That's what you are doing."

"I'm trying, but your yapping is interfering with my thinking."

He chuckled. "Come on. Let's go get some really shitty coffee from Oscar over there."

I looked at the small stand that did not appear to be all that inviting. I followed him, each of us getting a small coffee before sitting at one of the mismatched table sets dock workers would normally take their breaks at.

"How did it go with Kade?"

"Good, really good. I introduced him to Evie."

His eyes widened. "No shit? That's a big step."

I shrugged. "It wasn't that big of a deal."

"It sure the hell is a big deal. Did he hit on her?"

"He didn't dare. I would have beat his ass if he did."

Charlie laughed. "Yes, I'm sure you would have."

"Kade wants me to go up to Oregon," I said, kind of testing the waters.

"Are you going to do it?"

"I doubt it."

"Still don't want to see your dad?" he asked.

"No. I don't know. For so long, I have felt like a failure in his eyes. I have felt like I wasn't worthy to be in his presence. Now, I'm not so sure about that."

"What's changed?"

"Evie. Evie has made me feel differently about the whole thing."

I didn't miss his sly smile. "Color me shocked."

His sarcasm was warranted. "I know you've been saying it for years, but you are not as pretty or as eloquent as she is."

He laughed. "I'm not sure that's an insult."

"She called me selfless." I didn't want to brag, but it was the first time in my life I had been called selfless. I had been called selfish more times than I could count. Even when I gave to charity and the grateful members of one board or another would call me generous, selfless felt completely different.

"Does that make you happy?"

"Yes, asshole," I muttered.

"Just checking. You are an odd duck. I never know what gets you off and what pisses you off."

"I'm not that odd. She said I'm selfless because although I didn't go into the Marines and go kill bad guys, I am changing the world in my own little way."

"Dude, I've been telling you that for years," he said with disgust.

I shrugged. "I guess I wasn't listening. You aren't as pretty as she is. When she said it, it meant something."

"It meant something when I said it," he protested.

"You sound like a jealous lover," I warned him.

"You are changing the world. If you can figure out this rudder problem, you will not only change the world but change my life. I'll have weekends off. I'll get to work a normal eight-hour day. I might even get to take a real vacation."

"I don't want to put you out of work," I teased.

He laughed, shaking his head and pointing toward the harbor. "There are a lot of old ships out there. I've got enough work to last me three lifetimes."

"This is true."

"It really is a game changer," he said. "What you are doing is going to just make life easier for the world in general. People want goods faster. They don't want to pay ridiculous shipping fees. You are making it all the better. That award you won is just the first of many. I'm sure you are going to have yourself a Nobel prize in the near future."

I sipped the horrible coffee. "I have to admit, I never did any of this because I wanted to change the world. I didn't do it because I was thinking about global warming or climate change. The designs just made sense. I don't need awards or recognition. Selling my ships is enough."

"Yeah, because you make a lot of money."

ALI PARKER

"That doesn't hurt," I answered honestly. "If people are willing to pay, I'm willing to do my part for mankind."

"And you are a scientist," he agreed. "Scientists look at facts. You saw a problem and you fixed it. You weren't looking for accolades, awards, or a pat on the back. You got rich for the right reasons. You weren't screwing anyone over.

"No, I wasn't and I'm still not. I would like a little acceptance from my father. And hers. I would like for them to be able to admit I'm not a total loser. They don't even have to tell me I did something good. I just want them to look at me with decency and not complete disdain."

"You are not a loser. I don't think anyone actually thinks that. How can they? You are the most successful guy I know. You are right up there with Gates and Jobs."

I laughed. "I don't think so. I wouldn't want to be. That's way too much pressure."

"You are whether you like it or not. You've only been doing this for ten years. Just think what you will come up with in the next ten. Like this rudder problem. You are going to fix it and it is going to revolutionize the shipping world. I bet you'll have it so good, these ships will come into the harbor like a Ferrari. Tight corners, speed, and steering like they are on rails."

"Yeah, I don't see that happening. If you think that's possible, you have no business doing what you do."

"Like it or not, you are doing selfless things. You can call it making sense, but you choosing to make ships more efficient is pretty fucking cool."

"Thanks."

"It makes you just a little less of a dick," he added.

"Gee, just a little?"

He held up two fingers and put them very close together. "That much and that is being generous."

"Call me when you get that thing up and out. I'm going back to my office to work on some stuff."

"You mean my new rudder. You are going to work on my new rudder."

222

I got to my feet and shrugged. "It isn't like it's going to just fall out of my head. Even if what I'm thinking does work, it's going to take some time. You know that."

"I do know that and I'm okay with waiting. I know you'll do it."

"I'll talk to you later," I told him and headed for my car.

I had an itch to sketch. My brain was being bombarded with a hundred different ideas. I didn't know what would work and what wouldn't, but I was going to solve the issue. It might not be tomorrow or even the next month. I would figure it out. I was looking forward to having something to work on, to fixate on.

I drove to the office, forcing myself to focus on my driving. I did get a little distracted when I had a new puzzle to solve. I could get obsessed. I tried to tell myself to keep it in check. Maybe things would be different this time. Evie would keep me from getting too wrapped up in the project. She would force me to leave the office. She would make me eat and shower.

And hopefully want to distract me in other ways.

When I got to the office, I closed the door, making it clear I was not to be disturbed. I was going to give the project my full attention for the day. I rubbed my hands together and pulled out my yellow pad. That was where it always started.

I had to purge the millions of thoughts pelting my brain. Once I got it on paper, I could begin to sort through it all. I reached for the fresh pack of Post-its. My office was about to get very messy.

I grinned, thinking of the coming days. It had been a long time since I'd gotten to design. It was like taking a hit from my favorite drug after giving it up for a long time.

CHAPTER 36

EVIE

It was just after five when I pulled into the shopping center. I had tried to get off work earlier, but with the day off on Monday, I was swamped. I couldn't neglect my friends. At least, that was what Nelle had said when she demanded I take part in some retail therapy. I called her to find out where she was.

I walked into the clothing store she was at and quickly spotted her. "I like it," I said as I walked up to where she was holding up a pretty blouse.

"Who are you?" she asked without looking at me. "You sound a lot like my friend Evie, but I think she fell off the face of the earth."

"Ha ha. I'm sorry. I've been busy."

"Not too busy for your man," she said.

"Actually, I saw him Monday and that's it. Well and Sunday, but that doesn't count."

"You are forgiven, with one stipulation," she said.

I groaned. "What would that be?"

"Have dinner with me," she answered.

I burst into laughter. "Yes. I'm free for the rest of the night."

"Good. Now, I need a skirt to go with this."

I began to browse the racks and not only found her a skirt but found myself a few things as well. I usually did the bulk of my shopping online. I never had time to spend a leisurely day shopping. It was nice.

We made our purchases and moved on to another store that specialized in accessories.

"What did you guys do Sunday?" she asked. "That's your decompress day."

"It is and I did decompress with Xander and his brother."

She spun around so fast, she looked like a figure skater. "You did what?" she shrieked. "Evie, you have really, really turned a corner. I know I've been telling you to loosen up, but damn, woman. You dirty."

I rolled my eyes. "Are you done?"

"His brother?"

"Yes, his brother and there was nothing dirty about it. You need to pull your mind out of the gutter. I worry about you sometimes."

She offered a cheesy grin. "Do not worry about me. I'm a very healthy, happy woman."

"I know you are."

"So, what's his brother like? Is he wealthy?"

"He's a Marine," I answered. "His brother is fun. He's very different from Xander, or at least the Xander I first met. Now that I know Xander a little better, I have seen the more playful side, but his brother is like that naturally."

"Is he hot?"

"He's attractive, but Xander is better looking in my opinion. Although I'm sure some women would think differently. Kade has that vibe about him, you know? Like he was probably voted most popular in school and his contact list is probably filled."

She scowled at me, one hand on her hip. "You are a really shitty friend. I might have to rethink our friendship."

My mouth dropped open. "What? Why would you say that?"

"You met a hot, eligible bachelor and you didn't bother to call me. It's like you are hogging all the hot guys for yourself. That's not cool."

"Uh, he's in the Marines. He was in town for two days. He doesn't

225

have time for you. And I don't know if he is single. It's not like I chase them down."

"You could have asked," she pouted. "You know I'm not one to turn down a handsome guy."

I rolled my eyes. "That's for sure. If he comes back to town, I will definitely ask if he would like to meet you."

"Don't ask. Do."

"I did think about you, if that makes you feel any better. I do think the two of you would hit it off. He's spunky. You're spunky. We would have so much fun together. Maybe Xander will take all of us out on his boat."

Her eyes sparkled with excitement. "That would be fun. I like that idea. When is he coming back?"

"I don't know. He didn't know."

She popped out her lower lip. "That sucks."

"It does suck, and I think Xander was bummed," I told her. "I liked hanging out with them. It was nice to see Xander and his brother banter back and forth. And Kade did not hold back. He gave me lots of insight into Xander's past. I feel like I know him so much better after a couple of hours hanging with him and his brother."

She paused what she was doing and looked at me. "You are really falling for this guy."

I grimaced, wrinkling my nose. "I am. Is that bad?"

"Why would it be a bad thing? He sounds like a great guy. I'm practically falling for him and I don't know him."

"Great guy doesn't negate all the other things."

"What other things? I'm so confused. Good is good."

"Let's see. My dad hates him."

"Your dad isn't sleeping with him," she retorted.

"Gross," I murmured.

"Next," she said, waving her hand.

"We agreed to be friends. We wanted to keep things casual. What I feel does not feel casual."

She shrugged. "And why is that a bad thing?"

"Because what if he doesn't feel the same way?"

She looked thoughtful. "Your face says you are falling for him."

I was confused. "What does that mean?"

"You have told me many times you can read people really well. You can be just as guarded with your heart as you tell me he is. You are open and warm and loving, but you keep things on a very surface level."

"That's not true," I protested.

"When is the last time you were in love?"

I thought about it. "I don't know."

"Exactly. You haven't. Trust yourself with this. Don't start attaching a bunch of rules and hangups."

I sighed. "I don't want to, but it's self-preservation. I don't want to get hurt."

"Nobody wants to get hurt," she said.

"Definitely not."

"What are you going to do about your dad? You can't let him get in the way of your happiness."

I slowly shook my head. "I have no idea. I tried to talk to him. He isn't budging."

"Maybe try to explain to him Xander is important to you. He should understand love. He loved your mother."

The memory of his grief still tugged at my heart. "Yes, he did."

"What if that's why he is so against you getting together with Xander?"

"What? That makes no sense."

"He loved and lost, and it cut him deep. There could be a chance he doesn't want you to experience that same kind of pain."

"Plausible, but not likely."

"Fine, then back to the original question. What are you going to do?"

"I don't know. He won't talk to me. I've been calling him all week, and once again, he's dodging my calls. He's being very childish about all of this. It's really pissing me off."

"He's probably been busy writing his speech," she said nonchalantly.

"Speech? For me? I don't need another speech from him. I'm good. He said plenty."

She burst into laughter, tossing a few bangles into the basket hanging from her arm. "Not for you. His acceptance speech."

"What are you talking about?"

"The achievement award he's getting from the school," she answered.

She might as well have slapped me. "I didn't know he was getting an award."

"I saw it in the newspaper, way in the back, but I saw the name and read the article."

I shook my head with frustration. "I can't believe he didn't tell me!"

"I'm sorry. I assumed you knew."

"I should have known. I'm his daughter and he didn't have the decency to tell me! Rude. So fucking rude and childish."

She looked around. "Shh. Come on. Let's buy this stuff and go get some dinner."

"I can't believe him!" I exclaimed again.

She practically dragged me to the checkout. We paid for our things and quickly left the store. I was still pissed. Instead of wasting time and driving somewhere, we opted to go to the Olive Garden in the same shopping center.

"You need a drink," she ordered. "How about something fruity?"

"I can't drink. If I drink, I'm only going to get madder."

"I'm sorry I told you," she said.

"Don't be. I blame him. I'm so pissed at him."

We were seated at a quiet table.

"Let's talk about something else," she said. "Like work. How is it going? Any more gigs you need me to cover?"

"No."

"Any juicy details on some celebrities that are going to be getting married soon? You always get the earliest scoop."

"No."

She stuck her fingers in her water glass and flicked them at me.

"Hey!" I protested.

"Snap out of it. I get a couple hours with you. I am not going to put up with a sourpuss. Let's talk about Xander again. And his hot brother."

"How can I talk about Xander when my father has essentially disowned me?"

"Because talking about Xander is a lot more fun."

"Do you really think my dad intends on leaving me out of his life forever?"

She shrugged. "I can't answer that. I think you need to make him tell you."

"This is ridiculous. He's not talking to me because he doesn't like the man I'm dating. It isn't like Xander is a serial killer. He's done nothing wrong except be successful! For twenty-five years, it has just been me and him. He might have taken care of me for the first ten years, but I have been taking care of him since. I have bent over backward to make sure he has food and clean clothes. This is how he thanks me?"

"I'm sorry," she said, keeping her voice low. "It's not cool."

"No, it isn't cool. He is acting like a child. He's acting like I committed some horrible sin against him. I didn't do shit!"

Her eyes darted around the dining room. "Relax. Let's eat and then you can figure out what to do next. You don't want to try and come up with a plan when you're angry. It is not going to end well."

I leaned my head back and looked up at the ceiling. I took in several deep breaths, calming my nerves. "You're right. I need to cool down. If I talk to him now, I'll only say something that will definitely lead to the ending of our relationship."

"This is what I've been saying," she said.

I ordered my usual ravioli. I ended up pushing it around on my plate. I had no appetite. I was angry and hurt. My father should not be the one making me feel so miserable. He was supposed to be looking out for me and he was ripping my heart out. I made it through dinner with Nelle taking pity on me and releasing me from my friend duties.

I got home and kicked off my shoes, ready to drink a bottle of wine and block out all the feelings that were bombarding me. I felt abandoned by my father. It was a little dramatic, but it was how I felt. I blamed my lack of experience with the situation. My dad and I had always been so close. We rarely fought. I was certain it was why it was hitting me so hard now.

I didn't know how to handle the feelings. I couldn't ignore the situation. I couldn't wait until I calmed down. I snatched my phone and pushed the button for his number. I waited, listening to it ring and ring. When his voicemail came on, I hung up and redialed.

"Call me back," I snapped when his voicemail picked up again.

I tossed my phone on the couch. He didn't get awards so often that this was not a big deal. It was a big deal. I should have been his first call. This was him punishing me. He was purposely trying to hurt me, and it was working.

CHAPTER 37

XANDER

Charlie thought I was crazy. I probably was. He told me to come up with a way to save his ships' rudders and I had.

Well, I hoped. Maybe I did. I wasn't sure. I was still working out the details. Right now, it was all an image in my head. I wasn't sure how or if it was even possible to make it work out in real life.

Then again, the ship designs were once nothing more than pipe dreams. I'd made that a reality. I was sure there was a way to make the rudders stronger and more effective.

Charlie didn't say it, but I knew what he was thinking. He was thinking what Marsh had thought. What my dad thought. I was crazy.

He thought I was getting ahead of myself. People had been building ships for hundreds of years, and here I was, young and dumb, thinking I could change what had always been done.

I got in the car, checked the time, and figured I would see if Evie was free. I doubted it, given it was a Friday night, but I was going to try anyway. There was an elderly woman selling pretty flowers on the street corner. I bought a bouquet and parked my car before heading inside the building where Evie worked.

I hoped I wasn't being too forward.

"Hello," I greeted the young woman wearing a headset and sitting behind a desk.

"Hi," she said, her posture changing as a bright smile spread over her face.

"I am looking for Evie Marsh. Is she in?"

"She is. Should I have her come here?"

"Can I go to her office?"

She grinned. "Absolutely. I'll show you the way."

"Thank you."

The woman knocked on a door before pushing it open. Evie was sitting at her desk that was very organized and tidy. Her eyes lit up. "Hi!" she said and jumped to her feet.

"Hi," I said before turning to look at the pretty receptionist. She smiled and quickly excused herself.

"What are you doing here?" she asked with surprise.

I handed her the flowers. "I thought I would surprise you."

"These are beautiful. Thank you."

"You are welcome. Do you have anything going on tonight?"

"Nope."

"Would you like to have dinner with me?"

She nodded. "I would."

"My turn to pick the place."

"That works for me. You know, it's very good timing you showed up today."

I raised an eyebrow. "And why is that?"

"Because my car is in the shop. I was going to have to take a taxi home."

I grinned and stepped closer. "Does that mean you need a ride?" We both knew what I was asking. A little sexual innuendo became part of our normal conversation.

"I do," she whispered.

"I will be your chariot."

"Let me get my purse."

I took a second to look around her office that was sparsely decorated and very neat. A couple of minutes later, she was ready to go.

Once in the car, I drove her to the grocery store. She made no move to get out of the car. She looked at me with confusion on her face. "Uh, what are we doing here?"

"Grocery shopping."

She slowly nodded. "Okay."

"Let's go."

I grabbed a cart and began pushing it up and down the aisles, picking the ingredients I needed to make her dinner.

"I think I'm confused," she said.

"I'm making you dinner," I told her.

"You're going to cook me dinner?"

"Yes. I want you all to myself tonight. I don't want to be in a public setting. I want to leer at you and be completely inappropriate with you while enjoying a nice meal. I can't do that at a fancy restaurant, at least not without embarrassing both of us."

She laughed softly. "You make a good point."

With our groceries bought, I drove us to my place. I was hoping the night went well and I could convince her to sleep over again.

"Sit," I ordered once we deposited the bags on the kitchen counter.

"I can help," she offered.

"Nope. I'm making you dinner. I'll pour you a glass of wine while you watch me cook."

"You are going to spoil me."

"I want to spoil you."

"I think I like the sound of that. Spoil away."

She sat on one of the barstools while I poured us two glasses of wine. "How was your week?"

"Short," she said with a smile. "Taking Monday off made for a nice short week."

"I agree."

"What about you? Last I talked to you, you were working on some big idea."

I liked that she was interested in my work. "I'm still working on it."

"Do you want to share?"

I spread some olive oil in a pan. "I don't know. I don't want to sound crazy. This idea is very reminiscent of what happened to me in college."

"How so?"

I turned to face her. I felt like I could trust her. She wasn't going to laugh me out of my own kitchen. "When I had a wild idea in college, another Marsh was very unreceptive."

She winced. "Oh. I'm sorry."

"Don't be. It isn't your fault. It's an old beef and I shouldn't hold it against you."

"Speaking of Daddy Dearest," she started, and I flinched. This was the part where she told me we couldn't see each other anymore.

"I can't wait to hear this," I said with a sigh.

"He's being honored by his school. I guess he's receiving some big achievement award."

I nodded and went back to cooking the chicken. "That's cool," I said without any emotion. I wasn't going to say he deserved it. I didn't think he did. I didn't think he was a good professor. If anything, he was squashing more dreams than he was helping come to life.

She laughed and I turned to look at her over my shoulder. "I'm sorry. You don't care about that. Tell me your idea."

"It isn't that I don't care," I said, trying to think of a way to soothe things.

"It's fine," she said. "He wasn't nice to you."

"It isn't that he wasn't nice. It was more about me being young and looking for a little reassuring. I don't blame your dad for laughing at me. I was laughed at a lot back then. He was one of many."

"He didn't tell me about the award," she said, and I could hear the hurt in her voice.

"You two still haven't made up?"

"No. He won't talk to me. I found out about the award through my friend who saw it in the paper. I called him and he let it go to voicemail."

I reached for her hand. "I am really sorry he's this upset with you about me. If you want us to stop seeing each other or being friends, I will totally understand. I don't expect you to ruin your relationship with your father for me."

"No," she adamantly said. "He is not going to get to ruin this, whatever this is."

"This is us having a good time," I said, not sure what else to say about the situation.

"Right. Exactly. It's nothing for him to get his panties in a bunch about."

"Are you going to go?" I asked her.

"No! Why would I? He didn't even tell me about it."

"Evie," I admonished. "You will regret not going. This thing that's happening between you two is only temporary."

"I'm not so sure about that anymore. We have never not talked to each other. This is serious."

I turned around once again to look her directly in the eye. "If I am getting in the way, please tell me."

She stared right back at me. "It isn't you. This is him."

"Okay." I went back to my cooking. "For what it's worth, I do respect your dad as a person. What he did raising you is pretty impressive."

"Thanks."

"I'm serious. He might be a dick to me, but you said he was great with you. I respect that. I respect a man that can raise a kid all on his own."

"Part of me wonders if he's embarrassed. His behavior was pretty atrocious. He doesn't know how to walk it back and is choosing to ignore the situation."

"That sounds very plausible," I agreed. "He's a proud man. He would never want to admit he was in the wrong, especially when it came to me."

"Very true."

"You should go," I told her again. "I think you will regret it if you don't. This thing between you guys isn't permanent. Once you guys have made up, you don't want to regret missing such a special moment in his life."

She was quiet. Too quiet. I looked over my shoulder to make sure she was still there. "Want to come along with me?"

I chuckled. "Yeah, I'm sure that would go over as well as a lead balloon."

"What exactly are you doing over there?" she asked.

"I'm cooking our dinner."

I heard her feet hit the floor. I glanced behind me to see what she was doing. She was coming toward me. Her wine glass was in her hand. "Are we here alone?" she asked.

"Of course, we are."

"Are you hungry?" she asked as she walked toward me.

I nodded. "I definitely am."

She trailed a finger over my bicep and then traced my collarbone. "I'm so hungry," she whispered.

"I'm cooking as fast as I can."

She slowly shook her head. "I don't think you are. I'm ravenous."

Her words were spoken with such heat and desire, I knew she wasn't talking about my fried chicken breasts. I reached for the knob on the stove and turned off the heat. "I'm rather ravenous myself."

She put her wine glass on the kitchen counter before her fingers went to the buttons on my shirt. I braced my shoulders, preparing for the usual tug that accompanied her undressing me. There was no rip. I looked down and watched as she slowly undid one button after another.

"Evie," I growled her name.

"Shh, I'm starving but I think I want to savor my meal."

I dropped my hands to my sides and let her have her way. The shirt was pushed open and then down my shoulders. The white tee I was wearing was slowly lifted up my torso. I lifted my arms, and when she reached as high as she could go, I took over and pulled it off, dropping the shirt onto the floor.

She licked her lips. "You are so right. This private dinner is so much better than a fancy restaurant."

I smirked. "I agree."

I reached for the buttons on her blouse and gave her the same slow, purposeful treatment until her blouse was in a heap with my own. She was wearing a pretty blue-satin bra. It cupped her breasts, lifting the milky globes high while squeezing them together. The cleavage was delectable.

"Pants," she said, her voice a harsh whisper.

I lifted my arms, ready for her to do the honors. She eagerly obliged. The pants were pushed down until they fell around my ankles. I kicked off my shoes and kicked the pants to the side. Her own slacks soon joined mine. A simple blue thong that was the same satin as the bra greeted me. The woman was beautiful. Every inch of her smooth skin begged to be touched and kissed.

The kitchen was all wrong. While I would have loved to lay her out on my kitchen counter and feast upon her, I was looking for something a little more traditional. I wanted her in my bed. I wanted to ride her and watch her hair fan out around her as I pushed myself inside her over and over.

"I'm thinking we could have our meal upstairs."

Her eyes twinkled. "I think I would like that. My knees are still recovering from the floor."

I grabbed her hand and led her upstairs to my bedroom. There was something to be said for being totally boring. A bed had its benefits. I was about to take advantage of each and every one of them.

CHAPTER 38

EVIE

He was standing next to the bed, looking down at me like I was on the menu. My skin felt flushed under his gaze. I could practically feel his hands on me. I closed my eyes as a wave of passion washed over me, making me squirm on his bed.

"You're ready for me, aren't you?" he asked in a gruff voice.

I moaned, my lips parting as I reached up to cup my breast through my bra. "I am. I need you."

His eyes focused on my hand. I gave him a show, squeezing and plumping my breast. I brought my other hand up to help.

"God damn, Evie. Do you know how sexy you are?"

"I want you inside me," I told him with raw honesty.

"Not yet. You look too good."

He dropped to his knees and pulled me to the edge of the bed. My legs hung over, my feet dangling over the floor. He reached for my panties and started to pull them down my body.

With my position, I couldn't quite lift my ass to make the removal of the damn things any easier. That didn't stop him from getting them off. He yanked until my pretty blue thong shredded under his force.

I didn't care. He was planting a trail of kisses up the inside of my thigh. I could think of nothing else except what he was doing to my body. When his mouth closed over my hot core, I felt like I had been struck by lightning. Heat flashed through my body. His tongue lapped over my folds, parting me until he was moving it inside me.

"Oh god," I moaned. It was too much. I wanted more, and I wanted him to stop. I was going to die a million deaths if he didn't stop. No, if he didn't keep going.

My body writhed, shaking and jerking with every swipe of his tongue over my clit. He licked and suckled before scraping his teeth over the sensitive nub. I was convinced I would pass out from the pleasure. I couldn't take anymore.

My body erupted into a glorious fountain of ecstasy. It seemed to last forever. His mouth kissed my belly, moving steadily upward until he released the front clasp of my bra. Then more kisses over each breast.

I felt like I was floating, hovering above the bed as he loved me with his mouth. He moved over me, holding his weight off me with his strong arms.

I reached up to cup his cheek. "That was incredible."

"You are incredible. I think I'm addicted."

An electric shock zapped me, causing me to shudder. "I don't know if my body can survive anything like that again."

"I certainly hope so because I'm going to need that on a regular basis. Don't even think to deny me."

I slowly moved my head back and forth. "Never."

"Now, there's another little something I need," he whispered as he reached down to guide himself to my entrance.

I jerked, still sensitive. "I need you."

"You have me. Every last fucking inch of me."

He slowly moved inside me, both of us savoring every inch of the invasion. I closed my eyes once again and let my body do nothing but feel. I cleared my mind, focusing on his touch and the feeling of him moving deep inside my body.

"Like that," I groaned. I reached up to run my hands over the corded muscles in his back. I slid them down his sides and gripped his ass, yanking him against me. "Just like that."

"Damn, you make me feel so good," he whispered. "I can't get enough of you. I think about you—this—all the time. I get hard when I hear your voice over the phone. My body reacts to you like nothing I have ever known. You are dangerous."

A slow smile spread across my lips. "I like to be dangerous. When I hear your voice, I get this little tingling sensation between my legs. Sometimes, I think about going into the bathroom and touching myself while I think about you."

He grunted and jerked, and his erection grew bigger inside me. I gasped, the stretching triggering a new series of delicious sensations.

"Do you?" he growled. "Do you touch yourself when you think about me?"

I kissed him, sliding my tongue inside his mouth as my nails dug into the flesh stretched across his muscular torso. "Yes. When I'm lying in bed and missing you, I do it. I picture you over me, just like this."

He released a loud roar, pounding inside me. "Do you get off?" he asked through gritted teeth. "Do you make yourself come while you're thinking about me?"

"Yes," I whispered, dragging the word out as he continued to rock back and forth. "Every time. Sometimes, I don't even need to touch myself. I can close my eyes and think about you and it just happens."

He was shaking. His body was wound so tightly, I worried he would fall apart. "I want you to do it for me. I want to watch you touch yourself."

I shuddered. The very idea was unthinkable. It was too naughty. Too far outside my comfort zone. "Later. Right now, I have the real thing and that's what I want."

I couldn't believe I had just promised to do that for him. I actually wanted to. I could feel how badly he wanted it and I wanted to give him that pleasure. He made me feel safe enough that I could do it without being embarrassed. I would do it for him.

"Fingers or a dildo?" he rasped.

"Fingers. What about you?"

"What. About. Me?" His breathing was coming hard and fast. I could feel him getting close to the edge.

"Do you rub yourself and think about me?"

He smirked. It was a cocky little smile that almost made me explode. "All the fucking time, baby."

I gasped. The confession sent shockwaves of heat and desire through my body. I understood what he felt. It was a huge ego boost. It was erotic and sensual and so damn good to know he thought about me and pleasured himself.

"Do you think about my mouth wrapped around you or do you think about you inside me?"

He grunted, moving harder and faster. "Both."

"In bed?"

"Everywhere. I beat off in the shower. I think about you and stroke myself until I'm squirting my desire all over the shower wall."

His words triggered a visceral response that I had zero control over. I bucked, exploding around him. I shouted out his name and a lot of other words that made no sense. He was yelling right back at me. I heard him cursing, ordering me to fuck him and a series of other things that were lost in the fog of ecstasy that consumed me.

He fell on top of me, his hard chest pressing against mine. I couldn't breathe. I didn't want to breathe. I wrapped my arms and legs around him, anchoring his body to mine. He moved off me, breaking my grip around him with ease. He lay on his side next to me, facing me with a sexy smile on his lips.

"You are nothing like I expected you to be when I first met you," he said.

"You were expecting what?"

"I don't know. A good girl. A cold fish. A woman who preferred missionary style and never broke the rules."

I grinned, reaching up to cup his cheek. "And now?"

"And now I know you are a bad girl that breaks all the rules."

"Not all of them, but I have a feeling if I'm with you much longer, I just might break a lot more."

"Good. I want you to break them all. You never have to hold back with me. I will never judge you for being who you are. I know you are a little vixen. A horny little vixen."

I couldn't stop the silly giggle from erupting from my throat. "I am not horny."

He cocked an eyebrow. "Wanna bet? Woman, you try to climb me every chance you get."

"Okay, I'm horny for you."

"Good girl," he said and kissed my forehead. "Are you hungry? I've got that chicken halfway cooked down there."

I thought about it for a second. "I am, but I think I have something else I'd prefer to munch on."

He jerked, his cock springing to life against my thigh. "Dammit, woman. You have to let a man recover."

"You feel recovered to me," I teased.

"Stay the night and we'll see how fast I can recover."

"I have an event tomorrow," I told him. "I should probably go home and get some sleep."

"*Should* is a word one uses when they really don't want to do something," he replied.

"You are right but *should* is the word a responsible person uses when they are trying to convince themselves about what needs to be done."

"Stay," he whispered before kissing me. When he pulled away, he was looking at me with such tenderness I nearly melted. "I will make your toes curl and you will be screaming my name over and over."

"I have no doubt in my mind that you will, but I have to walk tomorrow. You are going to leave me worn out."

He winked, his silly grin making my heart skip a beat. "That sounds like a challenge."

I groaned. "No, not a challenge."

"Let's go downstairs and grab a snack. Then, I'm dragging you right back up here. I think you made me a promise, one I intend to make you fulfill."

The words I had whispered in the heat of the moment flashed through my mind. Now, I was embarrassed. "Xander."

He put a fingertip to my lips. "Uh uh, no takebacks."

I pulled away from him, stood up beside the bed, and looked down at his naked form. The man was hot as hell. I couldn't believe I was lucky enough to crawl into a bed with him. Better than that, he wanted me. He craved me. That would make any woman feel like they were queen of the world.

"How about I go find us something to eat and you lie there and recover?" I asked with a smile.

He grinned and reached down to grab his dick in his hand. "I don't need long. I'm already thinking about yanking you back down here."

"I'll be right back."

"I'll be right here watching the clock. Every second you are gone will feel like an eternity."

I rolled my eyes and reached for one of the pillows. I playfully tossed it at him. "That is so cheesy."

"But it's true. Hurry. I would hate to have to take the edge off myself."

I looked down, watched him stroke himself, and decided food could wait.

CHAPTER 39

XANDER

I dropped Evie off at her apartment and immediately headed over to Charlie's place. He was probably still in bed, but I was going to wake him up. I had an idea and I wanted him to be the first to see it.

After talking with Evie a little, I knew I was on to something. She didn't understand the mechanics and all the little intricacies of a ship's propulsion system, but Charlie would. He would be able to offer advice and help me make this thing real. My week had been relatively productive, and I couldn't wait to show him what I had.

I pounded on his apartment door. "Charlie, get up."

There was no answer. I knew he was inside. At least, I assumed he was inside. His car was in the usual spot. I supposed he could have gotten a ride. I slapped my hand against the door again.

One of his neighbors pulled open their door and glared at me. I smiled in return. "Charlie, I'm not leaving. Open the door."

I heard the lock on the door finally turning. When Charlie pulled open the door, he looked like hell. I winced, taking in the bloodshot eyes, the hair that was sticking up in the back, and the rumpled shirt that I had a feeling he had worn the night before. The odor emanating from him was damn near toxic.

"Holy shit. Death warmed over would be a step up for you."

"Fuck you. Why are you pounding on my door like you are the damn police?"

I gave a small shrug. "Because I wanted to talk to you."

"Phones, asshole. That is why we have phones. You call a person. They don't answer. That doesn't mean you drive to their house and pound on the door."

"So you did hear your phone?" I asked.

"Yes, and I hit the fuck-off button! That means leave me alone. It means the person you are trying to reach doesn't want to talk to you."

He did not look well. In fact, he was looking a little green around the gills. "You are grumpy. That's really no way to treat your best friend."

He growled, glaring at me through eyes that were barely open. "Xander, please go away. Go away and I will call you later."

"I don't want to wait until later, which is why I am here now. If you would have just answered your phone, I could have given you another hour. You didn't and now I'm here. Get up."

He whimpered, sounding very childlike. "What. Do. You. Want?"

I grinned. "How about I go get some coffees and something greasy and eggy while you shower? You stink. Bad."

He glared at me. "Did you come over here to insult me at," he paused to look at his watch, "nine in the fucking morning? On a Saturday?"

"I didn't come over here with the intention of insulting you, but you made it very easy. Have you seen you?"

He groaned, leaning his head against the partially open door. "Xander, I love you, and usually, your neurotic behavior is cute, but not today. Today I want to sleep. I want to do nothing but sleep and not think."

"Are you hungover?" I questioned, even though I already knew the answer. I needed him to admit his problem. I was sure that was the first step to curing the hangover.

He gave me a dry look. "No, not at all. I usually look like this first thing in the morning."

I shook my head, clicking my tongue at him just like a mother hen. "Aren't you getting a little old for this nonsense?"

"Again, why are you here? Can you just text me the lecture?"

I held up a hand. I knew what it was like to be hungover. Not recently, but I remembered the college years. Even then, I didn't remember ever being quite as bad as he looked. I liked a good buzz, not a good drunk. It was probably part of that need to be in control all the time. I didn't like my brain to be muddled and foggy. "I'm going to get the coffee and food. Take a minute for yourself. I'll be back in fifteen."

"Don't come back," he whimpered. "Please, drive across town and get the stuff."

"I'm coming back. Trust me. I have something to show you and you want to see it."

I walked away and went to retrieve the usual hangover cures. Greasy breakfasts were the ultimate cure. I was knocking on his door once again twenty minutes later. He opened the door with a towel slung low around his hips, his hair wet but still sticking up.

"This had better be fucking good," he snapped, snatching one of the coffees from the tray I carried.

I pushed the door open and put the food on his small table before pulling out one of the Egg McMuffins. "It is good. I think it's good. It's going to need some tweaking, but I got the general idea."

"Please, for the love of all that is holy, speak English. I can't under-stand geek right now. My brain feels like a wet sponge and my mouth a dry cotton ball."

"Sit, eat, and I'll explain."

He flopped down in the chair and grabbed one of the sandwiches. "My skull hurts."

"Did you at least have a good time?"

He grinned and nodded. "Of course."

"Is your good time still here?"

"Nah, I went to her place."

"Good plan."

He sucked down the coffee. "What's the thing you need to show me?"

I smiled and wiped my mouth. "Remember your problem?"

"Problem?"

"The rudders and the ships in the harbor."

He nodded. "Yes. Two separate problems."

"No, the same problem. Rather, both problems solved with one solution."

He rubbed his head. "God, you are exhausting."

"Eat and I will show you."

"Show me where?"

"Down at the docks," I answered.

He did not look impressed. "I don't want to work. I want to relax."

"You don't have to work. I want you to watch. I want you to observe and give me feedback. I trust you to tell me where it's wrong. I need a second pair of eyes and only your eyes will understand what you are seeing."

"Can you tell me what you've got up your sleeve?"

I winked. "I have to show you."

"Where's your girlfriend? Can't you show her?"

"I just dropped her off. She is working today, and she wouldn't understand like you."

He grinned. "You had another sleepover."

"I did."

"Damn, one more and I think that means you are official," he said. "I knew you liked her."

I wasn't afraid to admit it. "I do like her."

"Are you going to tell her?"

"Tell her what?"

"That you like her," he answered.

The conversation was very strange. It felt like we were in the sixth grade, talking about a girl. "I think she figured that part out all on her own."

He crumbled up a sandwich wrapper and tossed it at me. "Not like that, asshole. You guys were supposed to be doing this casual thing. Whatever you have going with her is not casual. Have you had the talk? You know, the talk about where is this going, and blah, blah, blah."

I slowly shook my head. "No. Not yet. I don't think we need to ruin things by trying to put a label on it. It's cool just the way it is."

"Maybe for you, but she's a woman."

"No shit. Well that explains a lot."

He shot me a dirty look. "You know what I mean. Women think differently. She's probably already picking out China patterns and redecorating your house. You better figure out what you want before you wake up one morning with two kids and a wife."

I rolled my eyes. "I don't think that's quite how that happens. We aren't there yet. We aren't even close to being there. It was a sleepover. I'm not going to be proposing anytime soon."

"That's what they all say, and then one day, they are wearing a tux and being dragged down an aisle to be shackled forever."

"You have a very twisted view on marriage. You should get therapy."

"I don't need therapy," he said, finishing his second sandwich. He was already looking a little better. The greenish hue had faded and now he just looked pale and washed out.

He got up from the table and returned five minutes later dressed and ready to go. I drove him to the docks and popped open the trunk to pull out my prototype. His dark sunglasses shielded his eyes, but I knew he was glaring at me. "You dragged my ass out here to play with one of your toy boats?"

"No, I want to see if my theory will work."

"What are you planning?" he asked, sounding a little more enthusiastic.

I put the boat in the water and used the remote to steer it while I explained my idea to improve speed that would allow better control. We messed around with the boat for a couple of hours. Each of us took turns controlling it.

"What do you think?"

He smiled and handed me the remote. "You are a genius. Do you think it will really work on a large ship?"

"I don't know. In theory, it should. But there are a lot of details to work out. It isn't just the rudder. It's the propeller and the thrust—"

He held up a hand. "I get it. I trust you to work it all out, though."

"I am going to keep working on it. I've been running it through my program, and every time I put it on a large ship, it fails. It's frustrating."

"You've been down this road before. You know there is going to be a lot of trial and error. You know you are going to have a lot of failure in your future. But just like before, you know it's going to work out. You know you are going to make it work."

I grinned. "And hopefully, you will be out of a job."

"Never going to happen. I'm going to be the guy making this new invention you're creating."

I clapped him on the shoulder. "I hope so."

"If there is a chance you put me out of work, I wouldn't be sad. I'm ready to retire."

"Retire?" I parroted. "You're thirty. You don't get to retire at thirty."

He shrugged. "My job pays well. Really well. I could retire. I've invested. I'm good."

"You are not going to retire."

"When do you think you'll have this ready?"

"I just told you I don't have any idea if this will work."

"Yes, you do," he insisted. "This is like before. Five years from now, you are going to be mega rich and getting another award."

I groaned. "I don't want another award."

"Yes, you do. It's why you do this."

"Not even close," I muttered.

We headed back to my car. I put the boat in the trunk and drove him back to his place. "Thanks for the free preview. I'm looking forward to seeing the final plans."

"I'll let you know."

I drove back home and locked myself in my study. I had a lot of work to do. After trying it in the water, I had a better idea of what needed to change. Charlie wasn't lying when he said I had a lot of trial and error ahead of me.

I wanted it to work. It would be nice to be able to tell my dad what I was working on. He wouldn't care. He would think I was full of shit once again. Just like Evie's dad.

He would laugh me right out of the room if I told him my new plan. It was more far-fetched than the first. Knowing they would not trust me made me want to work harder.

I was going to make it work.

CHAPTER 40

EVIE

I finished my usual morning walk. I went alone. I thought about inviting Xander along, but I needed some time to think. This thing with my dad was really screwing with me.

I didn't like us being on the outs. It made me feel icky. I couldn't shake the heaviness of it and it was affecting my work. I had to settle things. I knew there was a chance we would never have the relationship we once did. I didn't like the idea, but I couldn't change his way of thinking.

Just like he couldn't change mine. I felt we were both intelligent, responsible people and we were always going to have our own opinions. I could respect his and I needed him to respect mine. At least, that was what I was going to say to him. I had been practicing what I would say all morning.

I parked my car in the driveway and fought down the nerves that erupted in my belly at the thought of confronting him. I was nervous and apprehensive. I didn't stand up to him. The day in his office had been a first. While it had felt good initially, it was like a wound that was slowly festering and making me septic. It was time to clear the air and heal the wound.

Instead of walking in like I usually did, I knocked on the front door. That felt very weird. When he opened the door, he scowled at me. "Why are you knocking?"

I shrugged. "Because I wasn't sure I would be welcomed. This is your house and I didn't want to barge in."

He stepped back, opening the door wider. "Don't be dramatic. It doesn't suit you."

"Ditto," I said as I walked past him.

I sat down on the couch, waiting for him to take a seat in his recliner. It was clear he wasn't thrilled to see me. I expected as much, but I was going to make him listen to me.

"What brings you by?" he asked.

"Oh, I don't know, to congratulate you on the achievement award you'll be getting," I snapped.

He flinched. "Do you care?"

"Yes, I care!"

He shrugged a shoulder. "Your behavior says otherwise."

"I have been along on this ride with you my entire life. This award is special. I feel like I've been a part of your career. This is not something I would want to miss seeing you get. It's a big deal. You've talked about getting something like this for as long as I can remember. Why would you try and hide that from me?"

"Because I didn't think you would care. You have your life now. You made a choice and I have accepted your choice."

My mouth dropped open. "You are seriously disowning me because I won't date who you deem appropriate?"

"It's more than that and you know it," he snapped.

"Dad, grow up."

"I'll remind you I've been a grownup longer than you've been alive."

"Then you should act like it!" I shouted.

He held up one finger. It was the universal signal for *calm the fuck down.* "Rein it in, young lady."

"How can I?" I wailed. "What is wrong with you? Why wouldn't you tell me about the award?"

"You've been mad at me. Why would you care?"

I closed my eyes, silently counting to three for patience. "Because I'm your daughter. You are the one who has been mad at me. You are acting childish."

"I'm tired of arguing with you, Evie."

"You haven't argued. You have stated your opinion and I'm supposed to just fall in line. That isn't fair. You are completely invalidating anything I say or feel. Can't you respect the fact I'm a grownup now? Can't you let me make my own choices, whether they are right or wrong in your opinion?"

"I'm your father. My job is to protect you. I'm supposed to look out for you and steer you onto the right path."

I scoffed, shaking my head. "For how long, Dad? For the rest of your life? And when you die, then what? Do you plan on outliving me? What am I going to do if I have never been able to make a single decision in my life when you are no longer around?"

He looked as if I'd slapped him. "I trust you will know better by then."

"How do you know for sure? Is there a test I'm supposed to take? Tell me what I have to do to make you understand I'm not a little girl. This may come as a surprise to you, but I have been making decisions for a long time. I make careful decisions. For you to try and forbid me from doing something I want to do, it's asinine. You need to check yourself."

"Excuse me? Check myself? When you talk like that, I think you do still need my guidance."

I growled and threw my hands in the air. "Why can't you just let this go? Why can't you just let me live my life the way I want?"

"Because you are my little girl and I don't want to see you hurt!"

I saw the softness in his eyes, heard the genuine fear in his voice. I knew he loved me. He cared about me more than anything else in the world.

"Dad," I said, softening my tone. "I'll be okay. If I get hurt, I'll get better. This is part of life. I need to experience all life has to offer, even the bad stuff."

He shook his head. "You don't have to experience the bad when I can see it coming. Let me help you."

"Can we stop this?" I asked, my voice so soft I barely heard it. "I don't want to do this with you. I don't want to fight with you."

He took a deep breath and leaned back in his chair. "I don't want to fight with you either."

"Good. Let's agree to disagree and move on."

"Evie, it isn't that simple. I know this kid. He is bad news."

"I don't understand how you can say that. You don't know him. You knew him for five minutes in your classroom ten years ago. He is not the same person he was. I'm not the same person I was ten years ago."

He shook his head. "A leopard doesn't just lose his spots."

"What does that even mean?"

"It means the man is incapable of thinking of anyone except himself. He will hurt you. He's only using you. You are a pretty young woman and that's all he sees. I can't stand the thought of that punk touching my little girl."

"I get that this might be hard for you to hear, but there have been other men in my life. You have never reacted so strongly to any of them."

"Because they weren't him," he spat.

"No, they weren't. Xander isn't selfish. Not by a long shot."

"That kid thinks it is funny to disrupt things," he said.

"Things? Like what?"

"My classroom for one. He went out of his way to argue with me in front of the entire class. He tried to make a fool out of me. He thought he was so much smarter than me and everyone else. He was some young punk with no life experience and he was convinced he knew better. He refused to listen to history and reason. He was only about himself and proving his point."

"He was right," I said. "Do you know what he has done? How much he is worth because he listened to his gut and did what he knew was possible, despite you and everyone else telling him it was impossible?"

He shrugged as if it didn't matter. "It doesn't change who he is."

"Maybe in your eyes, but I see a man that is a modern-day Jefferson or any other inventor from the past. People laughed at him and told him it wasn't possible. A lesser man would have given up. A lesser man would have taken the harsh criticism to heart and let his dreams die. Xander didn't give up. He pushed through and I'm so proud of him."

"You talk like he is some kind of hero," he spat the words like they tasted bitter on his tongue.

I couldn't stop myself from smiling. "Maybe he is my hero."

He groaned. "He put you under a spell."

"I'm falling for him," I told him, looking directly into his eyes. "Not falling. I already fell."

His face fell. "I cannot condone a relationship with that man."

"That's your choice. Just like it's my choice to choose a relationship with him. I can't change your mind and I will stop trying to do that but I'm asking you to respect my decision. Stop trying to change how I feel about him. I know a different man than you did. I wish you would give him the chance to show you he isn't that guy."

"I have to trust my gut," he said. "I know in my heart he is not the one for you. He's going to hurt you and then I will hate him more than I already do."

"I'm sorry you feel that way," I told him. "Maybe he will hurt me. Things might not work out between us. I have to find out for myself. I will always wonder what if. This is something I want to do."

"Like you said, you are an adult. I can't stop you from making a mistake you will regret."

He wasn't going to budge. I should have known he wouldn't. My father was set in his ways. He seemed to dislike people in general. Again, he was so much like Xander it was crazy.

I had tried. That was all I could do. It felt a little lonely to be moving forward without my father's support, but there was nothing to do about it. I wasn't going to give up on what I felt was a good thing because he couldn't get over something so trivial.

"I'm going to be at your award ceremony," I told him as I got to my feet. "You can't stop me from being happy for you."

He offered a small smile. "I'll be looking for you."

"Goodbye, Dad. Please take care of yourself. No matter what you think about my decisions, I do love you."

He didn't get up from his chair. "I'll be just fine."

"Bye, Dad," I said, my heart feeling heavy in my chest.

"Be careful," he warned. "You are playing with fire. I don't want to see you burned."

I left the house without saying anything more. There was no point. He was never going to budge.

I might get burned. I knew that was a strong possibility. The problem was, I didn't care. I was a little infatuated with him. Oh hell, who was I kidding? I was a *lot* infatuated with him.

Every time we got together, I learned a little something more about him. I was seeing who he really was. I was getting to know the Xander no one else got to see. I felt incredibly privileged to be one of the few.

I knew Xander was still guarded. That was okay. I wasn't pushing him. I was okay with taking things slowly. I was convinced he felt something for me as well. I felt it in the way he touched me and the way he looked at me. I felt it in the little things he did, like bringing me flowers out of the blue.

My father couldn't see that side of him, and that made me sad.

CHAPTER 41

XANDER

I checked the time and cursed. I didn't know how to get myself to be where I was supposed to be at the right time. I was blaming the project this time. Once again, I had gotten caught up and lost all track of time. I whipped into the parking lot of the casual restaurant where I was meeting Evie for lunch.

I walked inside and scanned the restaurant. Her black hair immediately caught my eye. She was looking down at her phone, probably wondering where in the hell I was. I made my way to the table. She looked up and smiled.

"I'm sorry," I blurted out. "I tried to get here."

"You're right on time," she said, getting up and giving me a quick kiss before taking her seat again. "Your time, that is."

I laughed and sat down. "I have tried every trick in the book. I set my watch ahead. I have my phone give me ten-minute warnings. Nothing works."

"It's really okay. I plan for you to be a little late and get some work done while I wait."

I wrinkled my nose. "I really am sorry."

"Don't be."

"God, I feel like I haven't seen you in forever," I told her.

"It has been a while."

"How was your trip?" I asked.

She rolled her eyes. "Stupid. The bride makes bridezillas look like creampuffs."

"It has to mean something if she sought out your firm to do her wedding, right?" I asked.

She laughed. "Only because she has burned through everyone else in LA. My boss didn't give her an answer. She is mulling over whether she wants the hassle."

"Would you be on the account?" I questioned. We had been keeping up with each other via text and phone calls. She was a busy woman. Her services were in high demand, which made me feel an odd sense of pride that I couldn't quite explain.

She put her phone away. "I'm not sure. I don't think I want to be. I don't want to make weekly trips to LA and have to stay over."

"Couldn't you just make it a day trip?"

"Not with this woman. We got there on Friday and I'm sure we spent forty-eight of the sixty hours we were there listening to her demands."

"Good," I said with a grin. "I don't like the idea of you being away all the time. I'm a little selfish."

Her pretty smile hit me low in my gut. It had been too long since I had seen her.

"That's sweet," she said. "What about you? You keep talking about this big project you are working on. I'm a little worried you're turning into one of those mad scientists."

"I can get obsessive. I don't think I'm getting there just yet."

"You said it was something big?"

I quickly explained to her about the rudder and my plans to change up my current designs. "I am hoping, once I have all the details ironed out, it is going to be another big gamechanger."

"I have no doubt in my mind that it will."

I nodded. The excitement of being on the verge of a breakthrough was like drinking straight shots of espresso. "If it does, it will change the entire shipping industry. Not just for the United States. If my plan works, there will be fewer repairs. Ships will stay out on the water, transporting product and making everyone a little happier. Shorter shipping times and lower shipping costs are exactly what we need."

She was nodding her head and smiling. "I agree. I can't believe I'm sitting with the guy that is changing the world. You seem so normal."

"I am normal," I retorted.

"Not even close to normal. I'm normal. You are extraordinary."

"Be careful. You're going to give me a big head."

She leaned forward, eyes sparkling. "I don't need to do anything to make that happen. Your head is plenty big."

I closed my eyes and willed the erection that was threatening to split my zipper to settle down. "You are killing me."

She grinned. "I would never want to do that."

"Do you have to go back to the office?" I asked, hoping she would say no and we could squeeze in a little afternoon delight.

She sighed. "I do."

"Dammit."

"I'm sorry. Really, I am so damn sorry. What did your brother say when you told him about your new project?"

"I didn't tell him. I haven't talked to him except for once since he left here."

She frowned. "Why not?"

I shrugged. "I don't know. It's just how we are."

"I thought you wanted to change that?"

"I do."

"Then you have to do things differently than you have in the past. If you want to make a change, you have to change your ways."

"You are right. I'll text him. I'm not sure if he is still in the States or not."

"Good plan," she said with a satisfied smile. "I know he will be very proud of you. Just as proud as I am."

"Too bad our fathers didn't feel the same," I muttered.

"It is too bad, but it is their loss. They are missing out on the chance to know someone really special. You will be in the history books and they will be part of the group that tried to hold you back. I'm going to be in the group that cheered you on."

"I like having you in my cheer section."

"What about your friend, Charlie?"

"What about him?"

"Is he cheering you on?"

I laughed. "He is now. He wasn't quite so cheerful when I called him around three this morning."

Her eyes widened. "Oh no! Did you really?"

"I had a new idea and I wanted to run it by him," I explained, not really seeing anything wrong with the call. Charlie certainly had.

"Was he pissed?"

"He threatened to remove certain body parts."

She burst into laughter. "I might have to ask him to find other ways to get back at you. I like all of your body parts right where they are, as they are."

I grinned. "Me too."

"Is he helping you?"

"Yes, for the most part. The guy is a genius when it comes to the mechanical side of things. He could put together a boat with his eyes closed. He knows what will work and what won't. He's my sounding board. My ideas can be a little wild at times."

"I'm glad you have a friend like that."

"He's demanding a percentage of the profits," I told her.

"Are you going to concede to his demands?"

"Of course. I really couldn't have done it without him. I'm not going to tell him that. Not yet. I still have a long ways to go before I can get this on an actual ship and in the water."

"How long did it take you to get your first design sold?" she asked.

I blew out a breath. "Years. Probably about five years. Even after I got the design sold, it took another two years before it hit the water. None of this is fast. People think the government has red tape. They should see what it takes to build a ship."

"I can only imagine," she said. The waitress came by to take our orders.

"How are you and your dad?" I asked, broaching the subject that was still very sensitive.

She shrugged. "We aren't exactly talking."

"I am so fucking sorry," I said. "I hate that I am the cause of strife between the two of you."

"Don't be sorry. This is on him. I know it will take some time, but I think he will come around eventually. It's all a little raw for him right now, but he will have to learn to deal with it."

"Has he shown any signs of dealing with it?"

She grimaced. "No."

"I cannot begin to tell you how guilty I feel. I hate the way things have turned out."

"It's okay," she assured me. "I am okay with it. At first, yes, I was hurt and angry. I think I've reached the point of acceptance. I can't change him and I'm not going to try. I accept he can't accept my decisions. Does that make any sense?"

I smiled and sipped my soda. "It does, coming from you. What about the awards banquet? Have you decided if you are going to go?"

"I am going. He can't stop me. I'm not going to miss it."

"Good for you. Stand strong."

She blew out a breath. "It isn't easy. I think it's a very good thing I've been so busy. I don't have a lot of time to think about it. I just keep moving forward."

"That's all you can do."

"Do you want to go with me to the banquet?" she asked. "I know I've asked you before but I'm throwing it out there again."

I slowly shook my head. "This is a big night for him. I don't want to ruin it. He doesn't like me, and I get it. I have enough respect for him to let him have his night without any drama."

"You're right. I've thought that as well. I want to be there, but if he is truly that mad at me, I don't want to make it difficult for him. He should celebrate without worrying about me."

"He will want you there," I insisted. "Whatever he's going through right now is not going to be permanent. When he does calm down and you two do put your relationship back together, you'll both be glad you went."

"You're right. I just hope that realization comes sooner rather than later. I really hate not talking to him. I worry about him. I just know he is probably eating nothing but junk food."

She was a good daughter. It was too bad her dad couldn't see that. "I'm sure he's fine. It's going to take a lot more than a month or two of shitty eating to take him out."

"You're probably right. Eventually, he is going to have to cave in. He is going to have to realize I'm not changing my mind."

"About me?" I asked.

"Yes, about you. It isn't just you. It's me making decisions for myself without him butting in."

"Good for you," I told her. "You make a lot of decisions every single day for other people and you seem to have some pretty satisfied customers."

"Thank you," she said. "I appreciate your confidence."

"How could I not be confident? You are choosing me. That's a damn good bet."

She rolled her eyes. "Oh lord. Now you are proving my father right."

"How?" I asked innocently.

"By being arrogant."

"Only because I know this is right."

She slowly shook her head. "You are dangerous."

"Want to make a run for the bathrooms? As hard as I am right now, it will take less than three minutes. I don't want to brag, but in this moment, I am more than happy to be a minute man."

She burst into nervous laughter, her cheeks staining red. "You are so bad. Here I was thinking my dad might one day see you as the fine, upstanding gentleman I know you can be instead of the miscreant he thinks you are."

I shrugged a shoulder. "Even fine upstanding gentlemen have needs. I need you."

"When I get back to work, we are going to have a talk."

I frowned with confusion. "Why when you get back to work?"

"Because I need to check my schedule and find somewhere to squeeze in a little time with you."

"And then I can squeeze my way into you," I replied without missing a beat.

She bit her lower lip. "You are a tease."

"I'm not teasing. You name the time and place and I will be there."

"I will and you better damn well be there."

I winked. "I wouldn't miss a chance to be with you."

CHAPTER 42

EVIE

Nelle was scowling at something behind me. I turned around to see what had her encouraging premature wrinkling. "Will you stop?" I scolded.

"I can't help it," she muttered.

"Yes, you can. This is why I didn't want to come here. You are going to be picking apart that poor bartender all night. Give him a break."

"He sucks," she said. "No wonder he doesn't make any tips. I wouldn't tip him a penny."

I sighed, sipping on the drink that really wasn't all that good, but I was not about to tell her that. "If it wasn't for him, you would never have a day off. He is a necessary evil."

"Evil maybe, but I'm not sure how necessary it is."

"Pay attention to me," I demanded.

She finally looked at me. "You are a needy date."

I laughed. "You have no idea just how needy I am."

"Gross."

I shrugged. "It's true."

"I guess that means you guys still haven't managed to find some alone time this week?"

I groaned. "No. He had to go out of town to talk to someone about something that had something to do with a boat. He told me but I honestly have no idea what he was talking about. He gets really excited about his project and he speaks a totally different language."

"I'm sorry," she said, her eyes drifting over my shoulder again.

"No, you are not."

"Did you guys figure out what to do about your daddy?"

I rolled my eyes. "There is nothing to do about *Daddy*," I answered. "He doesn't want to be rational and I can't make him get it. He'll either come around or he won't."

"That is really too bad." She wasn't looking at me.

"Oh my god," I said. "Go. I can see you are dying to go say something to him. Just do it and bring your ass back here. With a fresh drink for me. I don't want another one from him."

"Ha! See? I told you! He's terrible."

"He is, but that's not our problem right now. Right now, me and you are catching up on girl talk. One night of bad drinks is not going to hurt anyone."

She scoffed. "I just want it made very clear I'm not the shitty bartender."

"No one would ever think that," I told her.

She disappeared behind the bar. It was always like this when we came in on her days off. She called me Type A, but she was just as bad. She was very particular about what she did and didn't like in her bar. It was very much her way or the highway.

She returned ten minutes later with fresh drinks for both of us. "There," she said with a sigh. "I feel much better."

"Good, now focus on me."

"Oh, you poor, deprived girl."

I grinned. "I like all the attention."

"Fine, let's get back to the daddy and boyfriend situation."

I wrinkled my nose. "That is not a pleasant conversation."

"Your dad is giving new meaning to the term overprotective father," she commented.

"It is so dumb. The more I think about it, the more I realize how alike they are. I think if my dad could pull his head out of his ass for five minutes, he would see how awesome Xander is. The way his mind works is incredible. I love to hear him talk about his project, even if I don't understand a word he is saying."

"You got it bad," she said as she shook her head.

"I do," I confessed. "I so do."

"I think you are doing the right thing, for what it's worth. Giving it time to cool down is the smart thing to do. I think if you keep trying to shove it in your father's face, he's only going to push back harder. Let him get used to the idea a little at a time. He'll soon see it's not as bad as he thought."

"I hope so. Xander is amazing."

"Of course, you are going to say that."

"He really is," I told her. "I feel like I must be wearing different glasses than the rest of the world."

"Why?"

"Because I don't see what my dad sees, or even his dad. Every time he tells me about his father, I'm just dumbfounded. Then I think about my dad, and I'm like, I get it. They hate him because he's rich and successful. They must have shared from the same bitter pills bottle."

"You do have on some rose-colored glasses, but that's because you are in love."

I flinched. "Don't say that."

"But it's true."

"I don't know if it is."

"I think it is," she said as if she was an authority on the subject.

"Maybe. I do miss him like crazy."

"Is he going to be back tomorrow?"

"I hope so," I answered. "I'm not sure. He was talking about giving a proposal on Monday, but he wasn't sure it was going to happen."

"For his new thing?"

"Yep."

"Your rich boyfriend is going to be even richer."

I smiled. "It's not about the money, but I do love that he is so successful. I just wish his family was around to share in it all."

"He has you," she reminded me. "But speaking of family, any more from the brother? I'm looking forward to my date with him."

I laughed. "I don't think the Marines grant leave for a first date. You are just going to have to be patient. That is assuming he wants to date you. You can be obnoxious."

She cocked her head to the side before waving a hand over her body. "Seriously, he would be lucky to get a date with me."

"You are right. He would be. Maybe he can come back for the holidays."

"I don't know. That's a lot of pressure."

"Eating a meal is a lot of pressure?"

"For a first date, yes. I don't want him to meet me and see me stuffing my face."

"Oh, that's a good point," I said.

"But I do want to meet him. You've got me excited to meet the little brother of your perfect man."

"He's a good guy. I like him and I know you will."

We sipped our drinks, our eyes drifting around the bar as it began to fill up. It was still early, but I considered myself an old lady. I couldn't stay out until the wee hours of the morning. I had to work tomorrow. I did not want to show up with a hangover. After learning a hangover was just really not worth it and completely preventable, I had made a conscious decision to avoid them like the plague.

"Do you think Xander is the guy that will father your future children?"

I nearly choked on my drink. "What? What are you talking about? Why would you ask me that?"

She shrugged. "I don't know. I was just thinking about our future."

"Our future, like me and you?"

"Yes. Me and you. You are pretty wrapped up in this guy and I don't blame you for a minute. I am a little jealous but I'm happy for you. You deserve a good man."

"I don't know what our future holds," I told her. "I would not even dare to speculate or fantasize about it."

"Why not?" she asked.

"Because it's been a month. We aren't that serious. I am not going to start thinking about marriage and all that stuff."

She looked thoughtful. "But do you think you might get to that point?"

"I honestly don't know."

"I'll say it. You love him."

"I don't really know what love is," I told her. "I have never been in love with a man. I have liked a few and been fond of others, but how do you know what love is? There isn't a definition or a test you take that tells you whether you are or not. This is a new thing and I think I might just kind of be in the mindset that it's an infatuation."

"I'm sure there is an element of infatuation to it, but I don't think it's just that. You are different."

I chewed on my bottom lip. "It feels different than anything I have ever experienced before. I do feel a little bit infatuated, but I also feel like it's more whole. Like it isn't just sex and it isn't just the fun we have when we are together. It's the total package. I can't explain it."

She offered a smile. "That's probably why people who are in love don't describe it. They just smile a lot and feel joy."

"I do feel a lot of joy. When I see his name on my phone or think about getting to see him, I get little butterflies in my stomach. This last two weeks has been the real test. Instead of me just being like oh well I have work to do, I miss him. I'm not worried about him forgetting about me or what we have fading away because we haven't seen each other. It's solid."

"Stop," she groaned. "You are making me so jealous."

I laughed. "I'm sorry. I wish I could explain it better. I want to understand it better myself. I want to know if it's love."

"Would it change things?"

"No. Yes. I mean, I think I would be more inclined to heal the major rift between him and my father if I knew it was love."

"That will come with time. Rarely does anyone like their in-laws. You are getting a head start in that department."

"That's an understatement. I wonder if his dad will like me."

"How could he not like you?" she teased.

"The same way my dad doesn't like him. He'll probably think I want Xander for his money."

She waved a hand. "That's stupid. I don't think you should worry about what anyone thinks. This is between the two of you. You guys get to figure out what comes next for you both. Don't worry about what I think or what anyone else thinks. For the record, I'm all for it. I'll miss you, but you've got to move on."

"I wouldn't ditch you," I protested.

"It's the girl code. It's the way it goes. You are going to have a man and you won't need me as much. Don't feel bad. I'll get a man one day. Maybe. I'm not sure I want one."

I laughed, pushing my hair back as I did. "When you get one as good as I have found, you'll want one."

"Probably."

"I should really get going," I said, fighting a yawn.

"See? It's already starting. You are ditching me at eight o'clock on my night off."

"I have to work tomorrow," I argued.

"Yeah, yeah, I get it. You are mature and responsible, and you have a real job."

"Damn the adulting thing," I teased.

She got to her feet and gave me a quick hug. "If I don't see you tomorrow, please tell your father congratulations for me."

"I will do that—assuming he will talk to me."

"He will. Are you going alone or are you going to take Xander?"

"Xander doesn't think it would be a good idea for him to go. He doesn't want to rain on my father's parade."

"He's got a good point."

"I'll be all by myself, the odd man out, but I'm going to do it anyway."

"Take care. I'll talk to you soon. Let me know what color my dress will be."

I stopped walking. "Your dress?"

"For when I'm your maid of honor. I don't do pink. Do not put me in pink."

I laughed and walked out of the bar. I was glad I at least had her support. It was too bad my father wouldn't give his. Thinking about a wedding just made me feel sadder. Would my dad walk me down the aisle? Would he refuse to participate?

"Relax, Evie," I scolded. I was getting way ahead of myself.

CHAPTER 43

XANDER

I was tinkering on my boat when my phone rang. I glanced over, ready to let it go to voicemail until I saw Evie's number. I quickly wiped my hand on my pants before grabbing the phone.

"Hello," I said, unable to stop the smile from spreading over my face.

"What are you doing?" she asked.

"I'm working on my boat."

She laughed. "Of course, you are. Your actual boat or the little boat you are using as a prototype?"

"My actual boat. What are you doing?"

"Well, my client canceled at the last minute. Turns out I have nothing to do on a Friday night. I was wondering if you were free."

"I'm always free for you," I told her.

"I like that."

"Come out to the boat," I said.

"Are you sure? If you've got big plans to tear apart a perfectly good boat, I don't want to get in your way."

"Woman, I'm free. You're free. Get your ass out here or I will hunt you down. You cannot put this man off another day."

Her sweet laughter came through the phone. She thought I was joking. I wasn't. I was so fucking serious. My balls were blue, and she was the only one that could cure the situation.

I had kept telling myself things would slow down after the presentation on Monday, and I would be able to see her more often. Just a few more days.

"I will be there. I'll stop by my place and change."

"No. Just get your lovely ass out here. You won't need clothes for what I have in mind."

"I'll be there in thirty," she said, sounding suddenly out of breath.

I smiled and put the phone back down. It was a little brazen, but that was the way we did things. I had never been quite so forward with any of the other women I dated. Evie was different. She made me feel like I could be that guy that was always locked down tight. I could tell her exactly how I felt, and she wasn't going to slap me or walk out. She was going to have a comeback that left me weak in the knees.

I got back to work on the motor, losing track of time until I heard her soft voice behind me. "I always get very worried when I see you working on this thing. Don't try to tell me you are working on the radio. I don't know much about boats, but I know the radio is over there."

I grinned and put down the wrench before sliding my hands down my pants again. They were still dirty. I didn't care. I had to touch her. I helped her onto the deck before grabbing her and giving her the kiss I had been dying to give for weeks.

"It's not a big deal, just a minor little issue," I told her when she looked over at the tools.

"Why don't you hire someone to fix it, or better yet, why not buy a new boat?"

I flinched as if I had been slapped. "Now why would I get rid of a perfectly good boat?"

"You keep calling it that, but you are always working on it."

"That's just for fun," I answered.

"I thought you would be working on your presentation for Monday."

I walked to the package of wet wipes and pulled a few out to clean my hands. "No. I'm done with it. If I keep fucking with it, I'm going to end up starting all over from scratch. I can get obsessive about it. I just need to go with my gut."

"Good plan. Did you tell Kade about it?"

"I called him yesterday and left a message. I haven't heard back from him."

"It's too bad he couldn't be here to see it," she said wistfully.

"He wouldn't know what I was talking about anyway. If I can pitch it right and I get someone willing to let me try it out on one of their ships, then I'll tell him."

"Good plan."

"Do you want a beer?" I asked her. "I wasn't planning on seeing you and didn't pick up any wine."

"A beer sounds good."

I headed downstairs and grabbed two cold ones before taking them back up. She had settled on the couch and kicked off her heels. She looked so damn perfect. She looked like she belonged on my boat.

I looked around the marina, disappointed to see it was a little too busy for me to have my way with her on the couch. I'd let her unwind for a few and then I would drag her below to satisfy the need I knew we both had.

"Here you go," I said and handed her the open bottle.

"Are you ready for your presentation?"

"I am."

"Do you ever get nervous before you do one?"

I shrugged. "Not really. I just say what I know. I don't try to be flashy. I don't give them a bunch of bullshit numbers. I give them the facts. They ask questions and I answer. I don't feel like I have to really sell them anything. I know what I have, and they can take it or leave it. In the long run, they are only hurting themselves if they decide to walk away."

She grinned. "There's that cocky side."

"Sorry. I don't mean to sound like a prick."

"You don't. You are confident. I'm attracted to your confidence."

"Are you now?" I asked, sitting down next to her and pulling her against me.

"I am," she whispered, her eyes dropping to my mouth.

I lowered my mouth to hers and gave her a leisurely kiss that left us both panting and wanting more. "Why don't we go downstairs?" I whispered next to her ear.

"Good plan," she answered, nipping at my bottom lip. We stood and were halfway down the stairs when my phone rang.

I growled, cursing the interruption. I assumed it was Charlie. I would call him later. I ignored the call until it started ringing right back without leaving a voicemail. "Fuck," I cursed. "Let me see who it is."

"I'll go ahead and get started," she said with a coy smile as she pulled her shirt from her pants, yanking it over her head.

I looked down at my phone and saw a number I didn't immediately recognize. Then it hit me. It was an Oregon number. "Hello?"

My dad cleared his throat. "Xander."

I thought about hanging up immediately. If I didn't answer, then he couldn't tell me.

"Dad," I said. Everything fell into slow motion.

Evie standing topless in front of me faded from my view. I saw nothing. I felt nothing. "Xander, it's Kade."

I gulped down the lump in my throat and turned away from Evie. I continued my walk down the stairs and moved to the edge of the room, trying to put some distance between me and her. I needed space. I couldn't breathe.

"What?" I asked, my throat feeling raw.

There was only one reason my father would call me. He knew it, and I knew it, but I wanted him to say the words. I needed to hear the words, or I wouldn't believe it.

"There was an accident," he said, adopting his formal tone. He could have been talking to a complete stranger. It was the same tone he used when my mother passed away and he was making the funeral arrangements.

"And? How bad?"

There was a long silence. With every passing nanosecond, I felt my blood growing colder. I shivered, my cold coming from the inside. "He didn't make it, son."

My knees buckled. I quickly regained my composure. I wasn't sure what made me more emotional, hearing him call me *son* or the fact that Kade was dead. "How? Is he here?"

"Training accident," he answered.

"What the fuck?" I breathed. My brain was in turmoil. He had been through war, literal war, and survived with barely a scratch. How the fuck did he die when he was on American soil?

"You know the drill," he said, sounding exhausted. "They aren't going to tell me shit. I got the visit and the fucking apologies. I didn't get answers. The family is the last to know."

I wanted to know. Was he shot? Did he drown in one of their rigorous water drills? Tank? I wanted to know. I needed to know. "Shot? Was it on base?"

"I don't know. Not yet. I'm going to make some calls. He was moving into one of those units that doesn't get to talk a lot."

I had suspected as much. He never said it, but I knew it was bound to happen. "But he is in the States?" I asked. "Where is he?" It was a stupid detail, and it didn't matter, but for some reason, I needed to know.

Once again, he was silent. "He'll be coming home soon."

I hated all the questions. I understood it, but I hated it. I craved details. I needed to make sense of it all. I needed facts. I needed to know the how and the why. I needed to know so I could put my grief in a neat little box with the loss of my only brother. Then I would tuck it away and move forward.

"Oregon?" I asked, not sure where Kade was calling home.

"It was his wish," he replied.

"Okay," I said. Who was I to argue? I didn't know Kade's plan. I didn't want to know. It made it too real.

"I'm sorry, Xander. Your brother was a good man. A fine Marine."

"I'm sorry too, Dad."

"I'll be in touch."

I ended the call without another word. I couldn't speak. There was a lump in my throat so big it was choking me. I tried to swallow it, but it wouldn't budge. I exhaled before sharply inhaling. The fresh breath helped dislodge the lump.

I knew my dad was hurting. He was taking on a stiff upper lip, but inside, I knew he was crushed. Kade was his favorite. I couldn't imagine the guilt my dad was suffering. Guilt for pushing Kade into the service. I hoped he was feeling guilty because I was feeling a little pissed. I shouldn't have lost my little brother.

I pushed the thoughts to the side. I was not going to pull that thread. I was not going to lose my shit and blame my father. It wasn't his fault. Kade made the choice to be a Marine. I had to respect his choice. He deserved to be honored for the sacrifices he made.

I wasn't sure if I felt better about him losing his life on American soil or not. Part of me was glad to know he was close but another part of me knew he would have wanted to go out while kicking the enemy's ass.

I couldn't think about it. I was bombarded with thoughts and images of Kade. His life was flashing before my eyes. I thought about the last time I saw him. What did I say? What did he say? How fucking horrible was it that I couldn't remember?

I slowly turned around to find Evie fully dressed once again with her hand over her mouth. I saw the pity in her eyes. I couldn't deal with it. I didn't want to see her pity for me. I didn't want to be pitied.

I wanted to be alone.

CHAPTER 44

EVIE

My heart was shattering into a thousand pieces. The look on his face told me everything I needed to know. I had heard his side of the conversation. I had seen his shoulders slump before he threw them back. He was trying to pull himself together.

"Xander," I whispered.

He had a blank stare on his face. "I, um, he—"

I felt a tear stream down my face. "Kade?"

He slowly nodded. "Yes."

I didn't want to make the wrong assumption, but I was pretty sure I knew what had happened. I wanted to believe I was wrong. I could be wrong. *Please, let me be wrong.* "Is he, uh, is he—"

"Yes."

I gasped. Hearing the confirmation made it all real. "I'm sorry," I breathed before stepping closer.

"It's fine."

"Xander, it isn't fine," I told him. I put my hand on his arm. He flinched and pulled away. "What can I do?"

"Nothing."

I could see him shutting down, pulling away. He was crawling into his corner to lick his wounds. "Can I get you a drink?" I offered.

I had no idea how to help him. I was grasping at straws.

"No, thank you."

"Do you want to go home? I can drive you home."

"No."

I could feel the retreat. I wanted to pull him closer. I couldn't lose him. We had come so far. I didn't want to lose all our progress. "What can I do?" I asked and reached for his hands. "How can I help?"

He looked at me, but I didn't know if he really saw me. "I need to be alone."

Not what I was expecting. "I can help you through this. You shouldn't be alone. If you don't want to talk, I understand. We can just sit. I'll be here for you."

"No," he said and pulled his hands away. "I want to be alone. There is nothing you can do to help me."

"Are you sure? You don't have to go through this all by yourself. I can be here. I can be a shoulder for you to lean on."

"I don't need a shoulder." He was completely cold and distant.

"Okay," I said with defeat. "Are you going to stay here?"

"Yes."

I bit my bottom lip, trying to choose my words carefully. "Please, call me if you need anything. I'm here. I wish I could make you feel better. I don't know how to do that but offer you support."

"Evie, I'm sorry, but this is something I need to handle on my own. I don't want to talk about my feelings and all that shit."

"All right, I'll go. Please take care of yourself. Can I call you later?"

"I'll call you if I need you," he answered.

It was a *no*. It was a *leave me alone, don't bother me*. I touched his arm once again, doing my best to infuse him with all the strength I possessed. "Goodbye."

I climbed upstairs and stepped off the boat onto the dock. I looked back, wondering if I was doing the right thing. I should stay with him. I should be tough and tell him he needed me. I couldn't quite bring myself to defy his wishes. Not at a time when he was already dealing with so much.

I walked to my car with a heavy heart. I didn't want to be alone. He might be okay with being alone, but I wasn't. I couldn't explain why I was feeling such grief. I barely knew the guy. But I felt like I had lost my own brother. I supposed Kade was about the closest I had ever come to having a brother.

I went to Nelle's bar. It was happy hour. Not that I felt happy, but I was hoping it wouldn't be too busy. She was leaning on the bar, chatting with an older man I recognized as a regular. She saw me and immediately came toward me. It was only then I realized there were tears streaming down my face.

"Portia, it's all you," Nelle hollered to the other bartender as she wrapped her arms around me. Her hug only made the tears come faster. I was beginning to understand why Xander wanted to be alone. I could see her understanding and pity. I was sure I had that same expression.

She guided me toward the back and took me into the small office. "What happened?" she asked. "Xander? Your father? Are you okay? Are you hurt?" She held me by the shoulders and looked me up and down, obviously checking me for injuries.

"I'm fine."

"Honey, this is not the look of someone who is fine," she said softly.

I broke into sobs. She quickly rushed to the desk and grabbed a few tissues before coming back to me. I wiped my eyes.

"Kade," I managed to choke out.

"Kade?" she asked with confusion. "The brother?"

"Yes, he—oh god." I couldn't say the words. I felt like I was going to throw up. No matter how hard I tried, the words were stuck.

"He what?" she asked.

"He's gone."

"Gone back to an ugly desert far, far away?" she asked. "That's okay. That's what he does."

I shook my head. "Gone," I said with a gasp. "He died. He's dead."

Her mouth fell open. "Oh no. How?"

I shrugged, bursting into a fresh new round of sobs. "I don't know. Xander wasn't really in a very talkative mood."

"Oh my god," she said again before going to grab a tissue.

I looked at her and saw tears shimmering in her eyes. "Are you okay?" I asked her.

"Yes, I'm just so sad for Xander and you. And maybe a little for me. I know we were only joking but I was really looking forward to meeting the guy."

I smiled through the tears. "He was such a good guy. I can't believe he's gone. It's strange to think of the man I got to meet now lying dead. He was young and healthy and full of life. It really isn't fair."

"Death is rarely fair," she said. "How is Xander taking it? Did he call you?"

"I was with him. I don't know how he is taking it. I would say not well. He wanted to be alone. He just totally shut down. I don't think he wanted to look at me, let alone talk to me. I didn't want to go, but he made it pretty clear he didn't want me there. I didn't want to make it worse."

"I'm sorry," she said and gave me a big hug. "I'm sure he wants you with him but he's in for a bumpy ride. He's probably just trying to figure out what to think and how to feel. That had to have been a huge blow."

"It was horrible. The look on his face. It was like he knew before his father even told him."

"Maybe he had one of those connections with his brother," she suggested.

I dabbed at my eyes. The worst of the sobbing was over. "I don't know. I think it was probably hearing his dad's voice. They don't talk. When you get a call like that, I think part of you senses what is coming. I can't say from experience, but I've gotten bad news before. There is always this kind of calm that comes over you. He got that weird calmness. Oh, my heart hurts so bad for him. What do I do?"

"All you can do is be there for him. Don't feel like you have to talk to him and make him talk. Just be there."

I nodded. "You're right. I want to do that but what if he doesn't want me? What if he asks me to leave again?"

"I guess you just have to dole out a little tough love."

"Maybe I can make him a casserole," I said, turning to the one thing I did know. Comfort food was called comfort food for a reason.

"He would probably like that."

"I think he is going to go to his dad's," I said as I replayed the conversation in my head.

"That would make sense. Are you going to go with him?"

"Oh shit," I muttered.

"What? What's wrong?"

"Tomorrow," I groaned. "Tomorrow is my dad's banquet."

She closed her eyes. "I get it now. Oh shit is right."

"What am I going to do?" I groaned. "I can't ditch my dad. He would never forgive me, even if he didn't technically invite me."

"No, you can't," she agreed. "You could offer to fly up to Oregon on Sunday. Nothing is going to happen before then anyway. My experience with the military is they move a little faster than a snail. They won't be able to have a funeral for at least a week."

I put a hand over my eyes. "I just can't believe it. Dead. It's so awful. Xander was just telling me he called him and never got a call back. I don't know why I'm feeling so sad. He wasn't my brother. I think I'm feeling Xander's pain for him."

"I'm sure you are," she said. "You are definitely an empath. It's what I love about you."

"I'm going home. I'm going to try and call Xander and see if he has changed his mind."

She gave me another hug. "I'm so sorry. Please tell Xander I'm sorry for his loss. It's a tragedy. You take care of him."

"I will if he will let me."

"He will. Just don't give up on him. You told me he was a hard man. Men aren't big on the feelings as it is. Make him a casserole and you will have an excuse to go over and see him."

I grinned. "Good plan. Thank you for talking to me. I'm definitely not a man. I do not internalize anything."

"Take care of yourself," she ordered. "I will call and check on you later."

I left, feeling a little better after crying it out. Xander needed to do the same. A little cry now and again made everyone feel better. I drove home and immediately called Xander. He didn't pick up. I was feeling very guilty for leaving him alone. On a boat. I winced. That was really not a good idea. I considered going back over there. I would refuse to leave until I got him home and tucked into bed.

That would never work. Xander did what Xander wanted. I picked up my phone to try texting him, hoping he would at least tell me he was okay. I waited with the phone in my hand, staring at the screen. He didn't text back.

"Shit," I mumbled. "Xander, please talk to me."

My phone chirped, alerting me to a text message. I snatched it, hoping it was Xander. It was my dad. It was my official invitation to the banquet. I smirked, shaking my head at the timing. Now my dad was talking to me and Xander wasn't.

I quickly texted my dad back and let him know I would be there. I had heard people tell me they were torn. I now had a very real under-standing of that feeling. I wanted to be with Xander. I wanted to absorb his pain. I also really needed to be there for my father. It was a once in a lifetime award. One he would never get again. Of course, Xander would never lose his brother again.

"Fuck, fuck, fuck," I shouted at the ceiling.

The timing couldn't have been worse. I knew that was completely selfish, but it made me want to scream. Instead, I opened my laptop and began to search for flights. Then I realized Oregon was kind of a big place. I had no idea where in Oregon his father lived.

I texted him again, praying he would give me some sign of life.

CHAPTER 45

XANDER

I had yet to sleep. I was afraid to sleep. Every time I stopped moving, I thought about Kade. I had spent some time on the boat and came home sometime around two. Then it was on the treadmill and then for a swim. I didn't want to stop. Stopping meant thinking. The rational side of me knew I had to think at some point.

My legs felt heavy, a sign my adrenaline was wearing off. Any moment, the crash was going to hit. I had gone through something similar when I lost my mom. Her death was expected. I was prepared for it. It sucked and it hurt but it wasn't nearly as bad as what I knew waited for me. Kade's death was going to hit hard. It already did, but instead of letting myself feel that pain, I pushed it away.

I could feel it creeping in now. I climbed the stairs, one heavy footstep at a time, as I made my way to the room he had used when he stayed with me. I walked to the dresser where the picture he had left me was still resting.

I picked up the picture, staring at the image of a time that would always be engraved into my memory. It wasn't just the memory of the moment but the memory of what he had left me as a reminder of good times. I carried the picture to the bed and sat down on the edge.

I couldn't believe I would never see his face again. I would never hear him laugh or see him smile. He would never tease me again. It just seemed impossible. Maybe if I went to sleep, I could wake up and discover it was all a really bad nightmare.

The doorbell rang, pulling me from my reverie. I wasn't up for company. The doorbell rang again, followed by the door opening. I got up, wondering who the hell would dare come into my house. I didn't have to wonder long.

"Xander?" Evie's voice echoed off the walls.

I should have texted her back. "Up here," I said before going downstairs.

"Hi," she said with a tentative smile.

"Hi."

"I texted and called, but you didn't answer. I got worried."

"I'm fine."

"Xander, you haven't slept."

I frowned. "How do you know?"

"You are wearing the same clothes you had on last night."

I looked down, only then realizing she was right. "Oh."

"Have you eaten anything?"

"I'm not hungry."

"Let me make you some breakfast," she said.

"I'm okay. I'm really not hungry."

She grabbed my hand and led me into the kitchen. I didn't have the energy to fight.

"Sit," she ordered.

I sat down on one of the stools and watched her move around my kitchen. She started coffee before opening the refrigerator.

"I don't want anything to eat," I said.

"I know you don't think you want to eat, but you need to eat."

"What are you doing?" I asked her.

She put down the carton of eggs and turned to look at me. "I'm making you coffee and breakfast."

"I don't want it."

"Xander, I'm here. I'm going to be here. I can go with you to Oregon. I can stay with you here today. I'm here for you. Whatever you need. I will make sure you eat and sleep and get some rest. You need to rest."

I shook my head. "I don't want or need any of that."

"Baby, you do." Her voice was soft and sweet. If the situation was different, I would have cherished her kindness. That was not today.

"I don't," I insisted. "I have never needed anyone. I have been alone my entire life. I'm better alone. I like being alone."

"Stop," she said. "You don't mean that."

I scoffed, looking at her through eyes that felt raw and gritty. "I do mean that."

"Xander, I know you are hurting. I want to help you."

"No."

She raised an eyebrow. "Why don't you go upstairs and shower, and I'll get you something small for breakfast? A shower and something in your stomach will make you feel a lot better."

I shook my head. I didn't want to be cruel, but she wasn't hearing me. She didn't get it. I didn't want to be near her. I didn't want to be around anyone. I sure as hell didn't want to be taken care of. "Look, I appreciate your effort, I really do, but I want to be alone."

"You don't have to be alone."

"I do. We have had a lot of fun but this thing between us isn't going to work."

She stiffened, her head tilting just a little as she looked at me. "What?"

"I was fooling myself. I'm not the guy you think I am. I'm a loner. The only person who has really ever understood who I was and how I was was Kade. Kade got it. He didn't push and he didn't try to smother me with attention and affection. He left me alone. That's what I want. It's what I have always wanted. I wasn't born to be the other half to a whole. I'm a lone rider. I always have been, and I always will be."

She looked down at her feet before her eyes met mine again. "I don't believe that."

"It's true," I said. I heard my voice. It was cold and unfeeling. It was how I felt. I had nothing left to give. I was an empty shell and I was convinced I would never feel anything again. It was over for me. My destiny had been written a long time ago and me trying to change it was futile.

"Please," she whispered. "I know this is the grief talking. Don't push me away. Don't shut me out. We will get through this together. You do not have to be alone."

I let out a sigh. "You are not getting it. I'm doing this for your own good. I'm not a man you want to be with. Trust me. Your father was right. I'm never going to be the guy that dotes on you and treasures your love. I don't love. I don't know how to love. If we had a relationship, it would be all one-sided. You would be putting in all the work. It would be a pointless exercise in futility. Just walk away."

"I can't walk away. I don't back down from a challenge."

"This isn't a challenge you can win. It will only hurt you in the long run. Walk away. I don't want this. We've had a good time, but it's time to get back to reality. This thing between us is finished."

"No."

That was not what I expected. "Evie, this isn't something you can reject."

"Yes, it is. You are in a lot of pain right now. You are a wounded animal lashing out. I won't let you push me away when you need me the most."

"You are wrong!"

"I'm not wrong."

"I want to be alone. I don't want to be a dick, but I need you to leave."

I could see the emotions running through her. I was being harsh. It seemed to be the only thing that worked. She was too fucking stubborn. "I will give you some time today, but I'm not going to abandon you."

"I will never love you," I told her and got to my feet. "I know that's what you think this is, but it isn't. I don't love. I'm not wired like that. Your father warned you. He told you I was selfish and self-absorbed. As much as I hate to say your father was right, he was. I can't do it. I don't have the energy to love another person. I don't want to try. I don't want to hurt you, and I'm really not trying to do that, but it's better if this ends now before things really get serious."

"Don't do this," she whispered. "Don't say something you will regret."

"I never do," I answered matter-of-factly. "This is who I am."

"I refuse to believe that," she shot back. She said the words with firmness, but I could see her bottom lip quivering.

"I'm sorry, but this is for the best. Please, just go. Leave me alone. I have things to do and I don't need a tagalong. I don't need you worrying about me. I'm fine. This thing I have to do does not involve you."

She used the heel of her hand to wipe away a tear that had slid out from her eye. "You don't have to do this."

"I do."

"You don't. You know I can help. You know I'm able to handle this. You know you are different with me."

I smirked. "Maybe, but that doesn't change who I am at my very core. Look at the last couple of weeks, Evie. I have barely paid you any attention. I've been caught up in my work. That's who I am. I don't think about others. I don't return phone calls when I should. I don't make time for people. I do what I want. What you experienced the last couple of weeks, that's who I really am. If Kade was here, he would tell you the same thing. He was my only fucking brother and I was too busy to call him or visit him. That's the man I am. Now go."

She wiped her cheeks again, her eyes flashing pain and anger. "I'll go, but I'm not giving up on you. You better believe that. I won't intrude on your grief, but I will be here. I will call you and I will check in on you. Believe it or not, I know better."

I turned and walked out of the kitchen without saying a word. I couldn't stand to look at her and see her pain. Pain I had caused. I heard the front door close a minute later and breathed a sigh of relief. She was gone. I didn't want her around me. I didn't want to hurt her. I didn't want her to feel the sting of my rejection and the absence of my attention when I ignored her.

Like Kade. My little brother had reached out over and over, and I always had one excuse or another for why I couldn't see him. He called me from fucking Afghanistan, and I was too busy to talk. That was a shitty brother. That was a shitty man. Evie was a good woman and deserved so much more than I could offer.

I walked out to the patio, and my gaze focused on the ocean. I remembered Kade standing in the exact same spot and daydreaming. I had known then he was dealing with some shit, but instead of asking him if he was okay or if he wanted to talk, I ignored the feelings. I didn't want to know what was bothering him.

My phone began to vibrate in my pocket. I couldn't deal with anyone else. I pulled the damn thing out of my pocket and threw it into the swimming pool. I'd said I wanted to be alone. Why was that so fucking hard for people to understand?

I wanted to run. I wanted to strip away everything and just run. I turned to look down at the beach. It wasn't too packed. I went back inside, took the stairs two at a time, and stripped off the clothes from yesterday. I pulled on a pair of shorts and my tennis shoes, not bothering with a shirt.

I headed out of the house, ignoring the coffee cooling on the counter and the carton of eggs still sitting out. I didn't stop moving. I practically ran down the steep stairs, hit the sandy beach, and started to run.

I ran until my legs burned. The exhaustion from no sleep was gone. I felt a new adrenaline rush as my legs ate up the distance.

At some point, I got hot. Too hot and I did the only thing I could think of to cool down. I ran into the ocean, shoes and all. I dove under, letting the water wash over me and pull me down.

I wanted to stay under the water forever. My body emerged from the salty water. I took several long breaths before diving back down and extending my arms. I wanted to float away. I wanted to get away from the pain. I begged the ocean to do that for me.

CHAPTER 46

EVIE

I slowly dressed, reaching for the zipper that ran up the side of the blue gown I was wearing to my father's award ceremony. My arms felt heavy and my fingers felt like they didn't want to work. The very last thing I wanted to do was get dressed up. My heart was broken. It literally felt broken in my chest. I stepped in front of the mirror and grimaced when I saw my puffy eyes and pale complexion.

Tonight was going to require extra makeup. I didn't want my father to see my suffering. Tonight was his night. I would not ruin it for him. I would sit at his table, a place of honor, and smile. I would drink champagne and make small talk with the other people seated at our table. I would play the gracious daughter and make my father proud.

I carefully put on my makeup, hiding the dark circles under my eyes and doing my best to make my complexion look bright and healthy. I left my hair down and put on some very simple jewelry. It took every ounce of energy I had to get ready. All I wanted to do was crawl into bed and cry my eyes out.

I kept telling myself Xander was worth crying over. A man that said those things wasn't worth a single tear, but he was worth it. I knew his words came from a place of immense pain. "No excuse," I said as looked myself directly in the eye in my bathroom mirror. "Don't make excuses for him."

I stepped away from the mirror, grabbed my purse, and headed to the hotel where the banquet was being held. I took a deep breath before stepping inside the ballroom. I scanned the room, looking for the table. As expected, it was near the front of the room. I hoped to sneak in, take my seat, and go unnoticed. I didn't want to mingle. I would, but I didn't want to do it if I didn't have to.

I sat down at the empty table, thankful I didn't have to smile and introduce myself. I was delivered a glass of champagne, which I eagerly accepted. After the first sip, I realized it was not what I wanted. The bubbles felt like little drops of acid in my stomach.

"Thank you for coming," I heard my father's voice behind me.

Showtime. I got up. "Hi, Dad." I greeted him with a smile before hugging him. "I wouldn't miss this."

"You look lovely tonight. I'm so glad you are here."

I forced another smile. "I wouldn't miss it."

He studied me with his eyes that always saw too much. "What's wrong?"

I tried to play it off. "Nothing. I'm fine."

"Evie, I know when you've been crying," he said, gently pushing me back into my chair before sitting in the one next to mine.

"Allergies," I lied.

"Evie, you don't have allergies."

I sighed and stared down at the napkin on the table. "You were right, Dad. I should have listened to you."

"I'm usually right about most things. You'll need to be more specific."

It was supposed to be a joke. I knew he was trying to make me feel better. I wasn't sure it was working. "Xander."

It was his turn to let out a long sigh. "I'm sorry," he said. "I didn't want to be right. I didn't want you to get hurt."

I shrugged. "Well, I did, and I have no one to blame but myself. I should have listened to you. I got caught up and didn't see who he was."

"What happened?" he asked in a gentle voice.

I could feel the tears burning the backs of my eyes. I did not want to ruin my makeup. I looked up at the ceiling, swallowing several times and taking several cleansing breaths. When I managed to push the emotions away, I looked at him. "His brother died. His only brother. He was in the Marines. I'm not sure what happened, but he died, and Xander wants to be alone. He ordered me to leave him alone. I wanted to help him. I know he's suffering, and I just wanted to help."

My father's face fell. "Oh my. That is awful."

"It is awful. I met his brother when he was home on leave recently. He is—was—so full of life. I really liked him. I know Xander loved him."

"Of course, he did," he answered. "I don't think I have ever told you, but I had a brother."

I frowned. "What? You did?"

He slowly nodded. "Yes, I did. I don't ever talk about him because to remember him is to hurt."

"What happened?"

"I was about fifteen at the time. He was ten. We lived near a lake and used to go swimming all the time. One day, I guess he decided to go alone. I think I was hanging out with my buddies or something. He drowned. The guilt I felt was tremendous. I shut down. I couldn't bear to be around my parents. I saw their grief and I was convinced they blamed me. I blamed myself."

"Oh my god," I gasped. "Dad, you never told me!"

He offered a small smile. "It didn't seem like you needed that kind of pain. You feel so strongly. I didn't want you to think about it."

"But Dad, you could have told me."

"It was in my past. There was nothing you could have done. Sometimes, a man chooses to leave those feelings in a dark place. I'm not saying it's healthy, but it is a coping method."

"Xander said he wanted to be alone. He said he isn't capable of love. He's wrong. I know you don't like him, and you don't believe me, but I know in my heart he felt something for me."

"Well, of course, he does. He'd be a damn fool not to love a woman like you."

I smiled, fighting back tears. "Thanks. I wish you could see he is a good man."

"I don't think I will ever sing the man's praises, but in this situation, I feel for him. He's in a tough spot. I might not like him, but I feel bad for him. You need to be there for him."

That was unexpected. "He doesn't want me around. He made that very clear."

"Make him want you. He needs you. He doesn't know it, but he does. He will push you away. I pushed everyone away. I didn't want anyone to see me as weak. I refused to cry. I thought if I cried, it made me weak. It took me a very long time to come to terms with my grief. It was actually your mother who helped me to see it wasn't my fault. Things happen. I had this idea in my head I was some kind of powerful creature capable of fighting fate. Your Xander is very much the same. He's stubborn and bullheaded and he has the same mindset. He thinks he can do anything. This is going to be a blow."

My dad had never opened up to me. He had never been so honest with his feelings. I leaned forward and hugged him. "I'm so sorry you had to go through all of that."

"I've coped. Now, it's time for you to help him cope."

"I don't know how to do that."

"Go to him."

"Not right now," I told him.

He smiled. "No, right now, I'd like to be a little selfish and monopolize your time for a couple of hours. Give him the night. He might need some privacy to grieve. Your relationship is fairly new, and a man will not be comfortable releasing his emotions in front of a woman he is still trying to impress."

"He doesn't need to impress me," I said.

He shrugged and smiled. "There is a reason cavemen pounded their chest. Men have a need to impress their women. It doesn't go away with time."

"You are so right."

The rest of the evening, I did my best to focus on my father. I smiled and shook hands with his colleagues and did my best to play the dutiful daughter. In the back of my mind, I thought about Xander. I sent a text message every hour, asking him if he was okay and letting him know I was thinking about him. I never got a response and I didn't really expect to.

I just needed him to know he wasn't alone. His words had twisted my guts and shattered me a million times over. I hated that he felt so alone. I hated that he thought he had to be that way for the rest of his life. In the moment, I didn't think arguing with him was the best approach. I let him say his piece and hoped we could talk about it again when he wasn't so raw.

I wasn't sure I would get the chance to tell him I understood his obsession with his work. I got the same way. I didn't feel neglected. He needed to know he had done nothing wrong. He was a good man. I just had to make him see it and believe it. I didn't think I could rely on his father to boost his feelings of self-worth. Maybe I was the one being overly confident and arrogant, but I was convinced I was the only person who could make him see he was worthy.

∽

Monday morning

I was being way too forward. I should mind my own business. I had no business being in his office, but here I was, strolling down the hall in my power suit, pretending I belonged. The receptionist told me the presentation was being held in the conference room and directed me to where to go. I told her I was the assistant to one of the attendees. She didn't question my story.

I never got a single text back from him all weekend. The gate at his house was closed and locked tight. I was going to track the man down and make him listen to me. He was going to at least hear what I had to say. If he kicked me out, so be it, but not until after I said what I had to say.

I walked into the conference room and took a seat. No one paid me any mind as they chatted amongst themselves. I waited for fifteen minutes, checking the time every five minutes. Xander was always late, I told myself.

After forty-five minutes, it was clear he wasn't coming. The others in the room began to leave one at a time. None of them were very happy. I went back to talk to the receptionist, who had a very worried look on her face. She had been calling him and never got an answer.

Alarm bells were going off in my head. I left and drove straight to his house. My heart was pounding as I pulled to a stop in front of the gate. I got out, looking for a way in. "Fuck!" I shouted, more nervous than pissed.

I drove to a parking area that would allow me to walk down to the beach. I took off my heels when I hit the sand, carrying them as I ran along the sandy beach. I found his stairs and did my best to haul ass up them. It was not an easy feat. By the time I made it to the landing that opened up to his patio, I was out of breath and sweating like a pig. I walked barefoot cross the hot cement of the patio.

My first thought was to check the pool. I was terrified I would find him floating in the damn thing. I didn't find him, but I noticed something sitting at the bottom of the pool. I immediately recognized the shiny blue case. It was his phone. That explained the lack of returned messages. I tried the glass doors, which were of course locked.

I found one of the kitchen windows unlocked and hoisted myself inside. He thought he was so smart by not having any neighbors. I was proving why there was something to be said for nosey neighbors.

I walked through the house. He wasn't there. I didn't feel his presence.

I headed for his bedroom, hoping he was sleeping. The bed was neatly made. He wasn't there. I went back down to the kitchen and saw the eggs still sitting out. The coffee I'd made him was untouched and sitting on the counter.

He had vanished.

CHAPTER 47

XANDER

I stared up at the ugly ceiling with the plain tiles. There was a hint of yellowing in one corner. It was to be expected in an environment like this, I supposed. I wasn't going to panic and demand another hotel room. I didn't care enough to move.

I'd made it to Oregon the day before and had yet to leave the hotel. I wasn't sure what I was doing there. My dad would not be pleased to see me. The moment of kindness, if it could be called that when he called to inform me of my brother's death, would be fleeting. I knew that as much as I knew the wind would be blowing at the beach.

The ringing of a phone disturbed the total quiet in the room. At first, I assumed it was coming from the room next to mine or above mine. Then I remembered it was my new phone with a ringtone I wasn't quite used to. The damn thing had been ringing pretty steadily since this morning.

I knew why. I'd fucked up. I'd blown off the meeting. It was an important meeting, but it wouldn't have changed my life, except make me a little richer and give me a little more cred in the world of ship design. I didn't care. None of that mattered. I never wanted to design another ship, rudder, or anything else.

The ringing of the landline in my room startled me. I stared at the phone with confusion. How and who? It had to be a wrong number, but if I didn't answer, the annoying sound was going to continue.

I rolled to my side and snatched the phone out of the cradle. "Hello?" I answered with zero friendliness in my voice.

Charlie's voice came through. "Finally."

"What the hell?" I muttered. "How did you get this number?"

"We call it Google search or something like that," he snapped irritably.

"Why are you calling me? How did you know I was here?"

He sighed and I imagined him pacing the small office he had at the warehouse. "Process of elimination. I knew where you would be. I just had to find which hotel you were in. I skipped the one and two-star motels and started at the top of the list of big ones and worked my way down."

That surprised me. "You've been calling all the hotels in Newport?"

"And Seaside and every other little town up there. If you made me go through the Portland hotels, I would fly up there and kick your ass."

"What do you want?" I asked. I was not in the mood to hear shit from him or anyone else.

"Um, gee, I don't know. You kind of left me hanging. Everyone hanging."

I climbed off the bed and moved to open the curtain blocking the sunlight from coming into my room. "Yeah, as it turns out, I had more important shit to do."

"I get it," he said, his voice low. "I'm so sorry about Kade. You know I loved him like a brother." I could hear his grief. I had sent him a quick text on Friday night, dropping the bombshell. That had been a shitty way to tell him, but I couldn't bring myself to actually say the words. When he tried calling me, I turned off my phone. Then I drowned my phone. And now I was ignoring his calls.

I gulped down the lump of emotion his words caused. "Thanks."

"I know you've got a lot going on. I get it, but man, you kind of left a lot of people hanging back here."

"Charlie, how can I care about that? Why would I care?"

"Because my future is on the line. The guys that work for me have been gearing up to begin work on this retrofit. You no-showed to a meeting you called with some of the top shipping magnates in the country. Hell, the world. They flew in from all over and you didn't even have the courtesy to tell them to fuck off."

"I don't know what to say," I answered honestly. "I really don't. I guess because I don't care. I don't give a shit."

"Don't say that. This is temporary. You are in rough shape right now, but you will get through this. Don't blow up your entire career."

I shook my head, anxiousness and anger boiling in my belly. "I don't care. Seriously, I don't care."

"Xander, come on, man. You know Kade wouldn't want you to destroy everything you've worked so hard for."

"You don't know what Kade would want," I snapped. "Kade would probably have liked to live. But guess what? We don't always get what we want."

He cleared his throat. "I don't suppose we do, but this is in your control. You can change this. You can do what you've set out to do. You have the design. All you need to do is show the world. The rest will fall into place. Me and my team are ready to put it to work."

"I'm sorry. I'm not interested in any of it anymore."

"Don't do this," he begged. "Take a minute and think about what you're doing."

"I have. Goodbye."

I ended the call and tossed the phone on the bed. I yanked open the curtains and stared out at the ocean. It was the same ocean that had captivated Kade's attention when he had been at my place. It was strange to think he would never look at it again.

I pulled myself out of the funk I was falling into. I didn't want to go down that road. I didn't want to feel distraught and sad. Somewhere over the last two days, I had found a place that was devoid of pain. I didn't feel anything. I erected a magic forcefield around me and was hunkering down.

It was time to face the very thing I came to Oregon to deal with. I was putting it off, but that wasn't going to make it go away. I grabbed the keys to the rental car I picked up at the airport in Portland and drove out to my father's modest house near the beach.

I knocked on the door, feeling an acidic burn low in my belly. When he finally opened the door, I immediately regretted my decision to show up unannounced. He was drunk. I could smell the alcohol coming off him in waves. His eyes were bloodshot, and it didn't look like he had showered in days. I doubted he had. Probably not since he got the news.

"Dad," I said, unsure of what to expect from him.

"What the fuck are you doing here?" he asked.

I shrugged. "What do you think I'm doing here?"

"You shouldn't have come."

He walked away from the front door. I followed him into the house and watched as he poured a glass of straight Jack before taking a drink.

"I came to help with the funeral arrangements," I said.

He scoffed. "You don't need to do a damn thing. It's already taken care of."

"What? How? You said he wasn't even back home yet."

He scowled at me with his lip curling in utter disgust. "It's been taken care of. The Marines have followed Kade's directives. He will be receiving full military honors."

I slowly nodded. I knew what Kade would have asked for. Part of me struggled to think of his body no longer in this world. He would have chosen cremation. I wasn't going to be able to look at his face one last time. I wasn't going to get the chance to say goodbye. He was well and truly gone.

A stark feeling of emptiness washed over me. It nearly dropped me. It was as if my insides had been carved out and I was a hollow shell. I looked at my father who had taken a seat at the kitchen table. His shoulders, usually thrown back with his chest puffed out, were sagging. His back was bowed. He looked deflated. I knew what I was feeling and imagined it was ten times worse for him.

I pitied him in that moment. His favorite son, his only son as far as he was concerned, was gone. His beloved wife was gone. He was left with me, his biggest failure. Life was not fair. Life fucked with people.

"When?" I asked, taking a seat at the table.

He looked at me bleary eyed. "What?"

"When is the funeral? Will it be here?"

"Yes. Wednesday."

I nodded. I shouldn't have been surprised to be left out of the planning of the arrangements. "It's all taken care of?"

"Yes."

"When? What time?"

He spouted off the time as if it took him a great deal of effort to say the words. "Don't bother coming."

"What?"

"You don't need to bother yourself by going to the funeral. You were too busy for him in life. Don't pretend you give a shit now that he's gone."

I felt like I had been kicked in the gut. Surprisingly, I didn't get angry. I was still in the emotional desert that stole away all emotion. That was probably a good thing. Fighting with him wasn't going to help. "I'm going to the funeral. Period."

He glared at me. "He was a good son. He was an honorable man. He died for his country. I am proud to be his father and I won't have you trying to steal his glory."

"I would never steal his glory. I'm his brother. I'm his only brother. I will be there for him."

He scoffed before taking a drink. "You just want people to think you give a damn. We both know you don't."

I shrugged, knowing it was pointless to argue. "I'm sorry you feel that way. You can be pissed at me if that's what makes this easier on you."

"I don't give a shit about you," he spat the words. His venom stung my battered soul, but I dug deep, pulling that invisible forcefield around me just a little tighter. "I'm not pissed. I just don't give a damn what you do. You made your choice a long time ago. You never cared about this family or the honor we all worked so hard to maintain. Go back to your mansion and your millions. I've got this."

I got to my feet. Staying would only cause more pain. Once the hard shell wore off, his words would be on repeat in my head. They would hurt me if I let them. My father was best in small doses.

"I'll see you later," I said and walked out of the house without stopping to look back.

I got in the car and drove to a section of beach that was packed with tourists soaking in the last days of summer. I kicked off my shoes and started to walk. I didn't know where I was going, and I didn't care. No matter how hard I tried to block them, my father's words echoed through my mind. It was like the little ticker tape on the bottom of a newscast. Things he said today mixed in with things he had said to me over the last fifteen years.

My mother's funeral had been bad, but I knew Kade's would be a hundred times worse. Maybe it was best I didn't go. I didn't like my father, and I knew he didn't like me, but I didn't want to make his pain any worse. I wasn't doing it for me but for Kade. Kade had desperately wanted us to find a way to be a family again. It was the last thing he said to me.

I didn't think I could honor his wishes, but I could keep from making the situation worse. It wasn't like Kade would know if I was at the funeral or not. No one would miss me. No one.

CHAPTER 48

EVIE

I cleaned myself up after discovering Xander's absence, but I was still a mess. I found myself randomly bursting into tears for no good reason. Half the time I didn't even know what I was crying about.

I just felt fried. My nerves were raw. Every little thing made me cry for no good reason. I stubbed my toe on a chair leg and I burst into tears. I looked at the ocean and I cried. I felt as if I was grieving the loss of not just Kade but Xander.

I'd lost him. I'd lost the man I cared for and someone I considered to be a good friend, a companion.

I wanted to help Xander. I wanted to know he was okay. I was terrified for him. I hated to think he was alone. I was imagining all kinds of things. I did have an active imagination. It was why I was so good at my job. In this situation, that imagination was not working well for me. I pictured him alone in a dark room, sad and distraught and hating himself.

I knew the relationship between him and his father was strained. Who did he have to turn to? Who was going to be there for him? I was probably giving myself too much credit by thinking he needed me. He didn't need me. The man had lived his entire life without me and had done just fine.

With the day coming to an end and still no word from Xander, I felt like I was going out of my mind. I needed some distance from the situation. I needed guidance. I drove to the bar, knowing Nelle would know what to do. She would talk me through the craziness I was feeling.

"Hi," she said with a soft smile when I slid onto my barstool.

"Hi," I said on a long sigh.

"Do you want a drink?"

I shook my head. "Just a diet coke please. I don't trust myself to day drink."

"What's going on?" she asked as she handed me my drink.

"He's gone."

She froze, her hand pausing mid-wipe on the bar. "The last time you used that phrase, you were telling me someone died. Please don't tell me that's what you're saying now."

"No, not that kind of gone," I told her. "Xander is gone. He didn't show up for a very, very important meeting this morning. Something is wrong. He would never miss that meeting. He's been working day and night to prepare for the presentation. Something isn't right."

"His brother died," she answered. "He needs time. I would think that would be a given."

"He didn't cancel the meeting. People flew in from all over to be there and he stood them up. That isn't normal. He would never do that."

She didn't look worried. "I'm sure he has a lot on his mind. It isn't really all that surprising that he would forget something like that."

I wasn't buying it. "Not Xander. He isn't like that. He's been consumed with this project. He wouldn't just forget it."

"Maybe he blew it off on purpose."

"Why would he do that?"

She shrugged. "People do crazy things when they're grieving. They can be irrational. Have you left him a voicemail? Texted him?"

I gave her a dry look. "Gee, why didn't I think of that?"

"Don't get snarky," she said with a laugh. "I was only making sure."

"I've been calling him since yesterday and have not gotten an answer, which isn't surprising considering his phone is at the bottom of his pool."

"It's at the bottom of his pool?"

"Yes."

"Then why did you call him?"

"I didn't know it was in the pool when I called," I explained.

"I'm so confused."

I looked away. "I kind of broke into his house."

Her brows shot up. "You did what?"

"I was worried," I defended.

"You broke into his house? Since when did you become a felon?"

I shrugged a shoulder. "His gate was locked. I figured he was holed up inside. I really wanted to see him. I wanted to make sure he was okay."

"How did you get in if the gate was locked?"

"I used the beach stairs and found a kitchen window unlocked."

"Wow. Breaking and entering. You are really taking things seriously."

I rubbed my fingers against my temples. "I'm so worried about him. He was not in a good way when I left on Saturday. He was distraught but not distraught, if you know what I mean. Like he was very robotic. He shut down and pushed me away. He wants nothing to do with me."

"He's hurting," she answered.

"I know but I can help."

"Evie, you know men are not like women. They don't want to talk about their feelings. They don't want to hash it out or cry it out."

It was not what I wanted to hear. "But he's hurting. It's his brother. His little brother. He loved his brother. In his eyes, he lost his only family. It would be like me losing my dad. I cannot even imagine what that would be like. I just want to wrap my arms around him and hold him close."

"Oh, sweetie, I know you do. He'll come around."

"I don't even know where he is!"

"Evie, I'm sure he went home to be with his father," she said, sounding so perfectly reasonable.

"But they don't get along," I said.

"I think in this situation, they need each other."

"The look on his face..." I trailed off, flashing back to the moment he heard about his brother's death. It gutted me every time I thought about it.

Xander was this big, tough man who rarely showed much emotion. In that moment, he looked like he had been cut in two. He was torn apart but didn't know how to say it.

"I'm sorry," Nelle said. "I can't imagine how hard it must be to feel so helpless."

She had no idea. "And now he's gone. He wants nothing to do with me. He's gone and that's that."

She rolled her eyes. "And you're just going to give up?"

"He's made his feelings abundantly clear."

"Would you want him to give up if the situation was reversed?"

"What do you mean?" I asked.

"Would you want him to be there for you if you lost someone important in your life? Imagine you lost your father. Can you imagine getting through it without him to lean on?"

That hit home. "No. I couldn't. I wouldn't want to be alone, but it's different."

"He might not know what it's like to have someone. He doesn't know what he's missing."

I groaned. "But I can't make him want my help."

"Evie, I know you, like really, really know you. You broke into the man's house, and now you're going to throw up your hands and walk away? That does not sound like you. Pity Party, party of one, sitting right here."

"I'm not giving up, but I'm not going to make things worse for him."

"Oh, you mean by being there for him? Being a shoulder to lean on? You don't want to make his life worse by taking care of him and making sure he eats and sleeps and takes care of himself. Absolutely. You're right. Leave him hanging out there all by himself. That's clearly the better choice."

"Your sarcasm is not appreciated," I said, pouting. "I don't know what to do. He pushed me away. Twice."

She reached for my hand. "I know, and while I'm sure that stung a little, I seriously doubt he means any of it. He's a wounded beast. You're the right person to help him settle. You're the woman that can heal his heart."

"I think I might have misjudged where things were going with us," I told her. "I had this idea we were an actual couple. I think I was wrong. He only ever saw me as a friend with benefits. I jumped to conclusions."

"Wrong."

"How do you know?"

"Because I know you," she said. "You wouldn't have fallen head over heels for this guy if you didn't think he cared for you as well."

I worried my lower lip. "It felt like it," I whispered. "I have to believe there was something. It was more than friends. I know it was."

"You are using past tense. Don't give up. Go to him."

"I can't do that," I groaned.

"I know it's scary, and I know it hurt when he rejected you, but he is worth it, isn't he?"

He absolutely was worth it. "Yes."

She smiled. "I guess you have your answer."

"But that doesn't change the fact I don't know where he is. He isn't answering his phone. Even if I want to help, there's little I can do."

She slapped her fingers on the bar. "Dammit, you are acting so defeated. You broke into his house. That tells me you are a resourceful girl. Find him."

"That is a little easier said than actually done. I'm not the FBI. I can't run his credit cards. I know he's in Oregon, but that is a really big state."

"Think about the little clues he has dropped during the time you've been together. I'm sure he gave you an idea."

I thought long and hard. "The coast."

She grinned, her eyes sparking with excitement. "There you go. Look at you, playing Miss Detective. You missed your true calling in life."

I felt a little better. Not a lot, but a little better and more confident I would be successful in my quest to find him. "Thanks. I was kind of losing my shit for a minute there."

She burst into laughter. "Yeah, you think?"

"I might have it narrowed down, but there are still thousands of places he might be."

"Start with the dad," she offered.

I wrinkled my nose. "I'm not sure he would go there. He might visit, but I am pretty sure that relationship is not the kind that would result in him staying with his father."

"So hotels."

"Just a few thousand, right?" I said dryly.

"I bet you are up for the challenge," she said with a grin. "You were always good at tackling big problems. Make a little spreadsheet or whatever it is you do and go from there."

I rolled my eyes. "It isn't quite that easy."

"It isn't supposed to be easy. You are saving a man from himself. That is going to be tough, but you can do it."

I mulled it over, trying to dig deep. Suddenly, a light bulb went off. I checked the time and hopped off the stool. "I have to go."

"Where?"

I smiled. "I know where to find him, or rather, I know *how* to find him, but it's going to take a lot of finesse and probably a great deal of begging to get the information. I'll call you later."

I rushed out of the bar, hoping I could make it before he left. I drove straight to the college, knowing my dad was teaching a summer class. Hopefully, he would be in his office. If not, I was going to have to beg him to return.

I practically ran down the hall to his office. I slapped my open hand against the door and pushed it open without waiting for him to invite me in. "Dad!"

He jumped up from where he was sitting behind his desk. "What's wrong? What is it? Are you okay?" He rushed toward me, his hands grabbing my shoulders as he studied my face.

"No, I'm fine. I'm sorry. I didn't mean to scare you."

He sighed. "Thank god. What are you doing here?"

"I need a favor. A huge favor."

"Anything you need, I'm here to help."

I smiled and closed the office door. "I was hoping you would say that."

CHAPTER 49

XANDER

I parked the rental car on the opposite side of the street from the funeral home. I got out and leaned against the driver's side door. A steady stream of mourners made their way inside. I had spotted my dad's car when I drove by the first time. He was one of the first to arrive. Technically, I was first but I never stopped the car. I had been circling the funeral home for an hour.

I couldn't bring myself to go inside. It wasn't like I would be viewing his body. There would be a big picture of him smiling.

No, that wasn't right. My father would have chosen a photo of him in his uniform. His celebration of life would be more of a celebration of his military career, something I was not a part of. I didn't understand a lot of it. I certainly didn't share in the joy of being a military man.

A young woman wearing a very small black dress openly sobbed. I didn't recognize her. Hell, I didn't recognize most of the people making their way into the home. I didn't feel like I belonged. I felt like I was an intruder at my brother's funeral.

There was no point in waiting any longer. I owed it to Kade to make an appearance. I had wrestled with going and not going for days. I was going. I needed to say goodbye, and doing it at the funeral seemed like the only way I could do that.

Preparing to walk across the street, I cleared my throat and threw my shoulders back, but that was as far as I got. I stood frozen in the middle of the sidewalk. The funeral would make it real. Part of me had been hovering in denial, not denying he was dead but refusing to cope with it. If I didn't admit it, I wouldn't have to think about it. I wouldn't hurt if I didn't acknowledge it.

A hand rested on my lower back. I immediately spun around to find out who dared to touch me.

"Evie?" I said with shock and disbelief.

"Hi," she said with a small smile.

"What are you doing here?"

"I came to be with you," she answered.

"But how? How did you find me?"

"That's not important. I'm here for you."

I didn't know what to think of her presence exactly, but I was glad she was there. "Thank you."

"Do you want to go in?" she asked.

"I have to," I said.

"You don't have to do anything, but I think you will be glad you did."

"This isn't going to be pretty," I warned her. "You should know I was uninvited to this."

Her eyes widened. "Oh no. I'm so sorry. He's your brother. No one can tell you not to show up."

I smirked. "My dad certainly didn't mind saying it."

"I'm here for you. I'm your ally."

"Thanks. You are probably the only one."

"I don't mind," she assured me.

"I still want to know how you found me," I said. Yes, I was stalling.

She winked. "We can talk about that later. I think there is something more important than that right now."

"I have a lot of questions and we are absolutely going to talk about it."

She reached for my hand. "Ready?"

"Can I apologize for what is about to happen now?" I muttered. "This is not going to be a happy family reunion. My dad has no filter. He says what he feels, and I can assure you, he isn't feeling good about me being in the same state with him right now."

"I'm fine. I can handle a crotchety old man. He's grieving. I'll give him a free pass."

I gripped her hand and began to walk toward the entrance. "He is a crotchety old man every damn day."

"I'll hang out in back," she said. "I will be there as an unseen safety net for you and you alone. I'm here for you."

Her words hit me hard. I had never felt so cared for. My mother had been a wonderful woman, but her allegiance was to my father. Evie was loyal to me, which made me feel worthy. My dad didn't give two shits about me and the pain I was suffering, but she did. We got in line with the other mourners. I didn't recognize anyone.

The number of uniforms inside the main lobby area was staggering. Seeing all of them looking somber and yet proud hit me hard. I actually stumbled backward. Evie was right there for me. She held my hand a little tighter. I took a deep breath and pulled myself together.

My father was standing between the two double doors that opened into the chapel area. He looked old. He didn't immediately see me, giving me the chance to study him. He was putting on a good show, but I could see the pain in his eyes.

He shook hands, offered smiles, and greeted old friends with a slap on the shoulder. Then he saw me.

"I thought we talked about this," he growled in a low voice.

I stood in front of him with Evie by my side. "*You* talked."

His eyes slid to Evie, giving her one of those hard stares he'd perfected during his days of training young Navy men and women. "You brought your latest flavor of the month to your brother's funeral?" he spat.

I felt Evie flinch. "She is here for me."

He didn't look pleased. "I always knew you were selfish, but this is a step up for you. It's disrespectful and I will not tolerate it."

"Evie is my girlfriend. She and I will be going in and you will give her the respect she deserves. You have no beef with her."

He sneered, showing his true colors. "She obviously doesn't know you."

"I know him quite well," she said calmly.

"Don't," I warned when he opened his mouth. "You can hate me. You can say what you want about me, but she does not deserve your hatred."

He shot me one last glare but didn't get a chance to say anything nasty. Someone approached him to offer their condolences, freeing me from being trapped in a back and forth with him. Evie led me away.

The moment I stepped through the doors into the packed chapel area, I saw his picture on a massive screen above a platform that was littered with flower arrangements. I didn't move. I stared at the picture of him smiling and wearing his BDUs.

It felt like he was looking directly at me. My heart lurched as I looked into my brother's smiling eyes. A sound escaped my throat.

Evie dropped my hand and put an arm around my shoulders. With a strong but gentle force, she began to lead me down the aisle toward the front row.

"No," I said, pulling back. "Not there."

"You are family. You should sit in the front row."

I shook my head. "I can't. I don't want to. I prefer to be in the back."

"Okay," she answered without pushing the issue.

I led the way to the far corner of the room. There were no seats available. I didn't care. I preferred to stand. I wasn't sure I would be able to make it through the entire funeral. I didn't want to disrupt it if I got up to leave. Evie stood beside me, her shoulder rubbing against my upper arm as we leaned against the wall.

I couldn't take my eyes off the image on the screen. It wasn't a picture I had seen before. It looked fairly recent, which told me it was likely from his most recent deployment. When the funeral director began to speak, I tuned out. I didn't want to hear all the generic phrases that were recycled for every funeral.

I barely listened as one man after another wearing dress blues spoke about him, applauding his bravery and courage. They all knew a different man than I did. They all called him their brother. I felt a twinge of jealousy as I realized many of them were probably closer to him than his real brother.

About a minute into the slideshow, I realized I'd had enough. I couldn't watch his life play out in a chronological order. Every picture was a memory. A reminder that we would never have another memory together.

"I need to go," I said and began to move.

Evie's hand gripped mine as we made our way out of the funeral home. I burst through the door, dragging in deep breaths of fresh air. The air inside the funeral home smelled like grief. The sniffles and the sight of hardened Marines crying was too much for me to take.

"Are you okay?" Evie asked.

That was a strange question to me. "No, I'm not okay."

"Would you like to talk about it?"

"No, I don't want to talk about it. I don't want to think about it."

"Okay. Would you like to go for a walk?"

I looked up and down the street lined with cars. "A lot of people loved him," I said.

"Yes, they did."

"I'm glad. I'm glad to know he had that many people in his life that cared about him."

"Just because there are a lot of people that loved and cared about him, it doesn't mean your relationship or your love for him didn't matter. You were important to him. I only got to know him for a very brief time, but I know he loved you."

"But did he know how I felt about him?" I asked.

"I think he did. He knew you very well, even if you don't think he did."

"I don't know," I murmured. "I just wish I could talk to him one more time. I want to tell him all the things I should have said when he was here. I want to apologize for not dropping everything and coming up here to visit him. I took him for granted."

"Xander, you are not the first person to realize they should have done this or should have said that when a loved one passes away unexpectedly. We know we should do better, and yet, we rarely do. Trust that he knew you cared about him. Don't try to add to your grief. Just accept the fact that he loved you and you loved him and you both knew it."

I wanted to believe her, but my heart wasn't there yet. "Thanks."

"Would you like to go get something to eat?"

"No, I hate to say this, but I really would just like to be alone. I appreciate you coming all the way here, but I don't feel like doing anything. I just want to hibernate."

She nodded without arguing. "Okay. I'll be in town."

"You will?"

"I have a room nearby. Do you have your phone?"

"I do."

"Same number?"

I felt a little guilty for not texting her back. That was a dick move. "Yes. I'm sorry I didn't text back. I've just been trying to figure shit out."

"It's fine. I'll text you the hotel and my room number. You don't have to text me back. You'll have the information if you want it. No pressure."

"Thanks. Really, thank you for coming. It helped."

"You are welcome. That's what friends are for."

"Did you drive? Can I give you a ride to your hotel?"

"I rented a car," she answered.

"Me too."

"I'll let you go. Please call if you need anything. I'm here Xander. I'm here for you."

"Thank you."

I wasn't sure if I was supposed to kiss her goodbye or leave it. It felt weird. *I* felt weird. I didn't have to worry about it for long. She turned and walked away, leaving me alone on the sidewalk.

CHAPTER 50

EVIE

I wrapped my hair up in a towel and pulled on my panties before walking into the room. I had waited all night for Xander to call. He never did, but he texted me a couple times to let me know he was okay. That was enough for me.

I was going to catch a flight home tomorrow. I wanted to give him one more day, just in case he changed his mind and needed me.

I flipped on the TV just to have a little noise in the room. It was going to be a warm day—in the eighties. I laughed out loud. That was an average to cool day where we were from. I stepped back into the bathroom to brush my teeth and was just rinsing out the last bit when I heard a knock on the hotel room door.

I froze, looking down at my undressed body and panicked. I rushed into the room, yanked on a pair of shorts, and managed to pull a T-shirt over my head with the towel still holding up my thick hair. I looked through the peephole to find Xander standing at the door, hands in his pockets.

I jerked open the door. "You're here. Did you text?"

"No, I thought I would surprise you."

"Come in," I said, feeling a little flustered. "You did surprise me."

"Did I catch you at a bad time?"

"Absolutely not," I told him. "I'm glad to see you. How are you feeling?"

"Good. Fine. Do you have plans for today?"

"Nope, I am at your disposal. I'm here for you and you alone."

"I was thinking we could go out on the town today," he said.

"I'd like that. I hear it's supposed to be a warm one today."

He laughed. "It is much cooler up here."

"I like it," I told him. "I can see the appeal."

He gave me a onceover. "We can go down to the beach, check out some of the tourist traps, and just have some fun."

"That sounds amazing."

"I'd like to take you to the best seafood restaurant in town. You will never want to eat clam chowder anywhere else."

I smiled, happy to see him behaving so normally. That was a positive sign. "I'll get dressed."

"You are dressed," he said with a smile.

He had a sense of humor once again. "True, but I think shoes would be good and I should probably remove the towel."

"I suppose if you want to be fancy," he said with a soft smile.

"Give me five minutes. Have a seat. Change the station if you want."

I disappeared into the bathroom to quickly towel dry my hair before pulling it into a messy bun for the day. I put on a little makeup and called it good before digging in my suitcase for a pair of sandals.

Xander was sitting on the small balcony that had a view of the ocean, if one tried really hard to see it through the buildings and trees.

"Ready," I declared.

He got up and came into the room. I could see he was still carrying that heavy weight of grief but was trying hard not to show it. My heart ached for him. It was clear he wanted to ignore the reason we were in Oregon. He was making it into a little vacation. I could go with that. I could pretend right alongside him if that was what he needed.

We left the hotel with him driving us down to the waterfront area. We walked around the many shops that essentially sold the same old

T-shirts and other items advertising a person had visited the Oregon beach. He didn't talk and I didn't push him.

"This is the restaurant I was talking about," he said.

"I'm excited to taste this food you've raved about," I told him, trying to stay upbeat.

We took a table outside. Thankfully, the bulk of the lunch rush was over. "Don't take this the wrong way," he said after a few minutes of silence between us. "But why are you here?"

"I told you I'm here for you."

"I know how busy you are. Why would you leave your work behind?"

"Because I wanted to be here for you. I have coworkers that can pick up the slack. I worked when I got back to my room yesterday. It's fine."

"I really do appreciate you being here."

"You are very welcome. If the roles were reversed, I know I would have liked having you around for me."

That seemed to confuse him. "I would," he said. "I would be there for you."

"Thank you. Hopefully, this situation is never repeated."

"I'm sorry for the way my dad talked to you yesterday," he said.

"Don't apologize for your father," I told him. "Your father is grieving."

He made a choking noise. "That's his normal attitude. He hates me and anyone I associate with."

"He can't possibly hate you," I insisted.

"He does. Trust me. He does."

"Grief is notorious for turning families against each other. It's an evil little demon that worms into a person's heart and soul. Grief rips your heart out and twists up all of your emotions. I'm sure he needs some time to process everything. Then he will be in a better place to talk."

"No, I'm serious. That was a normal conversation between us. He doesn't like me."

I felt my battered heart breaking all over again. "I am sorry. It's so hard for me to get my head around that. You're a good person. He should be proud of you."

"But I'm not a Marine or a Navy man. I'm not even a soldier. He would have tolerated me going into the Army, but Kade and I were groomed to become Marines or sailors from the moment we took our first breaths. I bucked tradition. I tarnished the family name. Apparently, our family's military service goes back to the days of the Civil War, according to my father."

"That's impressive."

"And I fucked it up," he replied without any real shame.

"You did nothing of the kind. You put your family's name on the map as one of the leaders of the future. Be proud of what you have accomplished. Don't let him take that away."

"I say that all the time, but it never really seems to sink in. Then I see him, and I remember why. The man is hard. He doesn't pull any punches."

"His opinion is his alone. He has a right to it, but it doesn't make it right. Not even a little bit right."

He seemed to brush it off. He took a drink and stared out at the water. The man drew strength from the ocean. He was a modern-day Merman. I watched as he collected his thoughts. His face, that had moments earlier revealed a hint of the pain he felt, was now devoid of all emotion.

"It doesn't matter," he said. "There's nothing that will bring me back here. He said what he needed to and that's that. Without Kade, there is nothing left between us. I won't have to listen to him and his ugly comments."

I felt the familiar twisting low in my gut. I could not begin to imagine the pain he was enduring. My father and I had been at odds for a few weeks and it turned me inside out. I knew my father loved me. Xander didn't believe his father loved him.

"You are a good man," I said again. I felt like I needed to say it a million times to make him believe it. "You are good and worthy, and you would make any father proud."

"Not any father. Not mine."

317

"He can't see it but that doesn't mean it isn't there. I see it. I know you are smart, capable, and generous."

"Thank you. I've made it this far in life without his support. I don't need him."

"You have me, for what it's worth," I said.

"It's worth a lot," he said, looking directly into my eyes. "It means more than anything."

I smiled, feeling like I had just won a gold medal. "Good."

"Let's do something we have never done," he said.

I raised an eyebrow. "Dare I even ask?" I teased before remembering this was not an appropriate time to flirt.

He didn't seem to mind. "I want to take you to dinner. A nice dinner."

"When?"

"Tonight," he answered.

"I'm going to have to do a little shopping," I told him.

"Shopping?"

"I brought the one funeral outfit and casual wear. I need something nice to wear for our dinner."

He shook his head. "You don't have to do that. We'll keep it casual."

"Oh no, you don't," I said with a laugh. "You don't get to dangle that carrot and then pull it away. I want to do dinner with you and I want to wear a pretty dress."

"Then, by all means," he said with that familiar smile I had been missing for too long. "Would you like me to help you pick something out?"

"Absolutely not. I want to surprise you. This is an official date, right?"

"It is."

"Then as soon as we are finished with our lunch, I'm afraid I'm going to have to ditch you."

As if the waiter knew exactly when to deliver our meals, they appeared at our table. I was already trying to plan my outfit. There wasn't a lot of shopping to be had in the small, coastal town, but I was confident I could find something. I wanted to knock his socks off. I wanted to make him want me. I wanted to remind him how good we were together before he cut and run.

We got through lunch, which was just as good as he promised it would be. "I'll see you at six," he said when he pulled to a stop in front of my hotel.

"I'll be ready and waiting. Don't stand me up."

He grinned. "I wouldn't even think about it."

I hopped out of the car, went directly to my own rental car, and set off in search of the perfect dress. I hated that I didn't have my expansive selection of dresses from my closet. I reassured myself a new dress was appropriate for the occasion. It was a new start to our relationship. Yes, I was totally getting ahead of myself, but I felt like we had turned a corner.

He was accepting me into his life and I was not going to forget what he said yesterday. He'd introduced me as his girlfriend. I was holding on to that with a white-knuckled grip. I was going to be his girlfriend. At least until he decided otherwise. I knew it was likely said as a defensive mechanism and he probably didn't actually mean it, but a girl could dream.

I would show him what it would be like to be my boyfriend. The moment I thought it, the familiar panic welled up inside me. Commitment was a big C word. I didn't like to use it. I was the one who said we needed to remain friends and here I was, trying to be his girlfriend.

I needed my head examined. Later. For tonight, I wanted to experience what it would be like to be his. I decided to think of it as a trial run. If it worked, great. If it didn't, we could still be friends with an occasional side of sex hopefully.

CHAPTER 51

XANDER

I was probably fucking myself over with this, but I was going to do it anyway. I couldn't resist her.

I thought I was over it. I'd ended things with her, but damn, the woman was stubborn. She didn't take no for an answer, and quite honestly, I was glad she didn't.

The rest of my life was imploding. I wanted to hold on to her for just a little longer. I knew it would never work long term, but having her near right then felt good.

I didn't want to admit I needed her. Technically, I didn't need her in the sense I wouldn't survive without her, but if she was here and offering her company, why not take it? It would ease my misery for a bit. I didn't have to commit to anything. We were having fun. We were friends. Casual friends. Nothing more.

Then why did I introduce her as my girlfriend?

That was a problem to be handled another day. I stepped off the elevator and walked down the quiet hall of her hotel until I came to her room door. I knocked, and when she opened the door, I felt my breath whoosh from my lungs.

"Holy shit," I said, barely managing to get the words out.

She looked down at herself and then me. "I'm not sure if that's a good or bad statement."

"It's a very good statement. Holy shit."

She smiled. "You said that already."

I couldn't believe my eyes. I knew she was beautiful. I knew her body was rockin' but seeing all her curves hugged and plumped in the red dress that was tight in all the right places was an assault on my senses in the best way possible. It was very Jessica Rabbit. All I could think about was stripping the dress from her body.

"You are hot. Gorgeous. I feel privileged to be the man taking you to dinner."

Her pretty smile created a stirring in my gut. If I stepped inside the room, we were going to miss dinner. I'd promised her dinner and I was going to damn well make sure she got to eat. All bets were off after dinner.

"Thank you," she answered with a little extra pink in her cheeks.

"Are you ready?"

"I am."

She grabbed her purse and we headed out. There were few fine dining choices to choose from, but I found one. I put my hand on the small of her back and gently guided her through the restaurant. I realized my chest was puffed out with pride.

Why not? I was with the most beautiful woman in the room. Hell, the state.

We sat down and ordered a glass of wine to go with our appetizer of stuffed mushrooms. "I know I asked you yesterday, but how did you find me?"

"I'm almost afraid to tell you."

"Why?"

Her eyes flashed with mischief. "Because there could have been a crime committed. I would hate to incriminate the other parties involved."

I was intrigued. "Now you have to tell me."

She looked guilty. "I asked my dad for some help."

"How would your dad know where I was?"

She bit her lower lip, her pretty little nose wrinkling. "Your school files."

I raised both brows. "What?"

"I was desperate. I didn't want to spend days calling every hotel in the city."

"Your dad broke into my school file?"

"Not exactly."

I could tell by her reaction there was more to the story. "Evie, what did you do?"

"My dad offered to do it, but when I realized just what I was proposing, I made him give me his password. Then I made him go get coffee while I did the deed."

I couldn't stop smiling. "*You* broke the law?"

"I did."

"To find me?"

"Yes."

"I'm not sure what to say," I said.

"I didn't mean to invade your privacy and I swear my dad had nothing to do with it. It was all me. I forced him into it. I bullied him and guilted him into giving me what I wanted. I swear I didn't look at anything except for your emergency contact."

"I don't think my father's Oregon address was listed on there."

She sighed, slowly shaking her head. "It wasn't. I did a little more digging and then more, and eventually, I found the obituary for Kade."

"I think you missed your true calling. How did you know I was here though?"

She groaned and finished her glass of wine. "I'm going to need another one of these before I can get into that story."

"I'm dying to hear it."

"It may or may not involve more felonies," she muttered.

I laughed, shaking my head. I waved the waiter over and ordered her a fresh drink, along with the special for the night. "All right, you have been given a fresh glass of liquid courage. I'm waiting to hear the story."

She blew out a breath before sucking in another one. "I went to the presentation at your office on Monday."

"I know you didn't find me there."

"No, I didn't. When you didn't show, I went to your house."

I tilted my head to the side. "And you discovered I wasn't there? It seems like an overreaction to enact your super-sleuth skills."

"Oh my god, I cannot believe you are going to make me tell you the whole sordid tale."

"I don't think going by my house is all that sordid."

She picked up her glass and took a long drink before putting it down. "I broke into your house."

"Doubtful," I said nonchalantly.

She shook her head. "No, I really did. I went up the beach stairs."

"The doors were locked."

Her perfect teeth nibbled on her bottom lip once again. "But your window wasn't."

"What window?"

"Kitchen."

"You went in my kitchen window?" I asked a little too loudly.

Her eyes darted around the room. The look of embarrassment on her face told me she wasn't making it up. "I did."

"Wow."

"I was worried about you. I did call—a lot."

"I didn't have my phone," I told her.

"I know. I saw it at the bottom of the pool."

I smirked, shaking my head. "You really were in the house."

"I was. I saw the phone and got very worried. I went in the house. It looked like you disappeared. I was worried."

"You said that," I said, doing my best to hide my smile.

"I'm sorry. I didn't mean to totally invade your privacy. It's just, well, when you didn't answer. I have a very active imagination. I got a little carried away."

"I appreciate the fact you cared enough to commit multiple felonies."

"I didn't snoop," she insisted. "I didn't dig through your drawers or anything weird."

"Good to know."

"This isn't my normal thing," she said, clearly flustered. "I don't stalk men. I don't stalk anyone. I was just—"

"Worried," I finished for her. "You were worried about me and stalked me to try and help me."

"Yes. That."

"Thank you. Sometimes, I can be my own worst enemy. At least that's what I have been told. I'm glad you came."

"I would do it all again," she said firmly. "I'm not trying to pressure you into anything. I just wanted you to know I cared and that I can be a friend. A silent one if you prefer. It's what friends do for one another."

"I'm lucky to call you friend."

"Damn right you are," she said with a bright grin.

"You know, I would not have expected your dad to help you find me."

She laughed. "You and me both, but I have to say, he was very helpful and very understanding. I did tell him about your brother. He empathizes with you. He's the one who convinced me to go to you."

"No way," I said, not believing it a bit.

"Yes, way." She smiled. "He was the one to convince me I had to get pushy. Well, him and then Nelle."

"Then I should thank them both. I'm glad you're pushy."

"Me too," she said with that sexy smile that always hit me right between the legs.

Our meals were delivered, taking my mind off the erection that had sprung to life.

"This is amazing," I said after taking a bite.

"Yes, it is. It's nice to share a dinner with you—while it is still hot."

"I'm glad we decided to come out for dinner," I told her. "I don't think I would have been able to think about food with you wearing that."

"You are too sweet."

"I'm speaking the truth. You look hot."

"Your flattery will get you everywhere," she whispered.

I looked down at her plate, then mine. The meal was great but I was no longer hungry for steak. I was hungry for one thing only.

"Would you like to go back to my room?" I asked. It was a bold question. A question I had no business asking but I would kick myself if I didn't at least try.

"I would love to go back to your room."

My arm shot into the air, calling for the check. When the waiter didn't immediately make his way to our table, I stood up and stuck my hand in the air. I didn't have a minute to spare. I wanted to leave. I wanted her naked and writhing under me. Now. Not in fifteen minutes. Right fucking now.

When I finally got his attention, I quickly paid the bill and practically dragged her out of the restaurant. I was trying to play it cool, I really was, but the woman was too much to resist. I could smell her arousal. At least I believed I could. I smelled her unique scent mingled with the floral perfume she was wearing. It was intoxicating and arousing.

I held her hand as we walked across the lobby of my hotel. I debated taking the stairs to my suite.

"Relax," she whispered when we stepped inside the elevator.

I growled and pressed up against her. Her soft curves rubbed against my body, sending me into an absolute tailspin. "I'm sorry," I breathed.

"For?"

"This," I said a moment before my mouth covered hers.

I ground my hips against her. Her body was held in place with my pelvis holding her against the wall. I heard and felt her soft moans and swallowed them. When the doors slid open, I didn't stop. I couldn't stop.

"Doors," she whispered.

Her word reminded me of where we were. I would have taken her right there if she didn't stop me. "Right, sorry."

"Don't be sorry, just hurry," she said breathlessly.

"You don't have to tell me twice."

I grabbed her hand and dragged her down to the end of the hall to my room. We burst through the door and I dragged her in with me.

"God, I have been dying to get you out of this dress all damn night," I said. "I want you out of it, but I want you in it at the same time. I like looking at you in this."

She smiled, that dangerous twinkle in her eye. It was the look that said she was thinking something naughty. I liked when she was naughty. "I think you might appreciate what's under this," she said coyly.

My dick stood at attention. "You're teasing me."

"This is not a tease. I assure you, I'm a sure thing. Why don't you take a seat on the pretty little couch while I step into the bathroom?"

"Evie, you kill me."

"Oh baby, you haven't seen anything yet."

"Go. Hurry."

She disappeared into the bathroom. I kicked off my shoes and shed my suit jacket before turning off all but the small lamp on the table under the TV. I sat down and waited. My cock strained against my fly. I wasn't going to strip. If I took off my pants, I would pounce on her the moment she stepped out of the bathroom.

CHAPTER 52

EVIE

I told myself I wasn't nervous. There was nothing to be nervous about. I knew he liked my body. He wasn't going to point at the little extra cushioning on my hips that felt extremely exposed and enhanced in the lacy red bit of lingerie I was wearing.

When he invited me to dinner, I'd claimed I needed a dress. I did but then I happened to come across the lingerie and decided to spice things up.

Spicy was one word for it. I fluffed my hair and pulled a few faces in the mirror until I was satisfied I had the perfect sultry pout. I hit the light and opened the door, slowly walking into the small living space with the kitchenette at my right. Xander was sitting in the chair, just as I ordered.

The lights were mostly off and there was soft jazz music streaming through the TV. The man knew how to set a mood. I paused and posed. I watched his expression as he drank in the sight of me wearing the tiny little teddy that had ribbons that crisscrossed over my belly and connected to slightly wider ribbons of lace that acted as a bra. It was definitely on the risqué side.

"Holy fuck," he breathed. "Have you had that on all night?"

I smiled and looked down at the lace. "I have."

"Holy fuck," he breathed again. "I can't move. If I move, I'm going to explode in my pants. Stay there. Don't come any closer. Give me a minute."

I loved that he was so turned on by me. I slowly turned, giving him a good look at the entirety of the outfit, which was really less than a few inches of lace and lots of ribbons.

"You look like you are in pain," I teased.

I ignored his demand to not move any closer. I stepped in front of him, staying just out of reach. His hands gripped the wooden armrests like he was afraid he would fly out of the chair. I ran my hands over my body, sliding one of the ribbons out of the way and giving him a little peek at my nipple.

I was turning myself on. My nipples pebbled under my own touch. I rubbed and teased and heard myself moan.

"Don't stop," he said in a raspy voice.

I moaned, dropping my head back and arching into my hands. I slid one hand over my belly and then between my legs. The lacy triangle felt damp. It was a combination of heat and my own desire. The man had a way of making me feel wet all the time. I lifted my head to watch him watch me. His eyes were heavy-lidded. The desire I saw there was so intense, I felt as if I would spontaneously combust. Or maybe he would.

I needed to touch him. I stepped closer, reaching for the tie he was still wearing. I tugged, jerking his neck forward until I loosened it enough to pull over his head. "You are wearing far too many clothes."

"I agree," he whispered.

I bent forward, letting my breasts hang loose as I began to work at the buttons on his shirt. His hands stayed on the armrests, never once touching me. I could feel him looking. I could feel the heat from his gaze as his eyes roamed over my body. I jerked the shirt up out of his pants and pushed it over his shoulders until he was topless.

I dropped to my knees in front of his chair, settling myself between his legs. His erection was very evident in his pants. I ran my hand over the long length, marveling at the steel rod barely contained in the pants that looked like they would shred.

I carefully undid the button before sliding the zipper down. He let out a breath like he had been holding it inside for hours. His cock sprang free, ripe for the plucking. I wrapped my hand around the shaft and squeezed. He grunted and his body jerked. I could feel the power humming in my hand.

I leaned forward and loved him with my mouth. I licked and sucked until I could feel him on the edge. The tension in his body filled the room with an electric energy that zapped me from head to toe. I felt tingly. I felt electrified and on the edge of my own climax.

He sprang from the chair. I would have fallen on my ass if he didn't grab me and yank my body against his. One minute, I was on my knees and worshipping his cock with my mouth, and the next, I was in his arms with his mouth plundering mine. He was needy and desperate. He carried me into the single bedroom in his suite and dropped me on the bed. He shed his pants and underwear in under five seconds and pounced on me.

His mouth covered mine before tearing away and attacking my neck with teeth and tongue. He was everywhere at once. His hands roughly rubbed over my body as his mouth attempted to keep up. It was an onslaught of wild sensations that left my body in sensory over-load. I writhed beneath him. I tried to run my hands over him, but he was too fast. He was sliding down my body with his mouth until he was at my heated core.

His mouth closed over the lace that covered my entrance. Even without direct contact, it was too much. My body was primed and ready, and the heat from his mouth and the feel of his tongue through the lace were enough to send me spiraling into a blissful abyss of electric heat.

The climax tore through my body. His fingers slid the lace to the side, giving him full access to the sensitive flesh. He lapped at me until I was on the verge of another orgasm. I wasn't sure I would survive the night if he kept up with his pace.

"Oh please," I whispered. I didn't know what I was asking for. Mercy? More? I didn't know.

He did. He rubbed his finger over the tiny, extremely sensitive flesh that sent me into another violent series of spasms as my body erupted again and again.

In a flurry of movement, I felt him peeling away the lace and ribbons. I was helpless to assist him. My body was tingling and vibrating with pure ecstasy. "Damn, woman, you sure know how to please me."

I managed a lazy smile and opened my eyes just enough to see him looking down at me. "I try."

"Try, my ass. I don't think I've ever been so hard. I feel like I have a tree trunk hanging between my legs. I don't want to hurt you."

I opened my legs good and wide. "I'm ready for whatever you want to give me. I'll take it all, every last inch. Show me how much you want me. Show me everything. Make me scream."

He growled before sliding one finger inside me. "You don't know what you're asking for."

"I do," I whimpered, squirming a little as my body clamped down on his finger inside me. "More."

A second finger slid inside my body that was swollen and slick from the first two orgasms. I knew he would give me a third and maybe even a fourth.

"How's that?" he asked.

I opened my legs just a little more. "Don't stop," I whispered.

"Let's make sure you're really ready for me," he said before he worked a third finger inside me.

I cried out with white-hot pleasure. My body stretched and slowly welcomed him inside. I moved my hips up, taking him deeper inside me until I felt his knuckles brushing against my skin. "Yes! I want it all!"

He pulled his fingers out, leaving me feeling empty. The feeling did not last long. He worked the head of his cock inside me. He was right. He was so much bigger than usual. I opened my eyes and looked down my body. He was holding his weight off me with one arm while holding the base of his cock in his other hand.

I watched as the length slowly disappeared inside me. I wasn't ready for the overwhelming sensations of the purest, rawest form of ecstasy. My body swallowed him up, welcoming him with a flood of juices as another orgasm carried me away. I was insatiable.

Walking tomorrow would be interesting. I didn't care. I couldn't get enough of him.

He began to move, adjusting his hips to slide over nerve endings deep inside me that had previously been untouched. "Don't stop," I whispered.

He was lost in the moment. I managed to pry my eyes open long enough to watch him for a few seconds. His face was contorted into what looked like sheer pain. I knew it was painful pleasure. I moaned, shimmying my hips just a little. It was an almost instantaneous reaction from him. He shouted over and over as his back bowed and he blew up deep inside me.

So much power. So much pleasure. I let myself follow him, riding the jerks and spasms of his cock buried deep inside me.

When he collapsed beside me, neither of us spoke. I didn't think it was physically possible to speak. My body was beyond sated. It felt like I had been treated to a luxurious day at the spa with an expert masseuse.

I wasn't sure if he was already asleep, but I wouldn't be surprised. I was barely able to stay awake. I snuggled against him, resting my head on his broad chest. His arms came around me, swallowing me up in his embrace. It felt so right being with him like this.

There was no doubt in my mind that I had absolutely fallen for the man. He was perfect and flawed and I knew he was the right man for me. His stubbornness and belief he was better off alone were not a turnoff for me. In fact, it made me want to get even closer to him. I wanted to crawl into his soul and stay there forever.

I was in trouble. I was falling in love with a man that didn't seem all that interested in loving me back. I told myself it was just his way. He needed a little more time. I could be patient with him. I could give him the time and space he needed to realize we were good for each other. I pushed hard already. I didn't want to push him any harder.

He had to come to the realization on his own. I wasn't sure how I would handle it if he didn't come to the same conclusion I did. I would worry about that later. For now, I was lying in the arms of a man who seemed to care for me a great deal. I would take it. I would hold on to every precious minute I got with him.

"Blanket?" he murmured.

"I'm good," I told him.

I didn't want to move. I didn't think I *could* move at that point.

CHAPTER 53

XANDER

Waking up with Evie's soft body draped over mine was probably one of the best feelings in the world. It was a little strange to me. I was not the kind of guy who liked the postcoital cuddling and the sleepovers with a woman snuggled against me.

I liked space in my bed. I liked to stretch out without worrying about another body being in my way. With Evie, I found myself clinging to her. In the middle of the night, I would wake up and find her just to pull her next to me.

I liked feeling her warm breath brush across my chest. I liked hearing her steady breathing. I didn't even mind the little bit of drool I could feel on my bare chest. It was all part of who she was. As it turned out, I really liked who she was.

It was dangerous. I knew it was a huge risk, but I felt myself falling for her a little more every time I spent time with her. She was so much more than a beautiful woman to me. She was becoming my other half. She was the person I wanted to talk to about anything that excited me and things that happened during my day.

What was supposed to be a casual relationship was morphing into something much more real. I had real feelings for her. I wasn't sure what to think about it or how to process it. I didn't want to do anything that pushed her away. I knew that for sure. I wanted to try to make things work between us.

"You're awake," she murmured, lifting her head and wiping her mouth.

"I am. Just for a couple minutes."

"Was I snoring?"

"Nope."

She turned her face to look up at me. "Are you lying?"

I leaned forward to kiss the tip of her nose. "No."

She settled back against my chest. "Good."

"Are you hungry?"

"I could use some coffee."

"I'll order room service. Do you want some fruit? Toast? A big breakfast spread?"

She pulled away, resting her head on the pillow next to mine. "I'm cool with whatever you want."

I turned my head to look at her. "I will tell you what I want, but it doesn't come from room service."

She slapped at my chest. "You have to feed me first. I'm not even sure I can move."

"You can move, baby. Trust me. You can move."

"Food," she said with a laugh before crawling out of bed and walking nude to the bathroom.

I ordered room service for us, suddenly hungry. Then I stepped out on the balcony in just my underwear and inhaled the fresh air. It was a little chilly, but it was wonderfully refreshing.

"There you are," Evie said. She stepped behind me, wrapping her arms around me and resting her face against my back.

"I like the air here," I told her.

"Isn't it the same air?"

"It feels cleaner."

She pulled away from me. I turned to look at her in the fluffy white robe that had been hanging on the back of the door.

"If you say so," she said.

"Room service will be here soon. I'm going to grab a quick shower."

"Okay."

The atmosphere shifted between us. It wasn't that it was an awkward morning-after scenario. It was the upcoming talk. I knew there were some things that needed to be said. I wasn't looking forward to the saying of those things.

When I walked out of the bedroom, she was sitting at the small table in the room with several plates of food. "It smells good," I commented.

She sipped her coffee. "It is *so* good."

I sat down and lifted the dome from my plate. The fluffy pancakes, scrambled eggs, and crispy bacon all looked amazing. I dumped syrup over the pancakes and took the first bite.

"When is your flight?" I asked casually.

"Three. What about you? Did you buy a round trip?"

I couldn't look at her. "No."

"When are you going back?"

"I'm not."

Time froze. "You're not?"

"No."

"What about your business? Your house? Your boat and car?"

I shrugged. "The house is being closed up and will be going on the market soon. I'm mooring the boat at a marina. It will stay there. I'll call someone to get the car."

"And your business? All the work you've been doing the last few weeks. What about that?"

"I don't know. I can work from anywhere." I finally forced myself to look at her. The pain and disappointment I saw there hurt me.

"Why?" she asked.

"I can't go back there. It's tainted. Everywhere I look in my house, I see him. I remember the exact spot he stood on the patio. I remember him sitting in one of the chairs by the pool. I remember him sleeping in that bedroom."

"I understand that, but that is part of grief. Those reminders don't have to be bad things."

"It's like living with a ghost. I can't be there."

"What will you do?"

It was a good question. A great question. It was too bad I didn't have an answer. "I don't know. I haven't thought that far ahead."

"Maybe you just need a week or two to process all of this," she suggested.

"I've processed it," I told her. "I don't want to go back."

"Do you plan to stay here? With your father?"

I shuddered at the thought. "No. I don't know. There are memories here as well, but they're not nearly as sharp as the ones from my house."

She pushed her plate away. My news had stolen her appetite apparently. "I don't know what to say."

"Honestly, neither do I. But I can't be there. It's not my home anymore."

"You could buy a new house. With your money, you could buy any house you wanted."

"True, but I've been doing a lot of thinking. I'm not sure I want to be there anymore. I'm not sure about anything anymore."

She was quiet for a while. "I get it. I understand you are going through something. Can I ask you to do one thing?"

"What is it?"

"Don't make any rash decisions just yet. Don't sell your house. I'm not saying you need to come back right away but give yourself some time."

"I'll think about it."

"My life is in San Diego," she said. "Not that it matters, but I guess you will know where to find me if you ever want to talk."

"Evie, this doesn't have to end between us," I blurted out.

"I live there. My father is there. My job is there. That's where I need to be. I understand you don't want to be there. I won't ask you to do anything you don't want to do."

"I'll make this work," I told her. "I don't want this to be over. I want you to be a part of my life."

She offered a small smile. "You know where to find me."

"I do."

I wasn't sure how I would make it work. I had heard all the stories about long-distance relationships and the fact they rarely worked. I couldn't imagine it working with the newness of our relationship. We didn't even technically have a relationship. At least not one we had discussed or figured out. It all felt very fluid, like we were just going with the flow.

She checked the time. "I should probably get back to my hotel. I want to shower before I go to the airport."

"I'll take you," I told her.

"To the airport?"

"Your hotel," I answered.

"Thanks."

She walked into the bedroom and closed the door behind her, a clear signal she didn't want me in there.

I'd fucked up a good thing. I knew it but I couldn't change it. Well, I could change it but that would mean going back home and facing memories I didn't want to deal with. Not yet.

I drove her to her hotel, and instead of leaving her at the front, I followed her up to her room.

"Can I wait?" I asked when she grabbed a change of clothes to head into the bathroom.

She offered a smile. "Yes, of course."

I found myself pacing the room. This was a pivotal moment in my life. I could feel it, and while I was pulled toward the option of going back to California, my mind was made up. I couldn't go back. I knew what waited for me there and I didn't want to deal with it.

"Feel better?" I asked when she came out of the bathroom looking fresh and clean and perfectly delectable. I couldn't touch her. Once I got started, I wouldn't be able to stop, and she would miss her flight.

"Much better," she said with a sigh. We were both trying too hard. It was stilted and awkward and I didn't know how to fix it.

337

She grabbed her suitcase and began to pack.

"Do you have events this weekend?" I asked her. I was trying to make small talk. I was trying to hold on to a connection to her. I could practically see the tenuous connection between us fraying with every passing second.

"I'm not sure. I cleared my schedule, but I might check in on things."

"Will you call me when you get home?"

She glanced at me over her shoulder. "Will you answer?"

I deserved that. "Yes."

She sighed, dropping the shirt she had been folding into the suitcase and turning to face me. "I am not going to ask you to come home, but I have to ask one more time. Are you sure this is what you want to do?"

"It is. I can't go back there."

She gave a brief nod. "Okay."

She turned back around and finished packing. I watched as she did the usual sweep of the room to make sure she didn't forget anything. I couldn't bring myself to leave. I should leave. I should go back to the hotel and let her go.

"Are you flying out of Portland?" I asked, stalling for time. I already knew the answer.

"Yes, and I should probably get a move on."

I stared at her, drinking in the sight of her, committing every detail to memory. I had a sinking feeling it could be the last time I saw her. I walked to her and pulled her into my arms. I held her for several minutes. Neither of us spoke. There was so much to say and yet nothing to say.

"Call me," I said when I finally released her.

"I will."

I grabbed her suitcase while she grabbed her purse and laptop case. I walked her to her car and waved as she pulled away. I stood staring at the back of the car until I couldn't see it anymore. She was gone. Just like that, I was all alone again.

With a heavy sigh and a heavier heart, I walked back to my car and drove back to the hotel I was calling home. I had no idea what I was going to do. I felt adrift. I was lost at sea with no idea where land was. I didn't know where I was going to land next or where I wanted to be. Living in town with my father was not an option. The place was too small, and we would end up running into each other.

Oddly enough, I ran away from home to get away from the memory of Kade but I didn't want to leave Oregon because it was where he was. Once I left, it was over. He was well and truly gone. In that moment, I felt completely alone. I went back to my hotel room and looked around at the dishes still sitting on the table. I could smell her in the room.

Maybe I would change rooms. I didn't have any more room in my head for memories and regrets. I wasn't sure I could deal with constant reminders of someone else I'd lost.

CHAPTER 54

EVIE

The plane jerked as the wheels hit the runway, signaling I was back home after a minor delay in Portland. I was anxious to get home and to the safety of my apartment. I needed my safe place. I wanted to be wrapped up in the things that made me feel safe and comfortable. It was hard to leave him behind. He said he wanted to make it work, but that was impossible.

My life was in California. My work kept me busy. It wouldn't make a lot of sense to fly back and forth to Portland or wherever he ended up going. I'd fought for him. I'd tried. Xander had some things to work through and there was nothing more I could do to help him do that.

I texted Nelle to let her know the plane landed. She was already waiting for me.

"Hi," she greeted me when I made my way to the baggage collection area.

"Hi."

"You don't look happy."

"It's a long story."

"I took the night off. We'll go back to your place and you can tell me everything over a glass or five of wine."

"Yes, please," I groaned.

Thirty minutes later, we were sitting on my couch, shoes off, candles burning, and full wine glasses in hand. "Tell me what happened."

I said a phrase that was becoming a little too familiar. "He's gone."

"Will you please stop saying that?" she snapped. "I know he isn't dead, but the way you say it makes it sound like he is."

"He's not coming back," I clarified.

She shook her head, clearly not getting it. "What do you mean?"

"He is selling his house. He isn't coming back to California."

"What?!" she shrieked. "Why? Where is he going? What did you do to the man?"

"I didn't do anything," I retorted. "Apparently when he fled here like a thief in the night over the weekend, that was his plan. He has no intention of coming back."

"Why? He has everything here."

"I know," I said. "That's what I tried to tell him. He doesn't want to be here with memories of his brother haunting him. The last place he saw his brother was here and it haunts him."

She slowly nodded. "I get that, but you would think he would want those memories."

"I guess not everyone likes to live with a ghost."

"What does that mean for you guys?" she softly asked the question I had yet to figure out the answer to.

"I don't know. He says he wants to make it work but we both know it won't. He doesn't even know where he is going to land. He's kind of lost and drifting."

"Why don't you go with him?"

I almost choked on his wine. "Well, for starters, he didn't invite me. Then there's the fact I work here. My job that I have worked very hard at is here. My dad is here. My life is here. I'm not running from any ghosts."

"But I thought we established you were into this guy," she said. "Isn't he worth fighting for?"

I rolled my eyes. "Uh uh. No way. You don't get to put that on me

341

again. I fought for him. I chased him down, after breaking several laws by the way. I did what I could. I was there for him. I let him know I was here. I have done everything short of shackle myself to him and I have a tiny bit of dignity left. I'm not going to do that."

"He's a stubborn guy," she reasoned. "He needs a little more convincing."

"I don't think he has it in him. He's made up his mind. He knows exactly what he is leaving behind."

"Maybe he didn't ask you to go with him because he didn't think you would want to," she suggested.

"I don't want to go with him. I have a job. A job I love. A job I have worked very hard to get to where I am at. I am not going to give all of that up."

She sipped her wine. I could practically see the little wheels in her brain turning. "If you give up everything to be with him and he wants you to be with him, I don't think you need to worry about working. He's ridiculously rich. Why would you work?"

"I am not going to mooch off him," I said.

"You wouldn't be mooching. It's a couple thing. Do you mean to tell me if things work out, you would insist on paying half the rent?"

"Well, no, but that would be different."

"How?"

"Because we would be a couple," I answered and then shook my head. "No, I don't even know if I could do it then. I just don't know."

"He has enough money to ensure your grandkids wouldn't have to work. You cannot tell me that isn't just a little appealing. I'm not saying you are after him for his money, but this is the real world. It's natural to want a man that can take care of you. A man that works hard and is financially secure is becoming harder and harder to find. I don't think you want to let this one get away."

"Yes, financial security is a bonus, but it isn't a motivating factor. I make decent money and I like what I do. I love working. I wouldn't want to quit."

"Here's a little secret for you," she said as she leaned forward. "People like to party. Every state, every country, people party."

"What's your point?"

"You could start your own company and be a party planner wherever you are. I bet your lovely man would be more than happy to make a financial investment in your company. This might be your chance to do the one thing I know you have wanted for a long time."

"What would that be?"

"To start your own company," she answered.

I did want to start my own company. "But my reputation is here in southern California. I have developed connections here. If I had to go somewhere else, it would be starting over. I would have nothing. No clients. No reputation. No anything."

"Everyone has to start somewhere."

"But I did already start. My dream is to start my own company here."

She waved a hand. "If you go somewhere else, you wouldn't have to compete with your current employer. You wouldn't have to worry about noncompete clauses and all that crap."

She had a good point. "I don't know. I went up there to be with him. I assumed he would be coming back either with me or shortly after. I never expected to be presented with something that could completely alter my entire life."

"Opportunities rarely send an advanced warning. They drop in your lap when you least expect it. This could be a huge opportunity for you."

"I think we are getting way ahead of ourselves," I said. "He hasn't even suggested we sail around the world or move to Bermuda or wherever he is planning on going. He could be done with this. It was kind of weird, but when we said goodbye, I got the feeling it was a *goodbye* goodbye. He said the right words, but I saw it in his eyes."

She popped out her bottom lip. "I'm sorry. I hope that isn't the case. I know he cares about you and you are madly in love with him."

"I am—" I was going to say I wasn't, but that would be a lie. "I am. I'm so screwed. I fell in love with a guy at the worst possible time in his life. I sure know how to pick them."

"Sometimes, things look bleakest just before they shine bright."

I stared at her. "Did you read that on the back of a magazine or something?"

"Nope, I just made it up. Well, it's a twist on something else I've heard, but it's still real. This might be your moment. This might be the moment you change your life. You might be staring at your crossroads."

"My crossroads?" I questioned.

"Yes. Go left, and it's the road you know. The road that keeps you here and at your job. The road on the right takes you down the bumpy road with Xander. It's filled with uncertainty, but it includes him."

"When you put it like that, I'm going to say I'm leaning left."

She nodded and licked her lips. "I get it."

The way she said it told me she didn't get it. "You have to tell me what's on your mind. I can see you have something you want to say. Just get it off your chest."

"Okay, I'll say it. You love your job more than Xander."

My mouth dropped open. "What? That's harsh!"

She offered a smug look. "Is it true?"

"I don't know. I can't make that kind of a decision. I don't have all the facts. I don't know if it's something he's even interested in. I'm not going to invite myself into his life. Not now."

"Your loss," she said.

It would be my loss but there wasn't much I could do about it. He had his own idea about the future and I was sure I was not part of it. "I know and I'm not looking forward to that loss, but I can't push him. I don't want to push him. What kind of relationship would that be? He would eventually feel like I was bullying him into being with me. That's not really how I want to win a man."

She shrugged. "I think you have to chase what you want. Sometimes, you have to bonk the object of your affection over the head. I think the cavemen were on to something."

That brought a smile to my face. "That is quite the image."

"I should probably get going. I need to catch up on my laundry."

"Don't lie," I teased. "You're going home to watch Vampire Diaries."

She giggled. "You know me so well."

"You are so predictable. How many times have you seen that stupid show?"

"I will never grow tired of watching my man," she said with that familiar dreamy look on her face whenever she spoke of the blue-eyed man that had captured her heart some ten years ago.

"Thank you for picking me up."

"You're welcome. I know I can't tell you what to do because you are not going to listen, but I would strongly suggest you call him. Drop hints. Make it clear you are his to do with as he pleases."

"Uh, not a chance in hell," I told her.

"Fine, then drop subtle hints that you would consider leaving everything behind to be with him."

I rolled my eyes. "You just don't give up."

"Nope, because I know this guy will make you very happy."

"He hasn't given me that idea," I retorted.

"He will."

I playfully pushed her out the door before closing it behind her. I leaned against the door, resting my forehead against it. I wanted to do what she said but I wasn't that brave. Telling him how I felt would make me vulnerable. I had already put myself out there once. While he was nice about it, he didn't necessarily say much.

He never invited me to stay with him. I knew him well enough to know if he wanted me to stay with him, he would have asked. We had spent a wonderful night together but that was all I could ask of him. I couldn't push myself on him. I had some pride.

CHAPTER 55

XANDER

I slowly pushed the lever, opening the throttle on my new boat. It was a ridiculous splurge and nothing that I needed but I wanted it. It was one of those things that just came to me in the middle of the night. Evie had teased me about my old boat. She was right. I could buy anything I wanted. I loved boats. I used to look at some of the other boats in the marina and get boat envy. Why was I envious when I could go and buy exactly what I wanted? And that was exactly what I did.

The wind blew across my face, sending a cold chill over me. I was still adjusting to the cooler weather. Not adjusting. I didn't want to adjust. I wasn't staying in Oregon. I was going to move on. I just wasn't sure where. I felt like a man without a home. Technically, I did have a home, but it didn't feel like my home.

I thought about Evie as the boat slowly bobbed up and down with a gentle sway. We had only spoken a few times since she left. There were plenty of texts between us, but it wasn't the same. I could feel us drifting apart.

Not seeing her was difficult. I wanted her in my arms. In my bed.

The idea of not seeing her again was weighing heavily on my mind. I wanted her, but I didn't want to be in California. She loved her work. I couldn't possibly ask her to leave it behind. There was a huge divide between us and I didn't know how to fix it. No, not true. I knew how to fix it, but I didn't want to do that. I wanted the best of both worlds. I wanted my cake and my ice cream too.

My phone began to ring. I patted the pockets of the cargo pants I was wearing until I found the thing. "Hello?" I answered, hoping it would be Evie.

It wasn't. "Where are you?" Charlie's voice came through loud and clear.

I sighed, shaking my head. It was the same fucking question he asked me every single day. He called me every day, and every day, it was the same conversation. "I'm out on my boat."

"Head in," he ordered.

"Why would I do that?"

"Because I'm sitting on the dock waiting for you."

I didn't know why, but I turned to look behind me in the general direction of the marina. I couldn't see the marina, but I was trying to picture him there. "What dock?" I questioned.

"The dock from which you left," he said dryly.

"In Oregon?"

"Yes. Holy shit, did you lose a few brain cells or what? Get your ass back here. We are going to talk face to face."

"Are you really here or are you just fucking with me?"

"I'm really here. Get your ass over here and you'll see for yourself."

I grinned, happy to lay eyes on him. "I'll be there in fifteen minutes or so."

"Hurry your ass up."

I slid the phone back in my pocket and hit the throttle. I was looking forward to seeing a friendly face. I truly didn't realize how much I missed my old life until he said he was there. I pulled into my reserved slip, and sure enough, there he was.

I shut off the engine and quickly tied up the boat before climbing onto the dock. "I have a lot of questions but let me say it sure is good to see you."

"Bullshit. If it was good to see me, you wouldn't be holed up in this tiny place. You would be back in San Diego where you belong."

"But you are here now," I said, choosing to ignore his comment.

"What's this?" he asked and nodded his head at the boat.

"Um, well, we call it a boat," I said with lots of sarcasm.

"Don't be an asshole. Did you buy this?"

"I didn't steal it."

He frowned. "I'm glad to see you think this is all funny."

"I don't think it's funny."

"You bought a new boat? Or did you rent it?"

I looked at the boat in question. "I bought it."

"Why?"

"Why not? There's some great fishing out here. Do you want to go out?"

He shrugged. "You may as well show me since I'm here. You're not going to get rid of me until we talk."

"We are talking. Come on. I've got extra poles already on the boat."

He climbed aboard. "Damn, this is nice."

"Thanks."

"You splurged," he said with surprise. "A lot."

"I know. I saw it and decided I wanted it."

"It's very unlike you," he commented.

"I'll grab us a couple of beers," I said.

I jogged downstairs, grabbed two cold beers from the fridge, and headed back up. Charlie was checking out the boat, running his hand over the control panel.

"Nice," he said.

"Thanks."

I fired it up and headed out. I found a place to set anchor and throw our lines in the water. I settled in one of the chairs that resembled barstools. Charlie was in the other. I knew he was there to lecture me. I was ready for it.

"Want to tell me why you're really here?" I asked.

"I would think that would be clear."

"You think I should be back in San Diego," I said.

"Yes."

"Are you taking a few days off?"

He grunted. "You could say that."

"What does that mean?"

"Look, I know you're going through some shit and I've tried to give you some time. I don't know if that was the right thing to do. I think I have given you too much time. I should have stepped in earlier."

"Stepped in? Is this an intervention?"

"I think we are past that stage," he muttered.

"Then what brings you up here? I don't get the feeling you're here for a friendly visit."

He let out a long breath. "I'm hoping I could appeal to your good sense," he said.

"My good senses are fine," I told him. "I'm embarking on a new stage in my life."

"What about the rest of us?"

I shrugged. "Why does what I do matter? I'm not asking you to do anything. This is what I have to do."

"Your design for the new rudder system was one of the hottest topics in our world. My company beefed up our maintenance and install teams. We ordered the tools and equipment that would be needed to retrofit the older ships. All we were waiting for were the orders. We knew they would come once you gave your presentation. We already had a few companies in line, ready to send us their ships to be outfitted with your new design. And then you bailed. You left all of us hanging."

"I didn't mean to cause anyone any trouble," I told him, feeling the bite of his anger.

"No, I know you didn't. That's not how you are. You are generous and responsible, and you have always thought about others."

"And you are saying I'm not doing that now?"

He didn't immediately answer, which told me that was exactly what he was saying. "I'm saying I'm grateful to you for everything you have done for me. Not just for me, but my entire crew. My bosses have gotten very rich because of your designs."

"Because you have become an expert at building them," I pointed out.

"I have and that has made me a lot of money. I'm only an expert because you let me into your head. You explained it all to me. I wouldn't be where I was without you. You made it possible for me to get my job and then rise in the ranks. I had inside information and that made me valuable."

I frowned. "I did not make you valuable. You are valuable all on your own. I'm just the guy that sends you an idea. You make it come to life."

"Not just me. A lot of guys are involved in that process."

"I'm not sure what you're trying to say. Why beat around the bush? Spit it out."

"I'm saying I've got a lot of guys that were depending on the work that was going to be coming in. We've got some stuff to keep them busy for the next thirty days or so, but if we don't get any new contracts, I have to let them go."

I slowly wound in my line. "You're saying I am to be blamed for those people losing their jobs in a month?"

"I don't want to put it on your shoulders, but it is mostly where the blame belongs. You got me hyped about that retrofit. You got the entire shipping world hyped. Everyone knew it was going to be good. Everyone was ready to jump on it the moment you made it official. Everyone was just waiting for the moment you made it available. Without you, a wonderful idea dies."

"I'm sure you could pick up where I left off," I told him.

He scoffed. "I would like to think I could, but I can't. I might be able to finagle something similar, but it wouldn't be a Xander Holland design. People trust you. They trust your name. They don't want the grease monkey presenting shit to them."

"You are not a grease monkey," I retorted.

"I am and I'm proud of it. I fix. I don't design. That's your half of this very lucrative relationship we had going. I'm going to be fine whether you come back or not. I have plenty of work, but the extra crew? They don't. They are going to be the ones going back to the unemployment office."

"I'm sorry," I told him. "I didn't mean to disrupt your life or theirs. What I'm doing is about me. I don't think I can handle thinking about what is best for anyone else right now."

"You don't have to worry about what's best for them, but you do need to think about the ripple effects your decisions have. You walk away from your company, assuming that's what you are doing, and the dominoes start to fall."

"I'm not walking away from my company," I told him.

"Are you sure about that? When is the last time you checked in with anyone?"

"They know I am taking a sabbatical. The company isn't going under. The designs are there. All they have to do is sell the damn things."

He was quiet for several minutes. "Man, you are really struggling, aren't you?"

"Why do you say that?"

"Dude, you abandoned your life. That is some crazy shit. That's the kind of thing someone does when they're having some kind of break-down. I'm not saying it's bad. I'm saying I'm here. I can help you through this."

I groaned and cast my line into the water again. "You sound like Evie."

"The two people in your life that are closest to you are telling you the same thing. That's pretty telling, don't you think? Shouldn't you maybe give what we are saying just a little consideration?"

"I get it. I know I left a few people in the lurch. I'll send them all checks. I'll compensate everyone for their time or whatever. This is about me figuring out what works for me."

In the back of my mind, I couldn't get the image of guys going home to their families and telling them the new job they just got was gone. I didn't want to be the cause of someone's pain. I didn't want to dump a bunch of stress on a guy just trying to do right by his family.

I had a feeling Charlie knew that, which was why he told me. He was tugging at my heartstrings. It was nothing short of a miracle that he didn't pull out pictures of crying kids to drive home the point.

My choices had consequences. This was one of the downsides to being wealthy and owning a company. It wasn't just me I had to worry about.

CHAPTER 56

EVIE

I couldn't shake the heavy feeling on my heart and mind. I missed Xander. Each day he stayed away served as confirmation our relationship was not what I thought it was.

He had his own life. He was making plans and moving on. His plans did not include me. I did believe he felt something for me, but it wasn't enough to bring him back to me.

"You look like you haven't been sleeping," my father said.

I looked across the table and offered a small and what I hoped was a reassuring smile. "I've been working a lot."

"I don't think that's the reason for your lack of sleep. If anything, you would sleep like a baby after a long day at work."

"I have a lot on my mind," I said with a sigh.

He sipped his tea. I could never understand how he could drink hot tea on a hot day. "Do you want to tell me what happened? You've been so busy—or maybe you've been avoiding me—you never told me if you found Xander."

"I found him," I said. My mind flashed back to the moment I found him at the funeral. Then to the night in the hotel.

"I'm going to go out on a limb here and guess things didn't go well."

"They went fine."

"Then why do you look like your world is caving in on you?" he asked.

I studied his face. "Why are you asking? You don't even like him."

He smirked, sipping his tea. "I don't like him. My opinion of him hasn't changed."

"Then we don't have to talk about this," I told him. "I cannot stand fighting with you right now. I don't have the energy."

"I'm your father. I care about you. I want to know what's bothering you. You can talk to me about your problems."

I took a bite of the pie I'd ordered after our lunch. I was eating my feelings and I didn't give a shit what that meant. Chocolate cream pie was exactly what I needed. "All right, I'll tell you but please don't judge me."

"You have my word," he said.

"I found him. I went to the funeral with him. His father and him have a horrible relationship. It was sad and crushed my soul to see him as an outsider at his own brother's funeral. He didn't make it through the whole thing. He chose to go back to his hotel by himself. I had to let him go."

He looked pained. "I'm sorry. I'm sorry for him. No one should go through that."

"The following day, he did seem to rebound a little. We explored the town and enjoyed a nice lunch, followed by an even better dinner."

His knowing smile left me blushing a little. "It sounds like you two enjoyed your time together."

"We did."

"Then why do you look like hell?"

I scowled at him. "Dad, you are not supposed to say that to a woman."

"You have circles under your eyes and you look exhausted. What happened?"

"He didn't come home to San Diego. He isn't coming home. Everything I thought we had is slowly fading away. He says he wants to have a relationship with me, but I can feel it slipping away. I'm busy and he has found things to do to occupy his time. The few times we do talk, the conversations are getting shorter and feel more stilted. I know it's only a matter of time before it fades away completely. We didn't have a solid foundation to begin with. There is nothing holding us together."

"You are really struggling with this," he said.

I had to fight back the tears. "I am. I don't expect you to understand or empathize. I suppose this is the part where you tell me you told me so. You can say it, but don't say anything bad about Xander. He is a good man, a very good man. He can't help the baggage he's been forced to carry around. He handles it the best way he can."

"I haven't said that."

"But you are thinking it."

"I'm thinking I see my little girl struggling. I can see how much you care about him. I am never going to be the man's biggest cheerleader, but clearly, you are. My allegiance is to you. I see you are hurting. I don't want you to hurt."

The tears were becoming harder to fight off. "Thanks, Dad."

"I think I have to concede in this battle. You are happier with him than you are without him. That means I have to accept your choice in men. Although I will struggle with it, I'm not the one that's in a relationship with him. I'm here for you. I want you to be happy. As your father, I want what is best for you."

"Thank you," I told him, and this time, I didn't stop the tears. "It means a lot to have your support. I don't know if it is going to be needed now. I think it's coming to an end. All that anger and arguing for nothing, I guess."

He released a small laugh. "I don't think it was for nothing. I'd like to think I learned from it."

"What did you learn?"

He looked at me and smiled. "That you aren't my little girl anymore."

"I'm still your little girl," I insisted.

"You will always be my little girl in one sense, but you don't need me guiding you and bossing you around. Like you said before, you have grown into a beautiful woman with a good head on her shoulders. I have to trust you to do what is best for you. We may not always agree but I will always support you."

My heart felt a little broken. I finally had my father's support and now it all seemed for nothing. "Thank you. It does mean a lot to me to know you trust me. I won't always make the right decisions. I'll be happy to have your help and advice."

"You will have it."

"Even if it involves Xander or another former student you don't like?" I teased.

He groaned, shaking his head. "Yes. I am not going to say I'll like it, but I will be there for you."

I blew out a breath. "I feel better. I'm glad we got to talk."

"You don't look like you feel better. You still look like you have the weight of the world on your shoulders."

"I just feel like I'm losing him."

"It's been a long time since I've been in a relationship," he said with a wistful look on his face. "I remember when I found out your mother was not going to grow old with me. I remember that feeling of just pure devastation. The two situations are not the same, but I think you really care about this man. Dare I say love him?"

"I don't know," I answered honestly. "I'm so confused. I think I do but then I question whether or not it is the real thing."

"But you are torn apart about the idea of not seeing him again. You are devastated by the thought of not being with him. That tells me it's real."

"I'm not sure if that makes me feel better or worse. In the end, the outcome is the same. I have lost him. I know that. Part of me thinks he might eventually come back but what if it's too late? What if there has been too much time apart?"

"Time won't matter if this is real," he advised.

"I think I am worried because we haven't really talked about what this is."

"I don't think you need to put words to everything. That's something women like to do. Men aren't always going around looking for a label to slap on something they are feeling in the moment. They just do it. You put pressure on yourself when you try to identify what it is you are feeling."

I heard my laugh escape my mouth and quickly slapped my hand over my face. "You sound so... I don't know."

He shook his head. "That's exactly what I mean."

I giggled again. "I'm sorry. I can't help it. I like things neat and tidy. I need to know what I'm dealing with."

"I get it. You want to know. Have you thought about asking?"

I chewed my lower lip. "No. I can't ask him that."

He laughed. "You are a direct person. It's a simple question. Ask him if he wants to be with you."

"It is not simple."

"It is. You'll rip the bandage off. You'll know one way or another. If he wants to be with you, then you guys have to figure out what comes next. If he doesn't want to be with you—and he would be a fool not to —then you move on. You start to heal your broken heart and you find another man that is worthy of you."

Even thinking about moving on hurt my heart. "You're right. I think I know what to do, but to actually do it freaks me out a little."

"Let me give you a piece of advice that someone once told me a long time ago. When you wake up in the morning, do you want to think about what you *should* have done? Or do you want to wake up in the morning and feel that sense of calm and confidence that goes with knowing you have done all you could do?"

"Well, obviously the latter," I answered.

He shrugged a shoulder. "I guess you know what to do."

"Thank you," I told him. "I'm glad we're speaking again. I don't like you being mad at me."

"I wasn't necessarily mad," he answered.

"You were angry with my choices. I get it. We will learn from this and move forward."

"All I ask is you don't start hanging out at biker bars. Do not bring home a man with leather and chains. I can handle a lot, but that might be pushing it."

"What about a rock star?" I teased.

He groaned. "I'm old, and you are trying my nerves."

"Thanks, Dad. I appreciate your wisdom. I better get a move on. I have to meet with a client and I expect it to be a long meeting."

"Take care of yourself," he said. "Don't let this eat you up. Find a way to get your answers and then move forward."

I got up from the table. He stood as well. I gave him a hug. "I will."

"Please reach out if you need an ear to bend. No matter what happens, I'll support you."

"I will. I've got an event Saturday. I'll call you on Sunday."

"Take care of yourself," he said as I walked out.

I got in my car and released a long breath. I was so glad we were back on track with our relationship. After seeing the relationship between Xander and his father, I knew how lucky I was to have a dad that loved me. I was not going to take him for granted. We would have our differences, but I wasn't ever going to let that happen again.

Now that I knew what to do, I just had to get the balls to actually do it. I was a straight shooter, but in this situation, I was terrified. I was worried about what his answer would be. I knew what I wanted but I didn't want to put myself out there and let him stomp all over me. No matter how confident I was, I still had my own hang-ups and being rejected by a man like Xander was one of them.

Xander was gorgeous. He was wealthy, and whether he chose to believe it or not, he was a good man. Women would line up for the chance to be with him. Those little insecurities I felt had been creeping up on me all week.

They were making it difficult for me to believe there was a future for me and Xander.

CHAPTER 57

XANDER

I walked out of the airport, and the California sun immediately warmed my skin. I didn't think I would ever be back, but here I was. Charlie's words had hit home. I needed to do something to fix the mess I created. I called earlier to have a car waiting for me at the airport. Charlie didn't know I was coming. I wanted to surprise him like he'd surprised me.

I was dropped off at the massive building where he worked. Thankfully, security recognized me and let me in. Charlie was not on the floor, but he was in his office, which worked out great for me. I knocked once before letting myself in.

"Excuse me," he said with irritation before he looked up and saw me. He wore a shocked look on his face. "Holy shit."

"I'll take that as a good holy shit."

"You're back!"

I held up a hand. "No. I'm here to see you."

"Oh. I'm afraid to ask why. Do I dare ask you to sit?"

"I'm going to anyway," I quipped.

I sat down and looked around this office. It was small, dark, and filled with books covered with greasy fingerprints.

"What's going on?" he asked, getting right to the point.

"I thought about what you said to me," I told him. "I'm here to fix it."

"I said a lot to you. I think you're going to need to be more specific."

"About your crew," I clarified. "You are right. I left you and them in a lurch. That wasn't cool. I want to try and make it better."

"Does that mean you're going to present your design to the shipping world?"

I winced. "No."

"Then what? I think you might have missed the entire point of our conversation. I wanted you to get back in the saddle."

"I'm not ready to do it right now, but that doesn't mean I won't eventually do it."

He sighed, shaking his head. "I'm glad you're considering it, but I have to say that doesn't do me a lot of good right now. Those guys out there aren't going to feed their families with *eventually*. I'm sitting on my ass in here doing nothing just so I have work for at least one or two guys to do."

"I get it. I know things are not great right now. I'm going to pay your payroll for the month. Keep them on. I don't know if you want them to deep clean the shop or organize bolts but keep them on. I'm covering their wages."

"I can't ask you to do that."

"You are not asking. I'm offering. No, I am doing it. This is how I am going to fix the problem I created."

"Xander, I never intended for you to do that. I only wanted to explain to you the ramifications of your decisions. You are not on the hook for this."

"I am on the hook. I've already talked with my accountant and the funds will be transferred to your business account to be distributed as you see fit."

"But how do you know how much?"

I winked. "I know people who know people, and when the situation was explained, no one was fighting the influx of cash."

"Thank you. Honestly, I do appreciate this but more importantly, those men will appreciate this. It's not a long-term solution but I hope you are willing to talk about what that looks like."

I nodded. "I am considering some different options. I am not willing to commit to anything, but you will be the first to know when I figure something out."

"Good. Will you be staying in town?"

I shrugged. "I don't know."

"Are you going home?"

"I am going to see Evie," I answered.

He smiled. "Gee, I'm surprised."

"She's a lot prettier than you."

"Are you going to stay?" he asked the question again.

"I don't think so. I don't feel like this is home anymore."

"What about your house?"

"I haven't decided."

"I'm glad you're back, even if it's only for a few days. Don't do anything rash. Not yet. Enjoy the weekend with your woman. I know she will be more persuasive than I could ever be."

That had me smiling. "That's for sure. Then again, I've been absent and neglectful. I'm not sure how happy she will be to see me."

"Does she know you're here?"

"Nope. I plan on surprising her. I'm going to cook her a nice dinner, and hopefully, she will forgive my neglectfulness."

"You don't think it would be wise to take her out to a nice dinner? Maybe impress her and properly grovel if you really want to smooth things over."

I leaned forward. "Trust me. I know how to grovel and my groveling is best done in the privacy of her home."

He burst into laughter. "Okay then. I get it. I suppose you do your best work without your pants on."

I got to my feet. "I do."

"Call me before you leave town," he shouted at my back.

I put up a hand, indicating I had heard him. I was anxious to see Evie. I was banking on her enjoying my surprise.

I quickly texted her as I walked to the waiting car. It was my usual text, checking in with her and asking what she was doing. She was working at home. I instructed the driver to take me to a grocery store where I picked up a few things to make her a lasagna I knew would knock her socks off. I was hoping it would knock a few other things off as well.

I made my way up to her apartment and knocked on the door. When she opened it up, I was hit by a myriad of emotions. I felt happiness at seeing her. Desire at seeing her. And a sense of relief I didn't know I needed.

"Hi," I said with a smile.

She was staring at me with her mouth hanging agape. There was a pen stuck in the mass of black curls precariously perched on top of her head. "I'm—you're here."

"I am here. Will you be inviting me in?"

"Oh shit, sorry, yes." She moved out of the way and gestured for me to go inside.

"I was hoping I could make you some dinner," I said and held up the two bags filled with my groceries, which was not easy with my overnight bag hanging on my shoulder. I felt a bit like a pack mule.

"You're here," she said again.

I put the bags on her kitchen counter before going to her and pulling her into my arms. I kissed her like I had not seen in her two years rather than two weeks.

"Damn, I've missed you," I breathed when I finally managed to pull myself away from her.

"I cannot believe I'm standing here looking at you. I'm floored."

"I wanted to surprise you."

"You definitely did that," she said with a laugh. "I would have put on something a little less frumpy if I had known I was getting some company."

I looked over the leggings and loose T-shirt she was wearing. "I think you look perfectly doable."

Her pretty smile melted my heart. "Well, that is one hell of a compliment. I'm afraid to ask, but does this mean you are back?"

"I'm here to see you," I said, dodging the question. "I would have been here earlier, but I had to stop and talk to Charlie."

I didn't tell her seeing Charlie and apologizing for fucking him over had taken priority over seeing her. She was a very good reason to come back, but obligation was the motivating factor.

"I'm very happy to see you."

"I was thinking we could have dinner and stay in for the night?"

"Does that mean you will be staying over at my place?" she asked.

"If you'll have me."

"I will absolutely have you."

"Great. I am going to make you my not so famous lasagna."

"I'll pour the wine. Let me put away my work stuff really quick."

I kicked my bag out of the way and began to unpack the groceries. Her apartment was nice. I loved the openness of it. As I expected, it was neat and organized with no random clutter spread about. It could have been the image in the brochure for the apartment building.

"I like your place," I told her when she stepped into the kitchen that was separated from the living room with a long, open, raised bar.

"Thank you." She pulled a bottle of wine from the little wire holder in the corner of the kitchen. She poured us each a glass and then leaned against the counter to watch me. "I cannot believe you are in my kitchen. I'm still in shock."

"I'm here, in the flesh."

"Can I help?"

"I'll need a pot to boil water and a pan to make the lasagna in."

She quickly retrieved both items. "What have you been doing these last couple of weeks? I know you have told me nothing, but you have had to be doing something."

I shrugged. "I bought a new boat."

"You said that."

"That's what I've been doing. I've been out on the water most of the time. I've done a lot of fishing and truly doing nothing."

"You mentioned Charlie went up to Oregon to see you. Was this visit to fix whatever you said you broke?"

"I almost broke his company," I confessed. "I fixed it. At least for now. But really, that was just an excuse. I came to see you."

She gave me that same pretty smile I had been missing for too long. We chatted about her work and recent news in the city while I showed her how to make the lasagna. Three glasses of wine later, both of us were feeling very full after our delicious meal, and we retired to the couch.

The city lights shone in the distance through the large picture window in the living room. She had lit a few candles, casting the room into a soft glow. She leaned against me. I wrapped my arm around her shoulders and simply enjoyed being near her.

"I've missed this," I whispered.

"Me too."

"I like when it's just me and you and the rest of the world is far away. When it's just the two of us, I don't have to think about anyone or anything else."

She sat forward a little and turned to look at me. "I like when it's just me and you too."

"It's quiet here," I commented.

"Not as quiet as your house."

"It's a lot quieter than I expected an apartment to be. Maybe because I've been living in a hotel for too long. I'm used to hearing my neighbors above me walk and the neighbor on the side of me shower every morning. It's very loud. I never realized it until just now."

"I imagine hotel living would be loud. You hear far too much in a hotel."

"How about here?" I whispered. "Will your neighbors hear us when I make you scream my name?"

Her lips parted, her eyes dropping to my mouth. "I guess we're going to find out."

She leaned forward and kissed me. It was just as I said. Nothing else in the entire world mattered when I was with her. The last two weeks without her had been fraught with stress and worry. With her lips against mine, I wasn't thinking about anything else except her. She was the salve I needed.

"Bedroom," I murmured against her lips.

She got up, extending her hand to help me off the couch. She led me down the short hallway to her bedroom. There were several candles burning on the dresser. The curtains were drawn, and it was just me and her.

I pulled her close and kissed her slow and deep, savoring every breath and whimper she released.

CHAPTER 58

EVIE

I told myself to guard my heart. That rational side of me was easily shushed and sent to a corner whenever he touched me. My body longed for his touch. I craved his kisses. I was addicted to the man in the worst way.

I could hear my inner dialogue as if I were a third party listening in. I bargained with myself. One night of passion with him and then I would stay away from him. Just one more night. I just needed him one more time to take the edge off.

"You are so beautiful," he whispered as his lips grazed my earlobe. "I dream about you every night. I think about touching you all the time. Sometimes, I think I smell you while I'm in bed, only to wake up and find myself alone."

His words sent shivers up and down my spine. My entire body erupted into gooseflesh. "I think about you all the time."

He ran his hands down my sides, stroking me through my clothes. He didn't appear to be in any real hurry to strip me. I was feeling just the opposite. I felt as if I would erupt into flames if I didn't have his skin against mine.

"I want you," he breathed. His hands slid up my shirt, sliding up the fabric until I was reaching my hands to the ceiling. With one quick lift, it was over my head. I instinctively leaned into him, my breasts pushing against his hard chest.

"More," I begged. "I need more."

"I'm going to give you so much more."

I rubbed against him like a cat rubbing against its owner. I demanded to be petted and stroked. "I'm so hot."

"Yes, you are," he teased. He pushed my pants down.

I very ungracefully stepped out of them and kicked them out of my way.

"You have too many clothes on," I pouted, still rubbing my body against his.

"Shh," he said before swallowing my complaints.

He slid his hand over my hip and circled around to move between my legs. The heat from his palm infused me with electricity as he pressed against my very core. I moaned, grinding my hips against his hand in an effort to seek more friction.

"More," I begged. I was on fire. I had been too long without his touch. I needed him more than anything else in that moment.

"Take it," he ordered. "I'm right here. You take what you need."

I reached between us and held his hand against me before rubbing myself against the heel of his hand. I gasped, pure pleasure shooting through me. "Yes," I whispered. I was in control.

I moved against his hand, riding it until I worked myself into a frenzy.

"Harder," he commanded.

"More."

"Harder," he said again.

I was trembling with need. My body felt frenzied. It wasn't enough. "More," I said again with more force.

He grabbed me by the waist and lifted me several inches before dropping me onto the bed. I scrambled backward, waiting for him to join me. He crawled beside me without taking off his clothes. I was about to ask him what the hell he was doing when he put his hand over me once again. He didn't move for several seconds, simply absorbing the heat emanating from between my legs. I writhed under him, desperate for penetration.

He pulled my panties away. I moaned, waiting for what I knew was coming next. His hand settled over my exposed center. When he didn't slide the finger I was craving inside me, I took matters into my own hands. I placed my hand over his, pushing him against me. More heat and friction coursed through my body.

He made no move to put a finger inside me. Once again, I took the initiative. I adjusted his hand over me, and with my finger on the back of his index finger, I pushed him inside my slick opening. He was watching me with a fiery gaze, giving me the approval to keep going. I rocked against him, riding his finger as I held it right where I needed it to achieve the most satisfaction.

"There you go," he growled. "Ride it. I know you can move faster."

I cried out, rocking my hips and sliding his finger in and out of me. I pushed another one of his long fingers inside me, the tips of my own mingling with his. I could feel how wet I was. My mind blanked as I furiously worked toward the only thing I could focus on. Ecstasy. I was after it, chasing it until my body exploded in a series of brilliant flashes of white heat.

I moaned, writhing against him, his fingers still planted inside me. "There you go," he coaxed. "That's my girl. Take all you want."

With the edge off, I was only getting started. I needed a lot more than a couple of fingers. I got up, pushing him to his back and furiously attacking him. First, it was his shirt. I yanked and tugged with no real thought to how I was going to get it off his body.

Once it was gone, I went after the pants. I slid down him, my feet hitting the floor as I tugged his pants and underwear off. I gave him no time to bark orders or tell me what he wanted. I knew what I wanted. I wanted him.

I slid my body back up his, trailing kisses over his defined abs and spending a little extra time on his chest before finally landing on his mouth.

I devoured him, rubbing my body against his. He reached up to unhook my bra, freeing my breasts. I purred against him, sliding my hard nipples against his chest. The crinkly hairs smattered over his chest teased and tickled.

Soon, I couldn't resist the urge to ride him. I sat up, looking down at the man who was looking up at me with pure lust in his eyes. "Fuck me," he said the words that nearly had me orgasming right then.

I moved, adjusting my body to take him in. With slow, purposeful moves, I swallowed him inside me. I moved my hips, taking the last little bit and leaned back, closing my eyes and relishing in the feel of him throbbing inside me.

His hands reached up, grabbing my breasts and squeezing and tugging. I began to move in a slow rhythm, taking the time to grind against his body. Sounds of pleasure echoed around us.

He wasn't bossing me now. He was letting me take the lead. Usually, it was breakneck speed to pleasure for me, but I wanted to savor the moment. I wanted to relish in every little spark of ecstasy and follow it until a new one caught my attention.

"Damn," he said. "You feel so good, so tight. You are so fucking hot."

A lazy smile spread over my lips as I continued my ride. I moved like I was on a leisurely stroll through a beautiful garden on a warm sunny day. I pressed my lips together, moaning with pleasure. "I want to ride you all night."

"Baby, you can ride me all week," he answered. His hands moved to my thighs, sliding up and down. I could feel his need building as he squeezed my flesh.

"I have to move faster," I told him. A wave of need overwhelmed me. I couldn't stop my hips. I rode him hard and fast. My breasts bounced as I moved. I was on a mission and nothing was going to get in my way.

"Faster!" he shouted.

I cried out with frustration and need. I couldn't seem to get fast enough for what my body was demanding. I tried. My hands settled on his chest, my fingertips digging in for purchase as I bounced harder and higher with every stroke.

"Oh god!" I cried out again when the orgasm slammed into me as if

I had run face first into a wall. It actually threw me back. My back bowed and I could feel my nails dig into his flesh. I was helpless to do anything but ride it out.

His hips were bucking off the bed, threatening to unseat me. I held on for dear life as the ecstasy coursed through my veins, setting my skin on fire. I could hear his grunts and curses signaling his own pleasure had been reached.

In a flash, the force that had been keeping me upright broke and I collapsed against his chest in one big heap. I struggled to catch my breath. My body trembled as his arms came around me, holding me close to him. I could feel his heart pounding so hard it felt as if it would pop out of his chest.

We had enjoyed countless orgasms together, but this one had been the most violent. The time apart had been too much for our bodies to handle. We were addicted to one another. I slowly slid off him, reaching for a blanket at the foot of the bed to cover our naked bodies. I had goosebumps and the shivering wouldn't let up. It had nothing to do with being cold and everything to do with being pleasured beyond measure.

"Run away with me," he said after several minutes of each of us trying to catch our breath.

"What?"

"I can support you. You don't need to work. Come away with me. We can go anywhere, do anything."

My heart jumped. It was what I wanted to hear, but now that he actually said it, I knew there was no way I could do that. "That is a conversation for another night. You are riding high on the afterglow."

"I'm serious," he said.

"I want to fall asleep in your arms. I don't want to think about tomorrow or next week. Let's just enjoy what we have right now in this moment."

He kissed the top of my head. "I can do that."

I said nothing more. There was a lump in my throat that prevented me from saying anything. I didn't know how to answer him. Nelle had suggested I run away with him, but I wasn't a runner. I needed to be grounded. Running from his problems wasn't going to solve anything. Whatever he was trying to work through was still going to be waiting for him when he got back. Running solved nothing.

As much as it was going to kill me, I had to let him go. I had to let him run free. He wasn't ready to settle down. He wasn't ready to face the demons that were haunting him. There was nothing I could do to change that. I didn't want to get caught up in the moment. Those demons would catch up with him eventually.

It would have been incredibly romantic if he was asking me to run away with him because he wanted me. I had a feeling he was asking me to run away with him because he didn't want to be alone. I was only a slot filler. I was a distraction. That was not going to work for me. I needed more. Sadly, I didn't think he was capable of offering more than an occasional night of really good sex. Not yet.

Maybe one day. *Oh please, let it be one day*. I could hold out for a little longer. I could hang on and pray he found a way to soothe his soul.

CHAPTER 59

XANDER

It was like *deja vu* waking up with Evie in my arms. It reminded me of the hotel room in Oregon. I remembered how I felt in that moment. It was good. Holding her in my arms was damn near as good as making love to her. I knew I wanted it again and again. When we were in bed together, I could forget about everything else.

I wanted the moment to last forever. Why did it have to end? I told myself we could pull the blankets up to our chins and cocoon ourselves for days. I sighed, knowing she would never agree to that. There was no putting a social butterfly back in a cocoon. She loved her job and her people. I would be selfish to take her away from the world.

Just then, I didn't give a fuck about the world. I wanted her all to myself.

"You are awake before me again," she said in a sleepy voice.

"I am an early riser," I said and wrapped her tighter in my arms. "I think I'm cursed. My father cursed us. If I sleep past eight, I feel as if I have broken the law."

She groaned and snuggled against me. "What could you possibly do before eight?"

"Let's see. I usually go for a swim, sometimes a run. Then I like to enjoy my coffee and browse the internet. I sometimes sketch out ideas that have popped in my head during the night. Sometimes, I just sit out on the patio and do nothing."

"Do you go for a swim in your pool or the ocean?"

"Depends on the weather," I answered. "I love a cool dip in the ocean, but I'll admit, I don't always feel that ambitious to climb up and down those stairs."

"I do not blame you. I did that climb. It's a miracle I had the strength to climb through your kitchen window."

I chuckled. "I still cannot believe you did that."

"A girl has to do what she has to do when things are desperate."

"I'm glad you did it."

"Have you been to your house?"

"No."

"Did you take care of the business you had with Charlie?"

I blew out a breath, my hand absently traveling up and down her arm. "I don't know. Not really."

"What do you need to do?"

"That's the thing. I'm not sure."

"Do you want to tell me what happened?" she asked. "You only said it was something to do with the business."

I didn't want to tell her because I felt like an asshole for my part in the situation. I shouldn't have left them hanging. I should have thought about what I was doing before I up and left. "That meeting I missed didn't just cost me a sale. Charlie and I have worked together a lot. He understands me and can read between the lines of my designs. Other mechanics don't always get what I'm trying to do. Because of that, Charlie's company handles a large chunk of the manufacturing and building of my designs."

"Does he own the company?"

"No, but he is one of the heads, even though no one would ever realize it. He's always got dirty hands and his head in an engine. He hired a crew in anticipation of business picking up with the new fan and rudder design I was supposed to present. The shipping industry is just as rife with rumors and gossip as an old ladies' book club."

"Hey," she said and slapped at my chest. "I used to be in a book club."

"And how much reading did you actually do?"

She softly laughed. "Good point. Go on."

"When I didn't show, it pissed off a lot of people. I didn't present the design, and therefore, Charlie's guys have nothing to build. They have plenty of other work, but that's the work that will keep his regular crew going. The extra team has nothing to do."

"Ouch. That's a lot of pressure to put on one guy."

"Maybe, but I feel responsible. I paid the payroll for a month to keep those guys on, but that's not going to solve the problem."

"Does that mean you're going to release that design then?"

I blew out a breath, staring up at the ceiling. "I don't know. I suppose I could have a proxy do it for me, but I don't think anyone can explain it as well as I can."

"Of course not. You are the designer. You are the mastermind. You are the one they want to hear from."

"Which is why I'm kind of stuck between a rock and a hard place."

"Why is that?"

"Because I retired."

She turned her face up to look at me. "You retired?"

"That was my plan."

"Oh."

"Not permanently," I clarified. "At least I don't think so. I sound like a nutjob. I really had not given it a lot of thought. I just knew I was done with the life I had. I wasn't sure where I was going but something had to change."

"I remember," she said, sounding disappointed. "Are you rethinking your decision?"

"I think I am. Unfortunately, judging by the emails I have gotten and the messages my assistant has passed along to me, I think my retirement might be inevitable. It isn't really my choice anymore."

"Why do you say that?"

"Because I burned some bridges. Not just burned. I blew them up. I imploded my own reputation. I'm not sure anyone will ever take me seriously again. The general consensus is something along the lines of I lost my shit and have moved to some hideaway. I'm a laughingstock in the industry. I don't think I could get anyone to the table, let alone get them to buy my new idea. They will laugh me right out of the room. It was a stretch when my reputation was intact."

She moved her head away from my chest and rested it on the pillow. I turned to my side to face her.

"I think your first question is to ask yourself what you want," she said. "Like really want."

"I want to fix the mess I made with Charlie."

"And to do that, you need to send work his way, right?"

"Yes."

"I'm not entirely sure how your business works, but the designs you have sold. Won't they speak for themselves? Don't companies always need new ships?"

I offered her a small smile. "Not when they are built right the first time. This new idea I had was more of a retrofit. I designed it with the idea of existing ships being fixed. It would save a fortune on future repairs and would be a hell of a lot cheaper than building a whole new ship."

"It certainly sounds like it would be a good investment for those shipping magnates."

"Yes, but now that my idea has been making the rounds, it isn't going to be long before some other dude figures it out and puts it on the market."

She looked irritated. "Do you think someone would really do that?"

"Oh, hell yeah. I have no doubt in my mind it's already in progress."

"Well, that's bullshit!" she exclaimed.

I grinned, leaning forward to drop a kiss on her nose. "I agree but it's the nature of the beast. You have to shit or get off the pot."

She wrinkled her nose. "Gross."

"Sorry."

She looked thoughtful, gnawing on her lower lip. It was her habit to worry her poor lip when she wanted to say something. I learned to sit tight and let her get it out when she was good and ready. "You are not the only guy my dad knows in the world of shipping."

"What do you mean?"

"We were talking the other day. He told me he is very good friends with a local guy that owns a shipping company. It isn't one of the biggest ones, but he does own a few ships."

I wasn't sure where she was going with her information. "Okay," I said, waiting for her to explain.

She looked worried. Or sick. "You could talk to my father and ask if he would be willing to set up a meeting between you and his friend. I could do it for you, but I think me acting as a go between would be a little ineffective."

"I would never ask you to do that."

"I would do it, but I think this is something you need to do."

I mulled over the idea. "I think I would have better luck getting the guys I stood up to give me another chance than I would at getting your dad to help me."

"You would be surprised."

"I would be floored if your dad wanted to give me a hand," I told her. "It's fine. I will think of something."

"Okay, but it is an option in case you run out of ideas."

"Thank you."

"I have to get up," she said with a sigh. "I have to get to the venue where my event is happening. The caterers should be arriving in about two hours."

I reached for her and pulled her close. "Are you sure? Can't you play hooky this one time?"

"That is tempting, but this client isn't the kind I can abandon at the last minute."

"Fine. I have some work to do myself."

"Are you going to leave?" she whispered.

"I don't know."

I saw the hurt on her face. I wanted to take it away. "You are welcome to stay here. I will leave you a spare key."

"Thank you."

She gave me another kiss. "Don't leave without saying goodbye."

"I won't."

She slid out of bed and walked to the shower. I got out of her bed and pulled on some clean underwear from my bag. I strode into her kitchen, vaguely familiar with where things were, and started some coffee for us. I wouldn't leave her hanging. I couldn't do that to her. Not again.

Now that I was awake and in the bright light of day, reality was crashing in around me once again. I walked to the huge window and stared out at the sea in the distance. The pull to stay was strong. I just wasn't sure I was strong enough. I sure as hell didn't feel strong enough. I felt fragile. I felt like my world would never return to the way it had been before losing Kade.

"Hey, you're still here," Evie said, coming to stand next to me at the window. "Do you know I usually find you like this? You're always looking toward the ocean, no matter where you are."

I smiled and stretched my arm around her shoulders. "It's where I find my inner balance."

"I believe it. I have witnessed it. I could probably stick around another hour if you'd like."

I turned away from the window. "No. I'm fine. Don't interrupt your day. I'll be fine. Can I take a shower?"

"Of course," she said. "I'll make you some toast. I might have eggs. If not, I can probably find a frozen waffle or something."

"Don't worry about me," I assured her.

I headed for the shower. I was lying about the things I had to do. I didn't really have shit to do, other than take care of all the shit I'd left behind. I wasn't looking forward to that.

Deep down, I knew I had to go home. I was going to have to face the memories head on. Part of me wanted her to be there with me when I did. Another part of me didn't want her to witness my vulnerability and weakness. I couldn't bring myself to let her all the way in.

Me holding back would ultimately destroy any relationship we forged.

CHAPTER 60

EVIE

I checked the time, mentally noting that everything was right on schedule. I walked to the bar being set up under Nelle's direction. The woman did not mess around when it came to setting up her workstation. There was a wrong way and there was Nelle's way. There was no in between. It was why she was so damn good at her job.

"Hey, drill sergeant," I said.

She turned to me, putting a hand on her hip and giving me that look that said she was going to murder someone. "I'm missing a case of liquor."

"Uh oh. Is that on my end or your end?"

"Mine. Not mine but mine."

I nodded with understanding. One of her minions had failed her. "Do I need to do anything?"

"Nope. I've got it handled."

"I knew you would."

"Walk with me," she said in a way that made it clear it wasn't a request.

"What's up?" I asked.

"I just wanted to make sure you are okay. I didn't hear from you last night and I got a little worried."

"Xander showed up at my door."

Her eyes bulged. "No way!"

"Yep."

"Oh my god! I'm so happy for you."

Before I could tell her it wasn't really all that exciting, the head of the waitstaff waved me over with the typical panicked look in her eye. "I better go put out the fire. Why does this happen every single time?"

She laughed. "Because you are the best and the universe wants to test you."

"I'll talk to you later."

I quickly handled the issue, only to be faced with another one and then another one. No matter how well I planned, these little emergencies always arose. It was the nature of the beast. Servers got sick, food got ordered wrong, or a tablecloth had a stain. My job was to do my best to prepare for every crisis. With my experience, I was used to just about anything. It took a lot more than an ugly coffee stain on a white tablecloth to freak me out. That was why they'd invented bleach pens.

The party got underway and things were moving along smoothly. I made my way over to where Nelle and one of her hired help were serving up drinks at the open bar. "Club soda?" she asked, knowing me well.

"Yes, please."

There was a lull in the line, giving her a chance to step back. "So you didn't tell me. What's going on with you and Xander?"

"I don't know."

"He surprised you with a visit. That's a big deal."

"Yes and no. He is in town to handle some business. I kind of feel like I was an afterthought."

"I don't believe that for a second."

"It's so hard to know with him," I complained.

"Did you guys talk or just bang all night?"

I rolled my eyes. "You can be so crass."

"So you banged all night."

"Stop," I admonished. "We talked a little bit. He asked me to run away with him."

"No way!"

"Yes."

"What did you say?"

I gave her a dry look. "What do you think I said?"

"I hope you didn't tell him no."

"Technically, I did not tell him no, but I told him it wasn't up for discussion. I don't think he is serious. I got the feeling it was off the cuff and he didn't really think about it. I can't run away for a week or a month or however long it takes him to get this out of his system and then expect to come back to my life. I'm not him. I can't run away and have someone hold my place. If I leave, I give up my job, my reputation—everything."

"You need to convince him to stay," she advised.

I shook my head. "Nope. Not going to do that. I am not going to lay a guilt trip on him or give him an ultimatum. I will not be that woman. He has to come home because he wants to. I want him to be happy. If he truly cannot find happiness here, I'm not going to ask him to stay. I'm not going to tell him we can't be together if he won't stay."

"Then where does that leave the two of you?"

I sighed before taking a drink of my soda. "I don't know. I think last night was a goodbye. We both know it isn't going to work the way it is going. I think we both want it but neither of us is ready to give up what we truly want from life."

"That sucks," she muttered. "He's a good guy. I like him."

"You haven't met him."

"But I like him from what you've told me," she said with a laugh.

"He is a good guy, but he isn't ready for a relationship. He needs to figure out what he wants and needs. I don't want to be the one pushing him in any one direction. He will never be happy if he feels coerced."

"Lame."

We were both watching the crowd of corporate executives mingle around the room. They were traders or something along those lines. I watched as the man that hired me made his way toward us. He was carrying a half-full glass of a dark liquid.

"This is a lovely party," he said and decided in order to tell me that, he needed to touch my shoulder.

I smiled at him. "Thank you. I hope you're all enjoying yourselves."

"Oh, we are. What are you drinking? Can I get you another?"

"It's club soda and no thank you. I'm on the clock."

He leaned in close, the booze on his breath giving me a contact drunk. "I won't tell if you won't," he whispered. "I'm very good at keeping secrets."

"From your wife?" Nelle snapped. "Isn't she the pretty blonde wearing the red dress and looking over here right this minute?"

"My wife and I have secrets," he said without taking his eyes off the minimal cleavage showing in the dress I was wearing.

"Really? Because the way she is looking at you, I would say your secret is out of the bag. Get lost, buddy. This lady is way out of your league."

I looked at Nelle, trying to tell her to calm down with my eyes. She wasn't getting the message.

"Excuse me?" he growled. "Aren't you the bartender? Why don't you make me another drink and do your job? I assume I'm paying you."

"You aren't paying me shit," Nelle replied without missing a beat. "This is an open bar."

"And I'm the damn owner of the firm that is paying for it," he snapped.

"Congratulations. I hope you have an excellent attorney and an even better prenup. Your wife is only with you for your money and I would guess she is tired of your secrets. You're about to be a very broke man. She looks like she could be a gold digger. She was just waiting for you to screw up, and here you are, giving her all kinds of ammunition. Good job. Enjoy your last party as a wealthy man."

He glanced over his shoulder, and sure enough, the woman was glaring at him. I hoped she knew I was not entertaining her husband's advances. I didn't date old, fat, balding men that fucked anything that walked. I had some standards.

"You will never work one of my parties again," he hissed at Nelle. His cheeks were ruddy, and he looked nervous.

"Thank God. You heard him. Never again will I serve this shitbag a drink."

"You insolent creature!"

"Creative, but far from the worst I've been called," she said with a dry expression.

He turned and walked away. I had to hide the smile on my face. "Thank you. I'm going to have to put a leash on you."

"I don't understand why men think that having a glass of whatever in their hands gives them the right to say and do what they want. It's not an excuse to behave like a pig."

"No, it isn't, but they do it anyway."

"Assholes," she muttered.

"Usually."

"You are lucky," she commented.

I was confused. "I'm lucky?"

"Yes, lucky. You have a great guy. I don't know your man, but would he ever act like one of these douchebags?"

I watched the crowd and immediately identified several douchebags. "No, he would not. Xander is not like that. He's far too reserved to hit on a woman so openly."

She smiled before stepping up to help a customer. "Good, because I would hate to have to kick his ass for treating women like the men I'm seeing here."

The young man waiting for his drink stared at her. He looked terrified. I knew she had purposely said what she did for his benefit. Nelle didn't hold back. She'd been in the bar business a long time. Her tolerance level for drunken antics was pretty low.

"You will not have to kick his ass," I assured her. "Now, I must make the rounds and make sure nothing is falling apart in the kitchen. I have a feeling I won't be getting a great review for this one."

"If that asshole gives you a shitty review, you let me know," she said and practically thrust the man's drink at him. He took it and ran like the hounds of hell were on his heels. The poor kid hadn't even seen Nelle mad. He would have really run scared then.

"It's fine," I told her. "I will soothe things over."

"Don't you dare!"

I smiled and drifted into the crowd. I blended in, quietly listening to the chatter. My ears were open, listening for any complaints about the staff, the food, or the drinks. I couldn't fix a problem if I didn't know about it. I found the best way to identify any issues was to blend in and pretend I wasn't listening.

I heard no complaints as I made my way around the room. I found a place out of the way to observe things. I was not all that surprised to find the owner of the company making moves on a pretty, very young woman. I felt sorry for his wife. He was a scumbag.

While I watched him flirt and make a general ass of himself, I thought about Xander. I knew in my heart he would never behave like that. I was confident he wasn't the cheating type. While I knew there was no way to know for sure, there was something about Xander that said he wouldn't. He was a proud man that didn't seem to be prone to temptation. He was practical and certainly did not appreciate the company of strangers.

I smiled as I thought back to our first interaction. It was like pulling teeth to get the man to talk to me. He was a hard nut to crack, but I was so damn glad I managed to do it. Then again, I would probably end up regretting the fact that I did. I just knew the man was going to break my heart. I knew it and yet I couldn't stop it. He was going to leave me. I'd felt it this morning in bed.

I needed to prepare myself for the inevitable. It was going to hurt. Dammit, I didn't want it to happen. I thought about texting him. I loved the idea of him at my place waiting for me. I had given him the key, but deep down, I knew he wouldn't use it. If he left without saying goodbye, I would never speak to him again. I refused to be tossed away a second time.

I felt sick to my stomach at the idea of not seeing him again. I sent up a silent prayer, hoping against hope that when I walked through my front door, he would be there with music playing and candles burning.

A girl could dream, couldn't she?

CHAPTER 61

XANDER

I got up and immediately knew I didn't want to be in the house. Last night had been awful. No matter how hard I tried, I tossed and turned. I couldn't bring myself to forget. I thought about taking Evie up on her offer, but I knew I had to test myself. Was there a chance I could come home? Not now. Not after my long, sleepless night.

I promised her I would tell her I was leaving and that was what I was going to do. I didn't want to wake her and found myself trying to kill time while I waited until it was an appropriate time. When nine o'clock rolled around, I felt I'd waited as long as I could. I was confident she would be up by now.

"Good morning," I greeted when she answered.

"Hi," she said, her voice filled with hesitation.

"I didn't leave," I told her right away.

"When you weren't here when I got home, I assumed you decided to go. You didn't answer my texts."

"I'm sorry," I quickly apologized. "I fell asleep early, and by the time I saw your message, it was late and I didn't want to wake you up." It was the truth. I had fallen asleep on the couch before eight. I slept for a couple of hours and then a nightmare woke me up. From that point on, sleep was elusive. I wasn't interested in trying too hard out of fear I would have more nightmares.

"I see," she said, and I could feel her hurt and anger in her voice.

"I came home," I replied. "I wanted to check on things."

"Oh?"

I wasn't going to get into it over the phone. "Do you have any plans for the day?"

"Not really. I was thinking about taking a walk, but not much else."

"Would you like to drive up the coastline a bit?"

"What does that mean?" she questioned with weariness in her voice.

"I was thinking we could find somewhere quiet and enjoy the day. Anything you want. I just want to spend some time with you."

"I would like that, sure," she said after several very long seconds. "I think that's a good idea."

"I'll be at your place in an hour. Does that work?"

"Yes," she said.

I was going to have to kill more time, but I wasn't going to do it in the house. I had already showered and gotten ready for the day, hoping she would agree to spend it with me. If she would have shut me down, I would have said my goodbyes and hopped on the first flight out. I was a coward and obviously afraid of ghosts.

I left the house, a cold shiver going down my spine as I headed for my car. I didn't know if it was mind over matter or if I was just plain crazy, but I couldn't shake the ghost feeling.

I got to her place forty-five minutes later. She was just finishing with her makeup. The moment she opened the door, I knew she saw too much. "Are you okay?" she asked right away.

"Fine," I replied. "Why?"

She pulled a face, gesturing for me to go inside. "You look a little rough around the edges. I take it you didn't sleep well last night?"

There was no point lying. "No, not really. It's tough being in that house. I know it's dumb but it's the way it is."

"It is not dumb. We are all entitled to our feelings."

I groaned, rolling my eyes. "I don't need my head shrunk."

She laughed softly. "I won't try to shrink your head. That would require a professional with a lot of experience to sort through all of that."

"You are right. I was hoping we could avoid the subject altogether. Hence my desire to do something fun and completely unrelated to the real problems I'm facing."

"What did you have in mind?" she asked.

"Do you want to play tourist?" I asked.

"And what would that entail?"

I shrugged. "I was thinking we could go down to the boardwalk, check out the aquarium, and just hang out on the beach. Or maybe we could drive up to LA. We could visit Hollywood and really play tourist."

"I've been to the boardwalk a few thousand times, but I've never been to Hollywood."

"No way, really?"

"Really. It's not exactly my dad's thing. I have thought about going a few times but then I always feel so cheesy. Then I tell myself I don't have the time and I end up not going."

"Then, let's do it," I said with finality. "Charge your phone. We want to make sure we are ready to snap pictures of any celebs we might see."

"They don't actually hang out in Hollywood, do they?"

I shrugged. "I guess we're about to find out."

She clapped her hands together. "I'm excited. This is a first for me. Do you want me to drive?"

"I have my car," I told her.

She raised an eyebrow. "I thought you were selling it?"

"I didn't actually do it. Yet. I will probably store it or something. I don't know yet." Yes, I was indecisive. I couldn't pull the trigger on anything. Fortunately, I didn't have to. I could afford to let things ride for a while.

"And your house?"

"It's still there," I teased.

"All right, I get it. You don't want to talk about it."

"I'm sorry. It's probably not the healthiest option but I need to put it all out of my mind for a while. I don't want to think."

She offered me a small smile and gave me a quick kiss. "Then that will be the goal for today. You will be a mindless puppet with zero thinking required."

A little over an hour later, we were parking the car in an over-priced lot. I took her hand in mine and we found ourselves almost immediately absorbed in a crowd of people. After about an hour of mingling with the crowd, we broke off and found a small café for us to grab a snack and a drink.

"I'm glad you and your dad are talking again. I hated thinking you guys were at odds because of me."

"We're good," she said. "Trust me. I don't want to pry, but can you give me a hint about what happened between you and your dad?"

"I was born," I said dryly.

"Stop," she said. "For real, what happened? Were you especially rebellious in high school?"

"Not really. I'm serious. I cannot name any one specific moment in my life that led to his dislike for me. It was kind of a gradual thing from the moment I was born. That is the honest truth."

"You are not a bad person," she insisted. "I don't get it."

"I truly believe it is because I didn't want to go into the military. He had this idea in his head that's what I was going to do. It was never an option. I was born and I was going into the service in eighteen years. Period. When I started talking about college and stuff like that, he didn't think I was serious. I disappointed him. My mom kind of buffered our relationship. She kept it at a place where we could at least be in the same room. When she died, it was Kade who filled in as mediator."

"I am so sorry."

"Don't be sorry," I told her. "It's old news."

"It might be old news but that does not make it okay."

"I think I have accepted it. I don't really think about it much. I was trying to keep things cool for Kade. I don't have to fake it anymore. Kade isn't here to try and make us a happy trio. I'm not going to go fishing with him. I'm not going to grab a beer with him. There is nothing more."

"Did Kade want you guys to work things out?"

"Yes," I answered. "He did."

"Do you think you should try for his sake?"

I smirked. "No. I think you saw how that would work out. Fireworks would be putting it mildly."

"It was a tense situation."

"That's how it is in every situation with him. Kade was the guy that settled my dad. He could reason with him. He could manage us. It was strange. I can't imagine how stressful and exhausting that was for him to deal with. If I could, I would apologize to him. I would tell him how sorry I was I forced him to be a referee. He didn't deserve that."

"Do you think there is ever a chance the two of you could find some common ground?" she questioned.

"No. I wish there was a chance. I just don't see it happening. I admire what you have with your father but what you have is special and unique. I'm not the only person in the world who doesn't have a relationship with their family. Sometimes, blood isn't enough. We might be related but we couldn't be more different."

She nodded as if she understood, but I didn't think she did. It was a confusing situation for someone who had never experienced my familial ties. We weren't the Cleavers or even the Connors. I didn't believe we were dysfunctional either. We simply were not meant to be the typical father and son.

"Okay, I will leave it alone," she said.

"Thank you. I appreciate you trying to figure it out, but I really don't need you to try and fix it. This is something that has been a part of my life for a very long time. I have accepted it and I'm okay with it."

"Got it."

"Now, would you like to go to the wax museum or stroll down the Walk of Fame?"

Her face lit up. "Oh my gosh, I want to do both!"

"We will. Let's start with the TCL Chinese Theater and then we'll head to Madame Tussaud's."

She clapped her hands together much like a child would do. "Awesome. I cannot believe I have never been here. How often do you come here?"

"Not often. I have been here a couple of times but not recently. I'm sure the sidewalk is going to be littered with new stars. Is there one in particular you want to see?"

She appeared thoughtful. "Is it too cheesy if I say Marilyn Monroe?"

"Absolutely not," I assured her.

"What about you? Whose star do you want to see?"

I mulled it over. "I wanted to see Clint Eastwood's star, but I found out he doesn't have one. In fact, very few of the stars I actually admire do. But I guess I would like to see John Wayne's star."

"We are old souls." She smiled.

"I guess we both appreciate the old-school ways," I agreed.

"Are you ready?"

"Let's go."

I wrapped my arm around her shoulders, hers going around my waist as we melted back into the crowds clogging the sidewalks. Despite being in the middle of a large crowd, it felt like it was just me and her. I was enjoying myself and could almost believe we were on vacation together. We were far away from home and the confines of our normal routines. We were far away from the heavy decisions that were awaiting me back there.

Stalling. I was stalling. I wanted to spend as much time with her before I left. I was going to leave. I had come to that conclusion sometime in the middle of the night. I had to. I couldn't deal with the ghosts. I had an urge to run. Not necessarily back to Oregon but anywhere.

CHAPTER 62

EVIE

W e were both avoiding what was really going on. I refused to acknowledge it. I wanted to pretend we were on a normal date for as long as possible. We laughed and played and joked with each other as we strolled over several blocks of Hollywood stars before heading to the museum.

"I think this is all a little creepy," I told him after a while.

"You don't like being surrounded by wax figures staring at you," he teased.

"It's giving me the heebie-jeebies."

He burst into laughter. "It is a little creepy. Cool but creepy. Do you want to check out some of the shops? We could go to the Dolby?"

"Do you actually want to go shopping?" I questioned. I got the impression he was trying to make me happy, doing things that he thought I wanted to do as a way to appease me. I didn't need appeasing.

"I don't mind browsing," he answered.

It wasn't exactly an enthusiastic answer, but I would go with it. We spent a few more hours doing absolutely nothing except walking around and seeing all there was to see.

"I think we crammed three days of sightseeing and shopping into six hours," I told him. I leaned my head against the headrest of the passenger seat of his car and closed my eyes. "I am exhausted."

"You and me both," he answered.

I turned my head to look at him. Of course, he was beat. He didn't sleep last night and had just spent a marathon day sightseeing. "I'm sorry. I should have remembered you were already tired. I would have been perfectly content sitting on the beach with you."

"No, this was fun. This was exactly what I wanted to do."

"It was a lot of fun."

"Should we grab dinner before we head back?" he asked.

"We don't have to," I told him, seeing the lines around his eyes and the circles under his eyes.

"We need food. I'm starving. We could grab something fast and casual."

"That sounds perfect."

We drove out of the heart of the city and found a little diner decked out in retro fifties gear. We were both dragging ass as we slid into a booth with a shiny red table between us. There was a jukebox playing old forty-fives and lots of fifties memorabilia hanging from the walls. "I bet they have legit ice cream shakes here," I said and opened my menu.

"Oh, I want chocolate," he replied.

We both ordered big burgers, fries, and the traditional shakes, which were quickly delivered in tall glasses. I tried to take a drink from the shake, but it was far too thick. I was desperate for a taste and moved the straw to the side to drink straight from the glass.

"Ah, so good," I said after the initial taste.

He reached across the table and swiped his thumb over my lips. "You had a little something there," he said with a grin.

I burst into a fit of giggles, encouraged by my total exhaustion. "Sorry, I really get into my food."

"Don't be sorry. It was cute."

In a flash, the mood changed. I couldn't pinpoint the exact moment, but suddenly, reality crashed down on us. We had both been playing a game all day. Neither of us wanted to address the giant elephant in the room. I couldn't operate that way. I needed answers. I needed to know what came next. I couldn't wake up every day and wonder if he was still around or if he had fled in the night.

"Xander, what are we doing?" I asked, looking directly into his eyes.

He stared back at me. I could see the turmoil and uncertainty he was dealing with. "We're having dinner," he answered.

I tilted my head to the side. "You know that's not what I mean."

"We spent a good day together. Does it have to be anything more than that?"

My father's words echoed through my mind. He said I put too much weight on labeling emotions. Maybe I did, but I didn't like the limbo. "That's it?"

My voice felt raw. In that moment, I knew I was in love with him. That wouldn't have been a terrible thing, but I was in love with a man that didn't want to be loved. I didn't know if he knew how to love in return. It was just my luck.

"Evie, I don't know. I'm not sure what you're asking."

"I think you do, but you're avoiding it. Today was all about avoidance. I went along with it, but don't you think we need to talk about what is really happening here?"

"Why don't you tell me what you think is happening?" he asked, irritation evident in his voice.

I shrugged. "I have no idea. I don't know what you want from me. I feel like I'm dangling on the end of a yo-yo. It's up and down, push and pull."

He rubbed a hand over his eyes. "I don't know. I honestly don't know."

"You have to have some kind of idea about what you are feeling. I just need a clue. I need to know which way to go from here."

The waitress brought us our massive burgers. She was way too cheery for my current mood. I thanked her and waited for her to leave. Staring at the hamburger that was the size of the damn plate it was on made me a little nauseated. I wasn't hungry anymore. Ten minutes ago, I had been famished. Now, I wanted nothing.

"I don't want to hurt you," he started, and I felt my heart plummet. It was not the way to start a sentence unless you were letting someone down.

He was dumping me. Again. I had to be some kind of idiot to keep putting myself in front of him just so he could dump me over and over. At some point, I had to learn a lesson.

"But you are going to do it anyway," I said with a sigh.

"That isn't my intention."

"Just say what you need to say," I murmured. It was better to get it over with.

"I'm not in a position to be with anyone."

I rolled my eyes. "Because?"

"You know me. I'm not good at this kind of thing. I'm not good at relationships in general. The one person in this world that I truly cared about is gone."

He may as well have slapped me. It hurt. His words tore at my heart. "I see," I said, nearly choking on the words.

"Kade got me. He understood me. He was... well, he was the one person that I could say I had a meaningful relationship with. He's gone. His death has turned me inside out. I can't do this again. I can't feel like this ever again."

"Grief?" I questioned. "That's what you don't want to feel again?"

"No, I don't. I can't."

I slowly nodded. "I understand. Your solution to your situation is to avoid relationships so you never have to experience loss. You would prefer to be permanently be alone than to know love and maybe feel some pain."

"I guess if you want to put it like that," he answered.

"I do."

I picked up a fry and dipped it in ketchup. It didn't help. I didn't want to eat. I didn't want to sit across from him while he kicked me to the curb and pretended everything was okay. It wasn't okay. I wasn't going to be his security blanket to pull over himself when he was feeling bad and then tossed to the side when he was over it.

"Evie, I'm sorry," he started to say.

"Please don't. In fact, if you don't mind, I think I'm ready to go home. I need to get some things done before tomorrow morning."

He slowly nodded. He had barely touched his own meal. It seemed like a waste but that was the least of my concerns. "All right."

We left our meals sitting on the table virtually untouched. As usual, Xander left more than enough money to cover the bill. We got into his car and neither of us spoke as we headed back to San Diego.

The ride seemed to last forever. Every passing minute in the car was full of tension. I couldn't wait to get to the safety of my apartment. I couldn't deal with being near him but yet so far away.

"Thanks for a nice time today," I told him when he pulled onto my street.

"Evie, I'm sorry. I didn't mean to give you the wrong idea about what was happening between us."

I shot him a dirty look. "Don't you dare do that. Don't try and make this out to be all in my head. You know that's bullshit."

He pulled to a stop in the parking lot of my complex. "It isn't in your head. I was going to leave yesterday. I chose to stay because I wanted to be with you. I wanted to forget about everything. Being with you makes me feel normal. It's an escape from my reality."

I could hear the pain in his voice and couldn't stay mad at him. I didn't believe he was intentionally hurting me. Unfortunately, it just came naturally to him. "I get it. I'm glad I could serve as a distraction."

"Stop. It's not what I meant."

"Look, you've got some shit to deal with. I get it. I've tried to be there for you, but this isn't going to work for me. You can't keep coming in and out of my life and making me feel things. You know where I am if you ever change your mind."

"Can I call you tomorrow?" he asked.

"No."

He didn't look surprised. "Goodbye, Evie."

I got out of the car and practically ran for the elevator. I made it into my apartment before the tears began to flow. I didn't believe he was trying to hurt me. I knew he cared about me. I was a danger to him. He was afraid to care about me because he didn't want to feel pain.

I didn't know how to navigate the relationship with the way things were. I wasn't a quitter, but damn, a girl could only take so much. Again, my father's advice flashed through my mind. Did I want to regret not trying harder?

"What else can I do?" I sobbed.

He was a broken man. Love and relationships had not been kind to him. The two people that had shown him unconditional love had died on him. I could understand why he had some hang-ups, but damn, I wanted him to move forward.

I stripped off my clothes and stepped into the shower. Our goodbye was not exactly the way I would have liked it to go down. I knew I wouldn't see him again. He wasn't going to call and tell me he was flying out. He wasn't going to stop by. The brief, slightly terse exchange in his car, that was our goodbye. For all I knew, he was on his way to the airport already.

A fresh wave of sadness bubbled up. I turned my face to the shower spray, letting the water mingle with my tears. I told myself I had to be strong. I needed to be patient. The man needed time to work through his issues. Was I willing to wait?

That was not my style. I was a fixer. I needed to fix what was broken. Unfortunately, I had a feeling the fixing was more of an internal repair job and I could do nothing to aid in it. I had to sit idly by, watching him destroy himself and hope like hell he could see the light eventually.

"Please, please let him come back to me," I begged.

CHAPTER 63

XANDER

This was probably one of the top ten dumbest things I had done in my life. In fact, it could be in the top five. I turned off the engine of my car but made no move to actually get out. I was still trying to talk myself into keeping the appointment I had made. I knew if I didn't call and make an appointment, I would never actually follow through with it.

I stared up at the building for several long minutes. I was a grown man. I was a successful, grown man. I should not be intimidated. I would not be intimidated. I could do this. I needed to do this. It wasn't for me. It was for Charlie and his guys. One moment of humility would not kill me.

I opened the car door and climbed out. My shoes felt like cement blocks as I made my way inside the building that was all too familiar. I followed the directions from the registry and made my way down the hall. I paused in front of his door and reviewed what I would say to the man that had tried to kill my dreams.

"Fuck it," I mumbled under my breath and knocked on the door.

"Come in," Professor Marsh hollered.

Just hearing his voice made me cringe. The last two times I'd seen the man had been akin to the start of a world war. We didn't like each other. I doubted we ever would. I took a deep breath and reminded myself jail was not the place I wanted to be. I needed to keep my hands to myself.

I opened the door to find him sitting at his desk. It was a flashback. He looked up, his eyes going wide before he looked at the computer screen. "You?" he asked. "You're my ten o'clock?"

I shrugged. "I didn't think you would see me if I used my real name."

Shocking the shit out of me, he actually smiled. "Maybe, maybe not. One will never know. Have a seat."

I was cautious. It was like climbing into a cage with a lion. I sat down, never taking my eyes off him. "Thanks."

"Why are you here?" he asked, skipping any niceties.

Evie was the one who'd suggested I go to him. I knew it was a bad idea. His feelings for me had not changed. He was still just as pissed at me as he had been all those years ago. Hell, recently as well. "Evie suggested I come to you with a situation I'm dealing with."

"Me?" he asked with surprise. That told me she hadn't told him about her idea. I didn't blame her. I wouldn't want to tell him either.

"Yes, I'm in a bit of a bind and Evie suggested you might be able to help."

"I'm supposed to help you?" he asked.

I cleared my throat. I could feel my pride and dignity slipping away. "Yes. Technically, it wouldn't be for me."

"That changes things," he mumbled.

I wasn't sure what Evie was thinking, but it was very clear his feelings for me had not changed. I was sure it was wishful thinking on her part. He hated me just as much today as he had ten years ago. Hell, probably more now that he knew me and his daughter had a thing. Maybe it was all a setup. He pretended to be okay with me in order to put her mind at ease. I was really beginning to think I'd walked into a trap.

"I have a new idea that was supposed to be presented to the shipping world. As you know, I had some personal matters to deal with and the proposal was never made. Because of that, the company that generally handles the bulk of the work is looking at some serious problems. Employees were hired to handle the expected uptick in business."

"But you screwed everyone over because you were too focused on yourself," he said.

I frowned at him. "I don't think you have that entirely correct. I did not tell anyone to hire a full crew. I have no way of predicting whether or not the design would have taken off or not. There could have been no bites for all I know."

"You don't believe that," he said and leaned back in his chair. "You were confident you would sell it and the company you are talking about believed in your confidence. This feels eerily similar to what I warned you about way back when."

I wasn't going to sit there and let him insult me. "Actually, yes, it does, but just like then, you would be wrong. I am confident in what I do because I'm good at it. You might not understand my designs, but they work. The success of those designs is all the evidence I need. I don't have to try and convince you of that. Do some research and you will find out for yourself. My latest project is worth getting out there."

"Then why did you drop the ball?" he asked.

"I didn't—"

"You did."

I took a deep breath, trying to remind myself I was doing this for Charlie. If it wasn't for him, I would not be taking the man's shit. I had to swallow my pride. "You know why."

He studied me. "And now you are ready to pick up where you left off?"

"I don't think that is possible. I just need a starting off point. Evie told me you are friends with a local shipping company owner."

"I am."

He was going to make me say it. He was going to make me beg. I shouldn't be surprised. He loved power. He loved making people bend to his will. "Would you be willing to set up an introduction?" I asked, the words bitter on my tongue.

"I'm not sure," he answered. Yep, he was going to relish the power. He was going to lord it over me and make me beg. I was going to need a shower and a stiff drink once I was done. I felt dirty.

"You aren't sure," I said with a shake of my head. "Of course, you aren't. What do you want to feel sure?"

"I want to know what your big idea is."

"So, you can shoot it down again? Because you don't trust me and my science?"

He shrugged. "I don't."

I didn't care what his opinion was. I knew better than him, whether he thought I did or not. I was the guy that had changed the shipping industry. I was the guy that the ship owners trusted. At least, I used to be that guy. One failed meeting did not mean I didn't know my shit.

"It's a way to keep rudders from being damaged. With my new design, rudders will last longer. It's all very technical, and I can send you the plans if you think it would help you better understand, but in a nutshell, it's good. It's really good. This is just the beginning. With existing ships being retrofitted with the design, ship owners will save thousands on repair costs. Shipping lines are going to be running smoother with ships staying on the water where they belong. Lower operating costs mean better prices for everyone. It's a good plan. It's a great plan and I know it will work."

"You sound very—"

"Confident?"

"Yes."

"I am. I know it will work."

"If your plan can do all that, why would you not want to present it to a wider audience? My friend only has a few ships. There are a lot of other companies out there that would be better candidates."

I cleared my throat. "Yes, probably, but it only takes one company to test the idea."

"Are you suggesting you would be giving away your design?"

"I'm offering the design. Your friend would need to pay my friend's company to complete the work. They are the best in the area and their reputation is spotless. Charlie would give him a fair price on the parts and labor."

He leaned back in his chair. "You can't sell it because you fucked up."

"I can sell it. I'm not interested in going through the necessary steps to get to that point."

"You don't want to grovel at the feet of the men you snubbed," he replied.

I threw my hands up in the air. I was done. I had tried. I would find another way. Groveling at the feet of ten men would be better than kissing this man's ass. "You're right. I don't. Thanks for your time."

I got to my feet, fully prepared to make a dramatic exit when he stopped me. "Sit down and let's talk about this like men."

"Are you suggesting I haven't been?"

"No. Sit. Please."

Since he added the please, I sat back down. "What is it? What exactly do you want me to say or do to convince you to put me in contact with your friend?"

"I don't need any more convincing. I understand you went through a difficult time but not showing up for that meeting was unprofessional. With one act, you degraded the reputation you have worked to build. You wouldn't need to give away something you should be charging for if you would have taken five minutes to reschedule the meeting. No one is so heartless they wouldn't have understood. I am willing to bet any of the people that attended that meeting would have been willing to reschedule. Have you personally reached out to any of them to apologize or explain?"

I slowly shook my head. "No, I have not."

"You need to do that. I don't care if you plan on walking away from your business, but as a man, you own up to what you did."

I felt like I was being grilled by my father, except my father would have a lot more colorful words and insults added in. "I will. You are absolutely right. It was not my finest moment."

"We all have those moments in our lives. The key is to own them and learn from them."

Now things were just getting a little weird. He was almost being nice. I wasn't sure what to think about that. "I will do that."

"All right, now let's talk about what you have, and I will see what I can do to get Jonathan in the room. He's not a wealthy man, and I'm not sure how much he can afford, but I'm sure we can work something out."

"I would really appreciate that. This is important to a lot of guys depending on the work this will bring. I'm hoping Jonathan will be the free advertisement we need. I won't have much to do with any of the process after this, but I need to make sure it gets off to a good start. I am confident in Charlie's ability to follow my instructions. He has never failed me."

"Is Charlie the same young man that followed you around like a lost puppy dog in college?" he asked.

I couldn't help but grin. "I'm not sure he would appreciate it being put like that, but yes, he is one and the same."

"I'm surprised."

"By?"

"You are loyal," he said it as if he just found out I was the king of some small country. It was a little insulting, but I had come to learn the guy knew no other way to be.

"I am loyal. I'm only doing this for Charlie. Quite frankly, I don't need any more money. I'm doing this because his guys need the work and he trusted me to make it happen. I'm doing this because I know my designs are good and I know they will change the world. Just like my first designs. All I need is a chance to prove it."

"All right, we'll do this, but if you fuck this up, I will not be happy. I am putting my name with yours and my reputation will not be tainted."

"I understand. Thank you."

I probably should have cut my finger and signed my name in

blood. I kind of got the feeling that was what he was going for. I reminded myself I only had to do this one last thing and then I would be free of my responsibility to Charlie and everyone else. I would be free to go wherever I chose without worrying about leaving anyone in the lurch.

CHAPTER 64

EVIE

The GPS instructed me to turn right. The roads were ridiculously narrow. I was glad I had gotten the economy car at the airport instead of the midsize I had my eye on. I wasn't sure I could have navigated the roads with anything bigger than the tiny tin can I was driving.

"I can't believe you are actually doing this," Nelle's voice floated through the car via the Bluetooth.

"I have to. This isn't for me. This is me doing a public service."

"Don't you mean you are doing this because you are hoping to fix him so you can have him?"

"No. That is not what I am doing. Me and Xander are over but that doesn't mean I don't care about him."

She let out an audible sigh. "You have such a big heart."

"I have a normal heart."

"Why don't you turn your little self around and drive back to the airport? Come home and let's talk this through."

"I'll be home soon. Once I do this, I'll feel better. It will be closure for me. It will give me what I need to move on, and hopefully, he will be able to move on as well."

"Fine, I'll see you when you get back. You're a good person, Evie. I'm proud to call you my friend."

"Don't get too excited. I might make things worse."

"But at least you will have tried, and that's what matters. It's the thought that counts."

I groaned. "I hope he believes that. I'm here."

"Good luck," she said before ending the call.

I pulled the car into the driveway of the modest house. I saw him come around the corner of the house carrying a large pair of scissors. They looked more like a weapon. I was seriously rethinking my decision.

It was too late to back out now. I turned off the car and slowly got out. He was standing in the middle of his small yard, holding the cutters and glaring at me. "What do you want?" he growled.

I wasn't sure what I was expecting, but I think part of me thought it would be different than the funeral. I was wrong. "I was hoping we could talk."

"Talk? Me and you?"

"Yes."

He considered it and apparently decided he was okay with it. "Fine."

He walked to the front door, dropping the tools next to the door before pushing it open. I walked inside the house with dark wood-paneled walls. It felt dark and nothing like a beachside cottage. I stood just inside the door and waited for him to tell me what to do next.

"Do you want something to drink?" he asked.

"Um, yes, please," I answered. I didn't want to be rude.

"Water?" he grunted.

"Sure."

He walked to the old-style fridge and pulled it open. He handed me a bottle of water and opened one for himself. "Have a seat." He gestured to the worn leather couch. "You obviously have something to get off your chest."

I took a seat and waited for him to sit down. He settled in the recliner that matched the sofa. "Thank you," I started.

"For?"

"Giving me a chance to talk to you."

"What is it? Did he do something? If he did, there's nothing I can do for you. You are barking up the wrong tree."

"Do something?" I questioned.

"If you're pregnant, go to him. He's got the money. Not me."

"I'm not pregnant, and if I was, I would absolutely go to him."

"Then what is it? What do you want?"

I took a deep breath, steeling myself to deal with what was likely going to be a trying conversation. "I guess I wanted to start by saying you have raised a good son. He's a good man."

He didn't look convinced. "That's your opinion."

"He is. Despite his success, he still needs his father's approval."

"He doesn't need shit from me," he barked.

"I'm sure that's what he wants you to think. He wants you to believe he isn't hurt by your harshness or your withholding the approval and love he desperately wants from you. But I know Xander. He needs both. He's too proud to ask for it."

He looked disgusted. "The only thing Xander needs is another mirror. He loves himself and no one else."

"That is not true. He loved his brother deeply."

That seemed to soften him a little. "I believe he felt something for his brother."

"He did. He cared about his brother so much. Losing him has turned Xander's life upside down."

"It has been difficult," he agreed.

"Sir, I don't want to stick my nose where it doesn't belong, but I care about Xander. I care about him a lot and I hate to see him struggling."

He shrugged a shoulder. "Xander chose this path."

"Did he choose to be emotionally abandoned by his father?" I shot back.

He rolled his eyes. "You are one of them."

"One of them?"

"Do you need a safe place?"

"No, I don't. Don't do that. Don't try and turn your anger on me. I won't take it. He has every right to be angry and hurt by your actions. He is your son."

"I had a son," he spat. "My son is gone."

"I only got the chance to meet Kade once. I understand why you are so proud of him. He was a great man. He was funny and kind and he loved his big brother. You have another son. You didn't lose both of your sons. You have a living, breathing son who wants to be in your life."

"Xander has not been my son in a long time."

"You can't just revoke your fatherhood. You are his father."

"He hasn't wanted me to be his father for a long time. He doesn't care for me any more than I care for him."

"That isn't true," I argued. "He is trying to protect himself."

"From what?"

"You!" I said a little louder than I meant to. "Your disapproval and refusal to give him just a little credit for a job well done has scarred him. I'm not trying to criticize your parenting, but I am asking you to open your heart just a little."

"You don't know what you're talking about."

I wasn't getting anywhere. I was probably just making the situation worse. "He lost his brother, the only person he thinks loved him in this world. You lost your wife and a son, but you still have a son who needs you."

"Thank you for reminding me of all that I've lost," he said.

Coming to Oregon was stupid. I shouldn't have interfered. "You have lost a lot. I cannot imagine what that is like. Kade was a wonderful man. I felt his loss and I barely knew him. You and Xander are both suffering. If you two could lean on each other, it would make things so much more bearable."

"Why are you doing this?" he asked.

"Doing what?"

"Why are you here? Shouldn't you be talking to Xander? You're his girlfriend. I don't know you. You don't know me."

"I'm here talking to you because I've been talking to him and I don't feel like I'm getting anywhere. I think you both need to swallow your pride and realize you still have each other. This is what Kade was trying to do before he died. He wanted you guys to get along."

That seemed to sink in. I'd found a chip in the armor. "Kade was always trying to arrange fishing trips or to get us to go to dinner together."

I smiled. "You can still do that. I'm not suggesting it will be easy, but I hope you guys can find a way to at least be on speaking terms."

"There's a lot of water under that bridge," he warned.

"I know. Like I said, it won't be easy. You've raised a strong, stubborn man."

"He probably gets that from me," he said with a quirk of his lips.

"I think you're right."

"Where is he? I didn't see him in the car."

I chewed my lip. "I don't know."

"You don't know where he is?"

"No. He's... well, he's been staying here somewhere. I don't know where he is now."

"I thought you were his girlfriend?" he questioned.

I looked down at the water bottle in my hand. "The situation is complicated."

"Ah, he already broke up with you. That's how he is. He's never been able to stick with a woman for long."

"It isn't like that," I insisted, feeling like I had to defend him. I shouldn't defend him. He made breaking my heart a habit.

He shook his head. "You don't have to try and make excuses for him. Xander doesn't think of anyone except himself. It's all about making him happy."

I winced at the element of truth to his statement. "In this situation, I do not blame him. I blame you."

"Pardon me?"

I was treading on thin ice. "I mean, he feels like he's unlovable. That's why I'm here."

"You want me to get you two back together? Again, you are really barking up the wrong tree, but I'll give you credit for trying."

"I don't want you to help me get him back. I'm saying I want you to help him get through this. He needs you."

"I have not seen him since the funeral."

"But I'm sure you could call him," I prompted.

"Why don't *you* call him?"

"That's not why I'm here."

"That's right. You've lost him. You don't know where he is."

"I don't but I'm not concerned about that."

He looked a tiny bit concerned. "Doesn't he own a house down there?"

The fact he didn't know told me just how broken their relationship really was. Once again, my heart hurt for Xander. It explained so much about the person he was. "He does own a house in San Diego. It's a beautiful house right on the beach."

"He always did love the beach," he commented.

"Yes, he does. I'm sorry I showed up here. I didn't know what else to do. I hate seeing him struggle. It's just me and my dad and we are very close. He says not everyone can be us, and while I believe that's true, I also think it's important to at least try."

"Xander and I have had our differences over the years. A lot of them. I'm not sure we are ever going to see eye to eye."

"You don't have to see eye to eye," I said. "You just need to try and respect each other."

I knew I was way overstepping. I couldn't seem to rein it in. I was acting like a mama bear protecting her cub. Xander wasn't even mine to protect.

"It's something to think about. I make no promises."

"All I ask is you do think about it," I told him. "I won't take any more of your time."

I got up, taking the water with me. He walked me to the door and offered a friendly wave as I backed out of the driveway. My stomach was in knots as I drove away. I couldn't believe I had just done that. If and when Xander found out, he was probably going to be pissed. He was going to be furious with me for butting into his life.

I was ready to take it. I would tell him I did it for him. It wasn't like he could do much more to me. What was he going to do, break up with me again? It seemed to be his MO. I drove through town, heading back to Portland. My work was done. I needed to get home and get back to my actual work. My boss was going to fire my ass if I didn't stop calling in every damn week.

No one except Nelle knew about my trip. It was our little secret.

CHAPTER 65

XANDER

I was back. It wasn't intentional. I told myself it was because my boat was here. That was all. I wasn't back in Oregon because I felt drawn to the place. It was just the boat.

Running away from home was not all it was cracked up to be. I missed Evie. I missed my house. I missed San Diego. I was a mess. I knew that. I was hot and cold, up and down, and everything in between.

My head was a mess. I wanted Evie. I wanted her more than I wanted anything else. I just couldn't bring myself to commit to living there. Being away from home had given me a sense of freedom I didn't know I was missing. My life had been so focused for so long, I didn't realize I wasn't really living. Everything with Kade and Evie made me rethink everything I had ever believed.

I debated opening a beer. It was early afternoon, but I was on vacation. At least that was what I was telling myself. I was on an indefinite vacation. I heard my phone ringing and ignored it. But what if it was Evie? I scrambled into the little kitchen and snatched it off the counter.

"What the fuck?" It was my father's number. Why in the hell would he call me?

I considered ignoring it but the chance there was another family crisis made me answer the call.

"Hello?" I answered. There was a small part of me that feared it would be someone else on the other end. A doctor or paramedic calling to tell me my father dropped dead from a heart attack or something.

"Xander," my father's voice came through strong and clear.

I breathed a sigh of relief. "Yes, Dad."

"Where are you?"

"Why?"

"Are you in town?" he asked.

"How do you know that?"

"Are you or not?" he asked in his usual gruff tone.

"Yes, I am. I'm not here to bother you."

"Why don't you come by the house?"

I blinked and pulled the phone away from my ear to make sure I was talking to the right person. "Your house?"

"Yes. Don't be an idiot. My house. I'll be home all day."

It wasn't what I ever would have guessed was going to happen when I opened my eyes this morning. "I'll be there," I heard myself say.

I ended the call and stared at the phone in my hand. "Well that was unexpected," I murmured.

I changed into jeans and a shirt without any fraying or holes. My dad hated when anyone left their house looking anything but put together. I wasn't sure what was coming next, but I figured it was best to get it over with.

I pulled up to the house. He let me in, leading me out back to his modest patio, and handed me a cold beer without saying a word. It did not bode well. I didn't think there was anything he could say or do that would mess with my life, but one just never knew.

"What's going on?" I asked when he sat down.

"Your little girlfriend paid me a visit," he started.

I almost choked on my beer. "What?"

"Your girlfriend, who is apparently not your girlfriend this week, paid me a little visit last week."

"Are you talking about Evie?" I asked. She was the only one I could think of.

"Yes, Evie. Shit, son, how many girlfriends do you have?"

I smirked. "None."

"She's sassy. A little too bossy for my liking and very pushy."

"She is a woman who says what's on her mind," I replied. "I would think you could appreciate that."

"I do," he said with a smile that actually reached his eyes. "She's a firecracker."

"Why was she here?"

"You haven't talked to her?"

I slowly shook my head. "No, we—well, I don't think we are seeing each other anymore."

"So you fucked that up."

That was the dad I knew and expected. "I suppose I did. Is that why you called me over here? Did you want to rub salt in the wound a bit more?"

"Don't get pissy," he warned. "That's not why I called you."

"What did Evie say to you?"

"She said a lot. Mostly, I think she called me an asshole."

"I'm sorry," I blurted out without thinking about it. "She sometimes says what she thinks without thinking first."

"I like that," he said. "I don't like fake people."

"Me either."

"I've been thinking a lot about what she said. I don't think she was wrong. I think I've made some mistakes. I don't think I can do much to change the past, but I would like to try and change the future."

"What are you talking about?"

"She told me I had fucked up as a father."

Again, I felt like I was going to choke on the beer. "She did what?"

"Not in those exact words, but after doing a great deal of self-reflection, I think she is right. I didn't give you and Kade equal attention. I always favored Kade. It wasn't necessarily intentional. It was just that I felt a connection to him. We had a lot more in common than you and me."

"I build ships for a fucking living," I said. "Where do you think my interest in that came from?"

"I see that now," he said. "I should have seen it then. Your mother tried to tell me, and Kade tried to tell me, but I couldn't see it."

"It wasn't just for you," I said.

"No, I don't suppose it was. You did it for yourself. You made something of yourself. I've kept my head in the sand, trying to ignore what you've been doing. I did a little research. You have changed the world, just like you said you were going to. You really did something remarkable. Your mother used to show me newspaper clippings with your name. I know I didn't say it, but I'm proud of you. I've always been proud of you."

I put the bottle of beer down. I could not continue to drink it if he was going to send me into coughing fits every time he dropped one of his little bombshells. "You are?"

"I am. I should have told you before. You are my son. I've said some pretty shitty things. I don't know how to make them go away but I was hoping we could try and start over."

I felt like I was being pranked. Maybe I was dreaming. In thirty-two years, my father had never believed I was worthy of his last name. "You want to start over? I'm sorry, Dad. This is all coming out of left field. I don't know what to say."

"I understand. You've hardened your heart and I'm about the last guy on the planet you want to be friends with. I don't blame you. I won't push it, but I just want you to know I think you've done well for yourself. Your brother was very proud of you as well. He was always bragging to anyone that would listen. He would tell his guys about his rich brother that changed the world."

That made me smile. "We had a really good visit when he came down. We talked about taking one of those fishing charters. He wanted the three of us to go. Maybe we could still do that, in his honor."

He smiled, pain flashing in his eyes. "I would like to do that."

"As it turns out, I have a lot of free time on my hands. What about you?"

He shrugged. "I'm retired. My days consist of pruning your mother's roses and bitching about the neighbor's dog that shits in my yard every damn day."

"Can I make the arrangements?" I offered. "I'll hire a private charter. I don't want to compete with anyone else."

"I forgot, you're a rich guy."

"I am."

"Tell me what the deal is with that Evie woman," he said.

I shrugged. "I don't know."

"I think you need to figure that situation out. She's a good lady. She's special. She is a lot like your mom. She doesn't take any shit. That's the kind of woman a Holland man needs."

I was happy for his advice, but it was a little too late. "I think I might have messed that one up. I don't see her welcoming me back into her life."

"She came all the way up here to try and get us to talk. I think that says a lot about how she feels about you."

"Maybe," I said.

"Son, I'm sorry. These last few years, I have been especially rough on you. I'm an angry, bitter old man and just couldn't seem to pull my head from my ass long enough to see what I was doing. I'm going to promise you that is over. I've lost one son. I can't lose another."

I was not going to get choked up. "I'm not going anywhere."

"So about this fishing trip," he said. I pulled out my phone and started a search. "Put it away, son."

"What?"

"I think we can take a raincheck on the fishing trip. I think you have some business you need to take care of."

"Business?"

"Your woman," he answered. "You don't need to go out on a boat with me. We can do that later, after you've fixed what you have broken with that pretty young woman. I don't want to get in the way of you being happy."

I put the phone down. "I'm not sure there is anything I can say right now that will make her understand."

"How did things end the last time you talked?"

"I dropped her off at her place. She told me I knew where to find her and then got out of the car."

He smiled. "There you go. That was your invitation to come back."

He had a point. She didn't tell me to fuck off and never call her again. I was the one who ended things. Again. "You're right. I have to go."

"I thought you might. Stay in touch."

"Come back with me," I heard myself say without even knowing the words were going to come out.

He grimaced. "I can't up and leave."

"Why not?"

"I'll come for a visit soon, but you are going to be busy trying to fix things with your lady."

He was right. "Okay, but I'm going to hold you to that. I'd like you to see my house. I think you would appreciate the proximity to the beach. The house is plenty big. You can stay in one of the guest rooms."

"I keep forgetting you are one of those rich guys. How many bedrooms do you have?"

"Only a few," I answered. "The house isn't all that grand, but the view is where the value is."

"Go," he ordered. "We'll see each other soon."

I stood up, and before I knew what he was going to do, he grabbed me and gave me a bear hug. At first, I was completely stiff. I didn't know what to do. I wasn't used to hugs from him. It was weird and good. I patted his back. "I'll call you as soon as I get things figured out. I'll send you a plane ticket."

"You don't have to buy me a damn plane ticket."

"I don't have to, but I'm going to."

"It's going to be hard to get used to having a rich kid for a son."

I smiled. "Get used to it. I've got a lot of money."

He chuckled. "Still the same humble kid."

CHAPTER 66

EVIE

I pulled up the images from a sweet-sixteen party I had planned about six months ago before I turned my laptop for the new client to see.

"Oh wow, that is stunning!" the mother exclaimed.

"I don't want pink," the spoiled princess pouted.

I smiled, remaining calm. "You don't have to have pink. You can choose any color you want."

"No," the mother quickly interjected. "We are not having black."

The girl scowled. "I wasn't going to say black."

I kept my smile in place. The affluent family had reached out to me last week. Initially, I didn't want to do it. I was in no mood to deal with a spoiled teenager.

"What colors were you thinking about?" I asked.

"Purple," she answered. "I want several shades of purple."

"Oh, that's very regal," her mother said with a relieved smile. "I like it."

"I was at a party you planned for my friend like a year ago," the young girl said. "She said you were really good. My party has to be better than her party."

Ah, teenage envy. "We will do our best."

"We've capped the budget at five hundred thousand," the father interjected.

I was surprised he even knew the rest of us were in the room. His face had been glued to his phone the moment he walked through the door. "That is a good budget and I have no doubt in my mind that we will be able to fulfill all your wishes."

The woman, Carla, nodded. "As you know, we own a number of businesses around the country. We are looking for an event planner we can count on to take care of the charity events we host and the many associated celebrations we put on every year. We are hoping to find an individual that understands our tastes while respecting our budgets and wishes."

My phone vibrated on the desk. I quickly silenced it, only to have it start vibrating across the desk again. I flipped it over and saw it was Xander. I sent him to voicemail and turned my attention back to the clients. "I understand what you are looking for. I'd love to help you get this very special young woman the party of her dreams."

"You know, if you were an independent contractor, we could hire you to handle our business. We would want you to be exclusive to us alone."

"That's a very generous offer. Why don't we see how this party goes? I would want to make sure we are a good match."

"Obviously, this will be a test of your planning skills and how well you take direction."

I was already thinking of ways I could intentionally fail the test. I didn't think they were the kind of people I wanted to work for on a daily basis. Working with them did not appeal to me. "All right, I am looking forward to seeing what we can create together."

The phone began to vibrate again. The father looked up from his phone, raising an irritated eyebrow. I silenced it again. "You must be very popular," he commented.

I offered a nervous smile. "I am."

"I told you she was the best," Carla said with a satisfied smile. "I know these things. I have a lot of friends and we talk about things like this."

"I'm happy to know my reputation precedes me," I said.

"Oh, it definitely does," Carla said. "Now, do you have any connections with any of the big names in the industry?"

"What industry would that be?" I questioned.

"Music. I want Justin Bieber at my party."

I almost choked. "I do not have those connections. I can put out some requests and see if I can get a manager to call me back, but I wouldn't hold my breath."

She popped out her lower lip. "But I wanted Justin."

"I'll make some calls, sweetie," Carla said, shooting me a dirty look.

I took control of the meeting. "I'm going to put together some color ideas and send you over some sketches. We'll talk about menus and music. If we can't secure your first choice, there are plenty of local bands and singers I work with on a regular basis. I can send you links to their websites and you can listen to their music."

The girl curled her lip. "I really don't want a nobody."

"I think you will be impressed with our local artists. Many of them are on the rise in the industry. You'll get to be a little part of their climb to the top."

"I suppose," she mumbled.

"We need to get going," the father announced. "I've got a board meeting. Send whatever and I will review it and make the necessary adjustments."

I held my smile in place. "I will do that."

They left my office. I shouldn't have taken them on as clients but I couldn't stop now. The contracts were signed, and unless they fired me, I was on the hook. I was used to working with difficult clients. I could do it.

The phone began to vibrate across my desk again. I flipped it over and saw it was Xander again. He was persistent. The guy hadn't talked to me in over a week and now he was suddenly in dire need to speak to me? I declined the call again and called Nelle.

"Hey," she said, sounding out of breath.

"Where are you at?" I asked.

"Just climbing off the treadmill. What's up?"

"Ugh, I just got done with a very difficult client meeting," I complained. "It's a sweet sixteen for what is probably the most spoiled kid in America."

"Don't do it."

"I have to do it and it could lead to a lot of future work if I don't kill them before I get it done."

"Eek, that bad, huh?"

"Worse. And then, to make matters worse, Xander decides to call nonstop during the meeting."

"Really? What did he want?"

"I don't know," I answered. "I didn't take the call. I was in a meeting. And it wasn't the kind of meeting that allowed me to answer my phone."

"Did he leave a voicemail?"

"Nope."

"I hate that," she groaned.

"Me too. If it was important, he could leave a message. The guy has fallen off the face of the earth again. He hasn't called or texted and now he blows up my phone? I'm not interested."

"Liar," she shot back.

"Okay, I am interested but I don't want to make it too easy."

"You know you're never going to be able to think of anything else if you don't call him back and find out what he wants."

"Won't that make me sound like I'm desperate for his attention?" I asked.

"No. The man called you. Calling him back is just polite."

Truly, I was looking for her approval. She had given it to me and now I was anxious to call him and find out. "I'm going to do it."

"Let me know," she said and hung up.

I held the phone in my hand, tapping it against my forehead. I needed to mentally brace myself to hear his voice. It was going to sting a little. I hit the button to return his call.

"Hey," he answered.

"Hi. You called?"

"I did. A few times."

"I was in a meeting," I answered. "Did you need something?"

"I'm in town."

I sat forward. "Town, as in San Diego?"

His soft laughter filled my heart with warmth. I missed him. God, how I missed him.

"Yes, San Diego."

"Oh," I said.

"Are you busy?"

"I'm at work." I couldn't bring myself to be friendly. I needed to keep my emotional distance from him.

"Evie, I get that you are angry. I want to talk to you. Can we talk?"

"Xander, what is there to talk about?"

"When will you be off work?" he asked instead of answering my question.

I didn't want to see him. If I saw him, it would be impossible to resist him. I would be right back to square one with him again. We'd hook up, spend a great night together, and then he would dump me. I wasn't the fastest learner, but after a few times, I figured it out.

"Xander, I think it's best we leave things alone. I can't take the up and down. It's too much."

"I get it. Can we please talk? I would like to try and explain some things."

I wanted to tell him no. I wanted him to leave me alone. Well, not really. "I'll be off work in about an hour. I think we should meet somewhere public. I don't want to be alone with you."

"Ouch," he teased. "I get it. Meet me at our spot."

I was confused. "Our spot?"

"Yes, the first place you took me. Our spot."

I smiled. "At the park?"

"That's the place. I'll see you in an hour."

I hung up, taking a few deep breaths to calm my racing heart. The man could turn me inside out. Would he always have that kind of power over me? I couldn't imagine what he wanted to talk about. If he thought he was going to talk me back into bed, he was so wrong. Bed led to feelings and I didn't want to feel like shit again.

I called Nelle back. "He wants to talk," I blurted out when she answered.

"That's generally why people call people," she said with a laugh.

"Stop. I'm serious. He's in town. He wants to meet up and talk."

"What do you think he wants to talk about?"

"I have no idea. I don't think I'm strong enough to resist him. He's going to look at me with those soulful eyes and I'm going to be lost. I'm going to want to touch him and then I'm screwed. Literally. Sex is confusing the issue. He doesn't want to be with me. I can't be his booty call. I can't be the woman he calls when he is passing through town."

"Then don't be," she answered.

"That is easier said than done. I'm drawn to him. I cannot resist him. I see him and I want him."

"Meet him somewhere public," she suggested.

"We kind of are. I'm supposed to meet him at the park. It's where we went on our first outing after meeting at that party. He calls it our spot. Isn't that so cute?"

She loudly groaned. "Cute is one word. I think it's romantic. Maybe he wants to try and work things out."

"Maybe, but I don't want to get my hopes up."

"Be strong. You can do this."

"I think I'm going to cut out of here early. I want to go home and change before I meet him."

She laughed. "Of course, you do. You can't meet him without primping a little."

"That's not what I'm doing."

"Yes, you are and that's okay. I think you should. Show him what he is missing. Let him see what he is going to be walking away from. Sometimes, you have to be a little bit of a tease to get a man's attention."

"Thanks, I will keep that in mind."

"You're welcome. Call me and tell me what happens."

"I will," I told her and hung up the phone again.

I needed to get some work done, but I was suddenly very anxious to see him. I quickly created the new file for the sweet-sixteen party and emailed it to myself. I would work on it later. For now, I was going home and changing into something more appropriate for the walk up to my favorite spot in the park.

Now that he'd dubbed it our spot, I knew I would never be able to think of it any other way. It would always be our spot.

CHAPTER 67

XANDER

I was so close to losing her. I sensed it in her voice. I wasn't expecting her to jump at the chance to see me, but I wasn't expecting such resistance either.

The sense of urgency I felt was making me anxious. I couldn't imagine my life without her. It had taken me way too long to realize how I felt about her. Anytime I thought about my life in a month or a year or in ten years, she was there. I wasn't sure how it happened, but I knew she was a person I wanted in my life. It wasn't even a want. It was a need. I needed the woman like I needed air.

I was prepared to chase her down if I had to. I would do whatever it took to make her hear me out. I knew there was still a chance she would kick me to the curb. I wouldn't blame her if she did. I had fucked up. A lot. I would spend the next year trying to convince her to give me a chance. I couldn't explain when things clicked but they had.

It was like the light went on. I hated that I was so ignorant for so damn long. I hated to think of the pain I caused her. I hated myself for not treating her right. I didn't deserve her, but I was sure as hell going to do what I could to be the man she deserved.

I paced the area, checking the time. The sun was beginning to set. Streaks of orange stretched across the sky, creating the most perfect backdrop. It was all perfect. Now, I just needed her to show up. She texted and let me know she was running late. That was a first. I had to believe it was intentional. I was late all the time.

I checked behind me. She still wasn't there. My little picnic basket was sitting on the bench. Fortunately, it was a weekday, and no one seemed to be around. Most people preferred not to hike at night. A horrible thought crossed my mind. I was putting the woman on a path in the fading light all by herself. Maybe not the best idea. I thought about meeting her at the bottom of the trail.

I heard footsteps and hoped it was her. I spun around to see her making her way up the trail "Hi," I said and walked toward her.

She was wearing a pair of shorts and a light jacket. Her hair was pulled back in a ponytail. There was a vulnerability about her that pulled at my heartstrings.

She smiled. "Hi."

"You look beautiful," I told her. "Damn, you are so fucking gorgeous. I swear you grow prettier by the day."

"You are being very charming," she said with a forced laugh. "I'm not sure if that's a good or bad thing."

"I brought some snacks," I blurted out and immediately felt like a jackass. "I mean, I brought a picnic. Of sorts."

"Snacks? I thought you said you wanted to talk. Why did you want to talk here?"

"Because this spot is special to us. I brought a picnic because I wanted to create a whole thing. I wanted us to enjoy a picnic with the sunset in our special place."

"You keep calling it our special place," she said warily.

"It is special. I will always remember the first time we came here. It was really the first time I got to see you for the woman you are."

"I appreciate that, but I feel like this is a lot of pomp and circumstance."

I shrugged. "I wanted to show you I can treat you right."

"So you brought a picnic?"

"I did."

"How long do you anticipate this conversation going?" she asked with a great deal of skepticism.

"I figured I would hope for the best, and maybe if things went well, there would be some star gazing."

She was being standoffish. "I'm not sure what you expect to happen here. I don't want to keep doing this. I keep showing up and you keep walking away."

She was killing me. "I know."

"Then I'm asking you to please, just tell me what's going on."

"I want to talk. Sit please. Can I pour you some wine?"

"You brought wine?"

I grinned and opened the basket. I pulled out the little bottle and poured two glasses, emptying the bottle. "I did."

"Why do I feel like I'm being seduced?"

"I'm not trying to seduce you."

She was still holding back. I could feel her trying to distance herself from me. "This definitely feels like a seduction."

I sat on the bench beside her. "I might be seducing you a little but not in that way. I want you to be willing to talk to me and I suppose that takes some seduction."

"You could have texted."

"Definitely not," I told her. I looked out over the park and remembered the first time she showed me her favorite viewpoint. "It is such a nice night."

"It is. What's going on Xander?"

"I'm coming back," I told her.

"What does that mean?"

"I'm moving back home. Into my house. I'm staying."

"For how long? You were home a couple of weeks ago and you left."

"Good point. But this time, I'm staying."

"What about the ghosts you didn't want to deal with?"

I shrugged. "I think ghosts can be a good thing."

"How so?" she asked softly.

"The memories I have of him here are good. They are some of the best memories I have of him. Running away from them was wrong. I need to be here. I need those memories to keep him near me."

"I think that is a very good idea," she said, a real smile spreading over her face. "I'm glad to hear it."

"I'm sorry I ditched you. Repeatedly. I'm the world's biggest asshole. I don't deserve your forgiveness, but I'm hoping you will give it to me anyway."

"Xander, I want to believe you, but I'm hesitant."

"I know. I expect that. It isn't just the memories of Kade that brought me back. You. Memories of being with you. Thinking about this place and our time together. Those are all really good memories. I want more memories like that."

"You are saying all the right things," she said with a smile. "You know I can't resist you."

"I'm counting on it."

"I'm glad you are back," she said.

"Me too. Does this mean you will entertain the idea of having a relationship with me?"

"I could be convinced," she said.

"I am going to work very hard to convince you," I vowed.

She sipped her wine. "How are you doing? Like really doing?"

"I'm doing a lot better thanks to you."

"Thanks to me?"

"You are a sneaky little lady," I told her.

She raised her eyebrows. "Me? Sneaky?"

"I got a call yesterday."

"Congratulations."

"Oh, you're cheeky too." I laughed. I opened the picnic basket and pulled out the small cheese tray and peeled back the plastic. "You hold that." I reached back in and grabbed another tray of an assortment of nuts and fruits and peeled the plastic back.

"Wow, you come prepared."

"It's not exactly a meal, but I wanted to wine and dine you while we watched the sunset in our special spot."

"I think I like this romantic side of you."

"Good."

"Tell me about your phone call."

I popped a grape into my mouth. "It was my dad."

The look on her face was one I would never forget. It was surprise, guilt, and dread. "Your dad called you?"

"Yes, he did. He told me you paid him a visit."

She looked sick. "I'm so sorry. It was a total spur of the moment thing. I've been worrying about it for a week. I shouldn't have stuck my nose into your business. I was wrong and I apologize. I made it very clear you didn't know I was there. I told him I was acting of my own volition and you didn't put me up to anything."

"Are you done?" I asked with amusement.

"Um, I don't know. Am I?"

"My dad and I talked yesterday. Actually talked."

"You did?"

I nodded, grabbing a few cashews. "We did. We are going to go fishing soon. I'm going to hire a charter and we are going to do the one thing Kade worked so hard to make happen."

I thought I saw a tear slide down her cheek. "Really?"

"Yes."

"I'm so happy for you."

"Me too. He apologized. He told me he was proud of me. I think that is probably the first time he has ever said those words to me."

"I'm going to turn into a hot, blubbering mess any second," she said as she laughed through her tears. "I'm so happy for you."

"Thank you. I owe it all to you. I don't know if we would have ever been able to work things out without a little encouragement from you. We can be pretty stubborn. You showed us the way."

She let out a long breath. "I'm so relieved. I have been absolutely stressing out about the situation. I thought for sure I royally fucked up. I kept thinking I pissed him off and he was going to hate you forever because I butted my big old nose into your very private family business."

"Just the opposite. I mean, it did take him almost a week to finally call me, but he did it. He told me he thought you were special. He approves."

"Wow, that's some high praise."

I offered her a grape. She opened her mouth and I popped it inside. "Did your dad say anything?"

"About?"

"Our conversation."

Her mouth fell open. "You talked with my dad?"

"He didn't tell you?"

"No! When did this happen? I feel like I've been living under a rock."

"I took your advice. I stopped by his office on Monday before I left."

She pressed her hand against her belly. "How did that go? Wait, don't tell me. I'm afraid to ask."

"Well, it didn't start out great, but things got better. I'm not going to claim we are best buddies, but he agreed to help me out. I still don't think he likes me, but I don't think he wants to kill me."

She closed her eyes and took several deep breaths. "I am just a little taken aback. This is a whole lot of information coming at me at once."

"I bet. I'm not done yet."

"Oh lord, have mercy." She downed the rest of her glass and held it out. "Please tell me you have more wine in your little basket of goodies."

I grinned and grabbed another miniature bottle. "I do." I filled her glass and watched as she took several long drinks. "More?"

"Not yet. What else? I don't even know where to begin to guess."

"I love you."

She blinked, staring at me without saying anything. "What?"

"You heard me. I love you."

"Oh my goodness," she breathed. "Oh my."

I took the wine glass from her and put it on the little cement pad the bench was perched on. I scooted closer, reaching for her and pulling her closer to me. "I love you Evie," I breathed the words before pressing my lips to hers.

She opened her mouth to me. My tongue swept inside her mouth, tasting the wine and the grape. She tasted like sweet ecstasy. My mouth opened wider, forcing her to open her mouth. I held her against me. All her soft curves pressed against my chest. I didn't intend to make love to her right there, but need was overriding all other senses.

"I want you," I whispered against her mouth.

"Please."

"Can I? Here? Please say yes. I need you."

"Yes," she breathed. "Yes. Here. Now."

It was the only approval I needed.

CHAPTER 68

EVIE

I was being terribly irresponsible. I was not the girl who got naked in the park and had sex. Unfortunately, when I was with Xander, all bets were off.

And he loved me. The words echoed through my mind over and over. He loved me. I would follow him into the fires of hell knowing he loved me. I didn't realize just how badly I needed to hear those words from him.

He loved me. I loved him. I didn't know what that meant for the two of us, but damn if I was going to pass up the chance to find out. The way he was kissing me was different. Maybe it was mind over matter, but I could practically taste the love on his tongue. It was in the way he touched me. The gentleness of his hand on my cheek, holding me steady while his tongue plundered inside my mouth.

"Over here," he said as he broke his mouth away from mine.

I felt a little dazed. His kiss made me feel drunk on lust. Again, I was ready to follow him anywhere if it meant I got more kisses like that. He took my hand and led me away from the bench that was in an exposed area. We walked through a narrow path and into the trees.

"Where are we going?" I asked him.

"I found this little area when we were here with Kade," he answered.

"Oh," I said.

The light was more filtered under the copse of trees. He pulled me against him once again. His mouth moved over mine, making me forget all about where we were. His arms were around me, making me feel like I was completely safe in his embrace. I was wrapped up in him and his love and it was the only place I ever wanted to be.

"I have never been so desperate for you," he whispered against my lips. "I have missed you like crazy. I haven't been able to think straight or sleep. I need you. I need you in my life."

"I'm here," I told him. I ran my hands through his hair. "I'm here for you. Always."

He growled low in his throat before taking my mouth again. I could feel his erection pressing against my belly. I pushed back against him, trying to get closer. I couldn't get close enough.

"This might be a little tricky," he said with a small laugh.

"I think we'll figure it out."

"I know we will figure it out. There is no way I'm going to make it back to the car or to your place or my place. I have to have you. I need you. I'm so hard. I'm so on the edge."

I looked around and came up with a plan. "Here," I said and took his hand, leading him a little deeper into the trees. I dropped his hand and very slowly undid the button of his pants and slid the zipper down.

I reached for him, feeling the hard strength of him, and wrapped my hand around his shaft.

"Fuck," he groaned. "It hurts so good."

He was straining. I could feel the tension in his body. My instinct was to make him feel better. There was only one way to do that.

I quickly undid my shorts and slid them down my legs, leaving my shoes on. Next, I slid my panties and very carefully put them on my shorts. I wasn't a big outdoors person, but I was not interested in whatever was on the ground making a nice bed for themselves in my panties.

"Goddamn," he groaned. "I need you. I'm sorry, but I need you so bad."

"Don't be sorry. I want this."

It was sweet he was thinking about me and my modesty. I had no modesty in that moment. All I had was a desperate need to have him buried inside me. I slowly turned and placed my hands against the trunk of a very tall tree. I looked over my shoulder at him and gave my ass a wiggle.

It was the only encouragement he needed. He stepped forward, nudged my legs open with his knee, and slid his hand up the inside of my thigh. He found my heated center. I was already wet and aching for him when he rubbed his fingertip over me.

I jerked at the contact. "Yes, please," I begged.

He dropped his hand, and a moment later, the head of his cock was probing at my entrance. With a little adjustment and me bending forward a bit with my hands braced on the tree, he found his way deep inside.

"This," he breathed. "This is what I have craved. Your warmth squeezing me."

I was caught up in the delight of being filled by him. I had convinced myself I would never experience him again. I was beyond thrilled he was back. I moved a little, adjusting him inside me. "I have dreamed of you every night."

"This?" he asked as he stroked a hand down my spine. "Have you dreamed of me doing this to you?"

"Yes," I whimpered as fresh new shivers of desire coursed through my veins. "This. Over and over."

"I love you," he said again and began to move. His strokes were long and purposeful. The usual fury of our lovemaking was gone. It was as if we both recognized we had time. We didn't have to be in a race. There would be a next time and a next time after that.

"I love you," I told him, realizing I had yet to say the words. I knew I loved him and had known it for some time.

The moment I said it, his cock grew inside me. My body tightened around him, squeezing him. I imagined myself holding him in my arms, hugging him tight. He gasped, sucking in a sharp breath as my body responded to his.

"I'm going to make love to you all night," he promised. "This is just the beginning. This is to tide me over until we get home. I want you in my bed. I want me inside you."

"Yes," I gasped, my head dropping to my chest as he slid in and out of me. Every stroke touched new places. Every stroke sent my body into a wild tailspin of desire and need. "Please. Please. Don't stop."

He didn't speed up his pace. He kept moving in that slow steady rhythm, sliding in, grinding his hips, and then gliding out and leaving just the tip inside me. The spasms rocking through me made it difficult for me to remain standing. I wanted to crumble in a heap at his feet with him still inside me.

"This is just the first," he said, his voice strained. "I can't hold back. Your body is milking me. You are too tight. Too hot. Too fucking wet."

"Don't hold back," I told him. I needed his release. I could feel mine hovering just out of reach as if my body refused to give in until it had his complete surrender.

He let out a long, low groan. I felt him explode inside me. I kept myself from screaming with the pleasure that was shredding my nerves. My brain was in sensory overload. I couldn't cry out. The very last thing I wanted was some Good Samaritan bursting through the trees to save me. I would kill anyone that stopped me from getting every last drop of pleasure from my man.

His arms reached around me, pulling me upright with him still deep inside me. The action spawned a new wave of tremors through my body. He grunted, sounding as if he had been punched as my body clamped down on him again.

"Damn woman, you are going to kill me if you keep doing that."

I softly laughed, resting my head on his shoulder as he nuzzled my neck. "I think that it's the other way around."

"I want to get you home. I need more. I have a long week to make up for."

"I think I kind of like this outside thing," I teased.

He stepped away from me and slowly turned me around. Our

bodies pressed against each other once again. It was a magnetic pull that was futile to resist. "I have a very private backyard."

"Oh, I like the sound of that."

"Get dressed. We'll go to my place."

He didn't have to ask me twice. I quickly shook out my panties, praying to god no critters had taken refuge in them before pulling them on. We both dressed before he took my hand and led me out of the trees. "I feel like a naughty teenager. What would we have done if someone came upon us?"

He smiled, his white teeth flashing in the moon that had made a grand entrance while we had been cloistered in the trees. "We would have told them to leave us alone and let us finish our business."

I giggled like a schoolgirl and helped him pack up his picnic. "I'm glad you chose to come back," I told him.

He looked at me, directly into my soul. "I didn't come back to the place. I came back to you. Wherever you are is where I would be. It isn't where I am but who I am with that I care about."

I sighed. "You are good."

"Good?"

"This is the part where I tell you that you had me at hello. Except, I think I said hello first. I knew from the moment I laid eyes on you, you were going to be a problem for me."

He quirked his lips. "A problem?"

"Yep. You came into my neat and tidy life and shook things up."

"I hope that's a good thing."

I hugged him again. I couldn't stop touching him. "It's a very good thing. It's the best thing. But know this. You are stuck with me. If you try to run away from me again, I am going to chain you up and lock you in the basement."

He grinned, his brows dancing. "Chains, huh? I didn't know you were into the freaky stuff."

"With you, I never know what I'm into. I wasn't into having sex outside in a very public park until I met you."

"I can't wait to find out what else you are into," he teased.

"Let's go. I'm already feeling like I might drag you back into those trees."

His soft laughter washed over me. It was like being wrapped up in love. I never dreamed I would have the love of a man like Xander. He was so perfectly flawed. I couldn't wait for us to learn everything there was to know about each other. I knew we would heal each other. We would correct the flaws and weave together a beautiful relationship.

As I followed him back to his place, I let myself dream of our future together. I was probably getting ahead of myself, but I could see us having beautiful babies together. I could see us sitting at our children's graduations and meeting our grandchildren together. It was a future I'd never imagined before.

And then there was Xander. Meeting him changed everything.

The bumpy road that Nelle recommended I take was turning out to be the best ride ever. I was never letting him go. I hoped he was ready for me to stick to him like glue. He was stuck with me. He could run, but I had already proven I would find him.

He was mine.

EPILOGUE

XANDER

One year later

Pride. That was what I felt in that moment. My ships were heading out to sea. Everyone else was already making their way back away from the dock. I couldn't leave just yet. I watched the ships navigate out to sea one at a time. I didn't have children, but I imagined what I was feeling was similar to what a proud papa would feel.

I felt a hand on my shoulder and turned to see Charlie next to me.

"This is a big day," he said.

"It is. You pulled it off."

"*You* pulled it off."

"What do you think?" I asked him. "Is it going to work? Do you foresee them falling apart halfway around the world?"

He shook his head. "My guys did excellent work. That shit is solid."

"Good. Those test ships seem to be holding up."

"Of course, they will. My team is the best. Your idea wasn't half-bad either."

"Thanks," I said, watching as one of the ships cleared the harbor.

"You know, you could have made a lot more money with that plan," he lectured.

"I could have but I already have a lot of money. This one was on the house."

He slugged my shoulder. "On the house my ass. You still cleared a few million."

"You and I both know it was worth ten times that."

"You should consider going into marketing," he said with a laugh. "I never would have given something away with the goal of it paying off like that."

"It's the oldest trick in the book," I told him. "I gave it to a small company, and when the big guys noticed, they all wanted it. It was basically my coupon."

"Your business does not need coupons."

"It worked though," I said with a grin.

"It did. That fleet represents the biggest shipping company in the world. You did what you always said you would."

"What was that?"

"You changed the world. I rub elbows with the guy that changed the world."

"Hey, you two," Evie said as she walked toward us.

"Hey, baby." I greeted her with a kiss. She was wearing a navy-blue dress that was supposed to go with the theme of our little celebration. She insisted we have a celebration. There was champagne and appetizers and even some music.

"You guys are hiding from the party. I have cars ready to take everyone to the hotel. Do not think you are escaping the party that celebrates the two of you. I will not have it."

I kissed her. "I wouldn't dare."

She hooked her arm through mine and led me to the waiting limousine. We climbed in with Charlie and a few of the other guys from his team. We were delivered to the hotel where a large crowd was already gathered in the ballroom.

"This is all for you," she whispered in my ear as we stood just inside the doorway.

"I feel like this is a little much," I told her.

"Of course, you would think that. This is a big deal. We are all here to celebrate you and your brilliant brain."

"Thank you," I told her.

"I have one little surprise. I know you are not fond of surprises but this one was a must."

I groaned. "I don't want to give a speech."

"You won't need to give a speech."

She led me away from the door. While my anxiety wasn't as bad as it used to be, I was never going to be a social butterfly. Never.

"Son!" I heard my father's voice.

I spun around, looking at my father. "Dad?" I questioned what I was seeing with my own two eyes. "You're here?"

"I would not miss this!" he said and shook my hand. "I can't believe you are the man of the hour. You are a big deal."

My chest puffed out a little. "I'm glad you're here."

"I'm happy to be here. I've met a few people and they all sing your praises. You are a really big deal. I feel like a fool, but I had no idea."

Evie looked up at me, her face glowing with pride. "He is a very big deal."

Evie damn near dragged me around the room, forcing me to shake hands and smile at a lot of people. She must have sensed the moment I was done with it all. She escorted me out of the ballroom and onto the patio lit by pretty lights hanging overhead.

"How are you doing?" she asked me.

"I'm doing good. I'm glad I have you alone. Finally. There are a lot of people in there."

"They are all here to celebrate you and what you have accomplished. You have made a big impact on the shipping industry. I don't really understand any of it, but I know they all love you for saving them a lot of money."

I shrugged. "I aim to please."

"Yes, you do."

"I didn't see your father," I commented.

"He's here. I can bring him around if you would like. He has a new lady friend I think you should meet."

My eyes went wide. "No way."

"Yes way."

"He never said a word to me."

"When did you talk to him?"

This was the part where I fessed up. I learned a long time ago not to try and hide anything from my lovely lady. She was smart, savvy, and downright ruthless.

"I stopped by his office yesterday," I told her, unable to hide my smile.

"You did, huh?"

I nodded. "I did."

"Well, aren't you two the best of friends?" she teased.

That was a bit of an exaggeration, but we were friends. Things had not been easy, but I felt like we had a mutual understanding. He wanted what was best for Evie and so did I. She was our main concern. "We had some business to discuss."

Laughter floated out of the ballroom behind us. I was glad everyone was having a good time. It was the culmination of a lot of hard work over the year. Every person in there deserved to celebrate their success, including Charlie's crew.

"What kind of business?" she asked. "Are you guys cooking up another scheme to make ships even faster?"

"No. I think I'm good for a while now. I have more important matters to focus on."

She touched my cheek. "I better be one of those matters."

"You are. You absolutely are."

"My dad is pretty excited to be a part of all of this," she commented.

"He should be. He made it possible, which is why I gave him a check for his cut of the profits."

Her mouth fell open. "You did what?"

I shrugged. "Without him, I never would have gotten those first few ships to try out the new hardware. He offered suggestions that made it work even better. He deserved—no, he earned—that money."

"Wow. Did he accept it?"

I laughed and nodded. "Oh yeah, he did. His name is also included on the patent. Your father is not going to have to teach another day of his life if he doesn't want to."

"You are amazing," she whispered.

"Nah, I'm just lucky to have really amazing people in my life that make me look good."

"I think you are incredible all on your own."

"There was something else your father and I needed to discuss," I told her.

She made a face. "I'm almost afraid to ask."

I reached into the inside pocket of my suit and dropped to one knee in front of her. She gasped, putting both hands over her mouth. "I needed to ask him a very important question."

"You did?" The words were barely audible through her fingers covering her mouth.

"I asked him for permission to ask you to be my wife. Evie, you have taken this old, wounded soul and shown me what living really is. You have given me a life I didn't know was possible. You have shown me light and love and I never want to be apart from you. Will you please marry me?"

I opened the box, flashing the ring I hoped wasn't too big but big enough to convince her to say yes.

She was staring at the ring, tears in her eyes. "Xander."

"Evie?" I prompted.

"Yes! Oh my god. This is so crazy! Yes!"

I got to my feet and pulled her into my arms to kiss her. I was sealing the deal. I was going to make the woman who'd changed my life my wife. After a heated kiss, I stepped back to slide the ring on her finger.

"I love you," I told her. "I love you more than anything in this world. I promise I will do everything I can to make you happy. You will always be taken care of and cherished."

"Xander, you are a beautiful man. I love you. I cannot wait to be your wife. I promise I will work hard to make you happy. I will love you no matter what comes our way."

There was a sense of peace that washed over me. We were forever bound. I knew there was nothing we couldn't handle together. We were a team and we always would be. "We should probably go back inside before they start looking for us."

"Or we could sneak away and go home," she said.

I kissed her again. "Woman, do not tease me. I will take you right against the wall if you let me."

"Home. Later."

I kissed her forehead, being careful not to muss her hair. "I'm going to hold you to it."

We made our way back inside. It wasn't long before the news of our engagement spread around the party. What was supposed to be a celebration of a lot of hard work and success turned into an engagement party. Evie insisted she was throwing one of those in the coming months. I didn't mind a bit. I would attend any party she wanted me to if it made her happy.

I liked having a purpose in life that had nothing to do with making money or being successful. My only goal when I opened my eyes in the morning was to make her happy. I felt I owed it to her. She had come into my life at a time when I didn't even know I needed her. She had made me whole. She had gotten me through what was absolutely the worst time of my life. Her love kept me afloat.

My dad came to stand beside me as I watched Evie work the crowd, flashing her ring to anyone that asked. "She's really something," he commented.

"Yes, she is."

"Your mother would have liked her."

I nodded, smiling as someone hugged her and congratulated her. "Kade knew. The moment Kade met her, he knew. I just wish he could be here to see it all."

"I'm sure he knew you two were going to end up together, no matter how hard you tried to screw it up."

We both got a small laugh at that. "I did do a damn good job making a mess of things. I'm lucky she loves me despite my many flaws."

"Yes, you are. Always remember that. When you don't feel like you can do anything right or you feel like you are tired and weary, remember she loves you. A good woman's love can carry a man through for the rest of his life if he lets it."

"I'll keep that in mind," I said as I watched her move around the room.

I watched her and the other people that had made an impact in my life. I had never been surrounded by so many people I cared about. They were all there. I had a family. A real family.

The days of being a lone wolf were behind me and I was never going to look back.

The End

ABOUT THE AUTHOR

Ali Parker is a full-time contemporary and new adult romance writer with more than a hundred and twenty books behind her. She loves coffee, watching a great movie and hanging out with her hubs. By hanging out, she means making out. The man is hot. Hello.

She's a creative at heart and loves coming up with more ideas than any one person should be allowed to access. She lives in Tennessee with her hubs, teenage son, two grown daughters and first grand baby (yes!). Telling a good story that revives hope, reminds us of love and gives a vacation from life is all she's up to.

Questions, comments or concerns? You can always email her at Ali@aliparkerbooks.com.

Also by Ali Parker
Baited

Second Chance Romances
Jaded
Jaded Christmas
Justified
Justified Christmas
Judged
Judge Christmas

Alpha Billionaire Series
His Demands, Book 1
His Needs, Book 2
His Forever, Book 3

Bad Money Series
Blood Money
Dirty Money
Hard Money
Cash Money

Forbidden Fruit Series

Forgotten Bodyguard
Bright Lights Billionaire
Stage Left
Center Stage
Understudy
Improv

Pro-U Series
Breakaway
Offside

Rebound
Homerun
Free Stlye

The Rules
Making the Rules
Bending the Rules
Breaking the Rules

My Creative Billionaire
My Creative Billionaire Book 1
My Creative Billionaire Book 2
My Creative Billionaire Book 3

Money Can't Buy Love
Money Can't Buy Love Book 1
Money Can't Buy Love Book 2
Money Can't Buy Love Book 3

Broken By Love
Broken By Love Book 1
Broken By Love Book 2
Broken By Love Book 3

One More Night
One More Night Book 1
One More Night Book 2
One More Night Book 3

The Castaletta Syndicate
Take Me Higher
Whatever You Need
Killing Me Softly
Tipping Point

A Lost Breed MC Romance
Ryder
Axel
Jax
Sabian
Derek
Caleb
Rhys

The Dawson Brothers
Always On My Mind
Wild As The Wind
Mine Would Be You
Don't Close Your Eyes
Stand By Your Man

My Fathers Best Friend
Billionaire Bachelor
Billionaire Boss
Billionaire Beau
Billionaire Lover

Shameless Southern Nights
Down and Dirty
Slow and Steady
Hot and Handy

Money For Love
Hundred Reasons
Forging Thousands
Making Millions

Regal Rights
Uncover My Secrets
Unwrap The Truth

Unwind My Resolve
Undo Me

The Casanova Series
Piper
Joshua
Wyatt
Easton
Miles
Jeremiah
Aaron
Cooper
Levi
Asher
Christian

One Hot Summer
Hot Summer Loving
Hot Summer Fling
Rule Breaker By Accident

Standalone's
The Billionaire Affair
Right Under My Nose
The Billionaire's Unexpected Wife
Marry Me For Money
Billion Dollar Man
Unworthy Of You
All Grown Up
Getting Lucky